The Hangman's House

THE HUNGARIAN LIST

The Hangman's House

ANDREA TOMPA

Translated by Bernard Adams

LONDON NEW YORK CALCUTTA

Seagull Books, 2021

Originally published in Hungarian as *A hóhér háza* by Kalligram
© Andrea Tompa, 2010

First published in English translation by Seagull Books, 2021
English translation © Bernard Adams, 2021

ISBN 978 0 8574 2 792 2

British Library Cataloguing-in-Publication Data
A catalogue record for this book is available from the British Library.

Typeset by Seagull Books, Calcutta, India
Printed and bound by Versa Press, East Peoria, Illinois, USA

CONTENTS

Acknowledgements

I wish to express my gratitude to the Finnish cultural association Nuoren Voiman Liitto for the use of Villa Sarkia, Sysmä, where much of this translation was made.

Bernard Adams

A Brief Note on the History of Transylvania

When the nomadic Hungarians crossed the pass of Verecke—traditionally in 896 CE—into the Carpathian Basin, the area that they entered became known as Transylvania; the name is first recorded in a document from 1075. 'The land beyond the forest', in Hungarian Erdély (from *erdő* 'forest'), thus became the oldest part of the Kingdom of Hungary. Its remoteness from the capital Buda meant that from early times it was governed by a viceroy, while during the period of Ottoman rule (1521–1685) it became a semi-independent principality. After the Turks came the Habsburg Empire, which absorbed Transylvania—not without opposition—and the principality was restored in 1765, only to be abolished in the Compromise of 1867; the region was ceded to Romania after the First World War on the collapse of the Austro-Hungarian Dual Monarchy.

In the late ninth century, Transylvania had been sparsely populated by Slav, Avar and Gepid peoples, all to be pacified by the occupying Hungarians. The latter were never more than a large ethnicity in the region, reaching a peak of 32 per cent in the 1910 census, when the largest ethnic group was that of the Romanians. A notable feature of Transylvania in the early modern period was the much more peaceful coexistence of Christian denominations than was seen in neighbouring countries, while the Jewish population rose to about 3 per cent after the First World War.

Romania came into being as a political entity as a result of the Crimean War. Under the Treaty of Paris (1859), the former Ottoman provinces of Wallachia and Moldavia were placed under the protection of the signatories and both elected Alexandru Ioan Cuza as their ruler. This gave rise to a personal union of the two, followed by the choice of Karl Hohenzollern-Sigmaringen as Prince (1859) and King of Romania (Carol I, 1881–1914).

Michael the Brave of Wallachia briefly ruled all three provinces before his assassination in 1599, and is regarded as a Romanian nationalist hero.

The term Greater Romania, however, is mainly associated with the Kingdom of Romania between 1918 and 1940, when the country was at its greatest territorial extent. Transylvania was assigned to Romania under the Treaty of Trianon (1920), though in effect the territory had already been annexed when representatives of the ethnic Romanians of Transylvania and other regions unilaterally proclaimed Union with Romania on 1 December 1918.

Many ethnic Hungarians migrated to Hungary, as they did from other neighbouring countries at this time, and much lasting ill feeling resulted between Hungary and Romania. Hungary maintained a close economic relationship with Germany during the 1930s in the hope of regaining some of the territories lost under Trianon, and in 1940 the Second Vienna Award restored the northern part of Transylvania, which included the major city of Kolozsvár. This award was annulled after the defeat of Germany in 1945; and under the communist regime that followed, Romania pursued a strongly nationalist policy, especially during the later years of the period when vigorous efforts were made by Nicolae Ceauşescu as General Secretary of the Romanian Communist Party (and from 1974 to 1989, President of the Republic) to expunge Hungarian language and culture. He was highly influenced by what he had seen in China and North Korea, and made much of the dubious claim that the Romanians are the modern descendants of the ancient Dacians.

The Hangman's House is set in the final years of the communist period.

Bernard Adams

The Hangman's House

THE CHOIR

So it's started—she looked from a distance, from the safety of the farther corner of the square, at the group of students in knitted sweaters and scarves who were shouting spontaneously, raggedly, *Aren't those Art College students? They're in the same year as Csapó*! she suddenly recognized them, and would very much have liked Csapó to be among them, that hefty, boyish sculptress, Juci's former classmate, she'd have liked her to be there simply so that that very afternoon, and the next day and the day after, when it was all over, and in the following twenty or fifty years, she'd be able to toss out casually, lightly and proudly: *It was Csapó and her crowd that started it all*, in Kolozsvár at least, because by that time in Temesvár it wasn't starting but was in full swing, blood had run in the streets, and that she could tell from two sources, firstly because a few days previously she'd come back on a crowded train from that still tense and silent town where she'd been visiting a classmate who, to his misfortune, had been posted there in the army, and secondly because every evening since then they'd tried to get Kossuth Radio on the old VEF set—the borders were closed now, help couldn't come from outside—and so as she heard the shouting in the street grow more rhythmical and organized she knew that this wasn't just a sort of ineffectual choir practice but the first genuine public outcry, *This is it*, she panted to her mother as she rushed into her office in Deák Ferenc utca, no longer afraid of her mother's colleagues, *It's started*, she exclaimed aloud, flushed with excitement, and in the office everyone had heard the first shots, *We shall win*, she went on, her breath coming in gasps, and suddenly all her mother's colleagues looked at her and realized what she was saying: on 21 December everyone could understand

3

Hungarian, but it was a good thing she hadn't seen Csapó, sweatered and good-natured, among the two dozen determined University students, at two in the afternoon she hadn't been facing the inferior but loaded weapons of the soldiers, who wore no badges, *There won't be a choir practice this evening, that's for sure, bang goes my solo*—thought the University student as she ran towards her mother's office, because she was turning the corner precisely at the moment when the first shot went off, bang went her performance, that is, in a few days' time she was to have sung the Hanukkah solo with the choir, that would have been the first solo she'd ever sung, true, it was a boy's part, but a real solo all the same, and she'd only been going to rehearsals for a couple of months, whereas Csapó sang in the choir in the Catholic church in the main square and said that a great-aunt of hers was a nun in a convent—it wasn't because she had a good voice or because she liked singing (though in the meantime she'd acquired a taste for it) that she sang in the synagogue choir, but because she'd had to find somewhere to go: after a few disastrous, completely black pictures she'd become bored with the photographic circle, just couldn't grasp the connection between light and exposure, and the classes were held in the Pioneer House where, as a proud University student, she'd found it painful to go, then she went to the cemetery a number of times in early autumn to call on writers, poets, travellers and men of learning, and mainly her father's grave in the Barcsay garden with its globular stone roses, but it had started to turn cold, and inside the cemetery walls she was always nervous and horrid exhibitionists used to lie in wait so as to pick the right moment to jump out in front of her and startle her with their purple male organs, even as a child she'd been afraid of them when at eight in the morning they hid panting between the pillars at the side of the church in Farkas utca and with eyes staring shook themselves at the little girls as they walked to school, and this little girl kept pebbles in the pocket of her dress because she planned to throw them but could never muster the courage as Csapó certainly would have done, and as an almost grown-up girl she used to go into the dimly lit second-hand bookshop in the main square to look around but seldom bought a book, which would have been a good idea, everything was there, nobody ever brought in new books, but among the books of people who had 'relocated'[1]—she'd often recognized them by monograms or dedications—sometimes one could find things, and she went into the church in the main square, but at such times it was like an icehouse even though the heating was on, and she often went to the theatre and there too kept her coat on, and sometimes there would be a power cut and then some actor would start swearing and there would be jeering in the almost empty auditorium, and sometimes friends would come up to the flat and they'd cook macaroni and put a sauce of tomato purée and bacon fat on it, Mother made it ever so well, and they'd huddle around the cast-iron stove in the fourth-floor flat sitting on cushions, smoking cigarettes, drinking tea and laughing, Lacika would imitate One-Ear,[2] would hold forth about factory visits and agriculture or read out the seventeen points of the July Theses,[3] and the ornate stove could be stoked with wood, it had been plumbed into the light well, Grandfather had brought it up in three pieces of 50 kilos each, and since they'd had it working friends and neighbours liked to come in, and sometimes she went to a concert in the Filharmonia, though she could scarcely bear to sit still for two hours in the unheated hall, *How can the musicians play in this cold?* she wondered, or sometimes she'd go to the neon-lit halls of the Academic Library, where she'd spent so much time a year before when she was writing her final certificate essay in the Humanities special school about the god Pan—a minimum twenty-five typed pages was the requirement, plus an oral exam, that

---

1 That is, emigrated to Hungary.

2 At one time, official photographs of Nicolae Ceaușescu showed him only in profile.

3 The July Theses (Romanian: *Tezele din iulie*) is a name commonly given to a speech delivered by Ceaușescu on 6 July 1971.

is, a defence—the essay had been about the god Pan, because according
to Herodotus Pan had told the runner, the messenger—*angelos* was the
Greek word, as she deciphered to her surprise—that they were going
to win, and he was to take the news and not to worry: they were going
to win, because the messenger ran from Athens to Sparta (246 kilometres, he left one day and arrived the next, then turned straight round
and ran back, was that physically possible? or was the whole thing a
myth? and why not go on horseback? she'd wondered, and looked up
the yearbook of the Kolozsvár Athletic Club, printed a hundred years
previously, but the longest race was the 100-kilometre Kolozsvár–
Marosvásárhely, so was 246 kilometres even a human distance, or was
it one for a god?), the journey had had to be made by a runner, said a
footnote, because a horse couldn't have done it, the forest was too dense,
and in fact over a long distance a man is stronger than a horse, and so
the runner had gone to ask for help for the Athenians in the Battle of
Marathon, but that wasn't why it was called a marathon, she read in
another note, and he hadn't even been able to bring good news home
because the Spartans were in no hurry to help because they said the
omens weren't favourable and they were waiting for the full moon, they
assured him, and the runner knew what it meant going home with bad
news: it amounted to death, and so when he reached Athens he told
the king that he'd met Pan in the hills—had he really, or did he just
make it up? she'd wondered, and the question remained unanswered in
the essay—and Pan had said: we're going to win, so we can start the
battle against the Persians, and, added the runner, the god Pan had been
surprised (and certainly offended, thought the Girl) that they hadn't
been expecting help from him, because in the past he'd often intervened
when they needed him, perhaps he was alluding to the fact that they'd
turned to the distant Spartans rather than to him, who was always at
hand, because not only could Pheidippides run (he was a Greek messenger by profession) but his life too was precious—and it is indeed
possible that he spoke the truth, he had met the god—and anyway the

6

Athenians believed the messenger, because Pan had said *There is no need to fear*, that was Pan's instruction: there was nothing to fear, and the battle had begun, and her essay, written in Romanian and impeccably typed on her father's Olympia typewriter, had been awarded a ten *cum laude*, and on that day the perspiring girl (wearing her glasses, which, out of vanity, she did only in the theatre and at oral exams) only failed to give the panel a convincing answer to one question, why Pan? *De ce tocmai Pan?* why had Pan been her chosen subject?, but she'd smiled so broadly and silently that it seemed that she hadn't really understood anything of what she'd written, just painstakingly gathered material and read in the cold, reinforced concrete building of the Academic Library, and eventually in early autumn Mihály, her former classmate with the nice baritone voice, instead of holding her hand when he saw her home one evening invited her to the choir, *There's a choir that meets in Brassai utca, are you interested?*, he said no more than that, and when she went into the low, over-heated prayer hall she found herself face to face with her singing teacher from school, the kindly, buck-toothed Kati Halmos, Auntie Kati, who wore thick glasses and could never keep order in class, and they looked at each other in surprise at the door, but Mihály, as a full member and host, proudly announced that he'd brought a new choir member, and from then on she too had been going to practices on Mondays and Thursdays, but Kati Halmos looked at her former pupil, who had been in the choir in secondary school, and drily asked: *Well, I suppose your neighbours are Jewish?*, because she knew exactly what her voice was like, and that she smoked, but she knew nothing else about her, and in her view everybody could sing a little and so anybody could join the choir, and Auntie Kati didn't wait for an answer to her question because there were also a few muscular Romanian peasants in the choir as well who wanted to emigrate to Israel and had already put in their applications, and who reckoned that active participation in the choir of the faith community would be an advantage, and the Romanian boys in their new velvet *kippah*s sang

7

with spirit and even knew the words by heart and made an effort to understand their meaning, but to Auntie Kati Halmos it didn't matter at all whether there were any Jews or not, it seemed that everybody had their pressing personal reasons for being there, *Is everybody here Jewish?* the Girl wondered, *Yes,* she decided, *everybody's Jewish,* and Auntie Kati just gave them the note, pushed up the thick lenses on her nose and there she was waving her arms which she liked to hold up high above her head, and two round patches of perspiration spread under the armpits of her sweater, but that evening, 21 December (it was dark at five o'clock), they didn't make a start on *Maocurjesuati ha-na-na-nalesabe-lesabe-eah,* she didn't comment on the next line or *Ha-ha-hazegmorbeshirmizmor hanukat-ha-amizbeah,* or the other one in which her solo would have been: *Giluhamakabim, giluhalaim, sisuvasimehu, somanvalaim*—they pronounced it like Romanian: *sisuvăsimehu,* and to the Girl the melody meant nothing either, she just sat from seven to nine on Mondays and Thursdays in the nice warm room by the big brown wood-burning stove in liquid, boundless time, in the synagogue choir, *Until—until—until—until—until* she thought of something better, she said perplexedly to Mihály on the way home, and he still couldn't bring himself to hold her hand, and she was going to go there until eventually something happened, until *the whole thing exploded,* but suddenly some people did think of something better, and not just anybody, but Csapó's fellow art students, and even before that the Temesvár students, because she hadn't long come back from Temesvár, and even before that the people in Brassó, years before, and so in Kolozsvár it would have been enough for the artists to lean out of the windows of the big, high studios, because the building of the high school overlooked the main square, and for them to shout in their desperation for *something* to happen, but the Girl looked in astonishment from a distance at the little group as it advanced purposefully across the square, took out her glasses with the hideous purple frames, of which she was ashamed but they'd been the best she could find, and as she watched them it appeared that they were chanting their own freshly invented slogans not as consciously and organizedly as the Temesvár people had, according to the radio, but good-humouredly, and they were advancing across the square making for the bookshop at the corner, and opposite, outside the Continental, motionless soldiers sealed off Jókai utca, not a badge of rank or indication of what unit they belonged to could be seen on them—she'd been to military training and knew for certain that these weren't real soldiers—and the students were chanting the same slogans that next day, and after the cancelled solo and the sleepless, gunshot-riddled night she was shouting and singing in the streets with everyone else for hours on end, processing through the town as if they'd been practising for months or years, because in fact they had been practising in silence, and in the first place the slogans were only about *Sinistru*[4]—the moustachioed Hungarian writer tossed the portrait of One-Ear out of the *Utunk* editorial office in Deák Ferenc utca into the street—he whom Father could have knocked off the train sometime in the early '60s, and then *there'd be none of all this*, said Father ruefully, because according to him they'd travelled to Bucharest on a packed train with people hanging on like bunches of grapes, and *he* had been behind him, and when she was a little girl she used to imagine that she was watching a scene from a film: Father, elegant, dark sunglasses, hanging on at the steps, his thick fair hair blowing in the wind, and his long, unbuttoned coat, the colour of dust, holding his pipe in his right hand and hanging on with his left, while behind him the squat, stocky gnome with his demonic grin, and the train going faster and faster, and then Father did what he had to, because that was his mission: with a light smile on his face and a determined jab from his elbow he knocked him off and with that distant, solemn look became a hero, and appeared as such in films as a real father who had saved his children and the whole country from the talons of evil, but if

---

4 Romanian for 'Horrible', 'Terrible' etc.

Father had succeeded in knocking him off, then, of course, there'd have been neither vampire nor film, nor would Father have become a hero but a foul murderer and might still be in Szamosfalva prison, but after the train journey Father had grieved for fifteen years over that missed opportunity, *I might have known, I had a feeling this would happen*, he would mutter to himself, filled with remorse like an alcoholic, *Oh, go on, Janó*, Granddad would wave it away, but that day, 22 December, it was bitterly cold, the sun was bright, and in the morning she and her sister managed to persuade Mother that they should all go out, because by then the night-time firing had stopped, and tired as they were they ran down the Kövespad, didn't even have a coffee, a lot of people were hurrying somewhere in the direction of the main square, then they made their way down to the market, then towards Dohány utca, and Granny must have been standing at the window all the time, standing and staring as the crowd surged up narrow Dohány utca, she'd stood like that in 1918 (when she still lived in Vásárhely) when she'd only been a little girl and hadn't understood what it was all about, and in 1940, when she'd waved a white carnation (in Kolozsvár by that time, in Apponyi utca), and in early May 1944 when people loaded with big bundles were being herded into the ghetto at the brickworks, and now too in December 1989 she listened to the crowd chanting 'down with the vampire' and the Dictator and his wife *and the whole stinking pack*, as Granny put it, and she and the other elderly neighbours stared out of the window as they were no longer fit enough to go out into the street: there were Auntie Buba and half-blind Auntie Pötyi and Uncle Dudus, who used to peck little girls on the cheek, and the dread Auntie Mózes, who used to give the children of the street injections, but suddenly the first-year University student, as she marched in the crowd, her face flushed, no longer caring that she'd missed her solo, felt that what mattered wasn't that she'd been disappointed, been deprived, because the chanting crowd had started a new movement in the music, even more *molto vivace* than before, shouting at the top of their voices

Down with communism! Jos comunismul!, and Mother was repeating it automatically, without really paying attention, but the Girl felt that that wasn't what they'd come for, that wasn't the idea at all, listen, but to finish what Father hadn't managed that day: at last to knock the vampire off the thundering train, but it had never seemed to her that this new turning point was a possibility, in eighteen years not once had it occurred to her that perhaps that was what ought to be shouted, was there another world, and if so what was it like, but Mother couldn't tell her either, perhaps she should have asked Father, after all, that was what he'd taught at one time, scientific socialism and Marxist philosophy, but now she couldn't ask him what other kind of world was there, for goodness sake?—it was the same in Budapest, wasn't it?—it was five years since they'd been there, there'd been the sickly smell of petrol in the streets, the smell of fresh bread and chocolate in the shops, and in Great-uncle's seventh-floor flat in the block, the prefab, as they called it, even in winter it had been so warm in the staircase that fat Auntie Mari had gone about in just a synthetic-fibre housecoat and there was simply always, always, hot water, she could have filled the bath all day if it would have held it, because they'd got such a little bath, and you could see very progressive films like *Another Way*—Granny had covered the teenager's eyes in the cinema—and there was a Hobó Blues Band concert and farmer jeans and coffee and heaps of good books and tinned luncheon meat and pork, as much as you wanted!, and tampons and Postinor for Mother, and on New Year's Eve the whole city had been drunk on petrol fumes, awash with petrol and champagne, and there'd been fashion, which there never was at home, because the shops had only school uniforms on sale and Granny made everything else, and there was always electricity and heating and hot water, and then she suddenly looked sideways, and there was her mother flushed and shouting, and her sister, both shouting their heads off, and now she too was chanting like somebody copying off the next desk because she hadn't done her homework, in her deep, rounded, boyish voice which it had taken her so long to get to like, as loudly as she could, along with the choir, *Ha-ha-hazegmorbeshirmizmor hanukat-ha-amizbeah*, or more precisely *Jos comunismul*!, even though on that soft, ever-warmer, finally almost spring-like December day she couldn't, according to her grey identity card, so much as imagine that other world as an adult for another six months, whereas scarcely six months previously, as evidence of her maturity, she'd written an original and acclaimed essay about the god Pan, who had sent word to the Athenians that naturally they were to give battle even without assistance, have faith in him, for he had helped them before, and that in any case, come what may, they were going to be victorious, although she, by then a University student of six months' standing who regarded herself as an adult, hadn't fully understood the Greek message or the Hebrew hymn or the Romanian slogans.

SQUARE

It wasn't the photograph of One-Ear above the blackboard in the class-room, as, with his floppy bow tie and sleeked-back frizzy hair, he had smiled benignly down for fifteen years from Monday to Saturday upon studious youth—the A3 prints weren't on sale in shops, but organiza-tions could obtain them from a central distributor, there was no way that they could be had for money, it seemed that it would have been impossible to attach a monetary value to them—nor was it his two-eared photograph on the front pages of textbooks, riddled by pencil- or compass-points, routinely adjusted to the form of swallow, devil, Lenin, Dracula or clown in drawings of great variety and sometimes considerable talent—classes handed down textbooks, inherited them from one another, and these too were not on sale—furthermore they were surprisingly similar in that in all of them the background remained impossible to obliterate, showing through even drawings done with the darkest ballpoint, in brief, it wasn't the pictures in text-books or classrooms that terrorized the long-haired, uniformed school-girl, but the morning scrutiny of the biology teacher: at seven in the morning, his mirror-smooth cheeks pomaded, his white coat starched and ironed, his gleaming shirt with downturned collar likewise, the grey, knife-creased trousers of his suit and his leather-soled pigskin shoes, Comrade Teacher Antal, like one first to arrive at the place of ceremonial execution of the criminals of the day to lead the chief offender to the scaffold at eight o'clock precisely, stood stock-still, hands clasped behind his back, outside the heavy wrought-iron gate of the school, signet and marriage rings on right and left hands respectively, never wearing anything over his crisp, almost paper-stiff laboratory coat even in the hardest of frosts because his sun-tanned body, as he never failed to stress every week in military training, was tough and resilient, and the most that Antal put on in the biting cold of January was a grey lambskin hat on his dressed, brushed-back hair; and he bent down ten times one after another with an audible intake of breath as he cast a keen eye over the class; there he stood at the gate, his feet apart, self-confident, checking the school identity numbers[5] on coats and uniforms, on the front for the girls, above the heart, as the saying went, on the arm for the boys, all stitched on with dark thread, not held by an elastic band so that it could be craftily pulled off after school, nor with a safety pin so that it should dangle and be easily hidden, nor yet with press studs, but well and truly stitched on, even on a sheepskin or leather coat, because they had two numbers embroidered in yellow thread on a dark cloth backing which differed from school to school in shape and colour; here at the Farkas utca school it was a black pentagon with the name of the school around the edge and in the middle a two- or three-figure number clearly visible at a distance, one on the coat, so that it could also be seen in the street—because the school presumed that its pupils would have only one coat for all seasons, and the possibility of more coats was excluded in advance—and one underneath, on the uniform for wear in school, and in fact (as Grandmother used to tell them) everyone used to be able to have the number made at their own expense, like the yellow star, but the identity number had to be obtained at a cooperative tailor or hatter on production of a school record-book, but that wasn't usually asked for because it was assumed that everybody was honest and would only ask for two of their own number, and they'd been to the corner of Egyetem utca and Florilor, opposite the church, because home-made ones weren't acceptable, and Comrade Teacher Antal further checked the blue man-made fibre uniform blouses and the girls' hair-ribbons, to see that their hair was tidy,

---

5 Schoolchildren had to wear their number and the name of their school on this badge.

and the stockings below the uniforms, because trousers were, of course, forbidden even when the temperature went below minus fifteen as was the case that day, and he checked record-books, that is, the very word 'check' meant just that he stood silent and motionless at the gate and assessed everybody with a single keen glance—was there a button missing, was clothing torn—and now he was looking over the 71s (her number showed her year of birth) and the quick-witted 71-er, who another time had happily turned back from the gate at 7.55 because she'd forgotten the hair-ribbon which she hadn't been able to put on her long, unruly hair in a manner calculated to satisfy Antal, or because she'd put trousers on again, or she'd come out in knee-length yellow-and-brown striped stockings that made her look like a gigantic bee (fat Uncle Zolti had brought the distinctive item of clothing, leg warmers, from Budapest), or perhaps it was 8.05 by the time she appeared in something unexceptionable, but then she couldn't go in, and then, like someone that had done all in her power, she would turn round and make for the tea shop in the main square, which opened at half past eight, and sit by the big, brown-tiled stove with two cups of sweet elder-flower tea—Lulu,[6] the town's favourite lunatic, also warmed himself there for a little while, didn't ask for anything but got a cup of tea with five spoonfuls of sugar, said 'thank you' in a hoarse voice, drank it quickly and went off about his business—and then she would go home by a circuitous route via the deserted marketplace: sauerkraut, fresh cabbage, potatoes, Brussels sprouts, carrots, tiny, wrinkled apples, eggs at an extortionate price and carnations in bud that never opened were on offer that day, and home she went to Dohány utca, where she never needed a key as there was always someone in, Grandmother, for example; but this time she hadn't even left her red record-book at home but showed it up at once because she always had it on her and at home never took it out of the bag that had been made for it from Grandfather's torn linen towel, *Yes, that's just the bag I wanted, Granny*

---

6 See below in the chapter *The King's Fool*.

15

(because for some peculiar reason a fitting cover didn't exist, such things were only made for elementary-school pupils, *Șoimii patriei*[7] and soldiers), and she forged her mother's signature wonderfully: the winter term had scarcely started and already lined up were Principles of Constitutional Law 4, Latin 10, Hungarian 9 for Jókai—the new Hungarian teacher was grey and boring, the previous one had been dismissed after a year, that is, transferred to the country because she'd applied to move to Hungary[8]—History 2, and a slap for smoking in the lavatory from the same history teacher, Ghiță (Gica, from Gheorghe), her ear had still been ringing that afternoon from Gheorghe Silaghi's big hand, but she'd managed to conceal the pack of Snagovs, and she'd got a 6 for a punishment test on the industrial geography of Hungary, but in fact had made her mind up, she wasn't going to do Geography any more, she'd decided, because she was offended and felt that the 6 was unfair, but she hadn't known the coalmines, only the bridges and rivers, and according to her grandfather, who came from a mining family, Hungary really had no coal to speak of, and what was more the teacher, the fat Aristid Nagy, had suddenly, just like that, from one year to the next, taught Geography in Romanian with an execrable accent, which he was not disposed to explain, and what had been when she was in Year Six *Tanár elvtárs, jelentem, az osztály létszáma* . . . a year later was *Tovarășe profesor, raportez că clasa* . . . because from Year Seven the subjects of History and Geography had ceased to exist in Hungarian[9] as hostile and uncontrollable sources of knowledge, and thus it had become a language dispossessed of a territory and a place on the world map, as of a past and a present . . . *It was the same in Dés after 1922, we had to do History and Geography in*

---

7 'Falcons of the Fatherland', a communist youth organization established in 1976 for children between the ages of four to seven.

8 The standard penalty for such disloyalty to Romania.

9 An example of the anti-Hungarian measures taken by the regime involved restricting usage of the language in bilingual schools.

Romanian as well, Grandfather assured her, he'd been good at Geography, *and the teachers read the lessons out because they didn't know Olah,*[10] *we were better at it than them, because I used to play tiddlywinks with my Romanian friends in the courtyard, but after we moved to Parajd the Székelys couldn't speak a word of it*—and in any case her mother's illegible, scribbled initials was there by the Girl's bad marks: something like 'Kut, Kut', even by the black mark for smoking which had led to her being put in Square and disciplinary proceedings, better not reveal anything at home, especially what the alcoholic gym teacher had written in unsteady capitals, that she hadn't been to a single gym lesson that year and hadn't brought a note, nor was she going to, thought the Girl, because the gym teacher groped the girls, *We haven't had any kind of mark this term, the total will be put in altogether,* she lied innocently at home, *It wasn't like that in my time,* her mother accepted it, she'd originally been a Maths teacher, but she was confident that if there was going to be any serious trouble the girl would say, and Granny asked in surprise at eleven in the morning how come there was no school that day, well, there wasn't, it was cold and they couldn't heat the school, or the rest had gone off on community work and she'd been excused because she'd got a temperature, *Then let me see that so-called temperature,* and that was why she'd drunk two elderflower teas in the Plafar in Deák Ferenc utca, the pleasant-smelling herbalist, 1 lei 50 with sugar, 1 lei if she didn't take sugar, but she always did, she told Grandmother, and Granny didn't ask any questions because she had a vague idea that there must have been something the matter with the number, it had to be sewn on as firmly as Auntie Lili's family's six-pointed stars which she'd cut out of an old quilt for the Salamon girls, and in the morning she'd asked for a safety pin for the number but she wouldn't let her have one, *You've already taken all my safety pins and shed them,* Granny had grumbled and fished out some rusty thing, or she must have upset the teachers with the thick, curly hair that she'd inherited from her, because

---

10 From the region of Wallachia; a Hungarian pejorative term for Romanian.

17

she wasn't prepared to wear it in a plait or a ponytail, nor would she let her mother brush it properly, and she'd gone out, after much anxious pleading, with her hair just as she'd got out of bed; Granny had shouted at her for ten minutes at the bottom of the stairs, and finally Grandfather had gone up to the attic, but now this number 71 had almost gone through the gate beside the biology teacher of average build, redolent of aftershave and cigarettes, as he stood with unwavering gaze directed not at her but at her uniform, and suddenly sprang upon her and seized her arm so that she cried out, because in fact no rule prescribed how long the man-made fibre uniform dress should be, in principle below the knee, at least to mid-shin, and Granny had begged her to let her raise the hem because it was a size 52 uniform, *Oh, mother, of course I can buy myself a uniform!*—she'd begged her mother at the end of August to be allowed to go to the shop by herself —*You can't be serious, I can do a thing like that!*—and her mother had very reluctantly handed over the 45 lei, but in the shop in Szentegyház utca she'd simply asked the assistant how big the largest uniform was, she was getting it for her sister, and they all had the label 'Made in Bîrlad', because invisible Bîrlad, which she couldn't even place on the map, was the holy city of uniforms, and when her mother came home that evening and saw the enormous dress she slammed the door of the room and told her: you're not going anywhere tomorrow, not even to your Grandmother's, and Mother could have exchanged the dress if she wanted, after all, she was in charge of the big department store, but the enormous ankle-length uniform couldn't fail to be spotted, last year's was a disgrace because *Your backside's hanging out, love,* said Mother, it had become so short, Grandmother sighed and turned it up for next year's uniform and never said a word when a certain Pisti, Juci's classmate, often appeared after school or in the garden at Father's, and she was put in Square because in fact it was knee-length, and there was a number on it, and the pockets hadn't been altered, but it was so tight, so close-fitting that she could hardly get it on and it was hard to walk in it, but she was so slim in the dress—*Ta, Granny*—because Granny had let it out very carefully at the side and put in an invisible, narrow zip from bust to hip on the left so that she would be able to get it on, and wearing it the Girl looked like her mother in her school-leaving dress, that checked dress which, as it happened, Grandmother had also made, but now at the sight of the ankle-length nun's habit purple patches appeared on the teacher's hitherto immaculate, smooth face, a tiny bubble of saliva came to his lips and his hackles rose visibly; he grasped the girl's left arm tightly, his sharp nails digging in just by the previous day's injection which the whole class had been given with a nice blunt needle, he held on to her, abandoned his guard-post, and without a word took her upstairs to the teachers' room, as the purple patches darkened on his face and veins stood out on his temples and his hand stung through the thin man-made fibre blouse as if she had some skin disease, and until finally he deposited her outside the teachers' room where a few others were already standing, heads bowed, Comrade Teacher Antal's morning haul, and there was still a biology lesson to come in the day, starting after break at 11.10, but during break, instead of eating her favourite mustard sandwich, she had to line up in the concrete yard for Square, where she could expect to be called out from VIII-C because of the uniform; the summons to appear before Square usually began with the little ones, and that day nothing unusual happened— they too were sent over to Square from the other building—but the biology teacher, in his pale pink shirt, sharply creased trousers and immaculate lab coat, made his own class line up in the bitter cold at 10.50, classes 1 to 4 on the right, 5 to 8 in the middle and the big ones, classes 9 to 12, on the left, with the class leaders in front of them, and finally the head teacher, the deputy, the teacher on duty that week and three other teachers, *Hope it lasts as long as possible*, thought the Girl, because then the biology lesson would be late starting, Antal took the list of names from his coat pocket, and when one's name was called out one went to the middle of the yard, VIII-C, she heard her name,

Uniform! he shrieked, and as she went to the middle of Square and stood in front of the victims of the day she heard laughter evoked by her uniform; but she couldn't be sure whether they were laughing derisively and scornfully at her or, on the other hand, with her, fulfilling her plan, but in any case Antal looked up menacingly in the direction of the laughter and there was silence at once, so he went on, X-A, goodness! her sister, well, what had happened? she wondered, and her sister was standing right in front of her, but Antal didn't lower his voice but went on through the list as if he were uncovering a whole gang of criminals: X-A, *Csapó*, and then X-A, *Palocsay—fighting*, the inseparable friends! and the girls went shivering out into the middle of Square, the VIII-C Girl looked with interest at those in X-A, Palocsay's lip was bleeding, her sister was holding in her hand a pocket torn off her uniform as Csapó had hung onto it, but Csapó was unharmed, looking very smart in the new, cyclamen-blue woollen coat which her mother had knitted, now smiling smugly as if the proceedings didn't matter to her because she knew that she was leaving to go to Art school, and the fight had happened as follows: in chemistry Csapó had written to Palocsay that the third member of the gang and DT had slept together and *she'd become a woman*, and so the two girls decided by letter to cut her out of the gang, not for sleeping with DT, after all Csapó wasn't a virgin either, but for keeping it a secret and not telling them, whereas the three of them had sworn allegiance for life or death, and when in break neither Palocsay nor Csapó answered her sister when she asked whether they were going for a coffee to the Arizona in Egyetem utca, she shrugged and went to look for Moravek—the fourth member of the gang, who was in XI-D—a pure Romanian technical class—who knew all about it and furthermore had done it and boasted about it, and Moravek had told her straight that she'd let them down and ought to be ashamed, then turned her back and went into the lavatory for a ciggy and then her sister had gone for Csapó in the loo as she was just having a ciggy with that idiot Ambrus, who was a Catholic and whom she never talked to, even though Csapó was a Catholic as well, but it suited her, when finally in came Palocsay as well, and her sister's classmate Pisti had tried to catch the Girl's eye during Square, looking amusedly at the floor-length uniform, it looked as if she'd been sewn into a sack and now was going to be thrown into the sea for punishment, but she didn't notice because her eyes were on the big girls and she was imagining that she was going to get in their good books, become the fifth member of the gang, and the biology lesson did in fact begin ten minutes late, and the forty-strong class of VIII-C stood tensely in the room smelling of paraffin when Doctor Antal entered with a great big class register bound in canvas with embroidered letters on it under his arm and slammed the door behind him as hard as he could so that first the lid on the ancient upright piano fell down, then after a second-long interval the portrait of One-Ear dropped with a crash into the gap between the blackboard and the dais, the glass cracked from end to end and on the teacher's blotchy head a vein swelled anew and started to throb, he flung the register and the canvas depicting the palmacea species which he hadn't finished teaching onto the desk and bawled *Who's the monitor?* and the startled Girl, because, as luck would have it, it was her turn that week, stepped forward in her long dress, over which she all but tripped when she slipped out from the desk at the back by the window where she chose to sit with the dunce of the class, the cheerful Csabi Ürögdi, *Who was that?* shouted Antal, beside himself, *Me,* moaned the girl, at which Antal, biology teacher of the century-old, elite Hungarian model school, once again pretended not to hear, and she looked down at the dark, oiled floor and replied calmly *Comrade teacher, it was I,* but she herself didn't know how to take it: whether she meant that she was the monitor, or that she was to blame for the picture falling off the wall and breaking: who was who, which was the picture and which the original, and what had in fact broken at a few minutes past eleven in the morning.

THE MOUTH

What part of him are you? asked Csabi Ürögdi, blue with cold outside the children's clinic at the 25 trolleybus stop, because they would go the same way to the Györgyfalvi district, but no trolley had come in half an hour and the tall Girl in her worn sheepskin coat, turned inside-out, would have got on the Number 4 to go and see her aunt and warm up, but there hadn't been a Number 4 either, her toes were numb, all morning they'd been standing in the stadium in the icy January wind because at the start of the month the announcement had suddenly been made that the school holidays had been extended and the blessed condition was to last not three weeks but five, because of the extraordinarily cold weather the schools couldn't be heated, but in the second week of January everybody had suddenly had to report at the school, 'in warm clothing and with food' the summons added, the assumption at home was that there was to be a public project, picking over frozen potatoes or carrots, but in the morning they were lined up in a square in the school yard and after a brief instruction sent off to the stadium, where they had now been going to practise for a week, *I don't know*, the Girl answered uncertainly, watching for the buses on Monostori út, but there was nothing coming, then glancing doubtfully at little Csabi, *Aren't we letters?*, and she looked at the swarthy, stocky, black-browed boy, who was always cheerful for no reason, with whom she shared a desk, she'd been made to sit with him as a punishment in Year Six because Csabi was the worst pupil in the class, and then she'd got 'satisfactory' results and could choose otherwise but stayed with him because they'd become friendly, *What colour were you wearing?* asked Csabi, because in the stadium they'd not been together, he'd been taken off to somewhere else as he was short and they hadn't seen each other all day since the time they were lined up in order of size on the football pitch, which was still covered with last year's dirty ice and patchy snow, and the biology teacher and the PE teachers—all three of the school's PE teachers smelt of *pálinka* and vile cigarettes in the mornings (the senior pupils also were said to bring in *pálinka* and tea with rum in it)—led them up into the stand on the south side, where they had to turn on the shout of '*La dreapta!*' (Right turn!); they stood on the seats, the shell-shaped plastic seats, where they were not allowed to take anything with them, their bags were piled by classes in the mud-blackened snow on the pitch, but the clothes were only given out a week later, and by then they had learnt to turn backwards, to turn their heads, the slogans and the songs: the pig-eyed history teacher Ghiţă stood down below on the edge of the pitch on the top level of a podium fished out of the store, marked with a 1 and intended for winners, and howled into an aluminium megaphone, trying as he did so to turn over folded diagrams in the icy wind that blew from the side, and the teachers in charge of the classes and groups at the ends repeated the words of command: this was the sign that they had to turn all together in four stages, and those in charge clapped their hands eight times: left foot outwards turn, right foot beside it (so far a half-turn), left foot outwards turn, again right foot beside it, and by now they were facing the other way), only all this had to be done on a fixed, plastic seat on which there was hardly room for their boots, it was next to impossible to turn, so somebody was always falling off or late because the seats were wet and slippery, those that were badly secured wobbled, somebody must have taken the screws out—*One side's blue, the other side's red*, she replied, and thought that it might be as well to start walking home, there must be a power cut because nothing was coming up the hill, although several people were waiting, but perhaps they were queueing for the shop behind the bus stop?—*Red? There's no red*, said Csabi firmly, and added *I've got black and white: white is the letter on one side, black is his hair on the other*, and he began to blow on his red hands, *Aren't we letters on both sides? That's what Year Ten told me*, asked the Girl, because no one had officially told them what they were portraying, all that they knew was that they were preparing for a celebration, and it was a great honour and distinction for the whole school that they had been chosen, and so the Girl hadn't thought about what the colours meant, she'd just been waiting every day to go home—*Shall we go?* she suggested, because she and Csabi often walked home—*Yes, let's, there's nothing coming. At one time we're white letters on blue, then the other side's the picture. Which side are you on most?* he asked—*You mean, facing the stadium? The blue. Where are you going?* she asked, because in the meantime she'd decided to go to Grandmother's instead, where there was always some lunch left over, and now she might get a hot milky coffee as well, but Mother wouldn't be home until evening, she'd said she was working out of town—*I don't know, don't mind, I'm not going home*—replied Csabi, *I'm with the white more, I'm the hat on the letter ă, you know, right at the very top, because the side of the stand's been extended to make room for the whole thing, the words and the picture, they say the other stadium was higher than the Kolozsvár one, they've welded bars onto the top railings*—they just hung about for two days while that was done, couldn't even go into the dressing rooms—*then the bars have been supported from underneath, little planks put over them, and we stand on those, there's only a rope behind us, and the shortest and lightest in the whole school have been chosen, there are some fourth formers as well, they haven't put anybody smaller up there because a stupid third former fell off, and the whole thing wobbles like this when we get up and turn*—Csabi demonstrated with his red hands—*everybody shakes, and they've put the smallest up there in case the whole thing collapses under the big ones, you see, we're very high up, makes you shit yourself, you can see the cross in Főtér, the whole of Fellegvár, the Kerekdomb and the station, the Szamos bridge as well, Donát út, the Kányafő, the Monostor, the cemetery, the covered-up lions on the Roman theatre, I'd never seen the town from so high up, and you can't hear what Ghiţă's shouting down there either*—because it was he, the history teacher, who was directing the proceedings from down there—*we've got Kriszti on the end of the row, he's really shit scared, feels sick all the time, so I'm the very highest of the letters, on the first ă in 'Trăiască'* (Long live), *and when we turn I'm his hair, see! when I've got my back turned and I look down I shit myself! and when we turn round there's the picture, then your back's black or white, you're hair, face, eye, but there's no other colour, I've not heard of any red, d'you want one?* And he took out a pack of Albanian Apollonias and offered it, and now they were passing the Ethnographic Museum in Unió utca, and Csabi's mother knew that he smoked and only laughed—*Are you daft? Here in the street? Here and now?* because before the holiday there were more police about, but you had to look out for adults as well, they might note your identity number, and they turned into narrow Ion Rațiu utca—*There were others wearing red*—said the Girl, because at the end of the practice they'd had to stand in line and hand in their things by colour, crumpled overalls, front and back different in colours, with press-studs and elastic loops on the legs and arms, two-coloured hoods, all pulled on over their coats, only they had to take their boots off before putting the overalls on so as not to dirty them (that morning everybody had been hopping about in the mud, pulling their overalls on), and the first day they'd taken off long coats and furs, because the new uniforms wouldn't go over them, and Marinka and Monduk had had the good luck to develop pneumonia, they were able to bring sick notes—only notes from the school doctor, Polónyi, were accepted, and anybody that was absent for a single day without a note would be expelled, roared Ghiță—and next day everybody came in short coats, and at the end of the practice they gave the things in by colours, they weren't allowed to take them home during the two weeks of practices, only on the last day, Tuesday 25 January, they had to take them home before the celebration and iron them, and Mother hadn't stopped criticizing the paltry material and the sloppy way the ridiculous gear was tacked together, *This get-up! You'll look just like a clown in it! What a crackpot piece of work!*

Never seen such rubbish in my life!—she turned it inside-out—and after use the overalls were stored in cardboard boxes, on which was written in felt-tip: *Cluj 26 ianuarie* (Kolozsvár, 26 January) and underneath, crossed out or pasted over: *Miercurea Ciuc 23 august* (Csíkszereda, 23 August), *Tîrgu Mureş 26 ianuarie* (Marosvásárhely 26 January), the three had been made into a six, only the names of the months crossed out, it seemed that only the towns and months had changed, not the years, they were either still in place or ringed, it made no difference whether it was '79, '83, '84 or '86, and the clothes were all one size, like a uniform, and little Ogrucán, in an enormous white overall, looked like a circus polar bear that had lost its fur, *How many reds do you think there were? How many piles when you gave them in?* Csabi asked suddenly, as if he'd just remembered that at the end of the practice the overalls were stacked in piles of ten, and he stubbed out the cigarette on the wall of a house because his hand was frozen by then, and put the long butt back in the box. *Look, I'm going to have to go to my mother's office, see you,* said the Girl, and turned abruptly on her heel, but she didn't make for her mother's office but, although it was out of the way, for her grandparents', because it has suddenly dawned on her that she could only be his mouth: the fleshy lips, drawn into a smile on the front pages of textbooks, the blood-red cherry lips on the classroom wall above the double poster, the smiling lips on the holiday front page of the newspapers—his teeth never showed in the smile—the mouth that ranted long speeches on the television, she was the mouth in the gigantic picture made up of another school's worth of children, which in birthday greeting would turn into a sudden, smiling portrait on the south side of the stadium, the mouth which would churn out catchphrases and cheer itself when the tiny original of the picture descended from the helicopter at the birthday celebrations in the middle of the gravel-strewn, red-carpeted stadium, and a chosen boy and girl would run forward and happily greet him—the best class in the school—and school governors had come in Pioneer uniform on the first days and practised in the dressing room—with flowers, salt and a huge, gleaming plaited sweetbread that no mouth would touch, step onto the edge of the rolled-out carpet, like the little ones, the Falcons of the Fatherland, in just blouses and skirts, and a bigger pupil would declaim enthusiastically into the microphone the poem entitled *Ce-ţi doresc eu ţie, dulce Românie*—What do I wish you, sweet Romania—the rest would sing and, standing on the plastic seats of the stadium, would suddenly turn round on the word of command, and then the picture would appear, because this portrait which hitherto had existed only in textbooks, classrooms, newspapers, every kind of special editions of books and on television for anniversaries would now become reality: the sixty-fifth birthday of the original of the picture would be celebrated in other towns too, he would arrive by plane and helicopter, finally go home in the evening to deliver his celebratory speech before crowds of thousands in the floodlit main square of the capital in his winter coat and astrakhan hat—*Perhaps he won't turn up*—Csabi Ürögdi called after her as she was just going under the house on piles (where wishes come true, the children's game came into her head, but perhaps Csabi didn't know it), *He won't come because he doesn't exist*, she thought, or perhaps his double will come because he's got several doubles who visit towns at the same time, and who would know except the pilot, because he himself would become immortal by means of others, and anyway he was only known from photographs and the TV, and it wasn't impossible that only the photographs existed, the doubles, not he himself, so then he wouldn't be able to die either as he'd never existed, somebody'd invented him and everybody else had believed in him, *They've invented him, like the Kolozsvár people have the Hangman's House in Petőfi utca, and nobody knows who thought it up or when so as to keep the town in a state of terror, and by this time we accept without doubt or hesitation that it's there and that there should be something for us to tremble at*, said the Girl to herself—she always walked on the other side in Petőfi utca for fear of that house—*Now I'm his disgusting mouth*, had suddenly come into her head, and she felt sick as she thought of herself and the overalls that she'd not long taken off, she felt as if cold, drooling lips were kissing her defenceless body, as if this huge frothing mouth were vomiting white, foaming letters over her, and she was becoming a bit of living, loathsome, pink flesh, torn off and displayed to public view, because *I am him, or vice versa, he is me*: I am his flesh, inseparably conjoined, he's taking root in me so that I shan't be able to wash him off, and his likeness has been burned into me like a brand, I am him, or more precisely we're all him, because we're all stood in nice, tidy order and we turn on the word of command and we're him: but he himself doesn't exist anywhere, nobody ever sees him, never: Tátá's seen him and my uncle Pista as well, they've sat with him at meetings, but now he's just pictures, pictures, pictures, not a person, just pictures, something that we've jointly made up and unknowingly formed from our bodies like people that have no idea what they're involved in or how long it'll last, because from close to we really can't see the trees for the wood just as that Year Eight schoolgirl can't see herself at that moment, only the crumpled clown-suits in which they turn in four movements on the word of command in an empty, echoing stadium where nobody's going to arrive, because even on his birthday he won't land in the middle of the stadium, but even if he does they won't see him because they'll have to turn their heads to the left so that first the blue, then the red side of the hoods is seen instead of their faces, because they no longer have their own faces, only his gigantic face is to be seen in the funnel-shaped stadium, but perhaps from above, from the Fellegvár with its patchy snow or the muddy Törökvágás, it will still be filmed as eternal evidence that he'd come among them, and they'd waste their time standing for hours on end in silence, motionless, waiting, they themselves would celebrate what they had unknowingly and helplessly invented, he didn't exist anywhere because he was just a dream, an icy January nightmare from which they must eventually wake or go to sleep on their feet and end up freezing to death, *I'm his mouth, I've got to stand still, like a statue, the lips will move with me, open and swallow me, or open to speak and speak through me, his words will start to pour forth because there are no others, only his screeching voice, because it is I, I, I in my blood-red overalls that keep him alive,* and he's Csabi Ürögdi, and apart from Monduk and Marinka the whole of VIII-C, the whole school, which is elite and still pure Hungarian but in the near future will start Romanian classes, because that's how the Romanianization of a school begins, and the wood-industry school, the music academy, the technical school and all the rest, the chosen few, all of them, because it's they who give the blood for it—this blood transfusion, this children's blood which the demon receives every week to keep him alive—when they hear from the end of the row the military word of command: '*la stiiiinga!*', the middle syllable falling menacingly away, long drawn out, and the third suddenly back up to pitch, 'left turn!', and they've become a picture, mouth, hair, skin, eyes, floppy bow-tie and ears, but they can't see it, can't hear anything, aren't looking at anything, saying nothing, nothing, nothing, *If you turn to the left you become him at once, and now* 'left turn!', and they feel no pain in the January frost.

ONO

Her high heels now clattered on the stairs, now slowed as she reached the upper floor and went down the corridor with her mincing steps, one foot carefully set in front of the other as if she was treading dangerous ground; after the lunch break a tense silence in the classroom awaited the fiftyish, swarthy, lightly boned teacher of Romanian, luminary of the school named after Ady and Şincai, in her long knitted skirt with a scalloped edge and her stiletto heels, tall, delicate, well groomed and solemn, with thick silver rings like heavy fetters on her slender fingers and two wedding rings besides—the talk in the school was that the childless literature teacher's husband had been an officer, perhaps a colonel, had died in some catastrophe, and she'd then had a breakdown, because the laconic, passionate and explosive Ono had the reputation of a dread and learned teacher at the new Humanities school and taught things that weren't even heard of in other schools—world literature, aesthetics, general linguistics, literary theory and, of course, Romanian literature, as now too, on this listless October day, when she clutched the essays written the day before as punishment between the register and her big, theatrical, envelope-shaped, fine leather handbag, and when she put the pile down on the shabby teacher's desk and they flew in all directions, covering the dais, and Vica, the monitor, a hefty girl who came in daily from the country and invariably smelt of sheep, waited uncertainly by the dais for the order to bend and pick them up or not to, Ono stood there for a moment, looked balefully at the sheets of paper on the floor and said in an undertone: *Ia-le* (pick them up), then wearily raised her narrow, angular face, looked round the twice eighteen-strong tenth-grade class, a fraternal class of half-Romanians, half-Hungarians, and sorted out with her slender, brown fingers the essays which by then Vica had carefully gathered up without looking at them, cleared her throat and, as if it hurt her to speak, forced out: *Habar n-aveţi de Caragiale*, whispered it scornfully at the silent class —You've no idea about Caragiale—his play *A Night of Turmoil* was to be put on at the Hungarian theatre in the pedestrian precinct that winter, and the most hair-raising scene wouldn't be the one in which the lovers play hide-and-seek so that the cuckolded husband, previously half-witted but now totally deranged, shan't catch them, but the one where the lovesick poet has a basin of cold water poured down his neck, at which the spectators, teeth chattering in their overcoats in the auditorium, two or three dozen people in the vast hall that seated eight hundred, would hiss as they felt the cold, and the director, so an actress had told the schoolgirl, was putting on the rumbustious, humorous play for a mere 400 lei, and the new girl pupil of the Humanities specialist school, of the same name as the director of the Caragiale play, went to see almost everything that was on, sneaked in through the door at the end of the courtyard (the caretaker said nothing to her, he knew her by that time) and although they even played to two people if that was all that came the play was often stopped or didn't even start because there was no electricity, and the audience would wait in silence for a quarter of an hour, half an hour, or would stay to the end of the imaginary performance, the one that eventually didn't even take place that day, like people that weren't in a hurry to go anywhere, as if time were boundless and lacked all urgent purpose, and it wasn't usual to ask for money back at the ticket office, which was shut by then, or to complain to the attendant in the auditorium, because the show had gone on in its own invisible way: *Paştele mă-tii!* or *Duceţi-vă la mama dracului!* an actor couldn't help swearing when everything suddenly went black halfway through the performance, said it in Romanian so that the person addressed was sure to get the message, although on that stage Romanian was never spoken (Your mother's Easter! Go to the devil's mother!—the fanciful nonsense rang out) and the performance was off, and eventually old ladies with electric torches would show the audience out, but at the time the new pupil hadn't had the chance of seeing on stage *The Lost Letter*, on which Ono had set the imposition last lesson: *Analyse one character in the play, you've got ten minutes*, she'd hissed, eyes gleaming, and now she bent and, bloodless lips pursed, glanced at a corrected essay, then looked up, raised her wan gaze to the pupils sitting on the right of the room and told them disparagingly: *Mi-e ruşine de voi, românilor* (I'm ashamed of you, Romanians) and began to give out the essays, reading out surnames as they came, all mixed up: Iordache, Vízy, Cornea, Boc, Horváth, Amăriei, Vălean, Vica, Szilágyi, Gönczöl (Gjontsol, she pronounced it) Covaci, Kovács, Váncsa, Vancea, Oltean, Oltyán—which all sounded alike coming from her as she forced herself to pronounce the Hungarian names as if reading them out was a task contrary to nature, an unworthy chore—everybody got three, four, five, at the most six, two of them, those that had handed in nothing got two, the essays with three were crossed out, those with four had at most a minute tick, but that was still reckoned a fail mark, and six was the top mark, Boc and Cornea had got that, and to Cornea's work she commented, after a pause for reflection: *Tu vrei să intri la actorie? Cu lucrarea asta despre Caragiale?* (You mean to apply for acting school? With an essay like this on Caragiale?) because she meant to go on the stage, and tiny Iolanda Boc from Nagybánya, who wrote talented verse and was one of Ono's favourites, likewise was in for it: *În loc să-ţi faci codiţe ca o fetiţă de cinci ani* (instead of going around in pigtails like a five-year-old), and indeed Iolanda, the new pupil's future friend, had that day turned up with two plaits, *M-m-m-m-da*, she added, as if uncertain of her own decision, *şase*, that is, Iolanda got a six as well, then Ono gave out the blank and half-blank sheets, hummed scornfully, Sângerean was next, who was as proud of his surname with the letter *â*, only used in old Romanian orthography, as if it were a kind of noble escutcheon: *Mă rog*, Ono flung at him, *nici nu mă mir, trei, dragă, trei, băiatule* (Really, nothing surprises me, three, my dear boy, three), and then, when

32

Pompiliu Sângerean, the red-haired boy, had gone shamefacedly to his place, Ono was left with only one essay in her trembling hand, hers that was waiting to feel the ultimate annihilating blow; Ono looked at the sheet of paper, paused for effect, then seemed to start but suddenly dried up like someone that can't make up their mind in what words to express the disgrace on the paper: *Să vă fie ruşine*, she said, and looked again at the desks on the right of the class, where the Romanian members of X-B were seated, *că singura lucrare ca lumea a fost scrisă de o unguroiaca* (be ashamed of yourselves that the only essay worth anything is by a Hungarian), then she added: *Nouă*, and the Girl, her face afire, was about to go up for the essay that had earned a nine when suddenly Ono remembered: *Care a mai şi lipsit primele două săptămîni*, she added crossly, that is, someone who, into the bargain, wasn't here for the first two weeks, because the Girl hadn't been able to arrange her transfer to the Humanities school and had been admitted without taking the entrance exam, and so she'd had to wait for two weeks for permission from the education authorities, for which she'd been running about all summer, her mother hadn't been able to help at all even though she knew someone in the education office, no chance, she shrugged, but the obstinate girl had pestered a tall, elegant Romanian literature specialist inspector with her hair in a chignon until she felt sorry for her —or had it been a matter of Humanities-solidarity?—and suggested that if she brought a doctor's certificate to the effect that she had asthma and couldn't stand the practical work in a factory that they had to do in the maths and physics lyceum—in the Humanities school the 'practical' would be speed-typing—she'd arrange the transfer for her, and next day, the first of August, she'd taken round the asthma certificate scrawled by Dr Löwy, their GP, but school started in the middle of September and she'd still had to wait for permission and finally got there one Friday morning, two weeks late, just in time for Romanian Literature, and the head of department, the tall, elegant French teacher, took her along and introduced her, but Ono didn't even turn round, went on writing on the board the analysis of Eminescu's poem *Sara pe deal* (Evening on the Hill), quantitative metre, evening tone, alternations of vowels, hidden symmetry of metaphors, cyclic framework of the poem, hillsides rising and swelling and willows trailing in the water and the moon, the shafts and rays, and all the time muttering the lines, and the new pupil sat down fascinated in the empty seat in the front, like someone listening for the first time in her life to a complex and risqué demonstration of verse-analysis, an orgy of the Humanities slowly released, and Ono was muttering words to herself, 'structure'... 'world-model'... 'musicality', and suddenly she simply drew a tree that reached up to the sky, heaven and earth, night and day, present and future, twilight and mist, until the blackboard and its surroundings became a cloud of chalk, an insoluble, pulsating drawing, and then suddenly the bell rang, Ono turned round, put down the stub of chalk, her dark palms gleaming white with chalk-dust like those of a gymnast who has performed a marvellous backward somersault in dismounting from the asymmetric bars on which she has achieved a score never before seen, dusted off her hands, took a deep breath and stared into space: *M-m-m-m-m-da*, yes, she said, scarcely audibly, looking anxiously at the students as if they had just unexpectedly appeared: *Pe ora viitoare se citește Scrisoarea pierdută de Caragiale*, she set the homework in an impersonal manner never before heard by the gaping new girl (For next lesson you are to read Caragiale's *Lost letter*), *plus citiți* (and also read) and she named a further three things, and then in the course of the first term she came and stood more and more often beside the new girl, tapping her notebook with her pointed fingernail as if speaking only to her: *Mai citește acolo Pompiliu Constantinescu, Perpessicius, Adrian Marino—care o să-ți fie profesor la facultate* (and read Pompiliu Constaninescu as well, and Perpessicius and Adrian Marino, who'll be teaching you at university) and because Ono's sentence sounded like a prophecy or an explicit requirement the Girl had regularly taken the books out of the municipal library, and during breaks, when she walked aloof in the yard with her mincing steps, Ono checked with a casual glance what her disciple was reading but never commented, and the disciple never read Hungarian books in the yard because they didn't interest Ono, indeed annoyed her, and once she pulled a face and turned her head away in disappointment, until afterwards in the twelfth grade she suggested, as a mighty act of grace, that the Girl should give the world literature lesson on *Godot*: *Dar să nu-mi vorbești prea mult de Dumnezeu că mă plictisesc* (But don't go on about God too much, because I'm tired of it), because it had all happened *afterwards*, in May, towards the end of the year, before the university entrance exam, and perhaps she intended the *Godot* lesson as an apology, because she'd never handed over a single one of her lessons to anyone else before, neither to a colleague nor least of all a mere student: *I'll begin with the theme of expectancy, right?* the serious, self-conscious Humanities student, who had by then won literature Olympiads, proposed to Ono, *perhaps with Kafka*, to which Ono replied: You'll do as you please, *numai că, draga mea, așteptarea n-a început cu Kafka* (Only, my dear, expectancy didn't begin with Kafka), and the lesson was a great success in the by-then-purely-Romanian class (the Hungarian section had been closed a year after she'd arrived, a fortnight before the university entrance exam), she managed to draw on the blackboard as if it were Ono taking the lesson that day, and then too there was a world-tree and the sky and the earth, and the long-haired Girl quoted Hesse too when developing the theme of expectancy, but Ono, sitting motionless in a desk at the very back, had stared fixedly out of the window at the parallel with Hesse, and the Girl knew very well that there was no point in bringing in Hesse because, of course, none of the class had read him, but the reference was a personal score over Ono, because once, not so long before, one Wednesday morning in early April, Hermann Hesse had been there in the classroom under the second row of desks and Ono had asked *Ce citești acolo sub bancă?* and had held out a hand for the book, it had been *The Glass Bead Game*, which Éva had got from

35

Budapest, from the poet, and Ono had rapped out *Ce-i asta?* (What's this?), to which the Girl had replied *The Glass . . .* and then dried up, hadn't known how to translate the title, and in the end said seriously and a little proudly *Das Glasperlenspiel,* the original, but Ono had been so furious that she began to stammer, not just because she'd never before had the experience of the Girl reading something else under the desk and not paying attention, but it also annoyed her that *Das Glasperlenspiel* hadn't yet come out in Romanian and the pupil that was reading it in Hungarian had a kind of advantage: *Treci la tablă* (Go to the blackboard) she'd said curtly, at which the Girl put the pink-covered book down on top of the desk as there was no longer anyone to hide it from: *Structura romanului Frații Jderi* (The structure of the novel *The Jderi Brothers*), said Ono drily, and sat down at her desk, opened the register at her name, looked at the floor and waited, and the Girl had just stood there, stared at the oil-scrubbed floor like someone thinking of the answer, considering the structure of the said novel and who, as always, now too was about to come out with some original insight, begin with a startling metaphor or paradox, her usual trick, which she would elucidate in the course of the explanation, but Ono waited tensely, then, a little more loudly, repeated the task, this time calling her by her first name, because three years previously she'd explained how the Girl's name was correctly spelled in Romanian, and now she repeated: *N-auzi?* (Can't you hear?), at which the Girl, without looking up, told her that *N-am citit,* that is, she hadn't read it because she hadn't cared for it, and she'd borrowed *The Glass Bead Game* for a week, and she hated historical novels, and that was at least a thousand pages, and her sister, who'd specialized in Romanian, had told her that it was dull and gory and heroic and, naturally, anti-Hungarian, so she'd chosen *The Glass Bead Game* instead: *Treci la loc, unu* (Go to your place, one), Ono had said in satisfaction, she'd never before given her a one: *Ora viitoare răspunzi iar,* that is, You'll be called up again next lesson, at which the injured Girl thought to herself that if that day was Wednesday, she'd have to read the book by Friday, and she'd have two Russian lessons next afternoon and the theatre in the evening, *Hamlet* was on, and she was still only halfway through *The Glass Bead Game*, it was out of the question, and so she'd said in a matter-of-fact tone: *N-am să citesc pe vineri*, like someone turning down an unfavourable offer, that is, she wasn't going to have read the hefty tome even by Friday, and went to her place, while the startled Ono, who was just putting down the one in black in the register, raised her head and looked straight at her, then slowly stood up and, her eyes darkening, forced out between her teeth: *Tu sfidezi literatura română* (You despise Romanian literature), *pentru că eşti unguroaică* (because you're a Hungarian), and the Girl was about to protest, but then Ono, quivering, had gone on *Tu nici nu eşti unguroaică* (You're not even a Hungarian) *pentru că eşti evreică* (because you're a Jew)—not *jidoavcă*, that word the schoolgirl, who spoke the literary language, wouldn't have recognized, must never have heard it— and they'd both stood motionless and shocked, the Girl beside the second desk in the middle row, scarcely 4 metres from Ono as she stared at her from behind the teacher's desk, and the oppressive silence of suspense and expectation lasted for long seconds as if enemies were each waiting for the other to be first to reach for a weapon, when the Girl had suddenly picked up the Hesse from the desk, stuffed it into her bag, which her grandmother had made from two old linen towels, and left the room leaving the door open behind her, crossed Farkas utca, then Király utca, walked confidently straight to the ICS, the central shoes and clothing distributor, where her mother worked, and then, in the hearing of her mother's colleagues, told the whole story without the slightest emotion, and Uncle Nuszi, who worked next to her mother, smiled and gave her a good hug, *How does she know?* she tried to begin and looked at Uncle Nuszi, Uncle Nuszi who was always cheerful and whom she accepted as a grandfather-figure, but the rest of the sentence was drowned in her tears because she felt that now something had been taken from her, and what did she mean, she wasn't a Hungarian??? *People always do*, Uncle Nuszi reassured her, and hardly an hour went by and there they were outside the old Calvinist college, later the Ady and Şincai, and now just the Şincai school, in the doorway of the new building, where the ten o'clock break was just starting, and Ono came down with her mincing, sidling steps from her favourite, absolutely eminent, pure Romanian class XII-A, the Girl trembling with rage, and her mother waited behind the steps like a cat for its victim, pounced on the terrified teacher and shouted at the top of her voice that she was immediately and publicly to apologise for calling her daughter Jewish as an insult, and the headmistress, who by then knew all about it, had taken mother by the arm and escorted 'Doamna Kühn'—Kun, she pronounced it—into her room, while the Girl waited in the corridor outside the teachers' room, head bowed, like someone whose grave offence was being discussed inside, and teachers looked sympathetically at her as they came by and the white-haired English teacher, Fred, had actually winked as he went past—it was said that Fred had served ten years in prison, and that that was where he'd learnt such good English from an old professor—Fred, who smoked even during lessons, even then took a puff at his cigarette, his front teeth gleaming beneath his yellowed catfish moustache, *Dongiveashit*, he said in one word, but the Girl looked at him uncomprehendingly, she had Fred for English—that very week he'd got them to read a monologue from an Arthur Miller play, the prologue from *A View from the Bridge*, about human dignity—but Fred never used that expression in class, and at the start of the next lesson Ono had come in accompanied by the head of department, and mother was still there though the Girl had pleaded with her that enough was enough, it'd be all right, and Ono made an almost inaudible apology, to which her mother called out from the back row of desks: *Mai tare că nu se aude nimic* (Louder, can't hear anything), and Ono cleared her throat and began again her sentence beginning *Dragă . . .*' (Dear), at which mother spoke up again: *Tovarăşa profesoară Onofreasa* (Comrade teacher Onofreasa), *if that's how loudly you speak in this class I'm not surprised that the pupils don't hear anything from you, and they all get threes and fours. A teacher needs to open her mouth properly in class, doesn't she? I'm a teacher as well, I know. Surely you know that I used to be a teacher. After all, you know everything about us! Now let's hear this apology!*, but this time it would have been preferable to have hung her head in shame in front of the other thirty-five in the class, and Ono spent a long time looking for her for after her *Godot* lecture in May, when the Girl gave the lesson but afterwards didn't go back to her place, went straight out of the room from behind the teacher's desk like a real teacher, but in the lunch break she finally managed to track her down, and the Girl had been watching her from upstairs, through the window of the girls' lavatory, scurrying in agitation round the yard, putting her glasses straight, hurrying over the gravel, then she went back into the building, up the stairs, and opened the door to the girls' lavatory, didn't bother about all the smoking, went up to the Girl as she was insolently exhaling smoke and said quietly: *Ai uitat să-mi dai carnetul* (You forgot to give me your record-book), at which the Girl asked phlegmatically: *De ce, îmi daţi nouă?*, what was she going to get for the *Godot* lesson that she'd spent a fortnight preparing, a nine as usual? and grinned at her: *Nu, dragă* (No, my dear), said the indomitable Ono, superior and calm, *de ce să-ţi dau nouă?*, why would I give you a nine? *bunoăra*, she added, drawling her favourite word, all the same, Hesse didn't seem to add anything to the analysis, he makes rather too much of the lesson of mythology, and the preaching about human humiliation, *literatura nu e morală, da'mă rog*, that is, literature isn't a moral parable, but never mind, the moral content is quite valueless, so let me have your record-book, you'll get a ten, *adă carnetul, îţi dau un zece*, a ten, she repeated, then turned her back and went out, but there were only another two weeks of school left, full of upheaval, the school-leaving exam was coming and the difficult university entrance, and so about the ten promised in May in the upstairs girls' lavatory, like an excessive and infeasible promise, nothing more would be said.

HAIRSLIDES

Take these trays upstairs, dear, we've finished for today, said Lili, and the Girl with artificially curled hair took the tray of linden-wood hairslides which her mother and grandmother had just been glueing, and as the seven-year-old picked up the big, battered tin tray with the mass of crescent-shaped slides—which called for no little dexterity and balance —her nose caught the sharp tang of Aracset: mixing the white, creamy glue was Granddad's job, he knew how to dilute it, and in late afternoon the trays of slides were lined up on the larder steps, one tray on each, plastic and rusty tin trays one above another, but the slides also covered a big, old, cracked cake-tin and a perforated baking sheet, they were laid out in regular rows on the trays, two different tiny wooden pegs were glued at the ends of them, and after they were painted the curved wire that held the hair would be fitted onto these, they would be painted red and green and found in the shop, but all that they did was glue them, they usually started after eight in the evening after Lili's last pupil had left, cleared the kitchen table, hung the thick canvas curtain on the kitchen window overlooking the yard—Granny had made it from some striped material left over from a garden awning— that certain canvas curtain which they hung up on two occasions: when Granddad brought the shining copper still down from the attic in late autumn and made the plum *pálinka,* and when hairslide glueing was in progress, in which Granddad too lent a hand if he wasn't working elsewhere—he could fix anything at all, taps, electricals, furniture, he enjoyed varnishing and gardening, had a wide circle of regular cus-tomers, and in the evening wrote up precise accounts of what he earned because he didn't see anything of his pension, Granny received it direct from the postman—and sometimes the nine-year-old sister too helped with the glueing, but the seven-year-old played the part of a little servant: she would keep her balance seriously like an old-time high-wire walker so that the freshly glued slides shouldn't fall over and she would carry the trays up to the attic to set, and while they were working she would pile up the three constituent parts in front of everybody out of plastic bags, Lili had obtained the actual work unofficially from some co-operative, it paid 15 *bani* apiece for the glued slides, and the Girl, now in Year Three, could tell from the curtain being put up that slide-glueing was *an exciting and clandestine affair*, just as distilling *pálinka* was, which could, in any case, be smelt as far as the Dudus', three houses away, and as she went up to the attic with the trays on her shoulder to shut the finished slides away to dry in the little room, because in the loft the cats would knock them over as they gambolled, she counted up and it worked out as 460 for that evening, *as many as* . . . so she'd have to ask Mummy how many had been done that evening, how many of them Granny had made, how many Mummy, and how much she would get for carrying the trays, *Your share's 3 lei*, Mummy told her, *and you'll get it on the first*, and she could see in her mind's eye the shining 1-lei coins, magically potent with tractors and sunrises, *With the rest of what you owe me*, said the Girl, already running for the notebook to note down her latest earnings like Grandfather did, she recorded the small change in a stamp album, the first page of which was adorned by a brown 5-lei note, because she was very careful with money but would then spend it all at once on stamps, coloured pencils, purple ink or chocolate *parfait* at the Opera confectionery—at which Grandmother always remarked *That was nicely squandered*, since according to her, grown-ups *spent* money, children *squandered* it, but that evening Mother held out a prospect, saying *You'll rake it in tomorrow, it's Saturday, we'll start earlier, when I get in from work*, to which Juci exclaimed *I'm going to a birthday party*! and indeed, next day at four everybody was glueing, and Juci, before going to her schoolfriend's in

Zápolya (Dostoievski in Romanian) utca, where she was allowed to go alone, stopped in the middle of the kitchen and pointed above her two plaits, holding her fingers together and nodded towards them, pointing excitedly at something, which no one understood, but she was bursting with laughter, and Mummy just put down the slide that she had in her hand, wrinkled her forehead and asked *What ever is the matter?*, but Juci pointed even more excitedly to two red lacquered hairslides—the last type of slide that they'd been glueing—above her plaits, then suddenly burst out *Hajtsatok! Hajtsatok!*, then paused for effect, *See, Mummy? Hajtsatok! Hajtsatok!*, but Granny didn't get the joke even third time round and it had to be explained to her, and Juci's sister even then just raised her eyebrows and looked at her, of course, hairslides, and got their heads back down[11]—by six o'clock a pile of trays had accumulated on the larder steps, she'd had to tip the top one very carefully sideways so as to pick it up when they stopped work, *My back!* said Granny, and stood up from the kitchen table with its waxed canvas cloth, her bridge partners were coming for the evening and she'd still had to get the fruit ready, make the coffee, set out the remains of the spiced loaf—*What you girls have left of it*, said she—then she cleaned the sawdust off the table and took down the curtain while the little girl put the bags with the wooden bits on the floor in the larder so as to take them up to the room before she went to bed, *May I get some cherry cake and plums in rum downstairs?* she offered Granny willingly, because she too had had fruit cake in the company of the powder-scented old ladies, and she'd had milk specially warmed to go with the plums in rum, which she so liked, *Certainly not! You'll knock it off the shelf!*—in fact she could only reach it from a chair, and one couldn't take a chair into the narrow larder, *Laci*, Granny called into the living room, *come and get the bottled fruit down*, and Laci, who was at the desk, smoking filterless Nationals

---

11 There is a play on words involved here in the Hungarian. Juci says *Hajtsatok,* the plural imperative of the verb *hajt*, meaning 'Do it again!', which sounds virtually identical with *hajcsatak*, the plural of *hajcsat*, 'hairslide'.

through two short holders stuck together and at the same time drawing
in a notebook a bookcase that he was designing for the Gogomans from
sheets of hardboard, called out 'just a minute', at which Klári said to
herself I know what 'just a minute' means, because in fact Granddad
had to be called five times, and by the time that he came into the
kitchen the grounds for a quarrel were there, when suddenly the bell
rang, twice, deliberately, *Jesus and Mary! They're here, and I've not changed
yet, what's the time?* said Granny in a single breath, and looked up at
the enamelled pancake-timer in the kitchen, *Well, go and answer the
door,* she said crossly, because she had difficulty in climbing even the
two steps from the kitchen to the front room, and the little girl ran
happily to greet Auntie Gizi, Auntie Pötyi or Auntie Arany, though it
was always the childless, kindly Gizi Vályi that arrived first, who often
brought something for the grandchildren, and as she held the door wide
open three men walked in without so much as 'by your leave' and said
to Granny as she stood behind the Girl with a look of amazement *Bună
seara, sînt bzbzbz* (Good evening, I'm ... some name or other—the rest
she couldn't catch), *avem ordin de bzbzbz*—we have orders to ... , *Buná
szérá,* said Grandmother in her unmistakeable Romanian and looked
coldly at them as if keeping an eye on pickpockets, as they made to slip
through the open door into the middle room, *Somebody come, I can't
understand what they're saying,* but the three men didn't wait for the
somebody but went straight into the kitchen and through the middle
room into the big room, where by then Laci had stood up, then Lili
too came out of the bathroom, and everybody was standing rooted to
the spot: Klári in the kitchen, Lili in the middle room, Laci in the big
room, but the three men merely did what they'd come to do: one sat
down at Granddad's desk, the second started opening the three mir-
rored doors of the cupboard and turning out Granny's ironed tablecloths and bed linen, and the third began unloading the glass-fronted
bookcase in the middle room, the two cats vanished with a crash
through the cat-flap in the larder door and up to the loft—*They're going*

to jump on the trays, thought the Girl—and then they started on the rest: the bed-linen cupboard, the sideboard, the china cabinet, the night-tables, the cupboards in the living room, even opened up the big dining table, the sewing-machine case, the tool cupboard in the living room, the medicine cupboard in the bathroom, but the little girl cautiously opened the squeaky door of the larder, to which the man who was rummaging in the living room growled *Nu mișca!*—Don't move!—then looked that way and saw her apprehensive face in the open door, *Poți să treci*—You may go—he gestured, and she pulled the door to behind her and went silently on the rag carpet up to the bend in the stairs and picked up the tray on the top step first, the cats had in fact jumped on the trays, then she came down for the next and so on, but she didn't take them to the attic but to the back of the loft, where the cats yowled at night, as Granny said, but now they'd vanished, and she brought up all the trays and the bags, she left her slippers at the bottom of the stairs and went in stockinged feet, silently, on tiptoe, *In the larder we go silently, like cats*, she repeated to herself, though the two cats in the house at present, Balti and Szüri, were anything but silent, and finally she came down and on the way took down a long-necked preserving jar, she went and stood by her mother in the kitchen, *You've done that very cleverly*, whispered Granny quietly, and when the one man was making for the larder on the way he kicked the cats' milk dish, *Futu-i*, he hissed (Get stuffed), it was something that people kicked regularly in any case, and he looked apologetically at Grandmother, then opened the larder door, felt along the wall in the darkness for a moment with his right hand before finding the rotating light switch, stopped by the door and gave a long look of amazement: bottled fruit, cake tins, *kürtöskalács*[12] makers, pastry boards, an old coffee pot with a long spout, heavy ceramic containers, potatoes, apples and onions in baskets with broken handles, quinces on shelves, the bookbinding press,

---

12 A traditional yeast cake, shaped in a hollow tube in shape.

the bag of dusters and the big porcelain-headed meat tenderiser, but
mother was standing stock still, just as when they'd come through the
door, but now facing the open larder, Lili and Laci had come together
into the kitchen and the group of three statues looked at the motionless
back of the man in the overcoat, and from the narrow, lofty room there
wafted the sweet, tangy, softly decayed larder scent mixed with the
heavy smell of glue, *Gata*, said he without turning round, that's enough,
that is, the other two present were to stop, because he's found what he's
after, thought Lili, who first looked at her father, then at her mother,
standing rigid, then at the Girl, who was holding the jar of preserved
fruit under her arm and reaching up to her hair with both hands to
straighten the slide on the right, which had come quite loose with all
the bending and stacking, *This slide wasn't meant for your hair*, Granny
grumbled every morning when she struggled to do her hair, because
she had the same kind of thick, strong hair as well in which a little slide
like that was no use—*It's not worth 5 bani*, Granny turned it over in her
hand scornfully—it wouldn't stay in place but sprang out from her head
like a grasshopper, and the Girl wanted to tell her mother something
by that movement, and as she raised her hands she pulled a face and
winked reassuringly, but the jar of fruit slipped from under her arm and
crashed to the stone floor and shattered, at which the man by the door
turned and gave the order *Haide*, Let's go, and leaving the door open
set off through the kitchen and the living room without a backward
glance, and the other two followed, because the first house-search in
late November 1978 had consequently ended without result, and for
years everybody tried to guess what they'd been looking for, or who'd
informed on them, as Mummy suspected, *I know what they were after*,
said the Girl proudly, *but they didn't find them, because I took them up to
the back of the loft, to my secret empire, where everything is, the pálinka
still, old surveying seals, maps, some clothes of Granny's that she's making
for Uncle Fodor, and old magazines, broken pots, ball dresses, shiny globes,
bicycle parts, flower baskets which Mummy and Granny got when they were*

young and in love, some bits of lace, baby clothes, a broken piano stool, tennis rackets, skis, some enormous photographs, rusty swords which Uncle Zolti is going to take to Pest to sell, nail polish and a hat brush, love letters, cat baskets, torn Hungarian national dress which no longer fitted anybody, massive picture frames, railway permits, Hungarian passports and everything that is above the law, and happy, free cats, Baltazár and Szüri and their boyfriends, who romp about at night on the rooftops, and hairslides, masses of hairslides, on six trays, more than six hundred, out of which I'm getting at least 5 lei by today, Mummy, but they didn't find them and they're never going to.

THIRTY EGGS

It happened during the second act of *The Glass Slipper*, when the wedding was well under way and the cast were enjoying themselves at leisure with glasses of water in their hands and little Irma was getting tiddly on *pálinka*, wanting to give the little cat her breast as in the first act, and the storm was gathering in the stifling air: at the end of May 1987 there weren't very many in the auditorium at the guest performance by the Vásárhely Theatre School, friends, relations, prospective students of the School and a few members of Zsebszínház, the amateur company, which was bereft and had no director any more (Ödön, the interior decorator-cum-director had gone off to Sweden, and before that had played his last mime at the station, waving a white handkerchief from the train, then stiffening into a still), and the self-confident Year Ten Girl was sitting there among the amateur actors, a fortnight before her entrance exam, after the National Hungarian Literary Olympiad that had been held in the spring and at which she had carried off the special prizes given by *Young Worker* and *The Week* for her essay on *Bánk bán*,[13] and she felt that she had nothing to fear from the entrance exam for Year Eleven because for years there had been eighteen places allotted to Arts students in the Hungarian fraternal class in the Lyceum, and there she sat calmly in her seat in the middle of the fifth row, *I'm obviously going to be the first to get in*, she'd thought after the unexpected triumph in the Olympiad in April, but in the Humanities faculty of the University, where her sister wanted to go, a total of only seven Hungarian places had been announced and last year a hundred and seventy had applied, and her sister, who had opted for

13 A Hungarian classic play (1820) by József Katona.

the Hungarian–Romanian specialism, was having private tuitions that day with the best Hungarian teacher, old Auntie Juli, who lived near the Sétatér Theatre on the other side of the Szamos, *I might make the third act,* Juci had said that morning, perhaps she'll make the third act, thought her sister, because they both wanted to see their friend who had been accepted at her first attempt for the Theatre School, where there'd been only three places, so that for the examination performance they'd have had to put on a three-man play, the rest of the candidates laughed, they wouldn't even have been able to do *Godot,* and so now every year in the High School was performing, and in fact a few actors from Vásárhely as well to make up the full cast for *The Glass Slipper,* but during the act there was suddenly thunder outside and through the door of the auditorium they could hear the storm break a few minutes before the storm on stage, and the Year Ten Girl looked anxiously at her black velvet slip-ons which it had been her turn to wear that week; she was wearing the Chinese shoes belonging to Gyöngyi, her first-floor neighbour who was in Year Twelve, which the three of them —including Juci—took it in turns to wear, as they did the green-velvet cord Levi's, and the comfortable, one-size velvet slip-ons fitted Gyöngyi, Juci and herself perfectly well, as they usually took sizes 38, 39 and 40, the only thing was that the cardboard insoles were beginning to wear out and they were becoming smellier and smellier, and because they wore them without socks they sprinkled menthol powder in them, but they didn't dare wash them in case they fell completely to pieces, *I'll hang on and wait for the storm to pass,* she thought, but there was still an interval and the third act, then suddenly the stage storm too broke, and as it crashed down the wedding party began to run from it towards the covered veranda, and in the racket the Girl didn't even notice that the side door near her had opened; *Is my daughter here?* asked somebody, panting, and the old lady usherette pulled aside the heavy brown velvet curtain and turned her electric torch on the Girl as she bit her nails in the fifth row: her mother, soaking wet, excused herself and made a married couple stand up—they were Krisztina's parents, and it was because of Krisztina that she'd come that day—and sat down by her; her dress—the white polka-dotted red-and-dark-blue one with the shoulder straps, which Grandmother had made and for which they'd ticked her off that day at the Central Trade Distribution Centre, saying that such indecent clothing wouldn't be allowed in future, was absolutely clinging to her, and she was holding a completely soaked copy of *Igazság*,[14] all four pages of it stuck together in a single thick mass, and she bent towards the startled Girl and, still panting, whispered in her ear *the entrance exam*, but the rest was swallowed up by the thunderstorm, which had come in from outside before and then, to the delight of the spectators, continued at higher pitch on the stage, and on Mother's face raindrops were mingling with the tears that she was trying to hide—the hair that had been permed the previous evening had been completely straightened and her blue eye-shadow had run, so the rain had caught her unawares: the Girl leant quite close to her and looked into her startled face in the light from the stage, it seemed that she didn't want to make out the words from the severe, straight and now strangely pale lips, but the effect: Mother took the soaked, indecipherable newspaper in both hands and shook it, and, shivering from cold, repeated, this time aloud, *There's no entrance exam for the Ady*, the paper didn't list the school she'd chosen among those offering Hungarian, because that was the simple and direct way that a news item was made known—by silence and evasion it was announced that there would be no more Hungarian class in the former Calvinist grammar school, which had actually had nothing to do with Endre Ady, but all the more with Apáczai, who had begun teaching philosophy and theology there, and that day, three hundred and eighty years later, at the end of May 1987, had been shut down by a news item, *Fuck three hundred and eighty years! Why couldn't they have put up with it for another*

14 'Truth'; Hungarian language daily published in Kolozsvár between 1945 and 1989.

two? she stamped her foot at Grandfather, who for once didn't dare complain about the foul language, but this news couldn't be a printing error or an accidental slip of the pen, it was simply the long-established method of announcing a decision, which would seem innocent to the outsider: 'The register of lawyers working in Kolozsvár' had been carried in January 1941 by *Ellenzék*,[15] the forerunner of *Igazság*, and from that register Uncle Jenő had discovered that he no longer belonged to the company of lawyers working in Kolozsvár, but it seemed that the helpful newspaper only wished by this to inform its gentle readership, to extend useful information to the citizens of the town as to where they might turn, but Uncle Jenő had been deleted from the register, had simply ceased to be, just like his brother Pál's 'Stadion' sports-equipment shop, which the following year did *not* feature among the 'Christian trade sources' proclaimed by the paper, and the little business was then closed as a 'Romanian-Jewish global concern' and the owner himself made to prepare the inventory for the sale, but in the autumn of '46 the same paper wrote that Dr Constantinescu Neumann Erzsébet was not a member of the Romanian Communist Party, though she had served nearly a year in Szamosfalva jail as an illegal communist, and she (although by then divorced from her second husband too) had been able to pick the paper up and learn from it that she was no longer a party member, because everything and everyone was excluded and included in this way, just as the thick-walled, low, vaulted classroom of the fraternal Hungarian-language class in the Ady-Şincai Lyceum had been shut in the face of the hopeful Humanities student: that's done it, she thought, no more school, because she couldn't take the exam for the old maths and physics specialist school, she wouldn't be able to work up either subject in a fortnight, and now Krisztina, in her second year at Theatre High School, who likewise had gone into special school instead of Year Eleven because she'd failed the entrance exam, was now

---

15 'Opposition'; Hungarian language daily published in Kolozsvár between 1880 and 1944.

singing drunkenly on the stage about 'The pollen of my happiness, blowing in the breeze', because she'd been accepted with her certificate in cabinet-making, and her diploma work had been a piano stool which she'd seen for the first time the morning when she went for the exam as it had been made for really big money—500 lei—in the theatre workshop and had gone back there free of charge as there was no need of it at home, Krisztina had her own piano stool and upright piano, and now she was singing all false and rocking to and fro before the 'sweet poisonous' Lajos Sipos, played by the balding head of year, *Let's go home, dear,* said Mother next, but on stage the disconcerted crowd was frantically seeking shelter from the rain, which was only present in sound, because it poured from the loudspeakers, but through an unusual arrangement of the producer's not a drop fell on stage and the only person that was wet through was Mother, sitting in the auditorium, and nobody on stage seemed surprised or amazed or said anything or suddenly burst out swearing, but they said nothing and went on playing their parts in disciplined fashion, *The water's been cut off,* said Krisztina with a laugh in the interval when she went backstage to see her, because she'd stayed until the interval after all and said to Mother that she'd heard said that you could get eggs in Vásárhely and she was going down with the cast in the bus after the performance and she'd bring back at least thirty, that was how many there were in a tray, she'd go the one day, catch the night train and come back the next, and Mother, without a word, took out her purse and gave her two green 50-*lei* notes, then hurried back home to give a lesson, and it didn't matter any more whether she went to school next day or not, *There's nowhere to go,* she thought, as if school would never come again, because that toadying, loathsome poem which was always declaimed at moving-up ceremonies, usually by an awkward, bespectacled girl, and reduced everybody to tears with painful emphases in the pious silence in the school decorated with wilting wildflowers, that poem had suddenly come home to her with its personal, sharply piercing message: what would

there be if one day there were in fact no more school: the square building with its cloister-like corridors beside the church in Farkas utca,
with the tiny rooms with space for no more than eighteen, that is, half
a class, it seemed that the size of the little rooms had determined in
advance the future fate of the classes, in that only classes half the size
of so-called fraternal classes[16] could function, and next afternoon eggs
really were piled high in the empty butcher's in Vásárhely, and the
woman serving replied in Hungarian regretting that she couldn't give
her any packaging, and it seemed futile to bargain with her, saying that
she would pay for it, and she tried promising to take it back, but the
woman insisted, she had to account for the trays, please understand,
and she put the forty-five eggs into two bags and advised her to wrap
them individually in newspaper, especially if she had far to go with
them, *To Kolozsvár*, the Girl replied proudly, *Yes, I know*, the woman
commented sadly, as if speaking of a death, like someone that knew
that there were no eggs in Kolozsvár, *Eggs are rationed up our way, a
person gets seven a month, but you can't always get hold of any*, she'd have
liked to inform her, but by then there was another customer behind her
so she just put the money down and felt about the forty-five eggs, carefully stowed in nylon shopping bags, that it was going to be quite a job,
un tour de force, and if she reached home with the heavy burden of her
errand it would all have been a success, and she'd even had change from
the 100 lei, enough for a real Vásárhely melba, what was more, something that she'd never tasted, only Grandmother had often mentioned
the special Vásárhely dessert with eyes upturned to heaven: in the afternoon Krisztina and the director took her to the Lido patisserie in the
main square, *Three melbas, please*, said the director, a middle-aged man,
with a smile to the girl at the cash desk, *No melbas today, try again
tomorrow*, she replied regretfully and with a hint of encouragement, at
which there appeared from the back an elderly woman, who put an arm

---

16 Classes containing Hungarian and Romanian pupils, taught in both languages.

through the girl's: *You're in luck, director, we've just got three melbas left,* and she winked, *only just take them home, will you,* and she leant closer, *I can't even serve them on the terrace, there's been none for days, at least sit and have them in the back,* and she pointed to the dark depths of the patisserie, and the Girl, touched and astounded, paid for the melbas in gratitude for their putting her up, but she had simply no idea where she'd got to, into Grandmother's dreamworld of Vásárhely where there were eggs, this melba with whipped cream, apricot jam and ice-cream, and most of all Hungarian women behind shop counters, then in the afternoon they strolled around, looked at the theatre, the high school and the clothes shops, where the things were completely different from what was in Mother's store, so that there wasn't time to wrap all the eggs individually in newspaper before the train left, and what had taken an hour-and-a-half by bus took all night—in 1890 the 104 kilometres between the two towns, Grandfather had once shown her the list of results in the Kolozsvár Athletic Club yearbook, had been covered in fifteen hours and two minutes by the distance-walker János Kolozsváry, to achieve which he'd surely had to run—and this time there was a wait of more than three hours in the night for the connection at Kocsárd, as there'd been no direct link between the two towns in living memory, and you always had to change trains at the most impossible times: in the night or at dawn, so that only the most determined people should travel, those with serious business that could not be put off, if, for example they wanted to buy a whole heap of eggs by such a childishly simple method as shopping for them without standing in a queue, so she spent the warm summer night in the smoky, beer-smelling waiting room at Kocsárd, spent 6 lei on a plate of *paszulyfőzelék* (*costiță cu fasole* in Romanian), the only available dish on the list, haricot beans with sausage, and eating it in the small hours reminded her of the flavour of summertime camping: we'll take ten bottles of *kosztica* and go walking for a week, they'd say, because bottled *kosztica* was the most stubbornly lasting product in the shops, almost the only thing that one could always reckon on being there, and in the shop they would shake the bottles one by one, check them to see if there was any *kosztica* in them, that is, any sausage or bacon, but usually there was nothing to be seen in the cloudy liquid, or at least no meat, as on this occasion too, she thought, looking in disappointment at her chipped plate, and when she went to Vásárhely on the first of November Grandmother (whose parents lay side by side beneath a shared slab of concrete in the cemetery there) would never sit in the dirty, drunk-filled waiting room, but would rather stand outside in the chill of night while Grandfather and the Girl spooned up bean- or potato-*főzelék*, as if on a real excursion, just as now, when she'd carefully hung the precious nylon bags on the wooden arm of the seat, pulled the plate to her and began to stir its thick, hot, fragrant contents with the bent aluminium spoon, and to her surprise among the white beans there appeared at least 10 centimetres of slender sausage, real smoked sausage, but a man wearing a cap reeled dangerously towards her table and she kept her eyes on the two bags as if holding a shield in front of them, and by the time that the Iaşi–Temesvár express (its lights not working), so packed that no seat tickets were issued for it—the 'starvation train' on which people went several hundred kilometres shopping, Moldavians coming to Transylvania— ran into Kolozsvár station, dawn was breaking but the trolleybuses weren't running yet, so she set off down Horea út, turned off towards the market where the traders were already setting out their stalls, past the Romanian Theatre, into what used to be Zápolya utca (now Dostoyevsky), up the Kövespad (Pietroasele), where the *hóstáti* gardens had been long before, out past the new concrete blocks of flats, but stopped short at the corner of the last flight of steps: there was milk in crates, they were starting to deliver it, so she waited a moment, looked around, and in her soundless Chinese velvet slip-ons went up to the pile of crates, reached up and took a wide-mouthed litre bottle with its silver paper seal from the top crate: that is, she stole it, somebody wouldn't get their milk that day, she drank half of it before reaching home and the dawn was tinglingly chilly and comforting, *Blowing in the breeze*, came to her mind, the fragment from the play, *The pollen of my happiness*, she was feeling cold now from tiredness in the thin, flesh-coloured blouse that she was wearing for the third day, but the forty-five eggs in the grey plastic bags which she carried proudly as if walking a circus tightrope in soft ballet shoes reached home undamaged and triumphant at dawn on the Thursday, and the entrance exam began just ten days later on Monday morning, *It's beginning now*, she thought, confusedly and tiredly, *or it's over now, and tomorrow I'll have to get a copy of* Utunk,[17] *the essay that I won with is in it, and, they say, the photograph of me as well that Laci Kántor took*, and in a fortnight it was the holidays, she could move into the garden, or she and Juci could go camping by the lake, Mother had managed to find a lot of Globus preserves from somewhere, and there was going to be the Olympiad camp at Vargyas in Székelyföld, and Mother wasn't being given any summer holiday this year, only the bosses, she'd have to take time off in winter, and until September she'd be able to read as long as she wanted, all night, and sleep until midday, and she'd be able to visit Vásárhely any time, not just in November to light the lamp on the grave[18] but to see her friends, and when she got to the end of Színész (or according to Grandmother, Pillangó) utca, she looked up to the fourth floor where the neon light was on in the kitchen, perhaps Mother was waiting for her, or perhaps it had just been left on overnight so as to be more welcoming when she got back, and finally whatever the four-page newspaper said with its innocent-looking ash-grey letters, or more precisely, whatever it didn't say, when all was said and done it would say by default, because in those days the only reliable column in *Igazság* was the report of deaths, the 'deadly news' as it was called, and everything else the paper communicated by silence, annihilated, obliterated:

---

17 Our Way, the Hungarian-language cultural periodical of the communist period which became *Helikon* after the change of regime.

18 A reference to an All Souls' Day custom.

that there was to be no more Latin department at the University, which had been her dream, that the Ady had closed, that Juci wouldn't be able to take the entrance exam for the Hungarian–Romanian department though she'd spent two years preparing, and that Dr Jenő Neumann (1893–1978) could no longer practise his calling as a lawyer, and that Pál Neumann and Company no longer featured in the register of long-established Hungarian businesses and that Kocka was no longer needed by the Party, then too it was a different world, she thought, here, for instance, are forty-five eggs, a litre of milk, a sharp, silent, but hopeful dawn in Pata utca, a direct rail link between Kolozsvár and Vásárhely, you can be there in six hours at the most, and *paszulyfőzelék* at Kocsárd, it's a different world, she said, closing her eyes, but her mother didn't understand what she was saying, *And I'm not going to school today, and I'm not going to another school, I'm going to try for the Humanities school, I want to study literature with Ono, I want to calculate square roots in Romanian,* radical din doi (*root two*), *square it,* doi pe doi (*two squared*), *and study chemistry, though at present I don't even know the Romanian for hydrogen and oxygen,* from next day, she went on, she'd got thirteen hours of study ahead of her every day, and what the paper didn't say was all that was true, the rest was silence, but Mother laughed and said that in Year Eleven there was no more calculating roots, nor squaring, it would be integration, and you'll see, Juci took her certificate in a Romanian class and she's come to no harm, and by six o'clock, after drinking a hot Turkish coffee with a lot of honey, tucked up in a heavy woollen quilt in a bed made up in the big room, she'd fallen asleep.

SHORTHAND

The weekly two shorthand and typing lessons—which constituted the practical work[19] in the Humanities school—seemed like Heaven after the compulsory two weeks of heavy industrial *praktika* every autumn in the Armatúra, where, in the oily workshops, they only got in the way of the workers, who gave them dirty looks and never said a word, because the difference between the two schools was not limited to the identity number (pentagonal and black, brick-shaped and red respectively), but the typewriting lesson in particular promised to be attractive and mysterious, and scarcely had the new pupil obtained permission to transfer to the new school than she began to make arrangements: at the start of the week she found out who the shorthand and typing teacher was and went to see her in the staff room in the lunch break, introduced herself politely and said that she'd still been going to the other school—*Léméfé trei* (LMF 3, that is, No. 3 Maths and Physics Lyceum) in Farkas (Kogălniceanu) utca in the first two weeks—because she hadn't by then received permission, then she asked what she had to do to catch up, but she regarded that as just preparing the ground for asking the question that mattered: might she bring in her own typewriter to the lessons because she was used to working on that, she asked casually, at which the steno-dactylo teacher, as she was called, raised her eyebrows: *Cum adică, maşina ta?* (What do you mean, your own typewriter?), emphasizing the end of the sentence, and the Girl quickly corrected it, not her own as such but the family's, her mother worked part-time at the court, but she didn't add that the typewriter was effectively hers, she didn't have to share it with anyone, her mother had the

---

19 Pupils had to do a certain amount of 'work' in factories, farms, etc.

great big Victoria and the little Olympia portable had been her father's, but nobody had asked for it back, so there she was in possession of an unregistered[20] typewriter with which in principle she could have done all sorts of things, but all she did was type out her verse and 'my prose', as she said, and it was only later, in 1987, that she typed out, heart thumping, a copy of an article about *The Stalker*, the allegedly dangerous film, *Manual?* asked the grey-suited teacher, to which the long-haired Girl nodded, though she wasn't quite sure what she meant, *Oh, not electric!* dawned on her later, not like the secretary's in her mother's office where you hardly had to touch the keys and could write ever so fast, but the whole contraption shook and rattled as you wrote, especially when you scrolled down at the end of the line, your coffee would slop over on the desk, it was like the knitting machine at Aunt Ági's, which took up half the dining table, ah, I don't like things like that, *very well, bring it,* said Tovarăşa Steno, Comrade Shorthand, with her glasses, heavy make-up and lacquered hairstyle, and from then the new girl in IX-B had gone into school with it every Friday like a high-ranking diplomat in transit or a demi-goddess, as she thought of herself, a poet in disguise, a famous writer or a mysterious foreign scientist!, and she was never late on Fridays, not even when the day began with the boring shorthand lesson, and she carried the beige imitation-leather case containing the grass-green Olympia through the town, sometimes going as far as Unió utca on the 25 trolleybus or taking the Number 3 and getting off at the Sora so as to cut across Főtér, though she could have got off at the cathedral or the little market, and she often left home before half past seven, and in the afternoon, after school, there was always something in town to hold her up, looking round in the Russian bookshop or the second-hand bookseller's, standing around in the deserted shop with the conspicuous, important object in its case set down between her feet, or she would go up to her mother's workplace

---

20 Ownership of an unregistered typewriter was a criminal offence.

to scrounge a little money—*Don't come here again with that typewriter*, said Mother in a forceful whisper—or go in for an elderflower tea: *Ceai complet*, she would say and put her money down, because a 'complete tea' came with two sugars while an ordinary one cost 1 lei, or she would drop in to see Éva, who had a lovely upright Continental with a Hungarian keyboard, or call at Granny's, where she might be in time for afternoon coffee, and while the rest were practising on noisy, ancient Czech Zetas and Optimas she would delicately tap out the exercises: *asdf, asdf, asdf* the first week, everybody brought their own paper, or a week later for the left hand: *dada, dada, fafa, fafa, sasa, sasa*, or with both hands: *lala, lala*, and they were never told to write *kaka*, didn't actually practise *k* much at all because it isn't used in Romanian, and by the end of the term she was using all ten fingers quite nicely except for the little finger on her right hand because her sister had shut the WC door on it, and for weeks she hadn't been able to bend it, and at home she'd also practised on her mother's machine, while she was cooking she would dictate the citations and schedule of property from the divorce settlement (though there wasn't a word for such a thing in Hungarian, Mother had a second, quite well-paid job at the court), and as she dictated Mother would comment on the divorce: *They're sharing out a broken pot and the torn quilt covers!*, but the Girl didn't make much progress with shorthand though at first she'd found the straight lines and curves interesting as they resembled Georgian, Armenian or Tibetan, it had been amusing that vowels weren't marked except by dots under or above the signs—it seems that shorthand writers have stolen the idea from Hebrew, said Uncle Nuszi, her mother's colleague, when she showed him her notebook—and Romanian diphthongs and triphthongs were all sorts of open 'duck-bills', and when the soft-spoken teacher, distinctly enunciating the diphthongs, had dictated the rather improbable phrase *Oaia aia e a ei* (That lamb is hers) the whole thing had resembled poetry, and the little duck-bills opened in every direction, up and down, left and right, like a musical score, but by winter they had moved on to abbreviations, at first only those with two elements, such as five-year plan, socialist industrialization, fraternal countries, 23 August 1944, workers and peasants, July Theses, golden age, 26 January, 'We sing, Romania!',[21] and afterwards came the more complex ones, comprehensively developed socialist society, President of the Central Committee of the Romanian Communist Party, basic principles of the twelfth party congress for agricultural development, the community of nations of the developing countries, prolonged applause and the cheering of the chief secretary of the party, history written in letters of gold, the full and final victory of socialism, each compressed into a single solitary sign which had to be learnt, at the time the Girl was friendly with Gizi Horváth and by the end of the term was sitting with her, because Gizi was the best at shorthand, knew all the logograms straight off and had read some book in the neighbouring building of the Academy Library about the need for signs and for statistical checks to be kept on frequency, and she herself had begun to invent logograms in accordance with the rules, because Gizi worked on the basis of frequency and so devised her own, went through the newspapers and speeches and proposed special signs 'to indicate mistakes and the root causes of mistakes' and 'the raising of the educational and mental level of the people', and in her view 'the cornerstone of the reinvigorated dialectical theory relating to the revolutionary process leading to communism' likewise would have been reduced to a logogram, so often did it appear in the papers, but the teacher did not accept Gizi's proposals and said that the logograms were authorized by a central committee, and the Girl sat by Gizi in the final exam in shorthand too, and in return they exchanged papers in the typing exam so that the work of both of them was done on the little green Olympia,

---

21 A nationwide event involving thousands of people singing, dancing and performing plays; 23 August 1944 was the date of the ousting of the Antonescu government by Mikhail I and the declaration of a ceasefire; and 26 January celebrates Ceaușescu's birthday.

because the Girl had obtained written permission to use it in the exam, but nobody noticed the similarity even though in the typing test a number of corrections were made by overtyping with x's as the use of correcting fluid was not allowed, and as she was taking the exam the Girl's hands were shaking so much with nerves and fatigue, and in fact in the shorthand exam they originally should have had to take down the forty-minute speech delivered on 1 July from a tape recorder, and in the morning the huge machine and loudspeakers were brought into the examination room, but it wouldn't make a sound because the power had been cut off in the school and the surrounding area, and so after waiting half an hour the exam took place, with the permission of Bica, the headmistress, in a half-dark room, and the shorthand teacher had read for forty whole minutes while the Girl copied hard from Gizi, who had by that time won shorthand prizes at town, county and national levels and could take 240 words a minute, but in her copying the Girl left a number of signs clean out or wrote them incorrectly, and succeeded in getting an indulgent 8, because by chance what they had to take down was the same as the translation that had been set a week before by the Russian teacher, the delicately featured Tatiana from Gorki: the birthday speech of 26 January, because the Girl had been going to Russian lessons every afternoon in her flat, which was crammed full of books, dolls and icons, and they had prepared for the entrance exam to the university foreign languages department from the same texts, and the Girl had bought the Russian texts in soft-back editions at the 'Russian' bookshop in Főtér, speeches made at congresses, directives, five-year plans, visits, international links, which were available in all four of the examination languages, Russian English, German and French, only libraries bought the thick, leather-bound 'Complete Works', and when she was deliberately preparing for the examination she even bought the Russian propaganda paper *Koreia* with its coloured pictures of smiling children and adults basking beneath the free and happy sky of North Korea, and the pensioner Tatiana, who was proud to talk about her hometown, formerly known as Nizhny Novgorod, leafed dubiously through the publication and asked *Neuzheli khochesh' iz etogo?*—Do you want some of some of this—as if she'd really wanted to translate an article, such as one about an impending new omnibus edition of the works of Kim Il-Sung, but her sister, who'd tried for the English department, had had a harder time, it must have been more difficult to translate into the language of Chaucer and Swift, the language would have been, so to speak, more inflexible, or the result seemed no more than a parody, a cutting from the humour page of an American newspaper, and the Girl wasn't so worried about the Russian exam and it came as an unexpected twist that one could write a composition on anything at all under the title of *Nature in Russian Literature*: Pushkin's poem 'The Demons', Turgenyev, Levin's bees and a fragment from the banned Akhmatova would all be in it, she decided quickly, although the latter had nothing to do with describing nature, but she'd been given a book of Akhmatova for Christmas—her mother had queued for four hours to get it one frosty dawn—but before the shorthand exam her head had swum with a succession of signs for diphthongs and triphthongs, the sheep and the eggs, singly and in clusters (*oaie, oi, ou, ouă*), and the endless compound words, the mind-numbing expressions which had long since lost their collective meanings, condensed into single curving logograms, and finally it was a matter of luck that one could even write such things as repositioning of the delouser, general-supply delivery teams or cleanliness-checking filter examination, for which special logograms had obviously been invented, where did they get this compulsive urge to compound words from? she wondered, because there was analysis of compound words for the linguistic exam as well, and on the evening before the exam she'd sat and listened to the eight o'clock news by way of preparation, which had started with an account of the bumper crops of wheat and maize that could be expected in the summer of '89, and she'd tried to take notes about the *cséápé*, the CAP, but couldn't think of the logogram for 'collective farm', the sign of signs, and what did *cséápé* stand for come to that?, perhaps it ought to start with *cooperativa agricolă*, but what was the last bit? *Productivă?*—*landwirtschaftliche Genossenschaftsarbeit*, the lovely, super-fluous fragment of vocabulary had stayed with her from German lessons in Year Eight, 'collective farm' had been Juci's grinning rejoinder, at which the future examinee retorted triumphantly how pure and sim-ple the Russian *kooperativ* was, perhaps it had even meant something once, and then wintry shots had followed on the black-and-white screen, the laying of a foundation stone at a mine in Moldavia—East Romania, as it was put—which by that time had been built, and men in fur hats were shown breaking black coal and nodding their heads, and then the Girl went to sleep in front of the TV in the big room, the programme finished at ten o'clock and someone, perhaps her mother, switched off the TV, tucked her up, put the cats out of the room and pulled the door to so that she could sleep in peace, but in her dream there appeared a long line of black-and-grey fur hats, as if set out at a jumble sale, on the sort of table that was used for village weddings, the hats were in two rows, the smaller in front and taller and taller ones behind as far as the eye could see, looking from above like military divi-sions, while Grandmother, whose jealously guarded Astrakhan coat she'd never yet been able to put on although she'd promised it that year for her eighteenth birthday, had explained in detail, like a piece of ancient, precious knowledge, that the way they obtained the finest Astrakhan fur was to slit the belly of a mother sheep when her lamb was almost due, carefully with a sharp knife, reach in between the ribs, take hold of the beating heart—but Granny, despite this part of her consciousness that was still awake, couldn't so much as kill a chicken since Grandfather had got into trouble and in fact had been to prison for it, she didn't know the full story—you didn't have to squeeze the heart, just hold it until it stopped, and they took the little lamb that was in her belly out a good week before it was born, that was when the fur was at its silkiest and the skin at its softest, a suckling lamb was very tasty, they used to have it for Easter, the head made soup with tar-ragon and sour cream and the rest was roasted whole, like that, see?, and she pointed down the shining line of fur hats, bright, compact little curls and squiggles, like shorthand symbols, and the wearisome mem-ory of next day's exam returned, and she started to read back the sym-bols in the fur as words in a tremulous, hoarse voice, the same voice that *he'd* read in at the History and Philosophy matriculation, the short-hand and typing exam next day and the Russian entrance exam in two weeks' time, with a closed, southern accent, he'd read hesitantly, stum-bling, like the Oltenian peasants with melons in the market, slowly and deliberately at first, uncertainly, as if spelling it out, but towards the end of the sentence of squiggles his voice rose and he began to shout and scream, and then he just howled as if he were being flayed, then was lost in cheering that broke out, and finally his voice was swallowed up by the applause, rhythmical, unceasing, but not lasting so very long, at the most six months.

THE POET

Now you may ask, said the Poet, sternly but cheerfully, emphasizing the *now,* as if every sentence, question, movement or that day's thoroughly prepared walk had its proper time and place, and that time had arrived now, towards the end of June when school was closed and, in the shadow of the arcaded house on the main square, the teenage Girl, dressed in white, carrying a mysterious bag and brandishing a flower like a Field Marshal's baton, boldly put the deferential question that she had formulated in schoolgirl fashion and had been chewing over for an hour: *What do you think is impossible?,* but the question surprised the Poet just as much as the shiny packet had the Girl: *What's this?* she enquired uncertainly as she took the big, gleaming, hard, brick-shaped object from him, *You asked for some coffee, didn't you?* the Poet answered with a nonchalant question as if the packet was of no importance, but she had never seen such a big packet of coffee in her life, it must be at least a kilo and a half, perhaps all of two! the absurd hope flared up within her, fancy going home with two kilos of coffee!, and then she realized what she had in her hand as she read the foreign label, *one kilo ground Brazilian coffee,* because her youthful imagination, which exaggerated everything, must have thought that that one was a two, and, more to the point, there in the public street she daren't examine the strange packet, would have felt it improper, like costing a valuable jewel to the last *fillér,* and the packet itself was too conspicuous, because the Poet had asked her just two days previously what he could bring her when they went for a walk in the Botanical Garden—*Say something that isn't impossible,* he'd said, but *Why need he bring anything?* thought the apprehensive Girl suspiciously, as if it might be some kind of trap—

65

she couldn't even think of anything impossible, *What are you short of at home, then?*—*Peace and quiet,* she retorted sharply and laughed in embarrassment, because her sister had been playing that awful AC/DC record all day and she couldn't read, *and hot water,* but she kept quiet about the latter, she thought it risqué to mention such physical things to the Poet, and of course there were a thousand things lacking at home: in the first place, she hadn't got a room of her own, and Mother was never in, she worked non-stop and they weren't going on holiday that summer, and an absolutely awful thing came into her head, the day before they'd run out of cotton wool, *now of all times,* because the three women always had their periods at the same time and the cotton wool had run out on the second day, and fortunately there was a heap of old bedclothes at Granny's and they'd cut some up, and Granny (Mother said that she was sorry about the bedclothes) had mentioned that during the war there hadn't been even that, and they'd used the outer leave and cobs of maize—*Maize cobs?*—the Girl had been puzzled, *like tampons?,* because they sometimes got some from Budapest, *Silly,* her sister grasped the opportunity, *not in, just on, want me to get you some?,* because the school term in autumn started with them going harvesting maize, but she couldn't ask the Poet for cotton wool, nor for the cycle that she'd recently had stolen—if that hadn't happened the Poet wouldn't be seeing her home regularly—and that morning Mother had told her to get some cat food somewhere, and had left money, but it would be ridiculous to ask for that as well, why couldn't she think of anything ordinary, let's forget it, it was awkward, she ought not to accept anything, and she didn't like to return the Poet's steady gaze, could feel a drop of perspiration running down her spine, *Well?* the Poet was waiting eagerly and she'd sensed danger again and blurted out *Coffee*—because she'd finally thought of something sufficiently serious and adult that she'd be pleased to get for Mother—*There's never any coffee,* and she added to herself the sentence that Mother repeated every morning, *Well, when this goes we'll really be drinking the last,* and she smiled broadly because the Poet, unlike Mother, said that her teeth were nice, and after that she laughed more confidently even though in that too there was an alarming element of revelation as the pink of her gums showed, and now there she stood with a whole kilo of rock-hard coffee, and it shone like the cross on the church in the main square, such a mighty packet as she'd never seen, the golden paper gleaming in the sunlight that came in under the arcades—*You know, anyone that goes through under the arcades*, to which the Girl trotted out the appropriate response, that they have their wishes fulfilled, but the Poet raised his sparse eyebrows and corrected her: *No, won't pass the exam*, and the awful thought shot through her *Now am I supposed to walk through the town with a kilo of coffee in my hand?!*, which seemed an indiscretion, a greater display than it would be to walk around naked, *I'll pay you for it*, she said uncertainly to the Poet although she hadn't the slightest idea how much it might be, clearly, a kilo of coffee was beyond price, but it crossed her mind that in the pocket of her white dress with the pink trimming (what her sister called a 'goody-goody dress') there lay a folded, worn 25-lei note, her weekly pocket money, and a torn tenner, the cat money, and twenty-five was just the price in the shops of the quarter kilo of coffee substitute that one could sometimes get, and obviously Mother wouldn't be pleased if they had to pay for the coffee because she wouldn't have enough money, but what was she going to think if she went home with a kilo of coffee?, teenage girls didn't come by kilos of coffee unless miracles happened, but that was precisely what the Poet had intended: he meant to play the mysterious wizard to whom nothing was impossible, which was precisely what she wanted to ask him about, and here was this great big flower as well, she thought in embarrassment, the size of a tennis racket, because what was also quite obvious was that the Poet had broken off the only amaryllis flowering in the Botanical Garden's greenhouse and its four huge, open, dark pink flowers were as conspicuous as the kilo of coffee, *Flesh-coloured*, said he with a grin, and the Girl had hated carrying the excessively showy flower out through the gate, *Get me a lottery ticket in exchange*, he commanded suddenly, and made for the '*Loz in plic*' (Sealed lottery ticket) vendor seated by his little table, and she bought a 3-lei ticket, folded and sealed, which the Poet tore open, after a lengthy search for the big metal ring, smiling like someone who was sure in advance of the outcome, opened it out and immediately gave it back to the grumpy vendor who looked up suspiciously as if the scene hadn't been played in front of his eyes but, rather, the purchaser was showing him some dubious forgery, took the piece of paper, looked at for a moment, turned it over, smoothed it out on the table, then in an officious voice stated that payments in excess of 50 lei were dealt with at the central office, 'on production of the ID card', he added, and the Poet thanked him politely for the information and slipped the ticket nonchalantly into his shirt pocket, then smiled at the Girl, his small, regular teeth gleaming: *Thank you. Let's get some lunch, shall we?* and she was shaken, weren't the amaryllis and the kilo of coffee enough, and the ticket—how much had he won? a hundred? five hundred? he hadn't said—and the complicated rendezvous up in the Mikó garden: the arrangement had been that in front of the cactus house the Poet would give a sign for her to go down to the little bridge and they would eventually meet in the smaller palm-house by the water lilies, but if something went wrong he'd think up another strategy, and now they'd got to go for lunch as well! and the Poet, without waiting for a reply, made for the Continental, the smart restaurant on the corner which Granny kept calling the New York, *Do you like frogs' legs?* asked the Poet as he waddled beside her as if limping, which in fact he was, *Won't he be seen at a time like this?* flashed through her mind, why did he only have to hide in mornings and evenings? could he stroll about the main square in broad daylight with anybody he liked? *All you can get in any restaurant is frogs' legs!* said the Poet with a laugh, *Even Paris is nothing like it! They've had six tonnes of frogs' legs from Poland delivered at the central distributor's. Six tonnes! Have you ever had any frog? We've been coming here every day since. It's a pity I can't wait for the shipment of snails and lobsters from France, but I'm very fond of them. Comrades, I beg you*—and he looked around the high, gilded dining room, then his eye lighted on a suspicious, solitary man who was stirring his coffee and looking out of the window, and from then on he was addressing him—*I'd wait for the ostrich as well, because I've never tried it. But they say nobody eats frog, and it's light and tasty, and last week all they served at a wedding was frogs' legs, the hundred-kilo pig was delivered correctly, but the restaurant staff stole that and frog was served instead! It's nicer than chicken, you'll see, how many portions shall we have?*—but the Girl would rather have had a chicken leg, however scrawny, I'll have something else, she thought, and looked uncertainly at the waiter, then at the Poet, was there a menu, because the Poet went straight to the point: when the dinner-jacketed man stopped at their table, *Pui de baltă aveţi* said he, like someone for whom asking questions is superfluous because he knows everything, and the Girl was pleased when she heard the Poet not ordering frogs' legs (*broasca*) but talking about pond chicken or something. *What are you having?* she asked, puzzled—*Chicken? Some sort of game . . . chicken? Wild chicken?* at which the Poet began to laugh, because she hadn't known the expression: in Romanian, *it isn't called frog, but pond chicken, in the pond it's a frog, on the table it's a chicken, get it?* '*Aveţi un meniu?*'— Have you a menu?—the poet turned to the waiter, his lips pursed and curled to the side of his mouth, like someone who already knew the answer to that as well, and the waiter readily offered to fetch the menu, naturally he could, but everything on it was off, he said uncertainly, because today there were frogs' legs in the first place (and nothing in the second), 30 lei a portion, in which there were six pieces, he added patiently, as if reminding the guests that the price of this delicacy was exorbitant and so they should consider carefully, perhaps have something else, *we'll have three*, said the Poet in a voice that brooked no contradiction, *three portions, and a vase for the flower and a bag* (for the coffee), *I'll leave the flower here anyway*, thought the Girl, and the fried frogs' legs and rice and the sour-creamed salad that she hadn't asked for were really very nice, nothing about them to make her imagine frogs (she was only sorry about the tiny bones, that she couldn't take them home for the cats) and the journey home with the kilo of coffee was still a long way off and the Poet talked all the time, slowly and carefully, gravely and good-humouredly, like someone prepared in advance for a cheerful speech of farewell, because that's what it turned out to be, the last: he spoke of frogs, of light, white Enyed wines, of János Arany and Radio Free Europe, ate in small morsels, tucked his damask napkin into his collar, mopped his perspiring brow with a pressed handkerchief and promised that he would let her know from abroad how he was getting on, he wasn't going to give away how and when and from where just yet, he wouldn't sign the letter but she was sure to see the postmark, and he encouraged her to write, write and write, *Such lovely mouths as yours and your sister's, there isn't another pair like you in town*, he inserted, as if the remark had anything to do with the subject or with writing verse, and he told her who to show her poems to if he wasn't there any more, and to practice writing metrical verse as shown in the book by Gáldi which he'd given her (she could keep it) and descriptions, *For instance, begin with simple things: describe the taste of frogs' legs*, and that her great-uncle Jenő Neumann too used to go there, to the New York, in the '50s, the old staff still remembered him, he'd been the life and soul of the Duma-posta literary circle, the chairman—Gábor Gaál, Károly Kós, Miklós Spectator Krenner, Lajos Kőműves Nagy had been members of the special table in the coffee house—the chairs had been the same then, gilded and upholstered in red velvet, and *they* were irradiating the elderly writer who lived near Traian út *from there* at night, *they'*d invented a new method, irradiation,[22] that was how *they* meant to do for him, and that white dress really suited her, *Always wear light colours. Your sister's got one just like it, hasn't she?* he asked, and the Girl

---

22 The Securitate were believed to have some kind of death ray that they could aim at their victims.

looked at her plate and nodded, but the dress was one that they shared, Uncle Zolti had brought it from Budapest but Juci wasn't disposed to wear little girl's stuff, and she pulled the same face when she read the poem beginning with the 'I' *Girls' crowns of hair* which the Poet had dedicated to them, and Juci had just hair, not a crown of hair, and, added the Poet, pulling the second portion of frogs' legs to him, he wasn't going of his own accord, he would never leave there, but he was being *exiled*, he hissed, and she shuddered because she'd only met the word in Russian novels—was he going to Paris? London? Vienna? or Switzerland?, because he'd mentioned it last time, and now she didn't like to ask for fear of seeming inattentive: and now there the portly Poet sat in front of the fifteen-year-old Girl, exuding a sweet child-scent as if he had always just come out of the bath, he'd lent her the latest numbers of Budapest weeklies and periodicals, sent her a basket-ful of good things—dates, chocolate spread, raisins, Szeben salami, tea in a pretty metal box (though it smelt like burning tyres), three kilos of sugar and a litre of Hungarian oil—for the February masked ball, which had been held in the fourth-floor flat, and put a big, stiff mask on his head which made him into a grinning demon, and now he went on about how his leg had been broken in the police station when he was beaten up four years before, and in the evenings, when he escorted her home with his short, rapid steps from the Szamos-side house of their mutual friend, her former Hungarian teacher, it was as if they were playing hide-and-seek: they took sharp detours to lose his shadow, turned suddenly into one street, then quickly into another, then flat-tened themselves in a dark entrance and waited, and at such times he clutched the Girl's hand and stared at her as if he'd wanted to read the effect of the game from her face, *Frightened?* he would ask severely, and she was, but didn't admit it: frightened, fearful that he would kiss her on the lips, not the cheek, or hold her breasts, and afraid of Mother, who had once, suspicious and impressed, been introduced to the famous Poet, who had come to the girls' first masked ball, and now, he said, he'd thought over her final question, what was impossible, he'd answer it, but she'd have liked to apologize, it was no longer of interest, he'd kept her waiting so long for an answer, it had only been a frivolous question, she'd simply wanted to express her admiration for him, would just have liked to know, if a whole kilo of coffee wasn't the equivalent of impossible to someone, what, in the final analysis, was: *What is impossible is*—the Poet began syllabically and in a cold, magisterial tone, *for temperatures to be added together,* and in that instant he brought to an end the surprise lunch in the cool, small room of the New York Hotel, where perhaps poets still went in the May of '86, not only Ady and his friends at the turn of the century as Granny had said, he wiped his mouth with the gleaming damask napkin and gave her a long look: the startled girl, however, had heard of that sort of thing—*Which law of thermodynamics is it?*—in those detested physics lessons, when it was always her hair that was used to demonstrate in electrical experiments, her fringe always standing on end at the touch of the ebonite rod, bolt upright, the class shrieking in laughter as she grabbed the rod, but that temperatures couldn't be added together, simple and logical though it seemed, she knew from experience, because at home they heated the bathwater in a tub, and she was precisely aware of the third law of thermodynamics, but now the realization came to her suddenly, like a lightning bolt, that when all was said and done there were only very few things that were permanently impossible, and that to receive a kilo of coffee was certainly not one, *Would you like a coffee?*—asked the Poet after lunch, as if reading her mind—*A kilo of coffee . . . that's nothing . . .* he added, wheezed heavily and undid the napkin from his neck, *you see, coffee is nothing, even the smell doesn't appeal to me, I haven't drunk it for ages, so to answer your question,* he began ceremoniously, *it's impossible, for example, for temperatures to be added together, because only eternal things are impossible, for example, it's impossible for those swollen, purple clouds hanging low above the town, which are now touching King Mátyás' crowned head, to stay exactly the same even for a moment, and we beneath them, that's what's impossible, so in answer to your question the only things that are impossible are those which are eternal, and a kilo of coffee is never going to be one of them.*

FOR HER AGE

Theatre history—the History of the Kolozsvár Amateur Theatre, written in Stockholm—has recorded a certain thirteen- (-and-a-half-, for the sake of precision) year-old girl, looking as mature as possible, her breasts swelling under her sailor suit (handed down from her mother, she could hardly get into it)—*Mummy, my breasts aren't too big for my age, are they?* as she emerged from the bath and looked at herself in the steamed-up mirror, and the sentence became an embarrassment, her mother told everybody, this Girl, that is, with her long hair which stood up at the front in a quiff, as her colleagues said, because now she had colleagues, not classmates, appeared on stage for the first time in the autumn of 1984, not at the Sétatér Theatre, not in the summer stage circle, not at the Nemzeti nor the Romanian Theatre, but at the Railwaymen's Club: in her first performance she sat on a school bench, just like in the daytime when she was in class VII-B (the worst) at School No. 3, the hated maths and physics school (not for much longer), but now in the theatre performance it transpired that she came off the bench and recited the Modern Poet's poem, and this time she was appearing at the Pocket Theatre in the spring of 1984 and it became clear to her that Modern Poets did live in Kolozsvár, one of them not far from their house, down along (as the Hóstát people said) Pata utca (as in the anonymous jingle *At the end of Pata street pussycat cries, feeling piqued*) and the Girl with the 'tufted head' recited the poem written about her at the top of her voice, because she felt that that poem was hers, she recited *A bástya lánynak bokája is bástya, ajka szétlapul, ha száját mosolyra táccsa*[23]—not *táccsa*, my dear, sweet girl, not *táccsa*, that's

---

23 The director's complaint is of slovenly pronunciation.

how common people in the Hóstát district talk, Ödi called out at the rehearsal, but make the *t* clearer: *tátja*—I'll start again then, said the teenager, offended because she'd been interrupted, but she recited marvellously: *A bástya lánynak bokája is bástya, ajka szétlapul, ha száját mosolyra tátja*— The Bastion Maid's ankles are bastions too, her lips are broad, and when she stretches them into a smile—she stressed the *tj* furiously, stretching her mouth sideways with the *á, a bástya lányba, következik mármost, be-bejár egy furcsa alabárdos*—a strange halberdier, it follows, comes in and out of the Bastion Maid again and again—and the said halberdier, that is, the Poet, used to walk the budding Girl home after rehearsals, he doesn't *come in and out* of me and he's not going to either!! she added to herself self-consciously, it was no good his keeping on sending poems through the post, typed on coloured paper, about the secret meetings of the youthful actress''erotic little sandals' and his own red corduroy shirt!—there'd be no *in and out* then either!—and at the end of the 'Bastion Maid' poem her startled 'classmates' (everybody was at least twice her age) looked in amazement and malevolently at the 'Bastion Maid', he'd pulled, was having it off with her, because this was how Ödi worked: he'd given the thirteen-year-old the bad girl's part by casting opposites, he explained, but the adults would recite about an excursion, and a brown dove, *Imagine you're the Tailors' Tower*, was Ödi's instruction, because there was only the Tailors' Tower left in Kolozsvár by that time, and in front of it was enthroned the grim Baba Novac, otherwise a Romanian brigand of Albanian descent, according to the plaque a poor soldier of Mihály Vitéz (Mihai Viteazul), whom—Csabi quoted in the deep, broken voice of the stage school, the way that the princes of Romania were played in films—*Ucis de către unguri în chinuri groaznice*, because that was word for word what it said on the plaque: he was killed by Hungarians in terrible pain in 1601, but the statue had been erected when the *Bastion Maid* was no more than four years old and the Tailors' Tower precisely three hundred, because *Even then we Hungarians were being tortured and suffering, and the Romanians have always known that*, added the black-toothed Csabi with a cough and told the Baba Novac joke, the punchline of which everybody knew: *I've only just found out!*, but Ödi stopped her, *Imagine this*, he squeezed all his fingers together and explained in a tender voice, eyes transfigured, the way he would recite *Ady, you're the Tailors' Tower from 1473, you defend the city, the soldiers march in and out between your two feet, you are the City*, sang Ödi in the rehearsals: *The Baaastion Maid*, and from that *aaa* a splendid, great cloud issued from his mouth, as his huge, round, brown eyes lit up, his eyebrows rose, and a sweeping gesture accompanied the whole as if he were telling a story to children, *Get it?—No*, mumbled the Girl to herself, I can't play the whole city, and the Bastion Maid frowned, because she interpreted the poem quite differently, and *her ankles are bastions too* was very hurtful to her, because in her opinion the Poet was writing about her, very hurtful, just like when, in the middle of dinner, Juci's Levente had passed a comment, he'd glanced at her feet under the table, hidden in the new, ribboned, white, Italian patent-leather shoes (a single pair size 40 had come into her mother's store, which naturally became hers because her feet were too big for her age and the nickname for the patent-leather shoes became 'white loaves'), he'd looked at the shoes and came out with *Your mother must have been sitting near the piano when you were born—That really hurts*, she was to shout at the Attila József evening that was never put on, she could whisper it, scream it, mumble it, it wouldn't matter: the Attila József evening would never reach the public, they would merely stand, speak, live, glow, sweat, but nobody had yet been sent to *vet* it, people weren't vetted in amateur theatre, only received messages: it might open, it might not, as Ödi said, the copy of the programme would be marked APPROVED and stamped with the circular stamp of the *Comitetul de Cultură și Educație Socialistă a Județului Cluj* (Kolozsvár County Cultural and Socialist Education Committee), the Poet's ironed white shirt, which would be hung on a wooden clothes hanger on the black velvet curtain, would gleam reproachfully, emptily in the spotlight, and the actors would feel that they had found a powerful, mystic symbol, *a white shirt*, which was certainly not going to be permitted if anyone came and saw it, because the empty white shirt was that of simplicity and festivity, the working-class Poet's Sunday best, the Poet's, that of the Man who had left them to their own devices, moved out, gone off to America, each to his own America, and the ironed shirt was a lasting reproach and an uneasy conscience—*And a great big piece of kitsch*, Juci chuckled when her sister, almost unable to speak and with trembling hands explained to her—and now the Girl could choose Attila József's fragment that begins '*Only now do I understand my father*', as if she were her own director, because her father too had gone off to his own America, swindled his way to the land of promise itself, '*No, I don't want I've no father*', she said, *it's too well known, I'll find something new, something nobody's heard before*, but, the director might add, if he were still with them, it doesn't matter a bit because nobody's going to hear it because we shan't be allowed to put it on, but nobody speaks such things aloud so it doesn't matter which they *don't* hear, but even then she preferred *Only now do I understand my father* because she thought she could really understand it, and for her age she could, but theatre was only just beginning for her: it was the spring of '84, her father actually led her there by the hand, the theatre would 'sort her out', and now she was going twice a week to rehearsals in the Ironmen's Club (originally the Railwaymen's, that is, the CFR Club[24]), wouldn't miss a single one, she'd rather give up the piano lessons with the albino lady teacher or stop the ballet lessons with Aunty Emma Dombi, because after all the Bastion Maid *was just not cut out for ballet*, and the theatre was sacred: although there wasn't a single child there, in her own estimation she wasn't one either now, well, everybody had long ago left school and was working, some delivered milk early in the morning, or went to a factory, the Armatúra, or

---

24 CFR stands for Romanian State Railways

worked in an office, and there was a stagehand from the puppet theatre there, and her, and Ödi, the 'Transylvanian Latinovits', as he'd been called in an article even in the late '70s when he'd begun giving one-man shows in the vaulted cellar of his place in Horea út, Ödi too, the Transylvanian Latinovits, was a house painter with her father in the trade union, because from seven till four, Monday to Saturday, everybody was a worker or at school, but on Tuesdays and Thursdays from seven till nine an artist and a dreamer and an ACTOR!, Géza, for example, also wrote poetry, and not long previously there'd been auditions, but of course no children had been accepted because it was a serious grown-up theatre, only her, because they'd had to take her because Father was Ödi's boss, and he'd simply said that his daughter would be there, he'd bring her and that was that, she didn't even have to audition but she'd 'brought' a poem, by Ady, Ödi's favourite and her father's, *Ady's our idea of a poet*, said her father, and went with her to the little street opposite the Law Courts, *The Jewish theatre was here as well from '41*, he assured her, because she didn't believe that it was a real theatre, *that dirty little building*, the Vasas Club, and on the corner all her enthusiasm vanished, *It's worse that the Pioneer House*, she argued with her father because she felt that she was being cheated, and on the stage in the narrow hall Ödi raised his eyebrows and looked in silent uncertainty at her father, because he was thinking: *this girl's quite big*, so that *Jancsi, this is a . . .* and Ödi paused, *this girl . . . how old is she?*, all the same he took her on, and her father turned on his heel and left her there at the first rehearsal, and Ödi spoke up and introduced her to the company—they were all standing on the stage smoking cigarettes— *This is . . . what's your name?* and the Girl replied confidently, she and her father had practised, she spoke up with assurance, *right then, here's this young girl, her right to use a serious adult name doesn't start here at the Pocket Theatre*, that was the second disappointment that day, but if she was Ödi's boss' daughter then of course she could come, and come she did: she was a girl of thirteen, a child, and when they lined up at the front of the stage for an improvisation exercise—the spring of '84 was the first time that she'd heard the term—the rehearsal began at once: *Today we're going to improvise*, said Ödi, as he would at the start of every rehearsal for the next eighteen months, he read an Örkény *One-minute Story* and gave so-called instructions: *There are a lot of you in a room, there's no air*, or: *You're running slowly—Now we're doing sport again!*— the actors burst out, or: *You're travelling on a crowded bus . . . Come on, girl, there's nothing to look at, you do it as well*, and they lined up at the front of the stage, she found herself in the middle, only came up to the shoulder of Jutka, the shortest actress, then everybody had to learn an eight-line script, it wasn't poetry because it didn't rhyme, that was just the way it was written, Ödi had typed it out and passed it round, and everybody had to speak it, *And me?* She asked nervously, *You especially!* and then the exercise was: *We all stand on stage, look at each other and the audience*—there was never going to be an audience for the eight-line monologue, perhaps Ödi knew that, but it didn't matter, they could still rehearse as if it didn't mean a thing whether or not it was eventually performed—*we look at each other and the audience, and when the tension's built up, when you feel as if you're suffocating, my girl, then off you go: 'This age gives us birth and kills us . . .',*[25] and then *everybody'll look at you, turn slowly towards her and help her with your attention, as if you were saying it in unison, a kind of mute chorus, get it? Right, then!*, and the thirteen-year-old girl joined in, waited, waited until there was a pulsing in her temple, then kicked over the rules of the game, because she just had to recite!, and she came slowly forward to the very edge of the stage, she wanted to recite a poem, and she said to the invisible audience *'what we've got from it, like food for a journey'*, and the rest lined up behind her, Ödi just stood there concealing his surprise, his eyebrows in the middle of his forehead as always, and began slowly to conduct with both hands, mouthing the words along with the child, whispering and

---

25 The title of a book by István Örkény. The following quotation, which completes the sentence, is from his *Pisti a vérzivatarban* (Pisti in the bloodstorm).

helping, '*is that we can be heroes and murderers*', and by the time they'd got to the fourth line everybody was there on the edge of the stage, staring accusingly at the rows of empty seats in the Vasas Club, '*denouncers and denounced*', and in the middle the Girl in jeans and flannel shirt, her quiff standing on end, solemnly and ceremoniously, because they were rehearsing the first scene from a future performance taken from Örkény's one-minute stories, and perhaps she, yes, SHE! would begin the whole show, she dreamt and envisioned, '*doers of little and dreamers of much*', although according to Ödi they were slowly getting ready for the performance, *let's leave it open*, he said, *it'll be an open work, it can stay pure improvisation and so it'll come to life there and then*, just like here and now, and he, the director would keep it under control, but that sort of thing couldn't be used to apply for permission, the manager of the Vasas Klub argued with Ödi, and we can't put down that there's no script, just improvisation and these eight lines from a modern Hungarian absurd playwright, who's going to give permission for anything like that, they'll be suspicious of it straight away, won't come round and take a look, just stamp it 'Permission refused', for things to develop on the spot, in the performance, an unscripted piece of work, *Just hear what I say! The comrade director's gone crackers, what planet are you on?!*, but the rehearsal went on: '*saviours of others, our own destruction*', said the others mutely, mouthing in time with Ödi, like a chorus that had been rendered silent, as if the whole were speaking through just a single, surprisingly deep child's voice, and looking up at that child, heads on one side, and in the interval Ödi and the manager argued, he couldn't imagine them submitting Örkény one-minuters as the script, improvising on it, then translating it into Romanian! if that's what you want, because the way it would sound in Romanian, according to him, it would be like '*We've been born in a golden age and it will kill us*', and that they'll certainly permit, and we can simply put on the poster '*The Deadly Age of Gold*' and everybody'll have a laugh, with which the argument ended and the rehearsal went on, '*at one time, in one place and in one person*, and *one time* meant not that of the deferred and unscheduled first performance but that of a highly successful rehearsal, consigned to oblivion, which the Stockholm History of the Kolozsvár Amateur Theatre did not record, *in one place* was on the premises of the club run for the Romanian Railway Workers, the CFR, in the out-of-sight theatre at 17 Dobrogeanu Gherea (formerly Fejedelem) utca, where the Concordia Jewish Theatre had played from 1941 to 1944, and *in one person*: János, Ibi, Ödi, Jozefa, Csaba, Laci, Magdi, Edit, Géza, Jutka, the teenage girl and sometimes the Poet, *'each man for himself, accordingly . . .',*[26] but the Modern Poet evening, in which the Bastion Maid at a school desk recited, as she believed, about herself, was being put on (Father was no longer there, and never saw his daughter on the stage), and in the meantime she learnt if not to speak verse then to stand still on stage, to improvise spontaneously, to watch others, to be in a tableau, or stage presence, and she quickly learnt to smoke cigarettes—she practised that in private, a ciggy stolen from her father up in the attic—and on the early summer excursion to Dés she learnt to drink beer: because the Modern Poet evening went out 'down the line' to the CFR clubs at Dés, Torda and Hunyad—*We're taking it on tour*, announced Ödi proudly, and the Pocket Theatre company stayed in hotels, the Bastion Maid's first experience of a hotel: the doors didn't shut properly, there was no hot water, and in the night the doors of the six rooms occupied by the twelve members of the company opened and shut like a clown act in a revolving door, everybody—János, Ibi, Jozefa, Csaba, Laci, Magdi, Edit, Géza and Jutka—was in and out, having it off with one another, and her roommate changed thrice (Magdi, Edit and Jozefa took it turns to sleep in the next bed), because according to Csaba in technical terms of sociology and popular psychology the Great Transylvanian Hungarian Stud was at its best on the trip to Dés, Torda and Hunyad—*Csabi, dear boy, you shouldn't in front of the*

---

26 Here ends the quotation that began '*This age gives us birth*'.

Girl, you know, sighed Ödi, because only he and the Poet (who shared a room) and the teenage Girl were left out, and afterwards in the morning they sat in the now strong summer sunshine on the terrace of the Szamos restaurant in Dés, where at eleven o'clock the doleful waiter, in his stained suit, had to be persuaded: *Sîntem actori în turneu*, they explained, we're actors on tour, bring twelve beers for the company, to which he uninterestedly replied that there just wasn't any beer, and if there were any he'd only be allowed to serve it with food, and the haggling started, so bring the menu, Csaba wooed the waiter, as if they were in some posh place where there actually was a menu, or, Csaba suggested helpfully, just say what there is, that's just as good, but there wasn't a menu, or if there had been it would have borne no relation to the truth, but the waiter slunk wearily off to the kitchen to enquire whatever there might be to eat, *Never mind*, called Csaba after him, *The tripe soup isn't ready yet*, announced the waiter, *Ugh, I hate tripe*, Jozefa turned up her nose, *I can bring you some fishcakes*, the waiter went on, *they're yesterday's, but they'll be all right*, he used a technical term: *potrivit*, that'll do, that is, they won't be fresh, they're yesterday's, and especially if it means bread, it's rock hard, *And if we have some fishcakes, then there's beer?* Csaba bargained, *Yes*, and a big aluminium jug arrived with the twelve mugs, the fishcakes—if indeed there were any—remained in the kitchen, obviously nobody would eat them and there were no dogs about either—Juci had had some once, they'd been like tangy sawdust that smelt of fish, a salty, sour fried mush—because the twelve fishcakes appeared only on the bill, and with a glance at Ödi Csaba enquired whether he might now, for the Bastion Maid's benefit, tell the joke about Baba Novac, after all, there was nothing dirty in it, and Ödi gave a silent nod and Csaba started: János was found at Ion's house in a pool of blood, and the policeman asked Ion why he'd killed his Hungarian neighbour, whom he'd got on well with, and Ion replied: Well, they killed Baba Novac! The policeman shook his head, and said 'But that was three hundred years ago!', and Ion retorted 'But I've only just found out!', and now, that is, in early summer 1985, in June, when she ought to have been writing end-of-term essays, the Girl had instead proudly taken into school the official invitation to go on tour, and Csaba took the beer, which was clear, watery and cold with a thick head of froth, put his hand right into it under the foam, took out a handful and flung it onto the concrete, then looked up sternly, pressed the remaining untouched mug into the startled girl's hand for her to do the same, and so the teenager, who by then was smoking in public, learnt ... firstly, to drink frothy beer and to toss the froth off onto the floor with a quick flick, and then there was only a single improvisation exercise with Ödi, a real one-man show, as Ödi called it, the sort of thing that he used to do in the old days in his cellar in front of his friends, the one and only genuine alternative cellar-theatre in Kolozsvár, a show which likewise was going to have no audience but only partic-ipants, when in the biting cold of dawn Ödi climbed aboard the Baltorient Express and didn't stop before Stockholm, because he'd been getting ready to follow his wife there, who'd gone four years before, and the entire Pocket Theatre was standing there on the platform, and Ödi had got on, lowered the filthy window, raised his eyebrows and with that look of amazement regarded the empty auditorium—because in free Stockholm too the auditorium would be empty, he was really going to have no more audience—took out a large, pressed, white handker-chief as did the ten members of the orphaned company, who all took them in their right hands but did not wave them, merely: *we shall stand like a group of statuary*, until the train disappeared in the Swedish mist, Ödi, however, the Transylvanian Latinovits, would be able to follow his original profession in his new Swedish homeland, his career as a house-painter, so as later, in the tiny flat which he got from the Swedish authorities, to write the history of the Kolozsvár Amateur Theatre, doc-umenting it with photographs, newspaper cuttings, tickets and posters, which was a genuine though slim publication on theatre history, because by this he would be able to prove that he was entitled to apply for a Swedish-state retirement pension as an artist, not a house painter, and he had the slim, black-bound book printed at his own expense with his monogram on it, the round intertwined letters ÖD, like in the corner of a handkerchief.

A CHINESE TOWEL

At the time the rubbish had not been collected from behind the block of flats for two months, and Lili looked down from the kitchen window on the fourth floor at the enormous metal bin and the unappealing mess that was spreading all around it and thought that it was just as well that it was cold, she hadn't have been able to leave the window open in summer either, such a stink had invaded the flat, nor had it been possible to be on the sandpit or the playground with its rusty iron swings, and now there were only a few scrawny feral cats rummaging among the heaps, and Lili was anxiously watching what they were up to when she saw a man come from behind the block opposite by a very circuitous path, wait a moment, then quickly deposit the contents of a plastic bucket and hurry off, because at such times the occupants of the seven-storey, L-shaped Block No. 11 regularly took their rubbish to other people's bins, which weren't emptied either, and the people from No. 9 took their rubbish to theirs, and in the end the heaps round both bins grew equally, especially after holidays, but now Lili stepped back from the window and told everybody that the rubbish hadn't been collected for two months, *it's appalling*, she added with her much-used favourite word, heavily stressing the -*all*-, and derived some relief from the fact that she'd managed to throw '*it*', wrapped in a medium-size Chinese towel, into the bin while it had still been possible to shut the tight-fitting lid, but that same night she'd crept, candle in hand, down the dark staircase—the light bulbs were always being stolen—and picked the bundle out of the bin with the washing tongs because it had occurred to her that cats or dogs could pull it out, she'd taken it up to the fourth floor, didn't unwrap the towel but put the whole thing into a strong nylon shopping bag into which she also tipped half a box of strong-smelling Dero detergent powder, the sort that was only used for cleaning the staircase, then tied it all around nice and tight with wire and put it back like that, *My girl*, she'd said two months previously, *move up into the attic for the winter holidays, Juci's going to have to study for her university entrance exam*, which was in fact a life-and-death struggle, only seven places, get in or work in a factory, and the Girl, still in Year Ten, began to pack her things at once although Granny wasn't very pleased with her granddaughter in winter because it meant heating the attic as well, so she was forever watching the gas meter, worrying about the few cubic metres of the winter *kóta*—she mispronounced the Romanian word—*Because then they'll cut my gas off, and it'll be just too bad, nothing we can do about it*, but Granddad had made a clever gadget with two horseshoe magnets like tailors used ages ago (you couldn't get them by then, the demand was too great), and every evening, before the heating was turned on, it would be placed on top of the gas meter on the veranda and, because they were worried, in the daytime removed once the bathroom tank had warmed up first thing and everybody had washed, unless there was a lot of cooking to be done for some special occasion, because although there was a precious if dangerous water heater in the bathroom and in principle they could have washed and bathed at any time, several times daily or weekly—it wasn't like at home in the block, in the horrid bath of water full of one another's hairs and grey soapsuds, and the water had to be warmed in laundry tubs, and Juci absolutely always insisted on going first and poor mother was left for last, but being in the middle wasn't very nice either—but dearly though she loved her granddaughter Granny would have objected to so much bathing, and so the Girl didn't mind giving it up and had *her very own room* in the attic, had her morning coffee with Granny and Granddad, and could read or write until the small hours, and in the first days of January 1988 getting up at midday was the best present, Christmas included, that Mummy could have given her, so she moved at once as soon as she heard the suggestion, *I'll take the typewriter as well*, she announced, and for once Mummy made no objection, saying that she needed to work on it, and in any case there was the other one, her own, that old manual, but the Girl now realized that she could ask for anything as long as she just went: because ten days previously she'd shut the door behind her without saying a word and only come home late: she'd gone out in a hurry on hearing Mummy shout *What have I done to deserve this*! and even threatening to kill herself, *I don't want to set eyes on you again, how could you do such a thing*, and Juci went and hid silently for hours in the bathroom while she ranted and raved, *Don't let me see him here ever again, I'll kill him*, Mummy thundered, and went on making threats about *the ungrateful scum that had been the death of her* and *for whom she'd sacrificed her life*, because two days previously Juci had told her—not her mother, because she was scared to, but her sister, of whom she'd suddenly felt that she was really her big sister, not younger, and from then on that's what she remained, at which big sister had begged her to tell Mummy what she was expecting, and asked *You quite sure*?, but Juci said nothing, and *Does he know*?, and again Juci said nothing, *So he doesn't*, the Girl had ended the conversation, *then I'm going to tell both of them, I'll ring if you won't*, at which Juci burst out with *No, keep quiet*, but that evening nothing was said, and in the attic, days later, *bay-leaf brew* came suddenly into her mind; Krisztina's mother, who worked at No. 1 children's clinic, had told her that a girl had drunk a decoction of bay leaves in order to have an abortion, five bay leaves and that did it, she was rotting alive, *Pu-tri-fy-ing, do you understand*? Krisztina's mother articulated the syllables, they'd made her a special canvas bed in the hospital, and an older peasant woman had been brought in, completely brown from drinking cigarette stew, *Cigarettes*! Krisztina's mother had flung up her hands to heaven, *I'll rather stay a virgin*, the Girl had decided even though her girlfriends laughed at her for not going with anybody and taking such care of her virginity, the most you could do with her was kiss and cuddle, and at a party the well-meaning girls had warned Levente that it was a waste of time trying with her and he'd left her alone after the first night when they went camping to the lakes and gone straight over to Juci's tent, but she couldn't help feeling surprised that this was all happening now: not because Levente had been sleeping in their place regularly for the past two years, but because Juci had been born with a notice round her neck as the child that wasn't wanted and didn't want children herself, whose mother had had a difficult birth as well, and perhaps the series would continue: *That's what Juci has to thank for being alive,* Mummy always said, nodding at the TV, *because we weren't expecting her, she was born thanks to a C film which we got from Budapest, at the time it was said to be the most reliable form of contraception, so that's how Juci was born, because in those days you couldn't have an abortion any longer, the presidential decree came out in 1966,* and her sister somehow imagined that on the label tied to her sibling's wrist with a piece of bandage it hadn't said her name but *C film,* and underneath not her date of birth or her weight but *Decree 770 of 1966,* as if the new arrival had so been named —*C?* thought the Girl, *wonder what that means? Why C exactly? Why not some other letter . . .* afterwards Juci must have worn that little bit of card all her life, and in the Girl's chaotic imagination Juci was driven round the town on a cart with a wreath of feathers on her head and this C-film notice around her neck, like wicked girls used to be tarred and feathered, because aborting a child meant that the hangman would brand a letter on their shoulders in broad daylight and then turn them out of town never to return, because if they did they would go straight to the gallows, *Juci, my dear,* Mummy repeated in a high, piping voice, *you've got Him to thank personally for your life:* so Juci was in fact a decree-child, as they were called, as if speaking of a little abandoned lame duck or a bright-eyed drooling Down's syndrome baby: because in 1966 the Supreme Council had promulgated its Decree 770 under which pregnancies might be terminated only in exceptional, medically justified cases, otherwise all concerned went to prison: mothers, doctors and anyone else, but simply nobody made any provision concerning fathers, the strict letter of the law forgot about them as if they had in practice had no part in the act of procreation, in the decision on the life of a possible child, the yes or the no, only those wicked mothers, lascivious mothers, insatiable mothers, irresponsible mothers, who didn't even mean to be mothers and who were finally left to themselves with their terrible burdens, because as far as 1966/770 was concerned there were no fathers living, consequently they were not punishable, as now neither was Levente, only three women, and two of them still minors, and in the years that followed the number of births in the country, the birth rate, had increased spectacularly, and the Dr Stanca hospital at the corner of Pap utca and Magyar utca had become a dosshouse, because this C film was like an incantation, a seal, a self-fulfilling prediction: the unwanted child, who herself must not even have thought about wanting a child, as not for a moment did the question arise of her being able to support it—*Now? Where? At the age of eighteen? At university age? From Levente?*—the questions would have poured forth like that certain C film had done continuously since 1966 because justifications, reasons *why not*, could be listed *ad infinitum*, and such a question as why *yes* simply didn't exist because the hangman now silenced the yet unborn with his own hand, no questions asked—but her younger sister felt that she, who had seen the light of day in 1971, two days before the July Theses, was the son (or rather daughter) of fortune, it was as if by that time there had no longer been any decree in force, people had forgotten about it or had simply become used to it and acquiesced to it like everything else, including that prohibition, and the Girl thought that she had been born outside the law, in a sort of liberty which Mummy delicately entrenched because Mummy, so she said, had very much been waiting and wanting her: *But if you'd been a boy I was going to leave you in the hospital*, she always added sternly, *Thank you, sir, or rather madam, for making me a girl*, she curtsied impudently to her mother on her birthday, but Mummy hadn't understood,

89

and the two of them were still little, living in Dohány utca, it had been after the divorce, when Mummy had suddenly spent money on a terribly expensive trip to Budapest, she'd sent Uncle Zoltán a telegram saying that she was coming, and before that she'd been closeted in the big room with her mother and father, the double door had been pulled to which normally was never done, in fact it didn't shut properly, and again the conversation had degenerated into shouting and Mummy's voice had been heard: *And how often did Dr Fazekas give you a curettage? Until she said you weren't to go back to her, your womb had worn so thin?!*, and Granny had shouted something back, perhaps that she couldn't have had any more children, they'd been so poor at the time, but Mummy still might, at which Mummy had laughed scornfully and said *And you say we're not hard up now? Haven't I got two children? How many more am I supposed to have?*, but in the end she got a loan from Granddad's savings and went and caught the train, because in those days you could still travel at short notice and get a passport inside a week, but later Uncle Zoltán had to send a telegram from Budapest saying that old Mari had died, because she had been the only one to whom it could be shown that Granddad was closely related, but old Mari had already been dead fifteen years, and by that time a passport would only be issued on production of such a telegram, because Mummy needed to go again urgently and fortunately for her women weren't actually examined at the frontier by gynaecologists, it was just a rumour, *Why isn't your father going?* she was grilled at the police station when she applied for her passport, because it was his relation that had died, *He's old and senile, he'll never manage in Budapest*, she lied without hesitation (*E senil și nu se descurcă*), but in the winter of '87 it was no longer possible to get a passport inside a week, and when Uncle Zoltán really did die neither Granny nor Granddad were allowed out to the funeral, even though Aunty Marika sent an official telegram endorsed by an acquaintance in the Ministry of the Interior, but at the police station they said that cousins didn't count as close relations and they'd have to wait their turns, a couple of months, but in '85 Decree 770 had been stiffened up and after that only so-called hero mothers with ten or more children and women over forty-five could have abortions, and that terminating a pregnancy of more than four months' standing counted as homicide, and by that time everybody had learnt to control themselves when it came to life and death, and furthermore under that decree hero mothers could, in principle, be given an ARO car—of course, with the exception of Gypsies, who could have as many brats as they liked but got nothing for it—and hero mothers could travel free of charge on the railway and have an annual visit to a spa, *I'm a hero mother, then, Mama Eroină,* stated Mummy proudly and she wasn't just joking, because in the winter of 1987 she gave actual proof, and the younger girl that very afternoon had sternly ordered her sister, with the hardness of self-confident virgins and those reluctant to take chances: *If you don't tell Mummy at once I'm going to, understand, how long are you going to leave it?!* she whispered, because she was terrified that in her despair Juci too would drink bay-leaf brew or cigarette stew and turn black, and Juci asked for one more day, but after the fuss had died down and after not speaking a word to either girl for days Mummy took steps: it was going to cost 4,500 lei for the doctor who would perform the operation, and a kilo of coffee for the person who gave her the address, exactly Mummy's salary for a month, and she took out a ten-month loan, which was something that the firm didn't permit but which she and her colleagues paid off by monthly instalments to the cash office as if a regular but entirely illegal private bank were operating, with bookkeeping, statements and interest, but the firm knew nothing about it or turned a blind eye, because Mummy never had any money set aside, didn't save for anything, there was money in the house for a week at the most and she worked at three jobs. *You can come up with half of it,* she said calmly to Juci's friend Levente, whom she otherwise adored and frequently fed, *speak to your parents if you like, I don't care, sell the car or whatever else you've got, but the day after tomorrow you be here with*

91

the money, and not another word was said about it, it seemed that they could either shout or say nothing, and between the two arrangements had to be made and the *business* sorted out, but nobody shouted at Levente, the charming, good-looking boy, it was as if he'd had no part in what was happening, as if everything was only Juci's fault, but he came up with the money promptly and hadn't sold the car or talked to his parents, he'd made half of it from selling deodorants, soap and coffee at Ószer, sold his farmer jeans and jacket—that was Levente's sacrifice —and the rest he'd borrowed from a friend who bred rabbits in the block, and in the end it wasn't a doctor, as Mummy had thought, but a nurse who called when the younger girl had moved out to the attic, and next day it was all over, and Mummy had wrapped *it* up in a pink and yellow striped towel and taken it downstairs because the WC would have been blocked, and a week later she phoned Granny to say that her daughter could come home, but she wanted to stay there, and for once Mummy didn't argue or give orders, and it never entered the Girl's head that hitherto she'd always had to bandage every cut in the family, even put salve on Juci's tongue when she had an ulcer and it became infected, because Mummy felt faint at the sight of blood, an injury or a pool of vomit in the street, but now, all the same, she'd wrapped *it* up in the Chinese towel and taken it downstairs, because *You've only got one mother*, she thought, though she didn't know why Mummy looked so fixedly at the rubbish, because neither Juci nor she ever told the whole story, it seemed that it had never happened, and they threatened her, the 'blabbermouth', not to talk about it to Granny, but that's how it must have happened and only Mummy could have done it, only she could have taken *it* down to the rubbish, because that wasn't the nurse's job, that's the only way it could have happened, otherwise Mummy wouldn't have waited so anxiously at the end of February, when the cold weather had begun to ease up and the dirty snow was starting to thaw, for the rubbish at last to be collected from the back of the block, and for all that had accumulated around the skip to be shovelled into the empty one, because even for money the bin-men wouldn't pick it up, the people from the staircase on weekly duty had to do it, and by the time that the occupants had got it in, the empty bin was absolutely full, new rubbish began to pile up just as before around the rusty skip, everything could begin again from the beginning, and there was never an end to the unwanted births and those who, nevertheless, were born.

STEPS

The first-floor lesson began when Laci, who was studying architecture
in Bucharest, called graciously down—he happened to be doing nothing,
had no visitors—from their first-floor balcony where he was basking
half-naked in the warm March sunshine: *Hey, Tufty*—the name he
applied that day to what was to him a being of a lower order, the little
chick, whose uncombable hair towered above her high, prominent forehead because Granny had cut her hair in a fringe which had immediately stood on end and pointed skywards as if constantly touched by a
charged ebonite rod as in physics lessons, but Tufty, though still inferior
in Laci's eyes, had by then received her first love letter and had read it
with Juci, discovering forty-seven spelling mistakes in the two-and-a-
half pages, which she had self-confidently corrected in red and returned
to the sender by way of reply—*Hey, Tufty*, he called as he leant over
the balcony railing, *if you can guess what this music is, you win a sugar-
lump*, and grinned in challenge in the early spring sunshine, but the
absurdity in the sentence declaimed wasn't that Tufty would be able to
identify the record that Laci had just received from Budapest, which
was of course impossible, because his Gitta, a skinny, pimply geography
teacher (and according to Laci, frigid—*You know what that means,
Tufty? Wooden cunt*, rang out that very afternoon) who was going to
marry Laci and take him off to Budapest, brought him records, and
he'd only been waiting for the documents for two years, so obviously
Tufty wasn't going to guess what was playing full blast on the Bel-canto
stereo record player (which Mother had obtained for him), but even if
she did, at which, of course, Laci would click his tongue and comment
N-ai nici o şansă, dragă (No luck, my dear) in his harsh Bucharest

accent, because he went to Bucharest University and now spoke fluently the local gabbling, murmuring, sing-song dialect, which sounded as if everyone in Bucharest was in a hurry to impart their secrets, *Well, Tufty? Give up?*, no, it wouldn't have been absurd for the Girl in her yellow-striped socks and claret jacket as she grinned up at Laci, her eyes shining—because in her opinion she was actually a girl, as of that spring, a girl, not Tufty, even though in the matter of hair she was to have a serious bet with Laci next winter: she wouldn't wash her hair for three months out of rage and annoyance, because there'd been no hot-water supply in the Györgyfalvi flats for two weeks after Christmas, and partly to test Laci's opinion it would be a luxury to wash one's hair after a month, and so one month was the same as three, assuming that one could stand the itching, because the change to womanhood began with the hair—yes, the hair, and as she tried to cut out the inextricably matted bits at the back when the bet was over (the reason for it had been forgotten by the end of the three months, had it been a record? or a magazine?, in any case she got nothing apart from the acknowledgement) Grandmother tapped the coarse hair and said *This is horsehair, not hair, my dear, you've got horsehair on your head, when you were little you had such fine, straight hair, when did it turn into this wire?! It must have been when you started to menstruate, that's when it all changed, became curly and thick, see, it's man's work combing out this mass of knots for you! You'd better come over to our place and wash it, my dear, hair like this needs looking after*, because after that hair was a job, work—but the absurd thing wasn't that Tufty took up the university student's challenge and guessed that it was KFT's *Cat on the Road*, because they too had been in Budapest a couple of months previously and were given the record by their uncle, and they annoyed their mother with the cat number, singing to her in the kitchen *Cat on the road, it's done for now* and made Ludmilla and Belluka dance on their laps, which they endured nervously, but the real absurdity would have been if after all it had turned out that Laci's people actually had a sugar lump, but when Laci heard

the correct answer—that it was the KFT record *Cat on the Road*—he
turned pale, ran into the flat and really tossed down two lumps of daz-
zlingly white sugar wrapped in pale-blue paper bearing the words *Hotel
Intercontinental Bucureşti*, and quickly ordered the girl, a little confused
by her success, to come up at once, because he wanted to know what
records they'd been given or brought back, *I'll bet you've got KFT, Tufty*,
to which she added Queen—that had been in her mother's store,
because two copies of it came, and the Palocsays had bought the other
one—and they'd been given a Hobo from Budapest, AC/DC, but only
Juci listened to that, Mummy had got *István the king*, Hofi and Judit
Szűcs, that's *căcat de porc cu muştar* (leg of pork with mustard), Laci
exaggerated and lay flat on his narrow bed, giving Tufty a seat on an
old chest in which he kept his treasures, because there was nothing in
the little room but the record player, a bed and the worm-eaten chest,
and he informed her in leisurely fashion *Now I'll put some real music on
for you*, emphasizing the '*real*', and closed his eyes, at which *I'm an alien,
I'm a legal alien* began to play quietly, which Tufty had never heard and
which she listened to piously sitting on the chest, while Laci sang along
softly with his eyes closed, Laci, the Gypsy—Tufty never dared to call
him that—because he was short and swarthy with dark hair and eyes,
I'm 175 centimetres tall, said Juci's Levente, *Gypsy, how short are you?*
and burst out laughing, though Juci's permanent *pecitor*, her boyfriend,
was scarcely 2 centimetres taller, but Laci paused for effect and then
said with a serious, mysterious look *Little man packs big punch*, and Tufty
was gradually reaching her final height and was as tall as the student
who, to the fascinating melodies of a recording by the Police of
Bucharest origin, gave *her first introductory, theoretical lesson*, which Tufty
had earned by her musical education from Budapest, and Laci began
very softly, his eyes dreaming of nothing, as if talking to himself, first
only pronouncing a 'p' sound as if blowing a bubble, then he emitted
the 'p' at a variety of pitches according to whether he was thinking of
Kata, Krisztina, Anna or finally Zsuzsi, and there were big, rounded,

deep 'p's, little, rapidly bursting ones, many tiny, sharp sounding ones, throbbing and perfumed, intoxicatingly sharp-scented, with the aroma of snowdrops, or powerful, black-furred ones, with hidden depths, wild refuges, which all blossomed in his cold little room, decorated with fur of various colours, thickness and texture (Laci was actually going to be a window-dresser in her mother's store, temporarily, until his passport came through), because the theoretical lessons began in March and were repeated regularly, every time that Laci came home from Bucharest and hadn't any practical education to attend to, Tufty, on the other hand, who took the role of the pupil, as *tineretul studios* or studying youth, did not feature in the fluctuating series of Eszters, Katas, Krisztinas, Annas and finally Zsuzsis, she was still only studying theory, and received regular invitations to listen to music and be instructed, and she would sit on the chest, drink in Laci's mixed-language remarks, and they would listen to Police or 'Yesterday' in Laci's free, bilingual translation: *The day before yesterday I had no* deosit (*special*) *problem, now I'm very* obosit (*tired*) etc., and in autumn, after the partial opening of the Peoples' House in which he took part as a student architect, Laci developed a new programme for his pupil: *Dragi tovarăşi* (Dear comrades) the familiar reedy voice began the inaugural speech for the *Casa poporului*, the hangman's fabled thousand-roomed palace—nobody could imitate that voice like Laci, not even its original owner—and he sat on the bed, and as he spoke gesticulated with his right hand as if felling a tree, *După lupte seculare poporul român şi a dobîndit dreptul la pizdă. În epoca de aur a pizdei* . . . (After centuries of struggle the Romanian people has won the right to the cunt. In the golden age of the cunt . . .) and there followed the cunt of the five-year plan, many-sided advanced socialist cunt, the cunt of the working class and the peasant, the powerful cunt of the Peoples, and finally the cunt of Anna, his fellow student in Bucharest, that of his new Bucharest love, a Lipovan girl from the Danube delta, tiny, dark, slim and, sighed Laci, closing his eyes and sniffing at the air, pushing his nose into some unseen hole in the Lipovan-Danube delta from which came a delicate scent of smoked fish, *They speak Russian at home, Old Russian,* and he seemed to be speaking of some remote, exotic country where firm-breasted black girls danced in grass skirts in the blazing sun, Lipovans in Nigeria or the like, as if they lived in some infinitely large country, and in the celebratory speech he enumerated Eszter, the carefully guarded daughter of the writer, and Krisztina the actress, and the unconquerable Kata, the Old Russian Lipovan exotic flower, and finally the supple Zsuzsi, all were listed in Laci's interminable performances, the series of which lasted until late autumn, after which his room became an ice cave and he moved into their place on the fourth floor with the wood-burning stove where they waded through the Ferenc Bakos Romanian–Hungarian dictionary in search of ancient Dacian words—the school textbook listed a total of four—every one had 'z' in the middle, consequently *pizdă* (cunt) too was Dacian, stated Laci, and they drank tea and spoke Dacian beside the nice warm stove, and the girls spoke of when Mummy was teaching in the otherwise Romanian Almásszentkirály she had pupils named *Pizdăneagra* and *Pizdirică* (Black-cunt and Little-cunt) and never addressed them by their sur-names, but on the other hand everybody in the class was called Ion, so after all she had no choice, and that had been the greatest ordeal for that elegant, prudish, blond maths teacher, and finally Laci's theoretical lesson was put into practice in summer when they went off together camping by the lakes: Juci, Levente, Laci and his girlfriend Eszter, Kata, Krisztina, Anna or Zsuzsi, little Tufty and the rest had a barbecue (Kajla brought two rabbits) at which Levente and Laci had a competition at eating sharp paprika, and Laci held the blood-red *kápia* up in the moonlight like a communion wafer and bit it in two, at which Levente crumbled a whole dried *macska pöcse*[27] onto his aluminium plate and they sneezed and hiccupped and burped, and when the show was over

---

27 *Kápia* is a piquant variety of paprika; *macskapöcse* is a small, very strong type of chili.

they all went back to their tents for a rest, the responsible ones, and Tufty and Kajla were putting out the fire and packing up what was left over so that bears wouldn't be attracted when suddenly there was a scream and Krisztina—it could only be she, the actress designate—tore open the zip of the tent and with a piercing scream, like when a pig is killed, flung open the tent and raced down the slope straight into the lake, didn't stop, sat there waist deep and from there ranted *Gypsy, bugger you . . .! now I suppose I put my cunt on show*, and splashed about and cursed, and Gypsy went round proudly telling the story that the waters of Lake Tarnica hissed when Krisztina splashed in, and then in mid-October, by way of deepening their musical education he suggested going to a jazz concert, oh, not together, of course, *Tavitian's coming*, he said nonchalantly as if Tufty would know who that was, but her fringe was growing downwards now and she attached it to the rest of her hair with wooden hair-grips, but Laci didn't notice and off she went to the Music Academy—he actually bought a ticket—and Harry Tavitian performed, wearing a long beard and an embroidered cap, *He's the world's leading Romanian jazz pianist*, said Laci, *He's Armenian*, he added proudly, *Then he's your kinsman*, said the girl, because she was learning from him to mix her words cleverly, and she knew that Laci's family were also Armenians and made sour *angazsabu* soup, *That's quite another matter*, Laci snapped and frowned, because they were from Szépvíz, proud Armenians from Csíkszépvíz, *The two have nothing in common, understand? He's a Romanian from Constanța—But you just said he was an Armenian*, at which Laci crossly shot back *Why, you don't think we're* bozgors?!,[28] then calmed down and continued, now in his piping voice, the soft Oltenian dialect, *Bozogri împuțiți, asta sînteți voi* (you lot are the rotten *bozgors*), and at the concert the girl sat motionless in the back row and marvelled at the bearded Armenian in the embroidered cap who played as if he were alone in the unheated hall, with no

---

28 *Bozgor* is a pejorative Romanian term denoting a Hungarian.

one listening to him, and the music was like nothing she'd ever heard before, she could find no order or reliable direction in it, no framework or logic, just shreds of melody, constantly shifting rhythms, contradicting everything she'd previously learnt or heard, it was incomprehensible chaos its very self, now baffling her, now sweeping her along, but however much she paid attention they lost each other on the way, then suddenly came back together, Harry Tavitian, the bearded Armenian pianist in his embroidered *tyubityeika*—an Uzbek hat, Tatyana, the Russian woman, had one and proudly pointed out that she'd brought it from Samarkand—and the pianist with the Anglo-Armenian name would bend over the keys, then, as if resting, let his hand remain on them and look away, and from the big empty stage there blew a wind of freedom and chaos, and in the interval as she stood in the crowd looking confusedly for Laci she felt an arm round her waist which gently bore her forward: *Ma petite étudiante*, said the familiar voice, because that day, that very day she'd had her first German lesson in the new school: the bronzed German teacher, his hair and beard a dark blond, was smiling broadly at her, his white, faultless teeth gleaming like those of a predator, *moya studentochka*, as he supposedly knew seven languages, and he pronounced it *studentochka* as he couldn't pronounce the soft consonant (though it occurs in certain Romanian dialects), and he gently but firmly shepherded her to the circle where stood Miriam, the gorgeous actress from the Romanian Theatre—*Ah, that's completely different, they're Romanian Jews, nothing to do with us*, said Mother's colleague Uncle Nuszi afterwards, when the girl asked if he knew her—and Ursula, the middle-aged star of the Romanian Theatre, who was wearing a wig and (according to Mother) was said to have gone up to '*your father*' when Father worked in the Romanian Theatre and said: *Tell me, young man, have I been to bed with you already, or am I only going to?*, though it was hard to imagine of this short, stout, over made-up middle-aged woman that she had unceremoniously accosted blond, elegant Father and taken him home, only there were a good thirty years between the two images—and there she stood in the circle with the famous music critic, an architect, a set designer—and they smiled and looked at *Ma petite étudiante*, the *little Liv Ullmann*, the *frumusețea slavă*—the Slav beauty—because that morning, when he had come into class very late, the German teacher had thrown the register onto his desk, looked around, raised his thick, blond eyebrows in which, if one looked closely, could be seen hairs curling in various directions, and remained like that theatrically for several seconds because he had noticed the newcomer (that hadn't been difficult, only half the class was present, the rest had gone to French) and paced over in leisurely fashion to her and bent over her—he had a delicate, clean scent, his mouth smelt of sugar—rested his elbows on her desk and enquired *Wer bist du?*, where was she from, how much had she done already, and this went on for ten minutes, a quarter of an hour, and the rest were bored, chattered, went out, had a cigarette and came back, and the German teacher spent a whole lesson on her alone, set the rest something to do and then went out ten minutes early, but everybody thought he was mad, completely mad, and there was no need to be afraid of him, nor to work, because a student teacher that answered to such nicknames as Gilles, Jules, Jacques, Jim and so on was only there by accident and, obviously, temporarily, as a punishment, because the department—jazz—in which he ought to be teaching didn't exist and never had in the Gheorghe Dima Music Academy in Kolozsvár, but Gilles, the ever-smiling and perfumed poet and jazz-aesthete, continued to keep his arm around her waist while Miriam, Ursula, Mihai or Mihály—Good Lord! this was Juci's painter from the fourth floor opposite, because for a year Juci had been making eyes at—making eyes indeed!—going with the painter, and sometimes and secretly *was* with the big, fleshy, bearded man, who at first had only come out onto the balcony to smoke his pipe and had stood there stock-still, and they'd looked at each other in silence, Juci smoking a cigarette in the window with the cat rubbing against her and stalking up and down on the balcony parapet, and they looked at each other in that Esperanto language, the painter would come out, light his pipe, and Juci would notice almost at once, they'd stand, go inside, come out again, converse wordlessly or make signs, and her sister, peering from behind the velvet curtain in her mother's room, would guess, then Juci would open the window, lean out on her elbows, and in the end it took less than a fortnight for Juci to vanish to the painter's every morning, because her Levente too had vanished, his fiancée from Hungary had arrived, Mónika, whom he was to marry so that she would take him away, but first she had to obtain Hungarian citizenship and only then could she get a divorce, about another two years, and Levente too would put in his application, at the most another four, so a total of six years to wait, and at such times Levente would vanish but Juci was glad and she too vanished, went over to the painter's, allegedly modelling for him, but her sister would sing to herself *Moncsi, moncsi, moncsicsi, Mindig csak a moncsicsi* and show her her little brown monkey, at first she sang the words but later it was enough to sing the tune or wave the monkey and Juci would shout and slam the door—and in the interval, beside the smoke-wreathed actresses there stood Horaţiu the set designer, Marian the Portuguese teacher from the University and Ovidiu, a red-headed alcoholic poet, the entire Romanian elite of Kolozsvár, talking about where to go afterwards, to whose place, because it was only customary to go to someone's flat, and whether Harry would come with them, because this was the first jazz concert and the first German lesson, and a long series of both followed as she took more and more to jazz, and although she had better and better marks she equally quickly forgot the German—she'd done five years of German at the other school with old Jutka Daróczi when she came into the hands of Gilles, who taught her nothing, at least not German and not in school, and traced his artistic monogram on the improvisations: VM was made into a seagull with spread wings and snowy mountain peaks blended together as on a damask tablecloth, and he returned the Girl's exercise book with hidden poems in language incomprehensible with its embellishments, in which there were lines woven from unheard-of Romanian superlatives about the golden-haired Girl, glistening sunshine and exotic plants, while later in April, after Easter, on her name-day in break he presented her with a mighty bunch of laburnum in the middle of the school yard, and the others in her class laughed aloud and teased her, but Gilles had a narrow escape, this didn't reach the ears of the headmistress, and in fact everybody thought that he was mad, but Ono, the Romanian teacher, came into the next lesson in silent fury, she had evidently heard what had happened (the flowers were outside in the girls' WC and at midday the cleaners removed them), and looked contemptuously at the girl as one who had cheated on literature with a man, and ignored her completely all through the lesson like one whose mind was made up and in whose view her favourite pupil had made a poor showing, but Gilles whispered in her ear—his breath was hot and chocolate-scented—what would she like for her name-day, *goryachuyu vodu*, she retorted without thinking, hot water, although Gilles didn't know that much Russian, it would be nice at last to wash her hair because there had been no hot water since Easter, and on her sixteenth name-day Gilles brought her that very day the lace-edged Romanian towel embroidered with orange cockerels framed in blue and green grasses, and the *goryachuyu vodu* came about by a stroke of magic that same day, because in the block in Alverna utca lived *someone* because of whom there was always hot water, heating too, and so it was the same in Gilles' flat on the third floor, and after that she went round regularly every week for a bath, on Thursday, instead of going to classes on knowledge of materials and chemistry, political science and physics, round the corner she got into the yellow Dacia, which started first touch, the hot water was ready running and she could soak for a whole hour: because had it not been for that *someone*, *une sécuriste très importante* (not *un sécuriste*, but *une*, a woman, Gilles made clear), and Laci's attentive pupil Tufty or Beehive, the sixteen-year-old Girl with such long hair lay in the lovely warm water, and

Gilles brought in the linen towel with the cockerels and got in with
her, and after they had washed *not that*—Gilles' muse could only be
intacte, as he said, untouched, *szűz*, she tried to teach him the correct
word, because he spoke seven languages, seven *European* languages, he
emphasized, but knew almost no Hungarian although his parents
(long-established Romanian intelligentsia of Transylvania, he boasted)
spoke Hungarian—and as the Girl's legs, now becoming downy, hung
out of the bath (you'll have to start waxing them, Juci teased her), and
beside her lay Gilles, with his curly blond hair, even in winter chocolate
brown and fifteen years her senior, it sounded absurd but it was tech-
nically true: she was *intacte*, and only Laci wormed out of her the secret
of the Thursday baths, and he was jealous that Tufty had found another
teacher and looked at her astonished, as when she'd guessed the
KFT recording, that anybody could take her seriously—though he too
wanted to look at her breasts, *All right, I'll show you, but no touching*, she
retorted—and not just anybody, but Gilles, the poet and jazz-aesthete,
and of course he didn't believe the story about the muse, and Juci obviously knew everything, but Laci swore to keep silence, but Juci also
knew because she was her sister and called her *fürdős*,[29] and of course
the truth was somewhere in between theory and practice, Laci and
Gilles, because innocence had got lost somewhere between Laci's flat
on the first floor, Ivan's on the second, Gilles' on the third and their
fourth-floor flat (the Cobîrza family lived on the ground floor, they
didn't count, such a smell of soaking sheepskins and boiled bones came
from there that they held their noses when they went past), and so virginity was not lost suddenly and all at once but slowly, step by step, over
eighteen months, at the end of a party at Laci's at which *Sunshine reggae*
was being played and one of Laci's fellow students also noticed her
and finally she danced and smooched with a real university student to
Gimme, gimme, gimme just a little smile, but a week later Peti Hauszmann

---

29 Hungarian: bath-attendant. Fürdős also refers to a prostitute who goes and
'works' in the bath.

reluctantly said thank you (he was leaving Budapest for Sweden at the
end of summer, he was supposed to have some incurable disease),
and on the third floor on Thursdays, wrapped in the cockerel towel,
after bathing, as they still listened to music in Gilles' big bed and he
constantly explained and gesticulated, in 1988 they were listening to
the new Travitian record, the *East West Creative Combinations, ethno-
jazz, transcultural and postmodern,* Gilles explained and in his left hand
was the article, which hadn't yet been published, and under the big,
tickly, Máramaros blanket his right roamed her breasts, her belly, her
thighs and between her legs, and then it was back to the second floor,
when she had at last been admitted to the university (Laci had by then
gone to Budapest), she and little, sweet-smelling Iván with his yearning
look, who, although he was only a year younger than her, was just going
into Year Eleven at the same humanities school where she'd been, and
Ono and, of course, Gilles would be teaching him, on the day when
the results were announced at a joint party in Iván's three-roomed
deserted flat—his parents had already emigrated to America, his father
went out there to work and they stayed there, but the children hadn't
been allowed out in case they defected, but defect they did even so, and
young Iván was following them soon, perhaps a couple of months now,
the documents might come through by autumn, he'd had his application in for three years now and was going to wait seven altogether, his
relations were in the country and he, at the age of seventeen, was living
there alone, suddenly an adult and a boy at the same time—then in the
small hours, very tiredly in Iván's room—though the whole flat was
his—Iván, who was always blushing to the roots of his hair with love,
and laughed so that his pale gums showed, because now it was the Girl
who was teaching everything that she had learnt and imagined and
that worked between two, it was she that unbuttoned his shirt and her
own, he was quite hairless, not a hair anywhere, but he was slender and
muscular, and Iván gave a puzzled laugh, showed his gums like a nervous puppy, but while they were smooching his abdomen had started

to ache and he looked at her, begging her to do something, then next day he kept phoning from the second floor to the fourth and Juci laughed loudly when she realized, *So you're going to go with that kid now? That impotent Iván?*, but Iván wasn't impotent, just didn't know how and they couldn't get it together, so he remained a secret from Juci and Mother, and the summer came: Juci went off camping by the sea with Levente, an actor went with them as well, Mummy was at work, there was no Laci around, she didn't go to see Gilles, didn't need hot baths in summer, and anyway she was eighteen now, and Iván's family's big deserted flat was theirs all summer, they only went out now and then to walk the dog, they darkened the rooms completely because Iván was shy, and sometimes she even stayed the night, Mummy never asked any questions: she could please herself that summer, she'd been accepted for the university, and after all she was eighteen, Iván, however, burst into tears when things went badly, and said that perhaps he'd never get to America, but in the meantime nothing was heard of the documents, they were being seen to, drifting at their own speed from office to office, and eventually in the autumn of 1989 there was the actor with the cold eyes, conceited and taciturn (twelve years older), Mummy's intended, who'd been coming up to the fourth-floor flat for dinner since winter, Mummy had completely fallen for him and drank in his words, because of him she ignored everybody else, wouldn't even take Iván's phone calls because all she wanted was that elegant, poised, unfeeling actor who came round for the sake of her younger daughter, now a university student, although they never remained alone together, but he was her official *fătărău* (fataró, as Laci would say, but he was in Budapest now with no one to speak Romanian to any more), and on one occasion, after drinking a lot of *pálinka*, he deigned to stay and sleep at their place, in the big room, and the light had to be turned off, *Because that's what we always do*, he said in a voice that brooked no contradiction, and when the Girl tried to do things she'd learnt from Laci he said to her in a strangled voice *This isn't how we do things*, and that it was *disgusting*, and her classmate Boti also lived opposite, even in Year Three she'd always been able to talk to him about anything, but Tufty had been startled by him when they'd been playing doctors in Year Four, and he'd complained to her that he'd measured it and his prick was only 7 centimetres long!, 7.5 at the most, he was never going to grow up, and he encouraged her to measure her own but she didn't know what to measure or how, *Want me to put a ruler up, is that what you're thinking of? Are you crazy? I'm a virgin!*, but 7 centimetres was absurd, and somehow Boti had grown up in the meantime into a strapping, pleasant, hairy boy, but still frozen in that Year Four image of his pathetic 7 centimetres, and in the end she went back to the always phlegmatic Laci, the first, to the theoretical lessons that he'd given as he waved a big, shiny peacock feather about as if conducting a band, all about scents, liquids, Lipovan girls with brilliant skins, dark-brown nipples and fiery red hair, to Laci, who had rung the doorbell in agitation one morning in the winter holidays, *Say, Tufty, your mother hasn't got any Postinor?, could really do with one*, because after all Laci'd been waiting more than four years for his documents before Mummy got him that job as a window-dresser at the store, from where he could often take time off, he'd be able to do it, it was local, he'd have a job in Kolozsvár so that he wouldn't be relocated somewhere else as a punishment for putting in his application, so as not to be *repatriated* to Moldavia or the Bárágan or Dobrogea or the Danube delta, among the smoked-fish-smelling Lipovan girls, and it wouldn't be good to make Eszter, Kata, Krisztina, Anna or Zsuzsi pregnant when he'd married the frigid Gitta, *Tufty, you wouldn't have a Postinor to spare?*, and of course she had, teacher sir, but not for you unless you stop calling me Tufty.

SHAKESPEARE DRESS

In that luxuriant, dough-like permanence of anachronisms, one Tuesday afternoon in autumn, Granny's announcement, or rather tentative enquiry, sounded surprising to her granddaughter of identical figure— in Granny's opinion, therefore, with reference, naturally, to the impermanent present day—when, with a mouthful of carefully guarded pins with coloured heads, she spoke in the middle of a fitting: *This is not fashionable*, she pointed out, that is, she garbled the words between her teeth and the pins, and it sounded more like *Snofashnable*, with a rising intonation at the end as if she were asking a question, and in any case the sentence was directed to the puff sleeve that she was just pinning onto her granddaughter and the whole dress, which lay about in countless pieces, to the eye of the uninitiated, unconnected, and which she was making from cheap bleached linen so that at a later stage, when the dress was finished to the Girl's satisfaction, it would be dyed, lace, gussets, underskirt and all, a dark morello colour, *When you pin it up*, she directed her grandmother as she stood there in her stockinged feet, one white puff sleeve and—for the moment—a shapeless blouse, *put plenty of lace here on the shoulder and the ribbons that go on the shoulder, elbow and wrist loop-stitched to the end, and the neckline needs to be lower, and the ruff is to be fastened on with this button and well starched and the whole thing will be close-fitting but first I'd like some of the lace left over from that black veil all along the bust seam, and at the waist on the back*, at which point Granny interrupted, her mouth still full of pins, *Steady! At least wait while we finish the sleeves, I can't make a note of what you want*, at which the Girl gathered her hair in one hand so that the neckline could be chalked and stood patiently while Granny pinned up the Shakespeare dress which the Girl had designed all by herself, spent a month rummaging for details in the dusty, still loft, where she'd discovered things no longer of any known use in the wooden chests and cupboards—*chiffonières* was Granny's term—going back in time from Great-grandmother's day to the penniless, mad Pongrácz family, to Krisztina Pongrácz, who, in her mobcap, looked down on posterity with wild, staring eyes from a huge, black, frameless photograph which was turned to face the wall, and after school the teenage Girl would go up into the cats' exclusive domain and systematically examine all the hidey-holes that she had discovered, the two big cupboards and the chests: she opened drawers, matched up decorative buttons, found a big brass buckle for the belt, looked through the sacks of remnants and the chests with masses of shreds of lace, torn curtains, pieces of veil, moth-eaten wall hangings and blackout curtains, rags of tablecloths, tray cloths and lampshades, the boxes with elbow-length size six gloves, *There aren't any women with hands that size these days*, she thought, it was as if there hadn't been real people in the past but only shop-window dummies or little children, because when she'd come across the box at the age of ten even then she was too big for the gloves—*That's at least a size nine*, Granny looked at the child's hand, and then in the big cupboard she examined one by one the carefully mothballed evening and day dresses, worn to spider's webs, and there she'd found the stiff lace collar, crocheted in twisted silver thread and now almost black, which crowned the collection which she assembled for her plan, then she smoothed out the individual items and put the whole pile into a folder labelled 'Orders for the redistribution of land'—the careful hand had written the title and the date, 1890, in ornate lettering, but the orders had vanished just like the estates to which the enactments had referred, and she didn't take the barometer that she found in the bottom of the cupboard and which always stood at 'clear, sunny weather', she'd ask for it later, she thought, and then went down from the loft to discuss the new dress with Granny: *It'll be a Shakespeare dress*, she began to explain, and in the meantime made sketches on rice paper of how she envisaged her first historical dress, *Are you going to a masked ball?* Granny suspected, at which the girl was offended and replied that she was not, she was going to the theatre, to a première, *What's the play?* enquired Granny, *What do you suppose? Shakespeare, of course*, it was going to be Hamlet, she added to herself, at which Granny gave a sigh, *And when's the première to be?* she asked, but the girl shrugged: *Well, when it can be put on, they've been rehearsing for two months now, once it's been vetted and they get permission*, then she went on, standing in the same place in her Chinese cotton briefs marked 'Friday'—they'd only just received the set of seven, a different colour for each day of the week, she'd taken Monday, Wednesday and Friday, they'd tossed up for Sunday and Juci had won—*Let's not be fashionable, just beautiful*, she said quietly, irritated because fashion and the lengthy rehearsals made her think of the fashion shows of her childhood in the second floor of the Central shopping mall, when, two or three times a year, a dress had been made to fit her in the same sort of way and the 'Boss' two daughters had gone down the escalator from the second floor of the central store to the first, where a cordoned-off large crowd awaited them and the delicate, bespectacled Aunty Lia, her hair in a bun, wearing a close-fitting knitted suit of her own making, began to chant into a microphone as the little girls appeared at the top of the escalator, first with their feet firmly together as if lining up in school, then more and more nonchalantly and finally placing their left feet on the next step or with one foot coolly in front of the other, and Aunty Lia sang out '*See this preteen, wearing a light-blue pleated skirt and sailor blouse, available in all sizes from five to thirteen years*,' or '*Now this girl is wearing gardening pants with a plastron and a checked flannel shirt*,' as if the little girl had just happened to walk that way in her gardening pants and always wore such smart shop clothes, and Lia kept putting in how much everything cost, where it was made, what percentage of artificial fibre it contained, and went on so long gasping into the microphone with much ooh-ing and aah-ing (Granddad, who spoke perfect Romanian, had a special view of the language: in his opinion there were sounds in it—the vowels ă, â and î—

which Hungarians made only on the lavatory), and then she would continue '*Our little girl is wearing hot pants and a floral top in the summer holidays*' or '*A Norwegian-style ski sweater, product of the Someşul woollen factory, and matching trousers, 100 per cent cotton,*' or when Juci came on, '*Júlia has on a double-breasted coat, under which she is wearing a dark blue zip-fastening tunic dress,*' or '*Here comes Júlia in a printed dress available in sizes from twelve to sixteen years, price 72 lei, from the children's department on the second floor,*' or '*Júlia is now wearing check trousers and jacket of artificial fibre and high-heeled canvas slippers, available from the ladies shoes department on the first floor,*' and last of all, several times a year the two girls would come on together in the finale, identically dressed as twins (this they detested most of all), to display the store's seasonal products—Juci felt embarrassed, was not happy about wearing a swimsuit, and shortly dropped out of the compulsory fashion shows—but the younger daughter of the store's chief accountant was excited by taking part, the fittings, the inexhaustibly patient Lia's instructions on how to do a twirl, unbutton a coat or take off a cardigan and toss it over her shoulder, it was good fun choosing the clothes in the warehouse (she was given an increasingly free hand, later she could put on anything that she found), in the end walking down the escalator with all eyes on her, slowly promenading through the little space on the first floor outside the paper department, and the child mannequins were given parcels of gifts from the store, but when she was in Year Five the shows became less and less frequent and they appeared in clothes which were not even on sale, and the irritated sales staff made uninterested replies to purchasers who crowded into the children's department after the show—be in later, or sold out—and finally, imperceptibly and for no stated reason, the fashion shows stopped as if from the early '80s fashion had simply ceased to be and the clothes to be displayed had all gone, the daughter of Lia, the head buyer, didn't come back from a sudden trip to Germany, clothes began to be more and more alike, everything slowly became more uniform and indistinguishable like the

Pioneer uniforms in school, and long rows of light-and-dark blue dresses on hangers filled the whole children's clothing department on the second floor—only the orange of 'Falcons of the Fatherland' stood out in the gloom—and it seemed as if half of the essentially homogenous and timeless effect of the many colourful children's things, half or entirely of artificial fibre, which were displayed was an attempt to abolish fashion, the changing of the seasons, the superfluous luxury of differences between festive and everyday clothing, and by that means to attain the ultimate tranquilizing form, that of uniform, which would no longer call for display, *Turn sideways*, said Granny suddenly, as she chalked round the skirt section with a rod resting on the floor, and the threat of uniforms seemed already latent from the start in kindergarten and school clothes: in the group picture taken at the end of the kindergarten year one of the twenty-five children, a little girl, was showing her profile, having turned crossly sideways at the last moment when neither the teacher nor the photographer could do anything about it, as if she didn't belong in the picture, and her mother would melt on seeing it: *Look at that little girl, what an angel!*—as she pointed out her daughter, disguised in the Romanian folk costume of Maramureş: embroidered linen blouse, apron with metal strips, and at the waist ribbons in the national colours of red, yellow and blue, and on her feet sandals stuffed with newspaper at the toe, and with her short hair bound into a tight plait on top of her head she looked like the pineapple in the cartoon films, as the children—half Romanians, half Hungarians—moving up from the kindergarten in Majális utca performed the *Oseni* dance at the end of year festivities and draped a towel in national colours around the portrait of One Ear that hung above the little stage in the hall like they do to icons in the country, and had to move their feet quickly to the lively music from the Petreuşi Bros. tape-recorder, and it seemed that ever since she set foot outside the house in Dohány utca she'd had to wear uniform in kindergarten and school alike, either Maramureş Romanian or pseudo-Székely dress, in which she'd had to sing in the choir the folk song *Tizenhárom fodor van a szoknyámon* (there are thirteen flounces in my skirt)—*What's news in Budapest?*, enquired the town's leading poet prince in the deserted upstairs buffet, in the minutes before the long-awaited premiere, at which the teenage Girl became excited at the poet's remembering that they'd been to Budapest, she swallowed and considered whether she could make some unexpected, clever reply, then self-confidently said *There's a smell of petrol and . . .* then added: *fashion*, and smiled, with a tinge of regretful jealousy of the people of Budapest, *Fashion?* said the poet, who that evening too was wearing his personal trademark red corduroy shirt, he burst out laughing, liked her answer, and his white, regular teeth gleamed beneath his red moustache—*Fashion*, she repeated firmly, *it looks as if everybody's in uniform*, and then the tinny bell rang and the familiar voice of an actor called them into the auditorium, and the colourful crowd moved, some to the stalls, some to the boxes: and to meet them came the Kecset jacket of woven leather and the Fodor-style Indian dresses, which Granny had also made (that was where the gold thread used for the Shakespeare dress came from), and Réka came in her turquoise-blue pullover with leather on the shoulders, decorated with wooden balls and feathers, and her full-length knitted skirt, Kata wore an *A-line dress* of velvet and pieces of cloth, her mother a matching jacket and hand-bag, and Krisztina appeared in a close-fitting, white corduroy trouser suit and improbable white bootees—the whole family jumped about to meet her wishes, but never gave away the secret of where they found the clothes, but a fashionable corduroy suit could only have been bought from Arab students—and along came Aunt Ági, who had knitted her-self a striped, batwing-sleeved coat-dress on an ancient machine that she'd got through a fashion magazine—it was terrible—Juci had per-suaded Granny to make her culottes and a jacket out of small pieces of material (mother had brought the two thick pattern books back from one of her trips to the capital), and last of all, in the semi-darkness of the box of honour sat an expensive, quilted, floral Bartonek shirtwaister —one that the girl had seen several times before, and although Kati Bartonek had been in Budapest for a long time and was said to have set up in business near Váci utca, they failed to find the place, because the dresses which came into view in the big, dimly lit foyer all had their own histories and names, as in the old days, in the time of the great couturiers, something which now only Granny had known, because 'clothes maketh the man', as was said on stage that very evening, and it was a quarter past six before it became fully dark, the silver collar, starched in too thick a mixture of flour and water, was digging into the Girl's neck, but, she thought with satisfaction, she alone of the 813 members of the audience, plus those sitting on the steps, was wearing a Shakespeare dress, even if other people did not recognize the great English writer in the item that had been finished only that afternoon, and she placed on her knee her heavy bag, in which lay the barometer, recently begged for and which then too prophesied bright, sunny weather, and although Granddad declared that the mechanism of a barometer simply couldn't go wrong, it wasn't like a clock, the weather was always changing, you only had to wait, and the fact that the solitary hand wasn't moving didn't mean that there was something wrong with it or that it wasn't working, and in fact bright, sunny weather might be on the way if it wasn't there now, and it seemed that the barometer wasn't there to tell people what the weather was like, they could go outside and see that, but it showed what could be expected, hoped for, and bright, sunny weather was, when all was said and done, always, always, under all circumstances, to be expected, and clearly one would have to wait a long time yet, and the audience coughed and fidgeted a little longer, then in the gloom silence gradually fell and it was bitter cold, not a mouse stirring, and finally, on 23 February 1987 at seven o'clock up went the curtain and there was the empty stage, where it had struck twelve, as was said,[30] and a hard frost, a biting, merciless, sharp air.

---

30 A reference to *Hamlet*, Act I Scene 1.

MADAME CANAPÉ

The Hungarian teacher had been called Éva, then Julika, Julika once more and finally Éva again, because that summer, at the end of Year Seven, shortly after *that*, when she had enquired for her—at the end of August, when the tomatoes were ripe—saying *Is teacher in?* she had been indignant at home that evening: *Of course teacher said that I could call and see her*, because her mother had told her off, what did she think she was doing, dropping in on a teacher like that, but the Girl added in an offended tone that the teacher had said, in the final lesson, that they were to go, and the invitation hadn't been to everybody, just her and Kati Moscu, who also was good at Hungarian, a future Olympiad competitor, *Come and see me*, Éva had said, and Moscu knew her address, because she was leaving the school, *In future I shan't be teaching you*, she had announced solemnly and with a certain pride at the last lesson, but actually it had been known that the best Hungarian teacher was being kicked out of the school for putting in an application to emigrate, and a teacher that was emigrating couldn't be allowed to go on ruining the morale of the student body—two of the class also weren't coming in autumn—and now Éva was waiting in her flat in Dézsma utca behind the market for her actual passport for the move, and the Girl crossed the stony courtyard towards the last flat, to which a man pointed—he was stripped to the waist, doing some welding in the middle of the yard—*Not the basement*, he added, and she went up the wooden stairs and stopped on the top one with a bunch of zinnias from her father's garden in one hand and a bag of tomatoes in the other, not knowing which hand to ring the bell with, and then handed the lot to a kindly smiling, pasty-faced, over-rouged lady who opened the door,

I've brought these for teacher, when will she be in? she asked, and the lady looked at her blankly as if no pupil had ever before come to the door of the out-of-the-way flat and enquired for the teacher, then from inside a man's voice grumbled that there was no telling, and next afternoon the undeterred pupil appeared again in Dézsma utca, this time from the direction of the Vágóhíd, and then the teacher herself opened the door, praised the tomatoes, put the flowers on an old sewing machine in the window of the room overlooking the Szamos and offered her pupil some perfumed Lapsang Suchong tea, and that summer the name of the tea, which tasted of burnt tyres, became confused with that of the village where Éva was going to teach, one which the Girl didn't immediately register because she didn't know the villages around Kolozsvár, *We don't go to the country, we haven't got any relatives in the country*, she said a little shamefacedly, thinking that there could be no other reason for town people to go out there, *Nor do we drink tea*, she would have added, but by autumn she'd learnt that the name of the village was Szucság and had often repeated the name of the tea— *lábszag*, 'foot-smell', as Juci called it as she laughed aloud, or more likely was jealous—which came from France and which she was given every time until it ran out, from a real porcelain teapot and a wide teacup with a saucer—the glass cabinet at home was full of such things, but nobody ever took out the tea service with the blue grape pattern or the one with the brown swallows—on the bottom of the porcelain, Éva read out when she first visited her in the block of flats, was written in fine letters *János Seszták, Máramaros, 1890*, and from then on she too made a note of the name and date of the tea service inherited by her grandmother—and in winter, despite her mother's disapproving looks, she took out the delicate porcelain and drank camomile tea from it, *Are you unwell?* enquired Juci, and Mummy didn't miss a single opportunity of remarking: *I hate the very smell of camomile, it's what you should use for washing your backsides. It's children's backsides tea!* she squealed, and the Girl and Éva put sugar in the Lapsang from the tin caddy, until it ran out, and a couple of times the Girl brought half a kilo from home, it wasn't stolen, she was just taking her share, because Mummy couldn't make pastry and they didn't use a lot of sugar, but Éva, the Madame Canapé of Szucság as she called herself, lay back in her long, patterned dress on her bed, with the bobbin lace curtain and cushions with embroidered covers and read aloud, Örkény's *One Minute Stories* and Hungarian writers whom she didn't know, and after a year the Girl took her her first verses, and later her 'prose', and then in summer—at last there was no need to get up at dawn to catch the train to Szucság, from where the village was a further walk of a couple of kilometres because the stingy peasants hadn't allowed the railway through the village so that it should not stampede their cattle, because *All they ever think about is money*, added Éva—and in summer Juci and her friends went out camping by Lake Tarnica, she and Éva got into the inflatable and the Girl read Madame Recamier's letters in French, Éva had brought them with her and of course the Girl didn't understand a word, but Éva patiently corrected her pronunciation and they took it in turns to row *so that our breasts will be beautiful and firm*, but the permission to emigrate still hadn't arrived and even after two, three, four years—it was her good luck, thought the Girl whenever it was mentioned that she ought to go to Bucharest and get things sorted out once and for all—but Éva had no connections either at the Embassy or in the Ministry, nor the money to make any, and although everything was there and ready—letter of invitation from Hungary, guarantee of a job from a village school over there, *Well, it'll be just a dump like Szucság here, so I've done myself no favours, Ócsa, that's where I'll be teaching*, said Éva gloomily, admission to a school for her son (at first he was in Year Five, then Six, Seven and even Eight), a tied flat with two rooms, kitchen and bathroom, *Ah, right by the station, can you imagine*, she added unnecessarily, *And here's the Szamos*, thought the Girl, it kept her awake, and the telephone was transferred in Dézsma utca, the rest wasn't in Éva's name, not even the flat, because she had nothing and there was nothing for her to do but wait and go out to Szucság 'among the peasants' to give Hungarian lessons, because she'd only spent a year in the elite town-centre school and then had to put in her application, simply had to, she said proudly, I'm not going to rot here, altogether *she'd served one year*, 'a year in a proper school and a friendship', but after that endless waiting, and in November 1989 she'd been ready to buy her train ticket because it would be only another couple of months, she was promised, and her pupil went out every year in Years Nine and Ten as well and gave a lesson in the Szucság school, as she boasted at home, and at such times she stayed at the teacher's—Éva and her son lived in one room of the two-room house with no bathroom, her parents in the other, and in the kitchen there was only cold water from a lovely ancient wall tap until the pipe froze up in winter—only the Girl couldn't get used to the sound of the Szamos which ran outside the window and had a marshy smell in summer, or it was the strong Lapsang Suchong late in the evening that prevented her getting to sleep, but in any case Mummy didn't like her sleeping away from home, *She's jealous*, Éva dismissed it, and early in the morning they would squelch through the Szucság mud, and in the school she would be 'my pupil'—because that was how Éva proudly introduced her to her teacher colleagues, and at Éva's place in Dézsma utca there appeared a poet and a philosopher and an actor and all kinds of artists and a *gay* man, as Éva once whispered about someone (the schoolgirl had never heard of such things), exactly the sort of people that Mummy didn't know, sometimes foreigners too would appear unexpectedly, a Frenchman with long hair and a beard and a long, dirty, loud tie, Jean-Pierre, the travel writer, as Éva introduced the provider of the Lapsang Suchong in its elegant metal box and canvas bag, whose occupation sounded as absurd to the Girl as if he'd been a professional mammoth-or treasure-hunter: Jean-Pierre wrote travel books, going away twice a year to spend three months somewhere and then writing an illustrated book on the country in question, and he regularly presented them to

Éva, whom he had been courting for ten years, bringing unusual gifts, mint-flavoured chocolate, French literary magazines, an album of engravings of old Paris, he praised Éva's refined, eighteenth-century French, that dead language, and she obtained for him marijuana from the Arab students—he pronounced the word elegantly, with final stress—and according to her was a sixty-eight-year-old wreck who could not find fulfilment as a writer, condemned Western capitalism, declared himself a communist and was enthusiastic about Yugoslavia— the Girl was certain that it was only with them that he was critical —but in the end he didn't marry Éva and take her away because marriage—to him—was against his principles, he believed in free association, in the all-powerful and indomitable freedom of humanity, believed that everybody could choose their lover or place of residence and even the language in which to write and dream, and he explained to Éva that 'you Hungarians want to speak Hungarian and not Romanian, there are people like you in Paris,' and Éva was even preparing to choose her place of residence, Jean-Pierre explained, and that was freedom, and she didn't argue with him at all and didn't try to persuade him that that was different, that now she had no choice, and had never yet had any, nor had she chosen Hungarian, and nevertheless Éva forgave Jean-Pierre, the Jean-Pierre who *as a matter of principle* didn't eat meat, *We're vegetarians as well*, said Éva with a laugh, providing for the visitor was no problem—but she didn't forgive anyone else, not her parents, not the house in Dézsma utca, nor the schools, and most of all not Szucság, with its sharp, pigsty smell, where she had gone for punishment, nor the friends who had supposedly got her mixed up in something, some leaflets, some *samizdat*—she'd taught the Girl the word—and she forgave no one any more before she left, only the unwashed travel writer, the negligent believer in free love, and gradually ten years went by and Éva didn't get a passport, not even for a single journey, and to the Girl she alluded vaguely to having signed something in the early '80s, that was what was holding up the documents, and that the other signatories in the *samizdat* who previously used to come to see her had gradually dropped away and finally disappeared, they hadn't been merely signatories but authors too, some of them, poets, writers, artists, editors and philosophers, explained Éva, had soon got their papers and been able to go, indeed, even if they didn't want to go they were expelled—some had even been able to choose where to, like Jean-Pierre, the travel writer, she laughed sarcastically—and she waited a further five years, more and more offended, shrugging her slender shoulders in superior fashion, *Je m'en foue, they can fuck me about, I'm only a shitty Hungarian teacher, a nobody, they're not going to mention me on Kossuth radio, if I leave the country it's no great deal, and I can kick the bucket, go to muddy Szucság among the peasants for the rest of my working life or until I rot! And nobody will remember me afterwards!* and over the next five years Éva encouraged her to write, don't stop writing: letters, a diary— *Maintain a diary!* she said, not write or keep a diary, but as if you were keeping a chicken or a pig, so that writing is its daily sustenance— and the Girl had by then received the commission for her first book review—Éva would scribble all over the fair copy, already carefully done for the fourth time—and in the years that followed Éva would go every summer mostly to Marosbogát, where her taciturn father's fishing shack was, or in autumn to the market on Lake Fekete, where the Gypsies called the erect, long-skirted teacher with her proud bearing 'the countess', at which Éva would buy lace curtains from them, and once they even went to Szeben together because the following five years were spent between Suchong and Szucság, both black and corrosive, a drug that could be taken only with a lot of sugar, a smoky drug for every day including the working Saturday, as soon as one was on the train one's clothes stank, *I prefer not even to sit down,* Éva stated haughtily, Szucság and Suchong, two smelly and inestimably valuable luxury items: the one from the Chinese province of Szechuan, to France by ship, then by plane to Budapest, then on the Baltic Orient Express in an old-fashioned leather suitcase to Kolozsvár, the other 'a miserable teaching post' in a half-Romanian, half-Hungarian village in Kolozs county itself, *I'd better be glad they gave me this, a lot of people have got nothing when they put in their applications, must have gone to work in factories*, said Éva contemptuously, her thin lips compressed in rage, but the sugar ran out rapidly, and that impoverished, muddy, inaccessible Szucság, according to Éva peopled by peasants who were distinctly rich and mean, became the French and Hungarian teacher's place of exile in which there wasn't a single pupil *like you*, nor could there be, *these practising illiterates, look at their reading diaries!* she assured the Girl, and with a laugh brought out her old Year Seven diary, which she had been ashamed of for a long time and hid from Juci because Juci wanted to show it to everybody, especially after her verse was published, and later the Girl herself laughed at her own work and in the end gave it to Éva as a gift—Éva planned to take it with her to Hungary in her seventy permitted kilos—because the Year Seven reading diary was written by the sort of student that wasn't reading at all yet, never felt like reading anything, hated drawing as well, but could illustrate what she had to read, because the first reading diary, kept in the thick, monogrammed notebook, began and ended with the poem *The Captive Stork*: author, colon, underlined, next line: Contents:—here the pupil summed up awkwardly the content of the work that she had read—'The poem entitled *The Captive Stork* is about a stork', and that ended what she had to say, leaving three-quarters of the page blank, and there she'd drawn a huge black, white and red stork with a fetter on its leg and a weight the size of a cannonball, and with that the first summer reading diary was finished, the reading, the writing and drawing had taken half an hour altogether, because they'd done *The Captive Stork* at the end of Year Six, even before Éva's time, but when the new, elegant teacher with the aquiline nose and severe look opened the thick notebook, which had been meant for great things, she didn't burst out laughing but looked at it in surprise for a moment as if she could see some complex diagram which had yet to be understood, then said *Bring me a proper one by the end of October*, and by that time she was able to read an account of the novel *Golgotha* on the following page, which was marked by the pressure of the heavily used pencil, especially the first volume *Sisters*—perhaps she hadn't finished reading the rest, thought the teacher, but, nodded in recognition—*Why exactly did you choose that book?* she asked, but the Girl shrugged her shoulders, and didn't admit that she'd found it a bit boring, she'd skipped parts of it—there was so much description and hardly any dialogue, the pages were full from margin to margin—but she'd liked the sisters, cried a bit, Mummy liked this book as well, and the print was quite large, so that was why she chose it, and her father had persuaded her as well, and Éva turned the page: another whole-page conceptual illustration of 'The Stone Flung Upward', her father's favourite poem, which she knew by heart, *I've learnt that poem by heart, without the book, I can recite it*, and she pointed proudly to the well-executed drawing of a village on a hillside with sheep grazing and a church tower, and above it a grey, shapeless mass like a badly made snowball or overcast sun—the falling stone, symbolizing the poet, incapable of tearing himself from his native land and constantly returning in a great rage like the falling stone, but what had happened between the chained stork and the free-flying, upward-flung stone—a number of Hungarian lessons in which the strict teacher with the aquiline nose had looked out of the window of the ground-floor classroom and read poetry aloud, slowly, distinctly, repeating lines, pointing up similes, as if talking to herself yet so that others could hear—and after Éva's arrival the Girl entered a recitation competition for the first time and won second place with Petőfi's *Out of here, out of the town*, and if the Hungarian teachers after Éva were women, not men—they had either gone away or died, as a year later the Girl's father too died, and Éva had lost her husband long before in a motor accident —everything started with Éva, and they became men themselves: Éva, Julika, Julika and Éva, the Hungarian teachers: Julika, the one-time Hungarian teacher and writer, the mother of a friend in 1987, then another Julika, a successful teacher and literary wife, who coached the Girl for university entrance in 1988, and finally Éva, a university professor in the spring of 1989—and if they too had asked for a school reading diary as did the Éva that taught her in Year Seven they would have been able to leaf through one in a splendid, coloured notebook bestrewn with passionate descriptions and analyses of her reading experiences in the long summer and winter holidays, but by now they— Éva, Julika, Julika and Éva—only talked with the promising pupil, because the fifteen-, sixteen-, seventeen-year-old Girl, who by then seemed almost an adult, had become a professional reader, with an open book in one hand and in the other a cup of perfumed tea.

MOUSETRAP

You can't go, said the sixteen-year-old teenager to Claudius, but it was hardly an hour since she'd had the pleasure of being introduced to the great actor, who, on hearing her name, raised his eyebrows and didn't enquire *And you're related to . . .?* but let the end of the oratorical question tail off, like one who was not actually commanding but stating a fact and brooked no contradiction, but by then she knew, because they'd given the last performance: *They're always giving the last performance of Hamlet*, said Granny, or *They're always doing Hamlet one last time*, or *It's always the last time they'll be doing Hamlet*, but the producer had now crossed out the names on the left-hand page of the grey folder where the cast was listed, because by then Gertrude had gone, and Guildenstern (leaving Rosenkrantz behind), Polonius had actually died as in the play, and so he'd been crossed out, and Fortinbras and Osrick too had left, as had the Stage Queen and the gravedigger, Hamlet was preparing to leave the country and now Claudius was off, because actors were leaving: so far eight names had been crossed out in the producer's copy and the ninth remained, struck through with a firm line as were the names in the telephone directory at home of those that had died or emigrated, which for a telephone directory is all very well, and the producer crossed out the handwritten names with red or blue ballpoint before morning or afternoon rehearsals, because this shifting population was making the number of rehearsals limitless; *Hamlet* had gone into rehearsal on 5 September 1986 and it could have been ready a year or a decade later for all that it mattered, but they'd held a hundred extra rehearsals before the first night because after the umpteenth 'external revision' permission wouldn't be granted though every page of the programme was ready, stapled up, translated into Romanian, signed and sealed on every separate page by the director and the censor, but not yet finally printed, and during rehearsals there had been regular sessions of the Council of Workers, in the company of the 'external representatives', that is, the county censors, which had discussed the situation with regard to *Hamlet*, and meanwhile the Patriotic Guard had been on the rifle range, politico-ideological instruction had taken place, and the officials in charge, now Fortinbras, now Claudius or others had carried out inspections as on previous occasions too, and because of the many changes of cast rehearsals had had to continue even after the first night, because those weren't occasional substitutions but settled, permanent changes, and the producer, bent over the copy in his little den, ran down the official typed schedule of rehearsals and scrawled new names beside Guildenstern, Fortinbras, Polonius, the Stage Queen, Osrick, the gravedigger, Gertrude and 'a lord', but when he finally came to Hamlet he was uncertain and didn't cross out the actor's name because it seemed to him absurd that Hamlet should *exit*, as in the play, but Hamlet had by then received permission from Bucharest to emigrate but had had to stay for months until he had got hold of everything and made arrangements, and yet obviously could no longer take the role nor work anywhere else, and the producer eventually decided to write alongside the name that of the second actor who had been obtained from Vásárhely, perhaps he didn't believe that there'd never be another Hamlet with him, the marvellous, middle-aged actor who on stage was like a pain-racked saint, stammering in his despair, because in fact he often jumbled up his lines, made a lot of mistakes, left lines out and spoke them in the wrong order, and then one couldn't tell what he was talking about, but his agony was faultless all the same—the director, the Budapest critic was to write, 'envisages Hamlet as a creative artist, to whom theatre and real life are one and the same,' so wrote the reviewer, the secretive 'SO', in the November number of *Film, Theatre, Music*, because the critic, on a brief visit from Hungary, had to remain incognito so that he would be allowed into the country next time—because that Hamlet is a saint who even now walks among us, thought the manager, or—the vain hope flickered—he may yet return because he's changed his mind, and by that time the new Hamlet had been engaged and the show went on, and the two juxtaposed names gave the impression that the role was being shared, that a double casting was in effect, which could not have occurred in the company, by then shrunk to a dozen and a half, even so they were scarcely able to cover all the roles, a number were actually combined or eliminated, out of necessity but cleverly, and yet it seemed that several were playing Hamlet all at once, or that everybody might be *him*, a Hamlet, but the one Hamlet was commuting from Vásárhely while the other, together with his wife, the deep-voiced actress who portrayed the Stage Queen and the grave-digger, was packing the 70 kilos per person that one was allowed to take—in the past forty years, therefore, the allowance had risen 20 kilos: forty-three years previously, when the brickworks ghetto had been the designated compulsory abode of the 16,750 Jews of Kolozsvár, 50 kilos were permitted together with food for fourteen days, as the newspaper of 3 May 1944 stated—as everybody could leave for their new home-land with 70 kilos, and so Hamlet was giving away piecemeal his important and genuine library and his furniture, transferring water, gas, electricity and telephone services, to whoever, going to the second-hand dealer with his belongings, giving away and exchanging what he could, trying to send out a thing or two, and sometimes watching the show in which not long before he had been performing, for which reason his name had, out of kindness, not been expunged, it had simply been pasted over on the red-printed poster—the new name was longer, and easily covered his—since the show was constantly being renewed by the perpetual changes of cast, as if some people obdurately intended to keep alive the endless show, capable of being resurrected from its dead, but Polonius should no longer have announced to Hamlet *The actors are come hither, my lord*, but rather that they *had gone*, finished, none left, and if the same producer's copy had been marked up about the audience—at the first night, on 23 February 1987, the house was packed, after which audiences fell steadily until at the final performance in the chilly auditorium there were only a few spectators sitting stiff with cold and horror—among them SO the critic and the theatre-mad teenage Girl—so if the spectators too had been counted it would have worked out that they had changed in the same way as the actors on the stage, though in accordance not with the natural turnover of theatre-goers but with the laws of emigration, and the actors in the play too were preparing to leave the Mousetrap scene, the Stage King and Queen, whom Hamlet summons to play the murder of his father before Claudius, holding a mirror, as it were, to nature, displaying the peculiar form and imprint of the body of the age: in the performance there appeared rubbishy, worthless circus clowns, down-and-out, cheap show-men who had drifted this way in their wanderings and shortly moved on after finishing their work, that is, performing the Mousetrap scene, the decider of fates, without a backward glance: the mousetrap itself, as a practical item, had long been considered a rarity in Kolozsvár; this important piece of domestic equipment, made of wood and flexible steel, vanished from the shops in 1977 when, by presidential decree, the factories were transferred from civic to ministerial ownership and the ministry in turn changed light industry into heavy-machinery man-ufacturing, and from that point on they worked in accordance with the demands of central government, turning out only things which could be exported while the production of everyday things for the population, from stovepipes to mousetraps, came to a halt because the outside world didn't need Romanian mousetraps and at home they became simply no longer obtainable and anybody that wanted one made their own or kept a cat to deal with mice and rats, because a cat couldn't be taken off any-body and so cats began to assume prime importance, and after the Mousetrap scene the married couple who played Gertrude and Guildenstern also prepared to leave, and the latter had provided the voice of Fortinbras, to come on at the end of the play to proclaim the new, liberating powers, but the enforced and clever combination of roles produced the impression that in the end the traitor Guildenstern had returned in the guise of Fortinbras, and so there were no relieving force and salvation, but the devastation was just followed by a hopeless wait for something different, something new, and instead of salvation the circular logic, or rather trap, of history would remain, everything would begin again from the beginning as there was no way out, no escape, nor yet a mousetrap any longer to hold a mirror, and—as was the simple and unwritten law of the theatre—there was no hope-arousing Fortinbras to come to Kolozsvár: everybody perished in vain and needlessly—Polonius, Ophelia, Gertrude, Laertes, Claudius and Hamlet, and for the very first time the Father, the Spirit, because everything began with the father, and Fortinbras' voice howled only from the loudspeaker because Fortinbras had no longer come to Kolozsvár in 1919 either: on Tuesday, 30 September 1919, the last performance of *Hamlet*, which deteriorated into a demonstration and was cut short, was given in the beautiful National Theatre (designed by Helmer and Fellner) in Hunyadi tér (before that the less risky *Baroness Lilli* had been played three times to a large audience), and the anxious producer noted in the announcement in the programme merely that, that very day 'by order of the military commandant'—name and rank studiously omitted—but he could have written 'the company was driven out of the theatre by order of the military commandant'; the same hand had noted earlier, on 24 December 1918, in faint pencil so that he could rub it out at any time, that 'Romanian forces of occupation have entered Kvár', because the paper too wrote, and in the spring of 1919 wrote constantly, that 'Dr Ghibiu Onisifor, Secretary of State in the Ministry of Culture, had called on Dr Jenő Janovics to surrender the Kolozsvár National Theatre to the governing council in Nagyszeben as state property', and Janovics had protested in vain that under the terms of a legal contract he was not merely the tenant but actually the owner of the building, and that he could not unilaterally terminate a contract made with the state of Hungary, on the contrary he stood by it, and the obstinate director would on no account surrender the theatre and remained in it until 30 September, and in the spring, on the advice of his actor Mihály Fekete—who had, incidentally, played the Stage King in *Hamlet*—he went into the lunatic asylum for six weeks so as not to be arrested, because he'd played a madman on the stage and in real life, until finally the authorities expelled the company after the last Hamlet in the night of 30 September, and in that year 1919 the producer, for the sake of tidiness, noted down every reason that had led to the frequent interruption of performances in the National, and many and various they were: a strike, prohibition, lack of water, Romanian Easter and Romanian guest plays, and in March he wrote: 'From Thursday 13th to the 19th performances were suspended because of a Hungarian, K. Kilin, who had shot at a Romanian soldier', but then came the final performance, and Jenő Janovics, director of *Hamlet*, in which he played the title role, and director of the National tore out the last pages from his little pocket copy of *Hamlet* (the 1867 Budapest edition), and in thick, soft red pencil crossed out Fortinbras' entrance which the censor had prohibited on 30 September 1919, together with the great mono-logue, of which only the first line might be heard, and the play ended with Hamlet's dying words, and after those lines the actor playing Hamlet inscribed dynamically in blue pencil THE END, and indeed, for him, on Hunyadi tér, in the building which he had had built to his own specifications, it was for ever the end: after the performance a bus was waiting for the cast at the back door, to take them to Várad for *repatriation* to Hungary, but not a single actor got on board, nor yet did anyone seventy years later and it followed, therefore, that on Tuesday, 3 October 1919, the producer wrote 'Removal to the Színkör', because that was the first removal to the summer theatre, but in 1940 Janovics was no longer on the scene to be able to celebrate with his company his return to Kolozsvár, because he was no more desirable to the new, long-awaited liberating power than he had been twenty-two years before to the old one, and the newspaper was silent on the subject from that time on for five years, and the obstinately loyal great actress and wife, Lili Poór, who had played Ophelia in 1919, was likewise missing from among the members of what was once more the National Theatre but only appeared as a guest, on which too the newspaper was silent, and on Fridays and Saturdays in August 1940 the producer dutifully noted 'No performance, re-attachment of part of Transylvania to Hungary. Performances suspended because of Romanian demonstration' on a tiny, half-centimetre-wide scrap of paper, repeatedly pasted over, corrected and re-corrected and re-formulated, on which every producer, director, period and world view has left its mark, because this is the smallest imaginable palimpsest in theatrical history, and then on 12 September 1940, still in the old Színkör, *János vitéz* was staged: 'Festival performance, the entry of Hungarian troops', said the annotation, but there is nothing more that can be truthfully said in public about Jenő Janovics, because in the next *Hamlet*, in 1941, when, as the producer wrote, 'After twenty-two years of enforced silence the Hungarian language was heard again in the National Theatre in Kolozsvár', in the old theatre on Hunyadi tér which he had built, he no longer took part: at seven o'clock in the evening of 9 November 1941 the performance was symbolically recommenced at the line where it had broken off in 1919; she who played Ophelia in 1919 now played Gertrúd, he who was the priest in 1941 was the Ghost in 1987, and the son of the director of 1941 was the director in 1987; the Hamlet of 1919 was a Jew in 1941 and only returned to the town in 1945 when the new 'change of régime' was in place there, and the marginal note says 'between 1 and 13 November 1945 there was no performance because of the move to the Színkör', but Janovics, who had survived (in Budapest) and returned to Kolozsvár, was preparing for the first night of *Bánk bán* and had already written his introductory speech, but died on the day of the festival performance from a chill caught in the cold, unheated theatre, and had by that time lost the fabulous wealth that he had acquired through showing films and good business sense and that the theatre had consumed in the '20s: the beautiful Art Nouveau university cinema, together with, later, the high-class Select cinema was appropriated as Jewish property (in the teenage Girl's time the Arta, the Arts cinema, showed the best films in the '80s, as if the *genius loci* had remained ineradicable), but in 1987 no one referred to the Romanian Theatre opposite the orthodox cathedral as 'Hunyadi tér' any more, nor to the 'Hungarian-language Romanian Theatre' as the 'summer Színkör', and there the first night of the new *Hamlet* was to be held, and the teenage girl watched the performance with all the changes of cast and felt as if she were seeing something different all the time, as if the endless tale were constantly being renewed by somebody, and eventually she froze in the auditorium in her goatskin coat while the remaining Horatio —finally, he was the only one left—was rescuing his belongings from under the slowly descending Iron Curtain, the slowly, menacingly descending Iron Curtain, ponderous and insupportable, onto the proscenium, saving his guitar and some bundles of books—but nobody took a library with them, there was no room for books in 70 kilos, and those that remained picked them up cheap—and suddenly there was the rumour that there was to be a last *Hamlet* because *he* too was *off*, and everybody would then have gone, and on New Year's Eve 1987, as they were eating stuffed cabbage in the kitchen, the stubborn and self-conscious Girl said firmly to Claudius *You can't go*, addressing him with the familiar *te*, which caused a slight pause, but he—whose name the producer hadn't crossed out, nor had he written another alongside it, because that would be the end, it couldn't be done without Claudius, and the show would be taken off after the thirty-second performance— he gave the suspicious girl a gentle hug and smiled, as he might at an obstinate and sulky child who simply didn't understand, but she was thinking that it had been no use old Horatio—because he was old there was nowhere left for him to go—saving his *Hamlet* souvenirs from under the slowly descending Iron Curtain, and at every performance she had watched with bated breath so that the ageing actor could slip through the tiny gap for a few books or a handful of papers, a manuscript or some important official document, the sort of thing which people migrating would smuggle with them, but in the end he always emerged, and she thought that there were many Hamlets, everybody could play him, anybody, because there at that time it was the easiest role, there was no need to act at all, even she might go on, girl that she was, because everybody was crippled and incapable of action, Hamlet escaping into his books, and you saw, in fact another actor was found for the part, but he had seemed irreplaceable—it was said that he'd be taken on in Hungary, would act in the provinces like all the emigrants—everybody knew a Hamlet, but Claudius, without you there'd be nothing, the show couldn't go on, and it would mean not only that all the other scheduled performances would be jeopardized simply because *exeunt omnes*, but because there in Claudius' kitchen on New Year's Eve a complex and inexplicable feeling had come over the obsessed watcher of performances of Hamlet that only the tyrant could not be replaced by another, because if he too were *off* there really would be no going on: everybody was different, every possible Hamlet could leave, but without the jovial and merciless tyrant the world would finally collapse, and as on New Year's Eve 1987 the Girl clung desperately to Claudius' arm, Claudius', who was taking from her the first great, repeatedly watched performance in her life and was indeed no longer Claudius but the tyrant himself to whom she clung because he was about to desert her because he'd made up his mind to turn his back once and for all on the barbed-wire-fenced prison which he'd built up, leave his harshly brought up children to their own devices, just get up and walk out of the door, and now was grinning outwardly with an 'idiotic smile', as the critic SO wrote of him from behind his disguise, and the prisoner-king of Denmark would observe from outside how those remaining managed without him, perhaps designating a new tyrant for themselves, because the play must go on, because they knew nothing else, except that the hated hangman, murderer of Hamlet's father, must not be allowed to go away, must be prevented with all their might from going away, because without him there was nothing more, because he himself had invented this world and its creations, and in the dawn of the New Year, as she stood on the cold stone floor of the kitchen among the jumble of furniture, the Girl suddenly thought of the monkey kept in a cage which Granddad had read about in his old newspaper: a laboratory monkey had been taught to draw, and its first independent creation was a depiction of the bars of its cage, which might be pure chance or a symbolic coincidence, but no matter, and Claudius, as he was about to leave, didn't explain to the impatient and determined Girl, didn't take her around his spacious flat and show her what he was leaving there, didn't point out the rows of his posters and photographs, his whole previous brilliant career, nor did he refer to his sick daughter, nor complain of his none-too-alluring future in provincial theatre, but just stood in the kitchen, poured a beer, and, like a true tyrant, smiled inscrutably.

SOLDIERS, 10 DECEMBER

As they said goodbye, her friend said that he would meet her off the evening train, but the Girl self-confidently said not to, there was no need, she wasn't nervous (he lived quite near the station and it was arranged that she would sleep at his place), it would be cold, he needn't, she'd hurry along, but the elderly writer kindly made it clear, as he ended the leavetaking, that he would meet the Temesvár–Iaşi train at eleven o'clock on Sunday evening, *and don't forget, you're going to sleep in a writer's bed,* he added with an innocent, white-haired smile, noted down the seat number and said how she would be met at the station— *He'll have an orange shopping bag with him, he's got a moustache, about my age*—and as for the rest, the parcel of roast meat, morello cake, chocolate and cheese, and the glass tankard and the buck's grease for his soldier son's heels were nothing to do with him, his wife had packed the parcel, and on the Thursday afternoon the Girl left the thick winter army uniform with them, broadcloth greatcoat, linen underwear, boots two sizes too big, beret and belt, because she'd have to be at military training[31] by seven on the Monday morning and so she'd accepted the kind offer to sleep at their place after she got back because she could get there in time if she got up at half past six, they lived near the Arts faculty in Horea út, and she simply mustn't skip military training, she'd be kicked out of the university, as the female officer, red hair and nails, had threatened the very first time, and the student's military training was now in its fourth month, every Monday from seven in the morning when they paraded in the university yard, uniforms were inspected, buttons, shoulder-boards, the Romanian specialists were made to wash off

---

31 All university students, including women, had to do army training once a week.

134

all that eye make-up and rouge, and most of all berets in particular were inspected: *Băi, fată, părul!*—she heard every Monday at a quarter to eight, because that was how every week began for her: 'Hey, you girl, hair!' screamed the irritable voice, ever sharper, at which she had to step forward out of line because her hair just would not go under the minute beret—*It's like a yarmulka,* her mother said—*Data viitoare aduc a foarfecă şi ţi-l tai,* said the comrade officer, *tovarăşa locotenent,* with satisfaction—next week she'd bring scissors and cut it off 'for her'—but next week that hadn't happened, instead she'd made her take the hat off, undone the plait or ponytail and shouted at her to comb it, at which the Girl replied with false gentleness that she hadn't got a comb and the officer finally told her to tie her hair up and not stand there like that, and she got a thick elastic band and fastened the mass of ungovernable hair up after a fashion and stuck the beret on her head with a hair-grip, and now it looked even worse perched on top of her head, then she stepped back victorious into line, but in the morning she fitted the beret carefully on her head in front of the mirror—Juci was sleeping happily, she had no lectures to attend, had got out of military training, but mother laughed at the spectacle and suggested that her hair could be done in a tight French plait and tucked away, like the French resistance heroines in films, but the Girl didn't want to tuck it away, her boots, on the other hand, were size 43 and there was room in them for three thick pairs of socks, she'd asked for that size since that boy in Brassai Sámuel Liceum had been killed by his boots when he got septicaemia in military training and hadn't been taken to hospital, and then after inspection and reporting they were able to go firing on the outskirts of town or to theoretical training or, since the cold weather had set in and the Fourteenth Congress had started, to watch TV in the darkened hall of the Students' House, where three rows from the little TV one could get a good sleep and where—the Girl had started in alarm at the endless applause and cheering—it had been unexpectedly announced that the quota for consumption had been put up to

3,500 calories nationwide, but now there were still four cold and happy days until Monday's military training, with travelling and adventures, and she skipped Friday's Folklore lecture and thus on Thursday afternoon was seated excitedly on the train, which was extraordinarily full, for days it had only been possible to get a ticket but no seat reservation, and the writer and his wife were pleased that the student Girl was going to see their son and they could send him a parcel, and he'd got a forty-eight hour pass and he too was happy that he could meet his classmate, now his fellow university student—though because of military service he was only starting university the following year—and would at last be able to get a good night's sleep, and the Girl was mainly satisfied because she would be able to give the important writer pleasure, she could be off by herself, and because the words 'certainly I'll go and see him' just came out one day at the end of November, without any thought of danger, when she'd been having lunch at their place, and he'd been in the army for some time by then, and he'd introduced her to his parents, and according to the writer a girl who showed promise in every respect was sometimes invited to lunch to talk to the great writer about the university and her poetry and what she was reading —after the Girl's successes in the Iaşi Olympiad the writer had given her a copy of the book he'd had published in Hungary and dedicated it *To a young lady who deserves more*—and as a Calvinist he told her the story of the yarmulka that he had on the shelf: sometimes he would go over to the synagogue on a Friday evening if they hadn't got the requisite ten men, *Because I live nearest, and I stick it on with a hairgrip because it won't stay on my head*, said he with a laugh, and the Girl said that she too fixed that ridiculous army beret to her hair with a similar hair-grip, and the firm plan for the trip came within reach of achievement after that carelessly tossed out sentence: even next week, if she liked, and the Girl nodded, and the writer promised to obtain the ticket. *Take some papers with you*, he added seriously, *My ID? I always carry it*, said she, because that was what they called it, *not a passport*, joked his wife, because they hadn't got passports, those had to be requested from the police, and the trip was set for ten days' time, because for *going*, going anywhere, any time would do, even in early December in an unheated train, wearing thick boots and a Máramaros-style Romanian wool coat, as they called it, she wasn't worried about the cold, *You'll look like a Romanian girl*, said mother, but she'd bought it because it was the thickest coat to be found in the market upstairs, sold by the sellers of woollens and blankets for a tidy sum, 150 lei, and the Iaşi–Temesvár express was almost warmed by the mass of passengers—they were standing in the corridors, the connections between the carriages and even the lavatories, she couldn't find room for the parcel on the shelf above her seat but held it on her lap all the way, because the rack was full of baskets, bulging sacks and plastic bags, and the air was full of the stifling smell of sheepskin coats, and the Girl took her window seat on the train (which had already come a nine-hour journey from Moldavia) which a skinny old man vacated without saying a word, and she was disturbed the first time at Tövis and was drowsily getting the two tickets out of the red inside pocket of the woollen coat, but the fat peasant woman sitting beside her nudged her with an elbow and nodded at something, the Girl didn't understand what she meant, and only then realized that the man in uniform at the open door was not a guard but a policeman, and behind him was another and he asked for her ID. *Unde mergi?* he asked, using the familiar second person, where are you going? to which the Girl replied Temesvár, and what are you doing there, the conversation continued, visiting my boyfriend in the army, Oh yes? and what unit is he in? I don't know, she replied, and where are you going to sleep? I don't know, he's arranged it—*El a rezolvat*—and her face was burning, *Şi tu nu lucri?* he asked, don't you have a job? and it was explained that she was a student and had no lectures next day, *Da*, said the militiaman, and in satisfied fashion took out a thick, greasy notebook and entered her name and address, then wanted to know what faculty she was in, Russian, the Girl snapped confidently and proudly, it'll surprise you —she said nothing about studying Hungarian—and the scene was repeated before Déva when a second policeman questioned her, and this time she'd worked out that after saying 'Visiting my boyfriend in the army' she should smile mysteriously and coyly, and then the conversation was cut short, because she'd been on the Iaşi–Temesvár in April that year, as a Year Twelve pupil, when they went to Iaşi for the Olympiad and she'd won first prize in Hungarian literature, but previously she'd never been asked for her ID on the train, and the same thing happened on the return journey: two policemen stood at the front of the train, another two with a wolfhound at the rear, and before they left Temesvár passengers were checked as they got on and she had to give an account of the recent past—where she'd been and why, they'd been staying with a friend of her mother's, she lied and pretended to blush, Number 26 *strada Petőfi*, she said, hesitating over the number, because obviously there was bound to be a Petőfi utca in Temesvár, she thought, but the theatre director, in whose big, terribly cold block of flats they had in fact been sleeping—the Girl under two heavy blankets, he in the other room enveloped in his thick army greatcoat—hadn't gone with her to the station either, but they'd parted company two blocks away, and in the flat they'd talked of nothing but university gossip, who was going with who and who was the most boring lecturer, and what dreadful lacy dresses Daiana Zanc wore, and while they waited for the boy next day the director told her to wrap up warm and he'd show her the town, but on the Béga, leaning over the railing on the bridge from where they could see in both directions, the elderly, grey-haired director began to whisper quietly and seriously *and tell my dear friend*, and the Girl paid attention because it wasn't just a sentence that followed but a plethora of names and places, *he'll know, you needn't give such details*, he added, when occasionally she asked back which László or who's been locked up, or *they harass us, make it impossible, evict, dismiss and . . . would have come from Pest but they wouldn't let him into the country*, he went on, then there followed conjectures about the future, and she repeated quietly 'action' *by the statue*, 'action' was the word the director used, *we don't know anything precisely*, he ended at last, and over the Béga a keen wind was blowing—the Girl couldn't feel it inside her coat, but her legs in her jeans were frozen and by then her teeth were chattering as she listened carefully to the elderly man's quiet words and tried to keep track of them without being able to string them into a narrative, and she suddenly realized that she was in fact here on business, this trip was more important than it had seemed a week before in peaceful Kolozsvár, or perhaps she hadn't spotted the indications, because she'd known nothing and didn't even now, but she'd give the message to the writer, who would be waiting at the station on the night of Sunday 10 December in the same words in which it had been entrusted to her, because the university student— proud, winner of literary competitions and on friendly terms with great writers—had believed that she knew everything, but not that it was December, December 1989, the tenth to be precise, a Sunday evening, and imperceptibly a different reckoning was starting, they were at least on the threshold, and even when she got off the train she knew nothing, the writer was waiting for her at the station and asked questions all the way home, not about his soldier son with the great appetite but about the messages, as they wouldn't say a word once they got in, not even in the bathroom, and next day, and when she got home after military training, all that the Girl told her mother about were the ID checks on the train—she didn't mention the rest—and that on the Monday in military training they'd watched the Congress on the TV in the Students' House but the sound broke down, at which nobody dared switch it off and they watched it for hours like a silent film, and that she'd actually spent the night in the writer's bed, but he'd been in the other room, she'd slept in his son's bed, and she said no more because her mother wouldn't have understood, and what did they care, who were supposed to be Catholics, who the Calvinist clergyman[32] was in Temesvár and whether he was dismissed, but on Monday the

---

32 László Tőkes, the priest who is considered to have started the revolution in Romania.

eighteenth, at the next session of military training, everything was known: Mother was furious with the writer for 'sending' the ignorant girl to Temesvár, though she still didn't know about the conversation on the Béga bridge, while the Girl was secretly proud of her mission, and that day went in her uniform to call on the writer to enquire about his son, because in Temesvár the army were on alert, and he reassured her out loud that his son was well and sent best wishes, then he whispered that he and the students were only nine-month reservists,[33] hadn't been ordered out, and nothing had changed since that morning, nothing new on the radio, and finally at the door he added silently that the frontiers had been sealed—*Sealed*?, she pondered on the way home, what did that mean, because even before then they'd been completely closed—and, the writer added, he was really grateful for her help, and his wife gave her a kilo of sugar, some oil and a packet of Hungarian cocoa and some pudding mixture, and, swinging the shopping bag, the Girl set off for Dohány utca in her nice warm uniform—that day was the last time she wore it, she never put it on again, because four days later, on the Thursday afternoon, people in army uniform began shooting at the demonstrating students in Kolozsvár too, and on the Monday evening after leaving the writer she went round to Grandmother's with the valuable package so that at seven o'clock they could all listen to the six o'clock news from Budapest.

---

33 Male university students had to serve nine months full-time; non-students, eighteen months.

SILENT CHORUS

It was no use that Laci had kept all his documents: a whole bundle of *Testimonia baptisatorum*, originals and copies, dating from 1850, the original of his own birth certificate kept for sixty-five years, and something that he would have been prepared to show even at some risk of its being lost—the family tree, hand-drawn with tiny lettering, with which he could simply have proved by what logic the heap of tattered, illegible baptism certificates hung together—and the other thing, the official family tree certified before the Hungarian notary public in 1940, which declared that he was 'to the best of his knowledge not a Jew'— but he felt that now, in August 1984, it would be meaningless to produce that in the cemetery office, that wasn't what family trees had been for in the past, and so he'd made a new one, a third, leaving out occupations, titles, indeed, even largely disregarding the German or whatever various spellings of surnames, always opting for the simplest, but it was all no use at all: *Graves may be inherited through parents, siblings and children*, stated the cemetery administrator, without so much as opening the folder that was carefully laid before him, and Laci resorted to his ancient weapon: he just stood there mute, until the man who was filling up the charts put down his pen, *Who are we talking about?* he asked, but Laci was as silent as if he couldn't make out what he was being asked for: the name of the deceased, or what the relationship was or had been, or perhaps some other information, for example who the person in question was, 'somebody' or just a deceased, *My son-in-law*, he answered slowly, *In that case you may bury in the grave of his wife, children, sibling or parents, if any*—the fleshy man reeled off the list calmly, and Laci wondered to what 'any' referred: had the deceased such relatives or was there such a grave?, but the man went on calmly with his work, like someone letting the customer make up his mind what he wanted, but Laci spoke uncertainly, *They were divorced*, at which the man informed him that in that case there was nothing to be done, he'd have to buy a new plot, but Laci said that his great-aunt had a double plot up there by the Barcsay crypt, there were no heirs, he had all the documents there, *In that case no one has inherited the grave*—stated the official, at which Laci went on, as if he hadn't heard, that he thought that it would be best to bury him there, *It'll have to be transferred, can't be done until then*, said the man once more, at which Laci smiled and expressed the view that that was precisely the point, the grave could no longer be transferred either, *In that case, I'm sorry to say, you can have no interest*, said the man indifferently and unsympathetically, and Laci went on ... *and there's my sister-in-law's grave as well, my wife's sister's, unfortunately she died young in '34, there hasn't been a burial in that grave in fifty years—And who does that grave belong to?* asked the man in reply, and Laci shrugged and replied *Well, it's ours, the owners were my wife's parents, but they're buried in Marosvásárhely, they didn't transfer it, but his paternal grandfather is there as well*, and he fumbled at the bundle of documents, at which the man said, this time emphatically, *The point is, in whose name is the grave. If it's not yours or your wife's, you can't bury anyone there. It's not worth trying with a grave like that, fifty years old. But even if it were your own, you can't bury your daughter's divorced husband in it. He's not a blood relation, you see the point? You'll have to buy a new one*, and Laci cleared his throat and asked how much that would cost, but the man took a long, silent look over his glasses at the little, sunburned man standing in front of him as if astonished at the question, then, lowering his voice, said almost confidentially, *My dear sir, the question isn't how much it would cost. A lot. You can't buy a plot in this cemetery, because it's closed. Full, you understand? There can't be any new graves here, burials can only take place in the old ones*, and Laci went on that that was exactly what they wanted to do, because he wouldn't be able to afford a new one and of course if there weren't any there was no point, but on the other hand, he continued, there was the Vályi family's double one, his sister Klári's and Péter Kün's, *Try at the Monostor cemetery*, said the man, now becoming impatient, *or up at the Jews' place, there are hardly any burials up there, or I don't know, out of town somewhere, but in our cemetery there is nowhere*, and as Laci walked out of the cemetery administrator's gloomy, musty office, with the ancient gravestones leaning up against it outside, he stopped at the bottom of a shady hillock and just looked to his front, because it was now not merely a question of János but of himself too: it didn't matter that they had three graves in the cemetery, neither he nor Klári could be taken there for burial, and he suddenly felt that he had failed and must do something about it at once, when the administrator called out into the yard *Domnu . . . adică . . . Domnu . . . !!!* (Mr . . . I say . . . Mr . . .) because he'd called him by the surname of the deceased, then suddenly realized that father-in-law and son-in-law couldn't have the same name, *You've forgotten the death certificate*, he called after him, Laci went back into the office and the man asked him, over the open document, *Care e asta?* (Which one is this?), *E fostul . . . ?* (The late . . . ?) and didn't finish what he was thinking, just nodded his head, Laci shook his head gravely, no, that wasn't the *alispán*[34] or whatever, president of the county Party committee, *Nu e rudă cu. . .?* (Not a relation of . . .?), and Laci said yes, his brother, at which the man raised his eyebrows and suddenly spread out his arms, *Atunci care-i problema?* (Then what's the problem?) and went on jerkily, in that case why doesn't . . . see what I mean . . . that is, the other person, the *alispán* or Party secretary or whoever can surely arrange it, and Laci nodded and set off for the exit saying *Da, da* (Yes, yes), and next day indeed there was the grave: not that of the Vályis, as they lay peacefully side by side, nor that of poor Böske Soket, who'd died young, nor yet that of Péter Kün the gunsmith or that of Krisztina

---

34 The senior elected official in a pre–Second World War Hungarian county.

Pongrácz, born in 1835, whose name he hadn't even brought up, who was buried in the 24 square metre Korbuly plot, Number 67/111, as Laci had recorded on the family tree, but a brand new, terribly expensive grave in the Barcsay garden, close to the Vályis', to which Laci, without asking any further permission, had their solemn, Art Nouveau head-stone with the roses transferred for the fee of 100 lei and two bottles of *pálinka* to the gravediggers—the provident Vályis had had it moved from the grave of another relative while they were still alive—*Keep it dark*! Laci told them sternly (more precisely *Iar voi tacefi din gură*, or Keep your mouths shut!), because no more of the family were going to be buried in Gizi and Andor Vályi's grave until one day someone arranged to be able to transfer ownership of the uninherited double grave, long disused, and when Laci had had the headstone moved the plot, left there empty, was just a little patch of level, weed-grown ground, bereft, surrounded by rusty iron, because after the stone had been removed there was no trace left of the Vályis and only the fence commemorated the fact that people had once been interred there after whom there had been nobody to speak out and object, and after the stone had been moved Laci went down to the office again and made arrangements for the funeral: coffin to stand in the open air rather than in the chapel, it was too warm, no clergyman, ten minutes' worth of music, a eulogy to be spoken by János' best friend, a horse-drawn hearse up the hill, no more speeches up there, and so it all took place apart from the music, because after the fifth bar of the *Lacrimosa* the power was cut off and didn't come back on, expressions of sympathy were made, the children stood motionless between Klári with her slightly hunched back and their mother, a few friends, neighbours and col-leagues stood there in the blazing sun, János' best friend, the brown-haired Gyuri, who was called Indián on the collective farm because of his Gypsy appearance, was looking at the ground, perspiring and about to speak when suddenly the music cut off, nobody moved, it seemed that nothing unusual had happened, nobody ran to see to it or complain, nor would there have been much point: the power had been turned off and would either come back on or not, thought Laci, and so they listened to the utter silence: birds chirped and insects buzzed, a slow, silent ceremony followed, a motionless communal silence, until the imaginary *Lacrimosa* ended as the ever-heavier silence held the cluster of mourners together like a magnet, a group of statuary on a big plinth, that shared silence which nobody dared break with an expression of their sorrow, an exclamation, even a whisper, so that poor Janó didn't get that stupid *Requiem* either, which had scarcely begun before it was interrupted as if, beneath the open sky of the cemetery, a quiet, broken-voiced, timid choir had suddenly had their throats cut, and in the horror of the massacre nobody dared move, blink or shed a tear, and the silent choir, ashamed of its own lamed helplessness suddenly moved off after the heavily swaying, shabby hearse as it creaked along drawn by two scrawny horses, because in the end Indián had been unable to deliver his eulogy, not as if he had been forbidden, but the communal force of the silence swept him along with the rest, the silent *Requiem* meant never ever to end and let Indián's performance interrupt it, until the black-clothed gathering suddenly woke up to the fact that it was too late now, they had to go up to the grave because the cemetery workers had come in their dirty coveralls and Wellington boots, the gravediggers, reeking of *pálinka*, who stood for a moment in the crowd then went up to the one face that they recognized and bending to his ear, but nonetheless audibly, said *Tre să merem*, that is, they had to be off, had work to do, the next funeral was due at once, and there was no time left at the bier or at the open grave for Indián to speak, and with that shared silence the most important fact about the deceased was stated, and in the Barcsay garden the mourners, still together, could hear the unmistakeable sound of the ever-louder thumps of tiny clods on the lid of the silent coffin, flies and wasps buzzed on, sparrows twittered, a cuckoo was heard, somewhere a jay chattered, then suddenly it was as if an electricity pole started to make a noise, *The power's come on,* thought Laci, but it was only a cicada, a rarity up that way, singing loudly, somebody was watering the newly planted chrysanthemums, a squirrel dropped a pine cone, the cool chestnuts and pines of the cemetery rustled and the spade clinked, now only Nature had anything to do and say, Man stood rigid in the August heat and as mute as the chorus of the *Lacrimosa* on the spool of recording tape at JT's funeral.

THE INHERITANCE

That can't be all your father's left—she declared confidently, almost laughing, because she felt sure about the other half of the books, the ones that none of them had yet touched, and she glanced at the desk too, there, for sure, all sorts of things had yet to be gone through there, *though if I know him, he's more likely to have kept it in books*, she added, and dusted down her dark-blue skirt and brown blouse (she hadn't had time to iron anything black), then picked up the next book—one of the thrillers—and stretched it open, as if holding a bird by the wings, gave it a thorough shake and flicked through the pages as well, because, she'd explained to the two girls when they came into the flat that morning, these soft, worn notes always stick together, the paper they print them on isn't good enough, it's just like newsprint, *You saw in Budapest what real money looks like, didn't you?*! and as she spoke the older girl had just picked up a fat tome on Marxism–Leninism, because their father had propped his bed up on it—he'd broken the leg off when he fell against the wall drunk one day and knocked the light settee over, and for years hadn't got round to mending it—on the desk there still lay the crumpled, tattered 10-lei note and two 1 leis that the ambulance crew had found in his pockets before taking him away in the afternoon of the previous day, Saturday: and now they were having to tidy the house up—as Mother said: *We've got to tidy Táta up*—because on Monday she'd got to go to work, give lessons in the afternoon and do some typing in the evening, and the younger girl too obediently stacked up the books of verse in front of her, sat down on the bed, *that bed*, and quietly, thoroughly leafed through the India-paper edition of Ady, the cheap one of Attila József, and the bound ancient poets with their gilded spines, as if she wasn't really looking for anything, just absent-mindedly turning the pages as she used to do in winter when her father asked her to read aloud, *Perhaps he had some foreign money? Shouldn't think so, poor chap hadn't got the sense*—muttered Mother, *We aren't crying, girls, we aren't crying*—she assured them with a sniff, to deflect attention from herself as she was ashamed of her tears, and she started to look for the dog: *Where's the doggy?* and she went out into the yard and called it: *Doggy, doggy,* but Andrej had disappeared, and meanwhile the younger girl got some cold water from the well in an empty bottle and passed it round, and as she went by she scooped up the 12 lei off the table and pocketed them without anyone noticing, as if she alone had the right, she were the sole beneficiary, and of course because she'd always loved money, loved it passionately ever since she'd been little, and she'd made most money in this house: firstly at poker, at which she knew how to cheat, and she'd returned her father's ever-increasing number of empty bottles from the scullery to the corner shop, where they knew her, and she'd stopped being ashamed of her father's empties, and in autumn she'd earned a bit for chrysanthemums: because with the encouragement and supervision of Aunty Sándor next door she'd taken a lot of tiny chrysanthemums to the market at lighting-up time, and asked 8 lei for a bunch, but last autumn she'd finally discovered a real gold mine in the cellar, a hoard of bottles which, she suspected, her father's predecessor must have started amassing, as it included bottles for soft drinks, milk and mineral water and jars for preserves and pickles, the sort of things that her father almost never bought—but then her father expanded the collection of bottles to the point of impenetrability, and in fact when she tried to go down the few steps into the cellar to look around the bottles completely blocked the narrow entrance: because, thought the twelve-and-a-half-year-old Girl, the only benefit of Father's drinking is that the bottles can be taken back, and under the terms of their financial agreement she kept the proceeds, and in November and even December she washed them outside at the well, soaked them and rubbed them clean until her hands were blue, because even the local shopkeepers that knew her wouldn't accept them dirty or with labels, and there were a few there that were a great find from ages back: a Napoca brandy bottle in the shape of a peasant girl in skirts, for which she was given 15 lei, it hadn't been available for years and yet they took it back, and Father too had bought a bottle of Napoca brandy when she was born but hadn't managed to keep it until her eighteenth birthday, in fact he'd replaced it frequently and then forgotten about it, and indeed he hadn't managed to preserve himself until the Girl had grown up, and there were a good few bottles of 3-lei sparkling wine too, and by spring the diligent Girl had finished with the cellar, but Father had thoughtfully continued to pile up vodka and liqueur bottles in the dark, disused hole known as the scullery, and she'd loaned him part of the proceeds—*You're not to drink it!*, she said menacingly, but Father said, avoiding her eyes, that he wanted to buy maize for the solitary little pig that was left, and applauded Mufurcka, as he called her, for always having money, *The spirit of commerce is alive in you, you capitalist*, but the younger Girl loved money just for itself, *so as to have some*, she used to say, *so that one should have some money*, as Grandfather thought too, she didn't save up for anything, and the *pengő* and *fillér* coins[35] and over-printed Romanian *korona*s, out-of-date leis and banis with holes in the middle, and a big Russian banknote which she found in all sorts of old handbags of Granny's up in the attic looked just like the modern leis and the coloured game-money in the set of Takarékoskodj![36] from Budapest—a game she always won—and for a long time she kept old money and new together in a stamp album—and Granny had sometimes left a few valid coins in with the out-of-date

---

35 The unit of currency has changed from time to time in Hungary. The *pengőforint* ('tinkling' forint = 100 *fillér*) was the official name between 1927 and 1946. The name was often used informally and incorrectly to denote the earlier *forint* and *korona*.

36 'Save up!', a Monopoly-like board game of the communist era.

ones—and the treasured collection was pushed into the background for a while only in Year Four, when in playtime they played at shop-keepers with a new means of payment, the incredibly rare paper from sugar lumps and chocolate bars, because the wrappings of the vanishing sweets suddenly turned into money in school: the girls bought and sold the boys among themselves as there were not many of them in the forty-four strong class, and those that were ugly or fat were relatively cheap while the good-looking and the clever were more expensive, and the top of the class, for whom the Girl saved up, cost twenty rare sugar wrappers, and she traded to such an extent and stimulated the market in playtime with her buying and selling until one day she bought the best-looking and tallest pupil, Attila Zölde Fejér, whose thrilling name always reminded her of the Hungarian flag, and in so doing emptied the big, bright green, split leather handbag in which the coloured, indestructible notes were stored, carefully smoothed out, and for her the game was over because she'd acquired the best-looking boy and was not disposed to pass him on for any price, *Look very carefully, and if you see some unfamiliar money shout out!*—Mother encouraged the girls, and they shook the books and leafed through them so as to come across the inheritance, *because your father must at least have been picking up his dole,* Mother calculated, and in his house there'd often been small change lying on the floor, paper money too, where he'd dropped his trousers or shirt, *It's mine!* she used to shout, *I found it!* and it went straight into her pocket, because that was the rule that she'd made for money that was found: it belonged to whoever found it, and in winter, when there was nothing to do in the garden, poker went like this: Father would lend her some money for the game, which they played for stakes of 25 banis, the Girl would cheat, or simply win, call shame-lessly, irresponsibly, and take the pot, and as she now leafed through the much-thumbed volume of Ady she knew precisely how much the inheritance was that Mother was hoping for, and that it was all in her pocket, she had the entire estate and was telling no one, a mighty, once-in-a-lifetime inheritance, and she also knew that the strange money that she had found was now invalid, long out of date, and that Father had been wasting his time collecting it, cherishing it, worrying about it, keeping it hidden, now it was worthless, or at best an antique dealer would give a few lei for it, and now Mother was pulling out the desk drawers, she took out the thick, red plastic-bound notebooks in the front of which there were entries, and she went on searching in the hope that what she found would at least meet the funeral expenses, *It 's lucky we've got a plot in the cemetery*, she added, that's what she said, *we've got*, it's ours, the family's, and more, both here and in Vásárhely and Parajd and Zajzon, and she went on with the list, *we've got a burial plot and a house and a garden*, because Father's house had had to be sold in any case, a family has one house, that was the law, and the sale had produced money, and as the children were still minors it had had to be put into the CEC, the *check*, as she pronounced it, and *until the girls come of age*, as Mother had complained the previous evening to Grandfather, we can't touch it, that's another three years she sighed and looked at Juci, so there's no money for the funeral, *It's still lucky that we've got the grave*, Grandfather and Grandmother had added in unison, so Father's house and garden weren't 'ours' any longer, but the CEC's, the bank's and the state's, and the means of production, as he would have said, would go into communal ownership, and Juci had now picked up the thick, linen-bound second volume of *Das Kapital*, 1953 edition— which, incidentally, wasn't by Marx, as Father had taught—the book had always lain on the desk so as to be to hand, and when she picked it up and shook it white slips of paper started to fall out of it, raining down, marked with letters by Father and the younger girl, because in winter he used to read aloud from *Das Kapital* and explained it fervently, quoted examples, and in the Girl's head little scenes were enacted and once she stared at him and exclaimed *Somebody ought to make a film of it!*, and after that *Das Kapital* was read as a series of film shots, about the vampire, the exploiters of the lace and baking industries, world money, *Everybody's going to understand like this*, she assured him, and Father laughed and agreed, then inserted little slips of paper into the book and a filmscript began to emerge, and now the younger girl turned more pages, leafed through the Ady with its fine brown silk binding, in which there were all sorts of markers, a bay leaf, a badly done piece of cross-stitch saying 'To Daddy' which she'd had to embroider while still in Year Two—*this is a poor effort*, Mother had declared with her expert eye—an old label off a pre-war bottle of Zajzon mineral water—*Apă de Zizin* it said on it in flowery, sloped letters—and Father had underlined two lines in the book *'One must oppose Death, Oppose it, János, and charge, János'*,[37] then further on another foreign, brownish label and Father had underlined another line, it can only have been he, the line 'And I have not reached Death',[38] the Girl was surprised, Father had never scribbled in books, and she looked at the line, the hand had shaken in the middle and the line was broken, and meanwhile Mother was stacking the contents of the desk drawers in tidy columns and saying nothing to the Girl, who for a while did nothing, not turning pages, just sitting motionless looking at the marked line on one page of the book, and on the other page was the invalid, out-of-date banknote which Father had finally hidden away, that is, hadn't pulled out, because that book had lain there open both that day and the day before, and there he'd hidden the 100 koronas, because he too knew enough German to write *Quittung über hundert kronen* on the new, unused light brown note, not even folded in two, perhaps it had been so carefully kept, it must have meant a great deal to somebody for it to remain in mint condition forty years later, perhaps she ought to ask Mother after all whether it was valid, it might be so, and then Eureka!, because dollars too were valid for a long time, why might not something be valid that had been printed on 1 January 1943, *was it Jewish money?* the Girl

---

37 From the first stanza of Endre Ady's *A mesebeli János* (The mythical János).
38 From the first stanza of Ady's *Nem csinálsz házat* (You shall not make a house), alluding to I Chronicles 28: 2–3.

wondered, because there was also a six-pointed star on it as on the ornamental plate where Father kept the cufflinks that he never wore,
Theresienstadt, she deciphered, and *Wer diese Quittung verfälscht oder
nachmacht, oder gefälschte Quittungen in Verkehr bringt, wird strengst
bestraft*, ah, that must say that one mustn't forge money, she proudly
worked out, and on the other side a man with a big beard—like the
cantor on one of Father's records, who wailed so disturbingly—holding
Moses' tablets, just as in the Horea út synagogue, and—this too she
understood—the oldest Jew in the town signed the money, because that
was what they used to do, somebody was responsible for it, *Der älteste
der Juden in Theresienstadt, Jakob Edelstein, E-del-stein*, she spelt it out
once more, and went on examining it for a long time, this surprisingly
new money which in the end Father hadn't spent, it must therefore not
be a forgery or he wouldn't have kept it, and she said timidly, *Mummy
... I think*, and then for the first time held the discovery up to the light,
but there was no watermark in it, never mind, she thought, there isn't
one in the lei either, *I think I've found something, I think I've found it*,
she said, definitely now, and held the money out to her mother, *I thought
you'd be the one to find it, you're always lucky, you trod in the mud when
you were little*, Mother was delighted, then she looked at it for a long
time, turned it over, examined the new, light-brown note more and
more gravely and suspiciously, *Think it's valid?* asked the Girl nervously,
but still trustingly, *I don't know*, she answered quietly and thoughtfully,
and meanwhile Grandfather came in from the cemetery, out of breath,
his cigarette had gone out in the double holder, he carefully pushed his
bicycle inside and, pale of face, said that he'd been at the cemetery until
just then and they wouldn't permit burial in 'our grave', *Understand?!*
They won't permit us to bury him in our grave, he repeated, and sank onto
the bed, *Won't permit and that's that*, and he looked in front of him, 'And
it's possible that we aren't going to get any funeral expenses out of the
collective farm either, because it wasn't in the estimate,' Mother thought
aloud, because from 1983 not only those going onto pensions but also

the sick and the deceased had to be planned for annually, and that was the basis on which sick-pay and assistance were awarded, and a firm had an amount disposable for the sick and the deceased in accordance with these factors, and at this moment Mother held up the dazzling note from the mint at the star-fortress outside Prague, and like one that has seen the light exclaimed *This isn't money at all*! in a high-pitched voice as she always did when she was pleased at something, *it's a receipt*, she said, *a receipt*, *Quittung*, that's what it's got written on it: it's an acknowledgement for 100 koronas, it's what Jews used to give for their money to people who couldn't get it until they themselves had died, this worthless, unredeemable acknowledgement, pure as the driven snow, it's not negotiable: it's condemned man's money, it's what they'd push into the hangman's hand before he hanged them, *So it's a receipt*! said Mother a third time, with assurance that overcame all doubt and gave it back to the Girl, *It's yours, you found it, take great care of it, it's left you by your father*, but she took it uncertainly, *Then it isn't valid currency?*, but Mother was getting on with leafing through the papers in the drawers, and added seriously, weightily and quietly: *Oh, it's valid all right. And how. It's valid with us, we'll spend it together*, but the Girl asked again, A*nd how much is it worth?*, imagining that they'd accept just about anything at the dollar shop behind the Napoca hotel, but Mother couldn't answer because by then she was calculating mentally— how much it would be for the coffin, the mourners, the cerecloth, the ceremony, the laying-out, but the grave!, where am I to get that from?!, but the Girl was thinking: this note, this receipt or *Quittung* must be worth an awful lot, because that was her inheritance, her entire inher- itance, plus the 12 lei which she had pocketed in good time.

CUBE

'*Good morning, Comrade, I'm your son*'—the young man of medium build with fair, wavy hair in raincoat and sunglasses looked into the winged mirror, *No, I'll have to take the sunglasses off,* he said to himself, but the waterproof had no pocket and so he kept them in his hand, *This is stupid, I'd better put them in my jacket pocket,* and his green eyes shone in the dimly lit room, reflected in the triple mirror that came from a theatre dressing-room—the owner, a former ballet dancer, had kept the little bachelor flat in her heyday for assignations—*I'll have to speak up, Pista says that after being in prison she's a bit deaf in her right ear, so:* '*Good morning, Comrade, I'm your son*' *no need to say* maga,[39] *it's obvious I'm her son, that's why I'm going to see her, no need to over-emphasize, and*—he looked himself over—*shouldn't I put a tie on?* And he unbuttoned his coat, reached into his pocket, turned slightly sideways and looked at himself, *A tie's a bit lower middle-class, I've got a nice green cotton one, and my father always wore a tie, but I don't want her to think of my father because of me, and do I really need a raincoat?*—he looked out into Monostori út, on the far side patients were basking in the patches of sun between the trees in the hospital courtyard wearing just their dressing gowns, *Yes,* he decided, *it's smart and elegant, but all the same it's going to be warm today, and this is a great day!*—he smiled—*And it's the first of June. Perhaps I ought not to go today of all days—what number is it in Brassó or Brassai utca?,* he fumbled in his jacket pocket for the note that Pista had written for him, *And I wonder why she's gone to live in Brassó utca? Out of nostalgia for the shady poplars between Brassó and Zajzon? No,* he gestured proudly, *that's not Mother, she never turns back,*

39 The polite third-person pronoun. Its use here would be needlessly emphatic.

and Janó stepped out of the door of his first rented room in Kolozsvár, and one paid for with his own money, *the reason the road was planted with poplars was so that the sun shouldn't burn the heads of the delicate travelling public of the town while they were going the 24 kilometres down the asphalt road from Brassó to the spa at Zajzon, and to catch the snow and that accursed north-easterly wind, the Crivăț, that blows at us from the Romanian lowlands*, the prospective spa physician had explained when driving the young doctor who was his fiancée—'my fiancée, colleague and companion in misfortune'—to Zajzon via Négyfalu and Tarang a few days before his final exams in May 1920 to introduce her to his parents, *this won't be 24 kilometres*, thought Janó, *so I'll go on foot, no need to hurry*, and he sketched out the route in his mind as he was new to the town: down Monostori út, across Főtér, along Kossuth Lajos utca, turn left at the church towards the market and he'd be in Brassó or Brassai utca, *it's still quite a way from Monostori út to 15 Brassó utca*, he thought, and like the actor who, after long rehearsals, steps preparedly and confidently out of his dressing room and sets off for the stage, where in a few minutes' time the curtain will go up, he repeated once more on the narrow staircase 'Good morning, Comrade, it's me, your son', *do I need to say* me?—he was unsure—*Very much so, because I am her son, I, I, that's why I'm going, because I exist as well, there's not only poor Buci and Pista, of whom of course she can feel proud, because Pista's finished at university now and everybody says he's got a great future, he's got a lot going for him, in Bucharest these days, in the Ministry of Agriculture, his book's coming out shortly*, and he hurried down the stairs: yes, that was how he must greet her, in that soft, warm, deep voice that one uses to lovers or parents, that voice that comes from deep down, from right inside, not from the lungs but through the stomach, from the muscular, determined heart that means to live, and the sentence 'Good morning, Comrade, I'm your son' was going to burst from him as indubitable proof of the wish to live, to return and find the way back: and so he stepped out of the gloomy flat and felt that he had been lying motionless for years, gravely ill, and that at the two ends of his bed, like two mourning candles, the nightmare of the two white-coated doctors were staring in bewilderment because there was nothing they could do and they'd given up, but suddenly the patient's chest had risen as if something had lifted it up, as if someone, after a long hesitation, had worked the strings of the lifeless puppet, and the twenty-five-year-old man had decided to recover what he had lost—his mother, and he gave a sudden deep sigh and unconsciously took another deep breath because he had decided that he was going to turn to the right from his stagnant existence because he wanted to live, not to the left, no, not to the left, because after a long and irresolute waiting he had finally decided for life: because at last that day he was going to meet the mother he had never seen ... *Today is the 1st of June 1949, coming up to noon*—he stated, like someone synchronizing his watch for a coming attack, so that a new timescale could begin for him too—*never mind, I shan't keep count* . . . he added indifferently, as he was unwilling to allow the irremediable sorrow of numbers to come near him, *Or rather, perhaps I ought just to come out with 'Hello, Mum!'*, but he couldn't remember what they'd called her in those days, Mum? Mother? Momma? and these words all had a cold, empty ring, *Adults address their mothers differently from children*, he thought, names for mothers grew up as children did, but neither a teenager nor a young man could address his mother by name, *Or should I just say 'Good morning, Doctor!'*, *as everybody called her in Zajzon, but I'm not going to see the doctor!*, and he smiled inwardly, but that was just why he was going: to heal the past, *to see the doctor*, who hadn't taken her husband's name because she'd been too proud, and yet everybody called her that, simply Doctor Erzsébet, but they didn't like to use her maiden name, neither the so-called visitors who really were sick, nor the villagers who made a living from them, as it would have been uncomfortable to say the harsh, German-sounding name, but the name 'Concordia' was painted on the classical facade of the beautiful, wide, three-storey spa hotel in Zajzon:

It means the same in Latin and Romanian—harmony, father had explained to their son later, so after that the doctor's name featured only on her stamp, which she seldom used because in the spa they didn't write prescriptions or referrals to elsewhere, but in 1927 and afterwards, when certain visitors alluded more and more clearly to the doctor's origins, it made no difference, 'The lady doctor will practise somewhere else' came the official notice, and before he could take her with him to Zajzon her fiancé too spoke of 'Erzsébet Gizella' in a letter which, as a young doctor, he sent to his father, the local magistrate in Kőhalom, asking for his blessing: the intending husband introduced his Kolozsvár fellow student as hard-working and determined ('tough', Miklós wrote in the draft, but then crossed it out)—even in his student days he had experimented with treating back pains with acidulous water on her advice—and by this had meant to drop a delicate hint that after their marriage they wanted to settle in Zajzon as spa doctors, in which plan he reckoned on the support of his strict Lutheran father, and then he informed him that his fiancée too would soon be a qualified doctor, *At which we respectfully look forward to your presence*, but the proud elderly Székely, who was not enthusiastic about the marriage with the 'Jewish woman', took no part in his (now former) daughter-in-law's swearing-in, which took place much later, in 1928, by which time the three boys too could have been at the ceremony if they had stayed together—poor Miklós (Buci, for short) had been born at the end of 1921, then came Pista in 1924, but Erzsébet announced that she wanted no more children, and when the sickly, epileptic younger boy was four his mother had gone up to Kolozsvár and said that there were to be no more children, but by that time she was working in the Party and was there for two months claiming medical reasons, and in the spring of 1925 the unexpected Janó had been born, who now, aged twenty-five, had reached the corner of the Brewery and was thinking of a new line of approach, longer and more elaborate, but also more pleasant (he excused himself), and turned towards Sétatér, *I mustn't say Momma or*

Mother, or Ma as Pista called her, because I'm not going to see her, he told himself firmly and seriously, looking straight ahead, *because I'm her little boy, but to make her realize that I understand her, at last I understand her,* he cleared his throat and lit a cigarette at the corner of Fürdő utca, which he hadn't even recognized, looking in surprise at the bilingual street sign saying strada Băii, Fürdő utca, *I understand,* he went on, as if talking to someone else and explaining, *that there was nothing else she could have done, if she'd stayed with us she'd have put the family at risk, after all, she was working as an activist of an illegal party, but it was only her own life that she risked . . .what it comes down to is that she did it for us and I've got a lot to thank her for . . . that is, we have*—emphasizing the 'we' as if making a speech from a platform, and in his imagination his voice rose higher, and the warm voice in which he meant to greet Mummy now spoke from his throat and his head, and the words that he addressed to the invisible crowds rang out: *We have them to thank for our lives, those who gave up themselves, their families and professions, sacrificed themselves so that we might have better lives,* he quoted his own sentence from his first published article, because the winter number of the *Agitator,* carefully folded, lay in his pocket as did the application for admission to the University department of philosophy, so that at the right moment he could take them out and show them to Mummy, but by this time he was speaking to the comrade, the founder-member of the Party, the petite leading figure of the illegal movement, whom in his imagination he had seated at his side when he had spoken on the platform in the shoe-factory yard and with a smile, his eyes gleaming, spoken out loud and without a microphone to the Hungarian workers of the world-size tasks that lay before them, and the workers of the newly nationalized János Herbák Leather Works had listened in silence to the enthusiastic young man, who was now making his way slowly along under the chestnuts in the Sétatér, enjoying the cool shade, almost with a shiver, *I only moved to Kolozsvár recently,* he informed Mummy in his imagination, looking at the ground, because on leaving college just after the war he'd gone back to Zajzon, but from September 1940 suddenly it wasn't only the 340 kilometres between Zajzon and Kolozsvár that had separated them, but for the next four years a new national frontier as well,[40] because Kolozsvár had been restored to Hungary but Brassó had not, *You knew I'd come up, didn't you?* he suddenly asked Mummy out loud—*Then why didn't you come and look for me? At least now* . . . but he dared not open the bottle which he had filled full with reproach and accusations against Mummy, but rather went on defensively in a barely audible voice: *I too have only just thought of looking up my relatives*—but then it crossed his mind that he mustn't bother Mummy about 'relatives', not yet, that was Pista's advice, and he'd repeated what he and Mummy didn't talk about: any of Mummy's relatives, her brothers, Zajzon, Buci, father, the College at Nagyenyed, oh, and most of all the unpleasant school-leaving exam and the punishments, and all the tears in the room at the end of the top floor corridor in the College and in the grounds on the study trails, for which the rest had laughed at him so much, *I'll rather tell her what my plans are,* he decided at the corner of the Sétatér, as the future was full of possibilities and promises and seemed less risky than the brief, shared past, *because we're going to have a lot in common from now on, we're both on the same road,* 'We've got a single road before us,' Erzsébet said to her tubby, balding husband, who didn't like to budge from the village, while she regularly, on any pretext, used to escape up to Kolozsvár, where the centre of the organization was, but she never said how long she was going to stay and what she would be doing there, and the easygoing man couldn't understand what on earth his restless wife was talking about at such times: Hungarians, Jews, women perhaps, and all that he felt was that he, her husband, the morose, taciturn doctor who was running Zajzon hospital more and more single-handedly, had less

---

40 Transylvania was ceded to Romania under the Treaty of Trianon (1920) and restored in part by the Second Vienna Award of 1940. This was voided in September 1944.

and less place in that *what on earth* as did their sons, and that it was involving more and more alien, abstract thought, ideas, books, brochures, unexpected telephone calls and journeys, *It's very risky*, he would shake his head thoughtfully, *we've got three sons, think about it . . . taking risks, that's what you like doing, I'm not surprised you got the . . .* but at this point she would burst out 'Don't say it!, and as he emerged from Sétatér the young man was wondering whether that was why Mummy had been given that name[41] in the movement, because the strictly brought-up, courageous and restless girl had always enjoyed taking risks, in 1910 she'd enrolled as a medical student, forsworn her parents' religion because she couldn't forgive her father and brothers for praying every morning '*Baruch ato adonai eloheinu, melech ha-ajlom, shelaj osani isho*', a male mumble that had meant nothing to her until Jenő, her cheerful younger brother, had encouraged her also to give thanks for being a woman and that she shouldn't pray, for example, what the four of the seven who were male did: 'Blessed be Thou, Eternal God, that didst not make me a woman', and so then neither parent was present when Erzsébet and Miklós married in the Lutheran church in Kossuth Lajos utca, and of the family only Jenő, the law student, was there, because, thought Janó, Mummy always liked to live dangerously but the quiet of Zajzon, cool even in summer, impeded her in this: 'Live dangerously!' she ordered her sons, who looked at her uncomprehendingly, and indeed at the age of three Pista had been good at climbing trees and hadn't been afraid of dogs or the brawling big boys of the village, *But why am I talking about Mummy in the past tense?* Janó asked himself, *she's alive and I'm on my way to see her*, and he crossed the road and made a slight diversion towards the theatre and the recently opened State Hungarian People's Opera to take a look at the notices of the final

---

41 Erzsébet's Party name, *Kocka*, means 'cube, hexahedron' and therefore 'die'. From the latter meaning Hungarian derives the verb *kockázik* 'play dice', whence *kockáztat* 'gamble, 'take chances', 'risk'. As the Communist Party was illegal in 1924 in Romania, members had to use code names.

performances before the summer break and warm himself a little in the sun, because Mummy had suffocated in the safe medicinal-water clinic, where all year round the well-to-do, the 'select patients', came—artists, actors, among them even the great diva Lucia Sturza Bulandra—for whom the two doctors prescribed doses of water laden with compounds of iodine and iron, baths, long walks in the hills among the larches, lots of country food, rest and the mud-packs of which Mother smelt, Janó recalled with a shudder: sweet like mud, like damp earth after rain, and Doctor Erzsébet used to straighten spines by the Hippocratic method, fastening the patient to a ladder and turning it upside down so that the patient hung head downward relieving the spine of weight, then she would suddenly announce that she had something to attend to and rush for the train, even in the middle of the season when they were full with regular customers, until in the autumn of 1927 she stayed away for more than a month taking the middle son, Pista, with her and hadn't even come back by Christmas, and in 1933 Janó was enrolled at boarding school in Nagyenyed—like a foundling, he thought—sent to the same place as his mother and (her) brothers had studied, but the delicate boy struggled through school and the lady doctor vanished from Zajzon with Pista, shrugging off her name and past as a snake sloughs its skin: in the 1910s she had been known by her maiden name, in the 1920s as Doctor, and from 1927 only by her revolutionary name, in 1938 she married again, this time a Romanian church painter and for a few years used his name, and the secret name that had stuck to her revealed nothing of her origins or profession, not even whether she was a man or a women, indeed, it didn't even signify a human being nor yet even a naturally existing object as it wasn't anything that Nature had created but something Man-made, and Mummy became a notion, an idea, an abstraction in an insubstantial world, a geometrical concept, something in maths lessons, she acquired volume, surface, six sides, twelve edges and theorems that were to be learnt, at which Janó had done very badly in this topic in an exam at school and almost failed, *I saw her for the last time in 1927*, thought Janó, but could remember nothing of that autumn day, that too remained an unreal notion, an empty sentence, and now he turned towards Malomárok: there was hardly a trickle of water in the litter-filled bed of the stream, in the misty street there hung a faint, familiar smell of mud, and Janó suddenly realized that he was approaching his destination, but the face that he was trying to recall was like a featureless cloud of shining down in the spring sunshine like the dandelions which he had picked in the big, neglected garden of the Jancsi villa in the spring of '28, whispering many times a day the wish *Come home, Mummy!* and blowing as hard as he could, but by the time he'd done five all that remained was the stub, the bare stem, hard and dry and empty, instead of the face of which no more mention was to be made at home as slowly Mummy's photographs disappeared, and her clothes and everything melted away without trace in Father's stubborn silence until, in the spring of '45, father hesitantly announced, with his new Polish wife Hala Adjukiewicz at his side, to Janó and the staring, uncomprehending Buci that they were certainly never again going to see their 'dear mother', as by then all the survivors had come home, but Kocka had been arrested along with other comrades in October 1943, they'd been hiding in the town until then, the wife of János Bartalis the air-raid warden had hidden them in Deák Ferenc utca, and she'd spent the time in Szamosfalva prison (which her four sisters—Lotti, Mária, Berci and another whose very name was completely lost—and Lotti's children, a boy of four and a girl of three, did not survive, Kocka's one elder brother Pál was in the pulmonary ward and Jenő, the younger brother, the lawyer, grew a big moustache and took refuge in the country with the help of the cobbler Lajos Péter, disguising himself as a dairyman), and after nine months of questioning was taken out of the prison in the night of 6 June and loaded into a cattle truck, bound for Auschwitz with the seventh and last deportation from Kolozsvár, which was just being pulled out of the station when, on orders from Baron Braunecker Lamoral, the alcoholic

commandant of Szamosfalva prison, they were sent back to the interrogation camp although there was no rational explanation for this
reversal other than a miracle, had it not been for the news of the
invasion[42] which also arrived that same night, as that was the only occasion when Mummy had set off for somewhere and turned back, and
according to Pista she'd been beaten up in prison so often that she had
gone deaf in one ear, or pretended to be when she didn't want to hear
things, *And now she's an assistant lecturer in the School of Dentistry,*
thought Janó proudly as he came to the corner of Széchenyi tér, and
by that time he had taken off his raincoat, he shivered with cold but
salty perspiration dripped from his eyebrows, stinging his eyes, *How
close we are to one another!* crossed his mind as he neared the middle of
the market, *Perhaps I ought to get her some flowers, a bunch of zinnias, like
there used to be in the Jancsi villa garden, better not,* he hesitated, *I don't
want anything to come between us, just the two of us to be there, and give
each other a big hug. I'll bring some flowers tomorrow, because we'll be
meeting every day from now on, shan't we, Mummy?*, and he licked the
salty droplet from his thick, handsome lips—not perspiration this time,
but a very familiar tear—*That is, Comrade,* he corrected himself with a
smile, '*Good morning, Comrade, I'm your son, little Janó*'—*You're my little
Janó who plopped down from Heaven, because nobody wanted you at all,*
Mummy used to stroke his head firmly, and from the grey, patchy childhood which he had expunged from memory only this stroking, more
like a blow, came to mind, *No, never mind the 'little', Janó, Jancsi, János,
a serious, adult man who is responsible for his own life,* he thought with
satisfaction, as if he were bringing his mother a strange man as a big
present, kept for a long time and now raised to adulthood, *And it's been
twenty-two years since we met, to which Mummy may add, with a smile
'and nine months and ten days', but now we won't be parted again,* and he
added to himself *And I'm never going to desert my children,* and once

---

42 Reference to D-day, the Allied invasion in Normandy.

again he thought about the meeting in which two impossible existences, irrational survivors, were to confront each other: the one should never have been born, the other should have died, but the face of that other, like a pool that has been drained of water, continued to yawn, empty, colourless and awkward in Janó's memory, *Be sure, first off we'll call her 'Comrade'*, he said to himself the way one speaks to a child, *then perhaps in the next sentence 'Mummy'*, and by this time he was on the corner of Brassai utca, outside the stark, angular, four-storey Bauhaus building, *What was it Pista said, what's the name of that Romanian painter that Mummy married? What if the name isn't by the door?* the hope flared up that after all he might postpone the meeting, and he went in through the open door and looked over the battered letterboxes: on one someone had crossed out Neumann and the name of her former husband—as far as it could be made out—and the now-inappropriate Constantinescu too, and in childish scrawl there it said Kocka, second floor B, and he mopped his forehead with his crumpled handkerchief, *Perhaps I'll step outside and have a cigarette*, and he turned his back on the entrance, *I'll ask about her work, and what new jobs she's got in the Party, and tell her modestly*, he reassured himself, *that you're a member too, you haven't been given any serious work yet, but you're not expecting anything from Mummy or Pista, and that you're training to be a writer or theatre critic, and that we can be proud of Pista, but why have you never looked for me? You could have sent word, I could have come up from Zajzon any time, yes, it's taken me some time as well to make my mind up, and we've still got a long way to go together, towards each other, we've got a lot of things to catch up on, but Mummy, Mummy, why did you desert me?*—but this was no longer the voice of the forlorn child in the garden but that of a puzzled adult standing at the door of his despair, and in his paralysis lacking the strength to turn the handle, and then he heard the bell which he had involuntarily pressed at the tall, shabby door, and after a long, motionless pause the door opened but there was no one behind it, only a shapeless greyness, or it was just that his eyes, blurred by tears, saw everything as if it were crumbling, as if he were looking into a kalei-doscope, a big, empty terrace was next, *like the back terrace of the Jancsi villa*, he shuddered, an empty, dead theatre stage which the actors in a long-finished performance had left: two battered armchairs, a circular, cracked table, a narrow, hand-shaped ashtray, full of cigarette ends, some withered flowers in a chipped jug, and after that an entrance door which was now also open because the two doors were connected by a clothesline and the line was being pulled by a stocky woman who was a good three yards from Janó, wearing a dirty dress and worn-out slip-pers, she was as solid as a statue or a *Kocka*, the thought flashed through Janó, her grey hair was gathered into an untidy bun, in her right hand she held a thick, filterless cigarette while her left held the shining brass door handle, and she looked unconcernedly at the unknown arrival, but Janó cleared his throat and in a choked, dull voice, his eyes on the floor, embarked upon his much-rehearsed, perfectly polished sentence of greeting, at which she frowned and asked in reply what he was talking about, *We shall often sit here, on this terrace, and talk, discuss the work and plans that we have in common*, he thought, and looked out at the tops of the chestnuts and the treeless, sunlit Fellegvár, and that image went at once into the empty, echoing store of memories and imperceptibly van-ished into the oversized and now unfillable big room, and Janó spoke again: *Comrade*, he began loudly to declaim the well-practised sentence, *no, Mummy, I can't forgive you and I miss you very much*, and he breathed an all but inaudible breath, and ten years later, in the late spring of '59, he whispered the same into his mother's deaf ear at his father's funeral, *I miss you very much*, but nothing went into the deaf ear, only the warm breath tickled the hairs that grew out of its depths, and as she stood rigidly there she suddenly clapped a hand to it as if to drive away some insect, because then they were back together once more in Zajzon, burying Father beside all the relatives named Miklós, István and János, and the owners of the spa, the medicinal springs with their red, iron-rich water, the Concordia hotel, the Jancsi villa, the park, the larch forest in the Tatrang, Pürkerec and Zajzon districts, and the old disused water-bottling works, but Pista didn't go to the funeral, as he told his brother bitterly, as in his position it wouldn't do openly to mourn his father who was 'of hostile sentiments', but to Kocka that hadn't mattered for a long time, she'd disregarded the Party for fifteen years by then, ever since it came into power, and no one knew the little doctor when she went through the village, except the minister, who would have invited her to lunch because after the funeral they had an hour and a half to wait for the bus to Brassó, but she wanted to go for a walk and declined in a voice that would not be opposed as if she had not heard the invitation, and set off into the big, wild garden heading for the Jancsi villa, but a man using a scythe behind the house called out that there was no one in the collective farm office, which he repeated in Romanian, they'd all gone out to the fields, and went on scything, and in the humid, warm garden the dandelions were already in flower and Janó ran after his mother as she hurried, he was tired after the early train journey and because of the heat, his stomach was empty, and in the neglected garden he almost fell flat over the molehills as he tried to follow her as she hurried ahead with her resolute, short strides, but she just went on and on, almost running, and her youngest had by then been left far behind, calling in vain for her to wait, but she didn't turn round, her quick steps crushed the dandelions, knocking off the downy heads that shone in the sun, and in the big, humid, springtime garden her stocky figure began to disappear in the tall grass, and her human form diminished, shrinking more and more, blending with the forms of the trees, the distant houses, the grazing cattle and the haystacks until at last she looked like a distant rock, a shrinking cube, dissolving among the diffraction lines of the horizon.

MEAT'S MEAT

Janó lived in his garden with his steadily growing number of animals and his vegetables as if he had put the material world behind him once and for all: he only went into the two rooms and kitchen of the flat to sleep in a dark corner of what was called the scullery, where some years before he had even intended to put in a water supply and make it into a shower room, but now he just dumped his dirty clothes in a heap, the big aluminium washtub hung, covered in spiders' webs, on the wall and the youngest child, who liked to splash about by the well in summer and play at washing things, went there less frequently in late autumn and winter when there was nothing to do in the garden, the bulb burnt out in the little room and Janó sometimes went over to his former mother-in-law's, or on holidays to the children's in the block of flats, for a bath, and his few boxes of books were still tied up with string and unpacked, as if he were using the house as only a temporary refuge: but the rabbits and chickens multiplied steadily, and Ráchel and Sára had grown too: the two sisters had rather grown lengthwise like teenagers, and had no wish to round out and acquire a little womanly plumpness, when at the end of November 1983—Janó had by then stored the cabbage and went reluctantly into the office, but every afternoon shut himself in the house as if the garden had suddenly lost all interest for him for the next four months, took a French detective novel from one of his unopened boxes and uncorked a bottle of vodka or dark green Glacial to go with it, while the second volume of his brother's book lay open at page 100 and covered in dust—on the elder girl's birthday Lili announced, as if it were glad tidings, that for Christmas 'we'll kill a pig', Janó looked at the floor and objected, that was ridiculous, they were still hardly piglets, almost sucking pigs, *And don't people kill sucking pigs?* Lili asked with a mocking laugh, and next day after work she hurried down to see for herself: she went down the bare garden where there were only a couple of pumpkins and tall onions left for seed, and looked into the pungent sty: Ráchel and Sára appeared, slipping on the seldom cleaned floor and pushing each other to poke their pink noses between the slats: *Aren't you keeping them for the girls?* Lili enquired drily of the startled Janó who, in dirty trousers and gumboots, leant over the door of the sty and scratched Ráchel's ear, *God bless you, Lili, can't you see how big they are? I'll have to keep them for at least another six months*, and then he addressed the pigs as if to assure them that no danger threatened: *chika, chika*, but Lili turned on her heel and spoke over her shoulder in a choking voice, her lips pale: *If*—after the word she made a short, dramatic pause, drew breath, and as if she had reached the most weighty point in her speech of accusation—*if you want your children to have potatoes and pumpkins for Christmas, or toast, that's all right by me*, then she added more quietly and sadly, *Now what do you look like*, because Janó had appeared before the unexpected visitation of the honoured court to hear the verdict untidily dressed and unshaven—and if Lili had also seen his ragged, tattered nylon socks, which he'd put on inside-out!— and she strode resolutely out of the garden, but Janó ran after her, how much meat would she need, take a chicken, the cock even, if she wanted, Klári would kill it for her if need be, *Go on, take a look, they're lovely! Or there's that nice big white goose, what d'you say to that?* Lili knew it only from a photograph: her younger daughter was nervously holding the little white goose with a red ribbon on its neck, keeping it well way from her with straight arms among the brightly coloured dahlias and gladioli, and at the last moment the goose had turned its head to one side and the Girl, startled, had done the same, so that in the picture they were looking in opposite directions, *Would you prefer that, Lili, the goose?* and with a great effort he added *and I'll get hold of some pork, as much as you like, how much do you think? Three kilos be enough, or five, or maybe ten?* he panted, but Lili only wanted Ráchel or Sára, wouldn't discuss anything less: *Really, Janó, when have you ever got hold of anything? When there are these two pigs here, you've reared them for the girls, haven't you? Why won't you let them have them?* asked Lili in a softer tone as she scented victory, but Janó hurried after her, skirting the empty beds as Lili marched straight across the garden, the high heels of her red shoes sinking into the soil and leaving a regular trail of holes behind her as if she were dibbling something, and he caught her up beside where the tomatoes had been, and there they stood face to face in the bright, deep twilight among the myriad shades of brown, grey and black, and there had never been so great a difference between them: Lili, who had never been interested in philosophy, had never lived with an animal that she would have had to kill—she loathed blood, sickness and death—had only kept fluffy cats as decoration, and those too her father had taken to be neutered or put to sleep when their end came, and Janó, who had never lived with reality and only for a couple of years with the two children, the fanatical carnivores who ran eagerly to their mother not just for slices of roast meat but also for the most watery baloney, made with soya—which the girls called 'cemetery snails'—and which quickly went brown, just as now Ráchel and Sára ran to meet their dear, slim master, because Janó didn't live in his garden in accordance with the laws of natural rotation but like someone that wanted to stop time, take everlasting and motionless stills of Paradise there, and was now working on the details and the scenery: trying to create an ultimate peaceful state in which piglets, rabbits and chickens would remain forever young, just growing and growing, and spreading into a family tree with an infinity of huge, shady branches, in which death had been conquered—as in the little coloured booklets from the Jehovah's Witnesses which old Mrs Sándor next door passed over—because in that garden nobody ever perished under a knife held by the hand of man: it was a kind of Noah's Ark that had moored at 64 Budai Nagy Antal utca in the garden of the long, four-flat Hóstát house that had somehow escaped official notice and had incomprehensibly not been demolished, so that the occupants of the Ark might set out on the way to an inevitable multitude and carry worldwide the cheering news of the delight of eternal life, because Janó gave the rabbits away more and more often, but Ráchel and Sára, through the seller's error or intentional deception, were not a pair but were both girls, although Janó had two real teenage daughters, and for a fortnight Ráchel was known as Ábrahám, but when Janó took the black-and-white piglet in his lap and fed it on goat's milk from a baby's bottle he realized that he was holding a little girl and for days he put off exchanging it but in the end didn't take it back to the Ószer animal market just as, perhaps, Mother wouldn't have taken her baby back to the hospital as she often threatened, because according to superstition Andris had been expected, she'd been so big and he'd moved lazily and not very much, *When they're bigger we'll get them a boyfriend*, said Janó to his younger daughter, as he was planning to extend the sty towards the rabbit hutches so that there could be room for piglets, but now he bowed his head before Lili's unflinching, unforgiving blue eyes: he was unshaven, his breath sour from drinking, his tousled, wiry hair, long unwashed, stood on end, he had been wearing his checked flannel shirt for a week, and with his bad teeth he was afraid to smile in front of her as she told him every month to 'get his mouth attended to', and there he stood like a criminal awaiting sentence, looking at the ground and the dried-up tomato stalks, the sinews in his neck looking odd under his loose-fitting shirt, standing out sharply as if he were about to lower his head to the block, and it seemed that his whole body language was saying *I accept and deserve the verdict, and indeed, I turn to this stern and just court for a much heavier punishment, which I will carry out by my own hand*, but black-spotted Ráchel could not be killed in public view in the courtyard for fear of their being reported, so straw was spread at the back, next to the sty, and she was quickly killed early one morning, and Sára squealed as loudly as her sister, as if two pigs were being killed, and the big pieces were put in black plastic bags and hauled into the block, up to the drying-room on the fourth floor which nobody used, and made ready, but marvellous, big, whole smoked hams were not the outcome, such as the younger Girl had seen a year before, hanging in the village in her friend's grandparents' cool larder (otherwise only in story books and animated films), and which since then she had dreamt of though without making any connection between black-spotted Ráchel and Sára with the pink, curly hair, the link remained purely theoretical as if in practice the Great Ham could not be made by mere mortals, nor did they make any bacon fat because Ráchel hadn't any yet, or Janó hadn't been feeding her properly, and there wasn't any smoked sausage either because nobody in the courtyard dared keep a smoker, and all the meat had to be cooked at once as they didn't have a freezer—they hadn't been able to get one, though Mother sometimes got them for other people, but she thought that they didn't need one because they had nothing to freeze—and so Ráchel vanished almost unnoticed: she became cabbage soup and roast or fried meat, a big helping of blood-and-liver sausage for Grandfather, brawn from the head, the loin went into the cabbage soup and was mixed with other smoked meats in the pot, but it seemed that the 70-kilo animal had, in the end, not come up to expectation and Janó, in his last Christmas, sat silent at table like a man in the pillory and about to be beheaded, merely swallowing, not appearing to chew, and he offered to fatten Sára, the sole sorrowful eyewitness, on maize for Easter so that there would be fat bacon too, as Laci had been disappointed, and whatever the outcome he would make a smoker, and he promised the younger Girl a whole ham *Just for you*, and next spring he'd buy some more piglets, *and Lili, please, say when you're out of meat*, said he, his mouth closed and his lips smiling broadly, as if taking the decision of his life, making an undertaking in front of everybody not to drink any more, *Janó, you do talk rubbish! You know very well there's never any meat*, said Lili calmly without looking at him, as if speaking to a child, *I can always let you have a rabbit or a chicken*, Janó went on, feeling rich and happy at having something to give, and as he warmed to the festive meal in the five-storey block he began to lay more and more daring plans for his garden like a man with great deeds ahead of him, it would be up to him after that to produce regular material for the slaughterhouse, at last something useful and worthwhile had come for him to do, because he had begun to see himself as the children's benefactor, their saviour, who would feed his hungry progeny with meat sliced from his own body, and he offered Laci and Klári the big dish of pink meat as if he were at home, *Well, there's nothing like a bit of fresh pork* . . . said Laci in an encouraging tone, and with his big bone-handled fork picked up another slice of meat, pricked with garlic and cooked in beer, while Klári nodded in approval and cut off tiny, elegant morsels, *Good thing it isn't fatty*, she added, but the children could detect no difference in the meats, fresh or not, it was all the same to them, as were the brown-edged Bologna sausage with its perforations and the salami from Budapest with the faint dusting of noble rot, of which it was said that it contained donkey meat, and at first they'd regarded it with suspicion because of the fungus, they could tell no difference between Janó's yellow-skinned fowl and the purple chicken from the shop, *Meat's meat*, and they shrugged, they would eat it even if it were frogs' legs, dog or cat, they said to their mother's annoyance, even rat or baby!, and there was supposed to have been an English writer, not actually English but Irish, who'd recommended eating that, in fact it was the most nourishing, said Juci secretly one night, because from time immemorial the smiling face in the front pages of textbooks must have remained so youthful, smooth and animated because it drank children's blood: in his own hospital, allegedly, every fourth day he received a transfusion of the fresh blood of babies and children in a life-giving and rejuvenating operation that took all day, and children below the age of twelve were those used, and the younger Girl, who had only just turned twelve in the summer, watched the nine o'clock newscast in horror, and tried to work out when it was the so-called fourth day, that on which the patient paid no visits, received no guests, made no speeches, didn't travel abroad, and she checked the headlines in *Igazság* too, but could never work out when the operation was performed because the day didn't dawn when the face didn't appear on TV, and it would have made no difference if they ate the nervous, horrid turkey that was kept in a separate pen, Sára, who was in the end not fattened, and the big white geese too: but the geese weren't slaughtered, nor the red cockerel, nor the solitary turkey, nor the eternally filthy Sára, demented in her despair, Mazsola, the dear old, lame, bug-eyed guard dog, Andrej, the leggy spaniel, nor the family of hedgehogs that walked in procession behind the raspberry canes—father in front, little ones following, mother bringing up the rear—but Janó died in August, when the tomatoes are ripe at last and human flesh is at its worst, because it seemed that a real, great, long-awaited earthquake was beginning and the town had begun to fall apart: in the summer of 1984 the houses in the Hóstát around St Peter's church were demolished, the gardens were replaced by housing estates, and 25 Kossuth utca too, the lovely, classical, two-storey house that used to belong to the Neumanns, the sometime-owners of the sport shop, was swept aside in a single day: because Man is a killer and his body is the house in which he lives, for all kill, both Lili and Janó, meat's meat, it makes no difference, because one can always find someone weaker than oneself into whom to sink the sharp blade, whom one can devour, or if one seeks such and cannot find then certainly one has reached the end, oneself, because one is therefore at the bottom of the food chain, not the top, for one will not eat but be eaten and accordingly it follows that one will be slaughtered: each by himself, and the rest will butcher him, for Man is a killer and his house is his body.

TOMATOES

Nothing had to be done for the tomatoes, the hundred kilos of cooking-quality tomatoes, they just came from the light and the soil, and the soil too came about as unexpectedly as miracles, like the first-time gambler's jackpot that comes by pure chance to the winning number through a single chip tossed down negligently, without thought or reflection: the whole thing started with a small advertisement that hardly caught the eye: 'For sale: house, two rooms and kitchen, big garden, Budai Nagy Antal utca 8', no phone number, no price, just as in other advertisements there was no sum mentioned as if nothing had a price that could be expressed in numbers, only in exchange value—'I offer' was how advertisements usually began, followed by 'I want'—but Janó stirred himself and after work went along to look at the house, walked down the even-numbered side of Honvéd utca (as Klári's people called it), passed in front of the Institute for the Blind and the Institute for the Deaf on the other side and on this occasion avoided the cramped, smoky pub called the Zsil Valley where he had otherwise often waited for it to close at six in the evening,[43] but this afternoon had gone by slowly until he had finally been able to escape from the gloomy cooperative office in the middle of town, where he spent his time filling in printed tables on grey paper between two clumsy, silent typewriters, *This is dead work, as Marx writes in the first book of* Das Kapital, he said again and again, while above his head there hung a placard—the Girl always read it aloud—*In this office smoking is permitted on alternate days. Not today*, said the confident message, poker-worked

---

43 It may seem a strange time for a pub to *shut*, but this was intended as a measure against alcoholism.

on wood, below which Janó chain-smoked Snagovs and on bad days cheap cigarettes with no filters until his Rakéta with the broken glass showed three o'clock, *I'm popping out*, he said to the secretary, who balanced on her head an alarming, pitch-black coiffure, *Coming back?* asked Livia without even looking up, *Yes*, Janó replied decisively, *if it doesn't drag on*, though what could possibly drag on among the upholsterers he himself didn't know—he didn't dare complain to his brother Pista, who had found him the job in the central upholstery office, of how tedious it was, ordering in material, springs, nails, slats and foam from various places and distributing them on the basis of record sheets, and finally he bought in beds, settees and armchairs likewise by record sheets with three carbon copies, *It's the last time I'm helping you*, his uncle had said severely, who at first had helped the unemployed Janó, *Because you've drunk yourself out of everywhere*, Lili had said in front of the children, and the secretary knew precisely where her boss was popping out to—the Zsil Valley if he was alone, the Mushroom, Potato, Bean or Cabbage restaurants if colleagues joined him, the Vadász or the Ursus beer-bar if the weather was fine, the Casino in the pedestrian precinct if it was very hot, on payday the Melody in Főtér and at the end of the month the cheapest dive at the corner of Pata utca, or, after the shorter Saturday working hours, home to the flat in Monostori utca with a bottle of vodka, green liqueur or rum, because Livia, whose bosom took up the entire desk, told the Girl, if she looked in to see her father, *He's popped out*, and grinned, showing the pink gums above her tobacco-stained teeth, and she'd be ashamed in anticipation of the answer when she saw that his desk was unoccupied, and after that wouldn't appear again in the Szentegyház utca office for a week, *La revedere*, Livia now smiled amiably at the boss, as one that knows all but keeps quiet, but on this day she was mistaken: *What was the number?* Janó stopped at the corner of Budai Nagy Antal (formerly Honvéd) utca, if he turned left, he thought, towards Dohány utca he would see the cracked walls of his former mother-in-law's family house, where he often called, and the closeness of the two old folks had encouraged him at least to look at the long house with its eight windows, and so he opened the metal-sheeted gate and a big black dog which was chained there began to bark frantically, at which a man with tattooed arms, bare to the waist, looked out of the first flat and in response to Janó's question gestured towards the end flat: *Bathroom?* Janó was about to ask the owner, but he realized that he'd seen the whole place, so there was no bathroom, so he asked instead: *WC?*, at which the elderly man pointed with his stick through the kitchen window into the yard, at the end of which there stood four identical earth toilets, *The second one,* he informed him, *Aha,* Janó replied in a flat tone, *And water?*, at which the old man repeated his previous gesture, this time pointing to the left in the yard, to the outside tap, *That's where we get water from, everybody's got their meter, the charge for water is according to area and number of people,* then they stood in silence for a moment in the dirty kitchen, *The gas stove is staying,* said the old man, *I only bought it two years ago, but I'm not taking it with me,* then he cleared his throat and went on confidentially *This part isn't being demolished,* and Janó nodded as if he had already possessed that valuable information, and indeed he had made previous enquiries and knew that Pata utca and the odd-numbered side of Budai Nagy Antal utca were to come down, the gardens to be destroyed, and the present occupants to be crammed into blocks of flats, and it crossed Janó's mind that Klári's family too were always anxious, *Then I'll show you the garden,* said the old man seriously—until then he had not moved—as if now coming to the point, what had gone before had all been introduction, and gave a deep sigh, at which Janó muttered in answer, *No need,* and the old man raised his hands to his head, *You don't want to look at the garden?—No,* repeated Janó, *What d'you mean, aren't you interested in it? Then why d'you want to buy a house up here?*, to which Janó replied irritably that he wanted a house, not a garden, at which the old man gestured indignantly, a sharp movement as though knocking something out of the air, this fake purchaser was just wasting his time, it was a pity he'd even let him in, and he was just opening the kitchen door to let this frivolous enquirer out, adding in an undertone that he could have told from the address that it was a garden in the Hóstát that was for sale, not some villa with all mod cons or a weekend house or a flat in a block, *Then why didn't you say so in the paper?* Janó retorted peevishly, and the old man replied calmly that they hadn't allowed him to say in the advertisement that the garden was in the Hóstát because according to them there were only districts and micro-regions in the town, *And this is to be the Maraşti district, in case you don't know, sir,* he added acidly, emphasizing the 'sir', *Have you ever heard of the Hóstát?*! *It's the best soil in this town, I wouldn't sell it for any price, only I can't do it any longer, I can hardly see, my children have moved abroad, and I'm saying goodbye, I'm going to live with my sister in the country, her husband's died,* to which Janó, now at the door, replied that he'd changed his mind, he would like to look at the garden after all, and the old man, without a word, stepped into his gumboots on the porch, picked up the hoe that was leaning on the wall and led the way, walking quickly and unsteadily and saying almost inaudibly *This is mine, this is next door, chicken coop, loo, here's the garden, shed, tools are in the price, I'm leaving them, and a cabbage barrel, I'm killing a pig next week, I had it ploughed up again in autumn, vines, there are flower bulbs in the cellar but I'm taking those, you won't want them,* and from the pigsty a pair of bright eyes looked at the stranger, a young pig pushed its moist snout between the bars and gave a great snuffle into Janó's hand, *I'll take it,* said he drily, at which the old man didn't so much as turn round, *I'll only let the garden go to somebody who'll keep it up,* and he stood there rigidly, staring at the ground with his tiny, bloodshot eyes, *eighteen thousand,* to which Janó curtly replied that you could get a two-room flat in a block for that, at which the man set off towards the house and tossed back at him *nineteen thousand* to you, and Janó decided that there was no bargaining and he'd borrow what he needed from his uncle Jenő, he'd taken enough from Lili, half the price of the flat in the block, but then he'd not put anything in and they'd bought it with her grand-mother's jewels, *A garden?* Lili was astonished, *In the Hóstát? You'd be able to plant things, onions, parsley, spinach, whatever, at least you'd provide something as well as the money for the children, because we aren't going to get very far on that,* a third of Janó's earnings went into keeping the children, *I'll be the first in the family with a loo up the garden,* said Janó with a nervous laugh to his short, clean-shaven uncle, who couldn't be seen for books in his winged armchair in his imposing Kossuth Lajos utca office, *You mean, there's no flushing toilet?* asked Jenő with a broad smile, *One thing less to worry about, at least there won't be a smell in the house, but why are they asking so much for it?* to which Janó reluctantly replied *The garden . . . there's a big garden with the house,* whereas in fact there was a dark, damp dwelling with the garden, with no water supply or bathroom, *It's up in the Hóstát,* he added, with a searching look at his uncle's hairless face, as if that were the reason why it was so expensive, *And what d'you intend doing up there, Janó, old chap? Don't forget, the Hóstát people are all being turned off their gardens. Are you going to till the soil? That's nonsense, my boy, Jews don't know what to do with land even if they do lust after it, they're afraid of it because they know nothing about it, they gave it up ages ago, or were taken from it, because they've been exiled from their land and have been wanderers for two thousand years, and because they've chosen books instead of the soil, or whatever the reason, but we don't understand the soil, my boy, we don't even know the names of plants or anything, we stand there baffled at the sight of a bush, a bird, a rock or a cow, think about it, there are no descriptions of Nature in any Jewish writer,* and with his delicate white hand he pointed to his book-shelves, and Janó sensed that there was some truth in what his uncle was telling him, with his broad smile and immaculate new teeth, ges-ticulating with his tiny manicured hands to emphasize his point, only this wasn't a Jewish truth, and in fact he didn't know either how a river or a mountain started, how streams joined together, how shells piled up on one another, what the call of a quail or a pheasant was like, or what the wind was going to be, and what the connection was between the good soil in the Hóstát and the plump, scented, ridged, 500-gram tomatoes, and finally there and only there, in Uncle Jenő's company in the house and yard in Kossuth Lajos utca (Number 25, scheduled for demolition), did anyone think that he too was Jewish, *Turning into a peasant or something, Janó, old chap?* old Jenő Neumann asked and snorted with laughter, *It's just a sort of bourgeois nostalgia, my dear fellow*, said the old man, still a popular lawyer who even then was called on by clients and the wide circle of friends with whom he'd frequented the New York coffee house twenty years before, he had no children and liked to support the escapades of others, as on this occasion too: he stood up, took down the fourteenth volume of the handsome leather-bound Larousse and counted out the 4,000 lei in fifties in front of Janó, *Best of luck, mind you invite me to a good pig-killing, and most of all you don't have to pay me back*, which in fact Janó wouldn't have been able to do because all his money was taken up by the garden—seed, plants, bulbs, rose bushes, fertilizer, the water bill, the chickens, the two geese, the rabbits and the two piglets, because under the stern direction of old Mrs Sándor next door things suddenly started to sprout, and in the yard the Sándors were the real Hóstát people, first there was a working-class family who worked in the Armatura, then a family of Romanians from Moldavia with a pack of children, then the Sándors, proud Hóstát people: *I can still do Hóstát dancing, I've still got my polka-dotted dress, only I can't get into it these days, and I can do the waltz and the tango, you'll come to the Anna Ball with us, you can bring the girls as well*, said Mrs Sándor loudly as she leant on the battered green pillar on the porch, but an aberration had crept into her otherwise faultless Hóstát pedigree, as Father used to put it, because she was no longer a member of the Reform church but a Jehovah's Witness, though she didn't manage to convert the family and liked most of all to talk about seedlings and Abraham and his son and Nebuchadnezzar and the hundred and forty-four thousand elect who could enter the kingdom of God—as she called Paradise—and her husband went to market as he could no longer bend while she tended the vegetable and flower garden, they both did well, and in the evening, when the garden gate was shut and the little barrow had crunched over the gravel she could be heard over the fence: *Sándor, how much did you take today?*, and after the quiet reply she would start to grumble *I'd have given the things to the chickens and pigs at that price, I've made more selling dahlias on the corner,* and as evening came on she would often bring Janó the leftovers from lunch: cabbage stuffed with minced meat, because that was how they made stuffed cabbage, an apple doughnut, potato pancake and thick, sweet tomato soup with lots of noodles—*Tomato stew with macaroni,* said Janó, but he wolfed it down—and Mrs Sándor gave directions for the garden as if it were her own: *Plant a bit of spinach, lettuce and sorrel over there, where it's shady, my dear, I can give you some very good seed, and this little girl, isn't she clever, such a help to you,* because the supposed gentleman had become her best customer for seeds and seedlings, *Good health as you use them,* she said as she gave them to him with a broad smile showing only a single upper tooth, and sometimes she brought the girls an illustrated paper each, *From Hungary,* she added proudly—drawings of deer and lions basking in the sun of Paradise, *Sow lovage on the sides, it makes a good show, and there a row of carrots, celery and parsley, we don't plant paprika, we only use it in ratatouille, it doesn't do very well, nor do we plant aubergines, the Romanians do that in Oltenia, and here there'll be cabbage and potatoes, but why all that spinach, dear?* she wondered, *for the children, I see, pull up these raspberries, they only take up space, plant pumpkins instead, put about ten rows of cucumbers here, you don't have to do anything for them, just put the hose underneath every evening, a bit of maize is a good idea, and then this*—she drew a line with the heel of her cut-down gumboot around the heart of the garden—*this, look, is where the tomatoes will go,* she cried out in triumph, *I'll bring you fifty plants or so, real Hóstát tomatoes, they break the vine when they're ripe, they're so heavy, a bit of hoeing now and then and you can sit back all summer and just pick the great big tomatoes, they're so sweet I don't put any sugar in my ratatouille nor my tomato soup, but really it's a pity to cook them, you should eat them like apples, don't you think? Or like the negroes eat oranges, you want to plant a hundred? I'll get them, dear, then I'll sell them for you in the market if you like, there'll be plenty to do with it all, but you'll manage, or will you make juice?,* and without finishing the sentence Mrs Sándor changed the subject to Nebuchadnezzar and Our Lord Jesus Christ, and in spring Janó escaped more and more often to the garden from beneath the eternally unchanging notice that lied *No smoking today* and from the grey record sheets, but to the surprise of the corpulent secretary he went not to the Zsil Valley but to a newly discovered timelessness, the garden which depended on the changing seasons, sunshine and rain, one of the dwindling number of the hanging gardens of the Hóstát, and the Girl no longer came looking for him in the smoky office in Szentegyház utca but at home, in the garden, here she could water and pick things when they ripened and take them proudly home like treasure found on a mushroom hunt, or feed the rabbits, scratch the pigs' backs, look for eggs in the chicken coop—from which she picked up lice, and mother rubbed paraffin good and hard into her scalp and long, thick hair and she yelled for half an hour, feeling that her head was on fire, and couldn't go to school for two days—and Juci made a scarecrow with a red raffia skirt, long blond hair made of string and a stick pushed into a big ball-bearing which she stole from the Armatura at the next practical, and she mounted the whole thing on a bicycle wheel, and the spring breeze lifted the skirt and swung the huge doll about so that it was almost dancing in the bare garden—*It's like your mother standing there swinging her new polka-dotted skirt in the middle of Főtér ten years ago,* muttered Janó to the younger girl, as if to himself, and in spring he spent the whole weekend there: they dug the garden over, raked it, cut back the raspberries and the lilac bushes, Janó made her fetch the flower bulbs out of the cellar—there she looked at the empty vodka and brandy bottles that had accumulated menacingly over winter, from which she would make good money if she washed them and took them back, and the collection grew like a time bomb being slowly assembled —then they sat down to lunch, sweaty and covered in dust, at the table in the garden with a big brown loaf, half a side of thin fat bacon, two purple onions, a pot of mustard and some Borszék mineral water, *We've turned into real peasants!* Janó declared with satisfaction, but the garden was bare, motionless and full of scents, *Like the body of a young woman into which the seed has fallen*, thought Janó, because that was the moment that he was waiting for, that of conception, *And now we sit back and do nothing, as Mrs Sándor has told us, we wait for the hundred kilos of tomatoes to ripen*, he added, looking at the doll, swinging and dancing in its skirt, and then he spoke: *As Marx the poet says, let's get back to immediate contact with our means of production*, and he picked up the hoe that was propped against the bench, and the light, the soil and the tomatoes did indeed get on with their jobs, as had been promised, for a time, even a few years, as long as the tomatoes and the illusory life went on together, and the occupant obtained a few years of remission from himself in the garden which he had personally chosen and cultivated, until he became weary of the circling of eternity and withdrew into the flow of time.

THE CIRCLE

Freedom is circular, in any case—thought the Girl as she leant back on the unsafe bench of the rickety building in satisfaction at her discovery, after the giddying and extremely suffocating motorcycle display—*freedom is circular, like the circus,* and added conceitedly *and there are those that survive it and those that don't,* then she suddenly remembered that that was how Pisti made advances to her: *You've got a lovely round head,* indeed simply *you with the round head* was how he would address her, smiling, at which she was always cross; she would have liked a long face, a pointed nose, a thin, severe mouth, almond-shaped blue eyes like her grandmother, but all her features were quite the opposite: she'd inherited the thick lips from her father, but the round face—who was that from? Not Grandmother Kocka? And eyes that turned downward, round, of a nondescript colour, or grey on better days, *Jewish,* said Mother, broad cheekbones from Mother and Grandfather, a high, bulbous forehead unmistakeably from her father as were the bushy eyebrows, and the head, as flat as could be at the back thanks to Mother, who had been lazy and particularly so in turning the Girl over, and she hadn't turned over by herself—*Call this a round head?*! and she showed Pisti how flat it was at the back, she'd never be able to wear her hair short, but now at all events she breathed a sigh of relief because on that day everyone really had survived the display: they had been going to the Flea Market for two years now, and never before had she had the courage to buy the 8-lei ticket to go into the booth, which first trembled, then shook more and more and finally threatened to disintegrate with the din, and next to which people usually settled to sell the *loot* and the *gear,* and every morning the show was put on two or three

184

times, but on the outside, she felt after the performance, still remaining seated although the others were packing up, on the outside the whole thing was more frightening, more alarming, *freedom's more alarming on the outside*, because only on the outside could it appear that there was no physical explanation for the display, miracles must happen all the time, and so every display must threaten with death and destruction because two years ago now, as she looked at the rickety cylindrical building, improvised from sheets of tinplate and supported by iron girders driven into the ground, it looked like a biggish chicken coop and one had to go up a couple of flights of steps, and in the first place she had watched it with scorn for the cheap circus displays, the only people that went in were peasants and *prrroles* she said, trilling the *r* (that she got from Mother) and barefoot children, obviously without paying, and all manner of shabby people who had been seduced into town, who had never been to a real grand circus *like we have, to the Russian ice-show in the seal house in Budapest and on the TV*, and so every Sunday the motorcycle display roared into life two or three times, and before festivals, or if there was a big market, then four or five times with an ear-splitting din lasting for minutes, after which the acrid stench of petrol and the blue haze faded slowly, but even so merchandise was displayed next to the booth because a lot of people came that way, almost at the end of the Flea Market—though the Flea Market never had a distinct, designated end, but spread in all directions like a sort of amoeba, a living thing, a body that now tried to shrink, now to expand—but the booth drew the curious, those who had just arrived at the Flea Market, so thanks to the booth *trade was brisk*, and the round-faced Girl looked enviously at the short barker girl of her own age, as she took the tickets in a tattered ballet dress and silk slippers, who also sold the tickets and allegedly hurtled round in the cylinder with the elderly, bearded motorcyclist, though she couldn't imagine how they climbed to such a height without falling, until finally after the ambitious purchase of a ring she watched the performance, which left her dizzy for a few minutes, and when the man, in leather cap and glasses kickstarted his Java motorcycle—outside for two years they'd repeated the jingle: *motorcycle worth a lot, good to have one, better not,* but the motorcycle itself they never saw—and the ballerina sat behind him and they went higher and higher round the rusty, shaking walls, supported inside too, while the Girl stiffened into evermore daring poses: at first she merely stood on the pillion, then, leaning on the man's shoulders, raised first one leg, then the other, and the motorcycle went round and round with her at fantastic speed, and she, like a pink, slightly tatty and dirty silk ribbon, fluttered behind the speeding man, and then, as if a film were being rewound, she slowly put one foot and then the other back on the seat and, as the motorcycle slowly descended, sat back down, because the Flea Market—which had been on the edge of town as long as Granny could remember, on the road to Szamosfalva, at the end of Cukorgyár utca, on a patch of ground designated long ago on what had been Kölesföld, from which it had spread and spread—was a colourful blend of freedom and distended poverty, a vast and formless carpet of poverty covering streets and indeed railways lines which the many visible human hands laid in the dawn on Sunday as both sellers and buyers, hopefully and thoughtfully: the Flea Market started on the dusty, stony dirt road at the end of the Number Four trolleybus route, then went over the embankment—one line was always left clear, and one had to keep an eye out as one crossed since the trains to Tövis and Kocsárd went that way, and latecomers set out their stalls on the other, disused line—and all down the street, at the end of which admission was charged according to whether people came carrying bundles or empty-handed, and so were sellers or buyers, although by the time one had reached the marketplace one could either have sold everything or bought everything that one wanted, and the two teenage girls, who had started going to the Flea Market under the influence of Levente (and often in his tiny car), didn't usually want anything: just to sell for the best price they could clothes that they'd grown out of, toys, the horrible decorative objects that Mummy was given as presents, and the girls' own property too, whatever they could make money out of, and Levente's new luxury goods that he got or had brought from Budapest: soaps, black-market Postinor and contraceptives, deodorants and farmer jeans attracted purchasers from the town, whereas the girls' things were bought by country people and Gypsies—who usually bargained in Hungarian and, as they went away, cursed and complained in Romanian whether they had bought or not, and then continued among themselves loudly and garrulously in their own language—the younger girl could drive a hard bargain and sell anything, her method turned principally on getting people's attention, so that afterwards, in the late afternoon, she could go hunting on her own account with the money she'd taken, and she usually bought the same things that she could also find in Granny's attic, as the Flea Market was, like all markets before and after the war, an indiscriminate mixture of attic-style antiques and luxury goods, an indescribable assortment of rubbish and incredible worth, where prices did not reflect the value of things but the going rate of the moment in the internal world of the town, shortages and gluts, the past and the present, where a packet of cotton wool, an old, mended towel, men's underpants, a pack of coffee and a hundred-year-old hand-painted chalice were the same price, because at the Flea Market people looked for the cold comfort of objects which they couldn't find elsewhere, in the shops, and if the marketplace was threatened with being built on and made into a housing estate there was nothing there to be demolished, the Flea Market was not a place that could be done away with, not a building but a subconscious hope, a desire dreamt anew every week, which if not here would find its place elsewhere, always be reborn out of town, because there was always going to be such a place as 'out of town', licensed or not, though at one time it had functioned in the heart of town, in the big marketplace, so as to worm its way slowly outwards like some ragged, evermore ragged embarrassment, and in 1940 the municipal 'open-air market', as the local newspaper with its tendency to officialese called it, was crammed into a little area on the cattle market, next to the slaughterhouse, but as poverty increased the market people called on the city fathers and Dr Sebastian Bornemisza, the mayor (who was to surrender his office on 11 September 1940[44] to the new Hungarian authorities) to designate a new and bigger piece of land because poverty had reached such a level that the market had outgrown its site, and together with the animals it moved out of town: because animal and object, even if apparently a little farther apart on the marketplace, were still one, just like purchaser and seller, one's own and another's: because that same morning, when the Girl bent to inspect the embroidered peasant blouses among the items spread out on a black homespun cloth, a fat Gypsy woman with braided hair was sitting there on the ground— wearing a man's sweater and waistcoat in artificial fibre, a skirt of many colours, rubber sandals and a hat, and holding two chickens at her side with a string wound around her hand—and when the Girl casually picked up a heavy, old bracelet and asked—in the familiar form, because everybody addressed Gypsies so—*Argint ai?* Got any silver? the woman didn't even look at her but tried to take the solitary ring off her fat index finger, but it wouldn't move, so she put the finger in her mouth, pulled off the ring in her teeth and spat it out in front of the staring Girl, *50 lei*, she said in Hungarian, *Cinzeci*, she added, and the Girl picked up the thick ring, wiped off the saliva on a blouse, and saw that it was marked with vertically and horizontally incised crosses, *Twenty*, said she, but didn't put it on, *Fifty*, retorted the woman hoarsely, *give it back, fifty and gata* (that's that), *aren't you ashamed să-mi dai douăzeci* (to try to give me twenty), *I got it from my husband for our wedding, usca-mi-aş chiloţii pe crucea mă-sii!* (I'd like to hang my knickers to dry on his mother's tombstone!), *the drunken swine*, and something else in angry Romany, *Well, give me that twenty and take that blouse as well, that's fifty*

---

44 The date of the restoration of part of Transylvania, including Kolozsvár, from Romania to Hungary.

as well, cinzeci, go on then, and the Girl put the ring on her index finger and handed over the recently acquired green Tudor Vladimirescu[45], the 25-lei note, which the woman put away under her apron and was reluctant to give change, but still called after her to take the blouse as well, it was only fifty, *Come on back, take it, patruș cinci* (forty-five), *măi fată* (hey, girl), *come on, I'm not sitting here all day for you,* she threatened and made to get up to follow her, and the chickens too fluttered up, and afterwards the Girl, with the blouse and the ring, went and looked at the animal market, walking past a noisy, trilingual argument about a horse and the attendant avalanche of incomprehensible oaths, stroked the piebald goats, then set off back, avoiding the large cowpats, for their own pitch where her sister and Levente were selling the remaining things, drinking a beer and eating *mici*, spicy minced-meat sausages with mustard—because *mici*, in defiance of all shortages of meat, remained the staple food at the Sunday Flea Market—and as she was passing the covered concrete tables (the earliest arriving 'pros', as they were known, from whom only the gullible, fools, the inexperienced and novices bought things, gathered here) in the corner of the Flea Market—though that shapeless, irregular mass of people, animals and objects couldn't have 'corners'—a little back tent which she'd never seen before caught her eye: it was as high as a man, a circular, Turkish-looking tent, and beside it in a remarkable, carved armchair, almost a throne, sat a tall, middle-aged man in a hat, smoking a cigarette, he wasn't a Gypsy (though he was wearing striped corduroy trousers) and the Girl couldn't make out whether he was Romanian or Hungarian, and as she went over as a prospective customer might to clothes that he had laid out on the ground she could have stated nothing definite because such a person was the most uncertain, an unidentifiable customer, a stranger, a new arrival, a foreigner, the silly idea crossed her mind (what would a foreigner be doing here?), and now he too looked

---

45 A banknote bearing the likeness of the early-nineteenth-century Wallachian revolutionary.

fixedly at the approaching Girl, and on the basis of the tent and the remarkable throne she suspected that he must be some sort of fortune-teller, quack, palmist or magician, but this was countered by the fact that he was on the one hand a man, on the other hand not a Gypsy, and as she came closer she noticed a framed, printed sign on the side of the tent, the light shone on a sheet of glass and she would have liked to take a good look, but she was afraid that if she went up to it the man would speak to her and try to entice her into his little tent, but as she came towards him the man's stare softened, became almost gentle and friendly, and now she felt that the strange man had placed his throne to the left of the tent, quite close to it, so that he should in fact belong to it, yet he didn't give the impression of having anything to do with it, while the sign was on the right side so that the enquirer would be able to read it and wouldn't have to get into conversation if they didn't want to, or could avoid him, *nothing to stop me going up*, thought the Girl, without any obligation, confidently: *Dr Lazarro*, she read the big letters from a distance, and underneath: *Tränenhändler*, she spelt it out twice but couldn't make sense of it, Granny used to use the word *handlé* ages ago, but what *tränen* was (or were?) she had no idea, and below that it said: *One Person—20 lei, Two Persons—40 lei, Three Persons—60* lei the mechanical list continued, offering no discount at all, but the Girl couldn't imagine how four people could fit into the little tent, and underneath that it said: *sowie*: *Tiere, Objekte und andere*, furthermore: animals, objects and other things, that was clear, and finally at the bottom: *Offen*: *Sonntag am 10 zu 13 Uhr* (Open Sunday 10.00 to 13.00), silly to have a board showing opening times, that was when the Flea Market was open, thought the Girl, and only when she bent closer did she notice that at the very bottom it said in small letters: *Negustor de lacrimi*, and beside that someone had written in capital letters *Könnyárús*, and the Girl read that twice to make certain, *Könnyárús*, in other words *Tränenhändler, Negustor de lacrimi*, that is, *Könnyárús*, and the man, sensing that the Girl had finished reading the sign and was recovering from the initial surprise, nodded towards her with an encouraging smile, but she looked at him in confusion, and he reached into his coat pocket and held out a little printed piece of paper, according to which he, Dr Lazarro, Tear Man, municipal licence no. . . . , was open on Sundays between 10 a.m. and 1 p.m. on the Flea Market, consultation for one 20 lei, for two 40 lei, for three 60 lei, etc., discount and gift-tears for returning clients, relating to animals and objects for 70 per cent of the above price, because Dr Lazarro promised clients that he was able to rid them of very grievous and deeply buried grief, that he drew tears even from stone, the whole typed without accents on paper, and at the bottom in capital letters, underlined and with hyphens between the letters: F-E-L-T-A-M-A-D-U-N-K! We shall rise again! and the Girl thought that words in capitals, with hyphens and underlined had been an exercise in typing lessons, little finger on the shift key (she always used her left, right hand or left as appropriate for the letters, thumb for the space bar, for that she used her right hand, back to the start of the line, shift key, underline), and after reading the information in Romanian she nodded, felt for the remains of the day's takings in her trouser pocket—enough for two and a half, she decided—*Make it next week*, she thought, *I'll pay next week, for Father, I owe it to him most of all*, because she'd been there, to the Flea Market, ten years before with her father, and first they'd bought chickens, then two geese and finally two piglets which they'd taken home in a rucksack, then I'll pay for the piglets as well, and she recalled Ráchel, and now smiled reassuringly at Dr Lazarro, *Domnișoară, vă aștept săptămîna viitoare, La revedere!* (I'll expect you next week, miss. Goodbye!) said he with a strange accent, failing, like a Hungarian would, to make a difference between *ă* and *î*, but he couldn't be a Hungarian, and yet he spoke quietly, and it seemed that he had guessed her thoughts, and his voice was warm and velvety, like an actor's, but by then he had spotted another potential client coming into view, hanging his head, and the Girl twisted the new ring on her index finger and set off towards the cylindrical building where the girl of the same age as her was singing out the announcement of the next death-defying performance, starting in five minutes, which only the really brave would watch, those that scorned death, because today might be the last show, there might not be another opportunity, shouted the girl as she carefully counted out the change into the visitors' hands, just a few seats left, and the leather-coated man emerged from the cylinder and announced to her with a curt nod that they were starting, and a moment later the engine roared into life and the two girls—farmer jeans in front and ballet dress behind—stepped into the ring.

AT THE TEAR MAN'S

The performance in the Tear Man's tent consisted of a boundless, rich silence between two people at a price per person, one the listening seller: attentive, encouraging and severe, the other perpetually changing client who, after her eyes had at first looked one way and another in confusion, then looked away again and again and fastened on the black wall of the tent, finally finding relief in the Tear Man's gaze, a purchased arc that stretched from passionate beating of the heart to slow, even breathing, for she who was there had not come to talk, not to answer questions or offer explanations because that could be done outside, but to keep silence, and a single question brought the long, attentive and not inexpensive silence to a close, and then, at the end, when it was all over, *consummatum est*, because the Tear Man asked a single question: *What's your name?* enquired the man with the strangely foreign accent who sat facing her in the confined tent, and opened the big register that lay in front of him, the kind that in the old days printers produced to individual specification for tradespeople, businesses and the National Theatre, *I bet he bought it at the Flea Market*, thought the teenage Girl as she sat facing him, *because the tent too is in the back corner of the Flea Market*, and she looked aside and gave her surname, and the clean-shaven, middle-aged, man turned the pages, took out a screw-top fountain pen from an inside pocket and inscribed in printed letters the name that he had heard, only the surname, didn't put the date beside it, then shut the book again and said in a highly significant manner: *That's already on the list*, and the Girl was by this time about to get up, it was all over, picking up her little shopping bag from the floor, and as she did so asked casually whether her father had been to see him and when, but the man laid his white, manicured hand on the book—he wore a ring on his little finger, like the Gypsies—indicating that the contents of the book were a secret under his protection, *I don't know, we only note the surname, not the date,* said he, and, like in a novel by a bad writer, suddenly forgot his foreign accent—*two of your family have been to see me before you, a man and a woman, perhaps, one in my grandfather's time, because the first is in his handwriting and he started in 1904 and practised for the last time in 1938, so in that diapason of time, but not in my father's day, there's no entry, the other was while I've been here, but I don't remember, that's all I know,* he said, and the Girl was by then guessing in her mind who these might have been, perhaps her mother had been there, she too had kept the name, her husband's, for a short time, but must have come immediately after the divorce, although she had never seen her mother weeping, what would she want there, *Precisely that,* she thought, or perhaps her father had been, or Pista? what had he been ashamed of? or perhaps her sister had been in, she also came to sell things at the Flea Market, in any case, one of those born with that name, and she felt a burning desire to find out who and what they'd talked about there, and above all why nobody had told her that there was such a thing as a Tear Man, but in the Tear Man's grandfather's time it must have been her paternal grandfather that went—he'd gone up to Kolozsvár in the depths of despair to persuade his wife to come back home to Zajzon, to him and her sons, but it was also possible that people of the same name in the town, with whom they had only a distant, tenuous and uncertain relationship, had sought relief in tears in the little tent, release from the departed, those who had fled, been relocated, all that had gone, to confess their shame, because on the trilingual sign hanging on the tent the Tear Man promised to draw tears from even the hardest of people, but he put away in his snakeskin purse the two 10-lei notes which the Girl placed in front of him and continued to look at her in reassuring silence, like one that knew no more but did know everything *about them,* although neither he nor the thick book had any recollection, nor was he going to answer questions or offer help with searching in the past, he didn't regard it as his business, and with that the session was in fact over because the Girl's worthy forebears who had been there, men and women of the same name, had likewise remained silent in their language between the summers of 1904 and 1989, had been there for the same reason as this girl now, as she stood in front of the calm man with the otherworldly, vacant gaze, now a teenager no longer but suddenly a full adult, long-haired and, since the spring, freckled, who had been preparing to come here for eighteen months, ever since she first caught sight of the unusual sign, because she'd been thinking of coming as she'd wanted to watch the motorcycle display in the tinplate tent on the Flea Market, and as future clients were requested on the Tear Man's sign the Girl had brought with her a story, and more than one: *Tell the story that you've come with to yourself, in your head, tell it as if you were speaking aloud, and meanwhile look at me, but say the words inwardly, choose them carefully, don't let your thoughts drift, pick a point and make for that, speak to yourself in whole sentences, and in that way tell the story that you've brought*—was the man's instruction, and the Girl swallowed and began: 'The one is about the winter of '82, I was thirteen, and one afternoon I'd said to Daddy that I'd go and see him after school and we'd go to the cinema if there was anything on, and there was a Bulgarian war film on in the fleapit, the arrangement was that I'd go and see him first in the afternoon, but when I went into the flat I saw that he was lying there drunk and asleep, I could tell straight away that he was drunk, when he slept in the afternoon he was always drunk, the door was open so I wrote him a little note, there wasn't a scrap of paper anywhere so I tore a page out of a empty, red book and wrote: *Don't come round to our place any more, don't wait for me outside school either, I'm not talking to you any longer—"a."* because in those days I wrote my name all in little letters, and a couple of days later he came outside the school and was standing there by the statue which in school we called the three drunks, the three founders of Romanian science in Transylvania, know who I mean?, but when I spotted him waiting there I ran away, and another couple of days went by and he came up to our flat in the block, and said at the door that he wanted to speak to us, let's go for a walk, and Mummy was surprised, but perhaps she guessed what was the matter, because Daddy never wanted to "talk", and Juci came as well and we took the dog and went down to the lakes, and Daddy cried and apologized, but the wind was so strong that my eyes watered as well and I became angry because Daddy thought that I too was crying, *You don't impress me with your tears*, I told him, and I was angry, very angry, and decided that I wouldn't forgive, though I would very much have liked him to give me a hug, and he promised very, very seriously never again to get drunk, and he was going to prove that he was worthy of us, such a thing couldn't happen again, and I said I didn't believe him and I wasn't really crying, it was just the wind, and I didn't cry at his funeral either, and Mummy said how strong I was, not even to cry for him . . . I was very ashamed of my father, I think I was always ashamed of him, once even when I was in kindergarten. . . even then . . .' *Excuse me, this is another story, is it all right? I've just thought of it, may I tell it?* asked the Girl out loud, the man nodded, and she went on inwardly: 'it was late one afternoon, everybody had already been picked up from the kindergarten, and Auntie Czitrom was just waiting patiently, doing her knitting, and Juci was already going to school—and he came for me very late, I was the last, and then as well he was drunk, and we walked through the town and I was ashamed to be with him, and he wanted to hold my hand and I wouldn't let him, and he stopped at a shop window next to the Opera confectioner's and said he'd buy whatever toy I wanted, and I chose the most expensive Teddy, didn't like it all that much but I was sure it was the most expensive, just wanted to cost him money, 35 lei, said the man in the shop, but he hadn't got that much on him and so he bought a cheaper one in the end, a little Teddy with a big nose and a much sweeter face, but he couldn't compensate for the shame with a

Teddy, and there's no place in the world that I hated more than the Zsil Valley, I hated the Zsil Valley most of all, in Budai Nagy Antal utca on the odd-numbered side, down the Jiul from the courthouse, that filthy, standing-only boozer where he used to go because he could get home from there whatever state he was in, he'd feel along the walls, that's how he'd go, staggering, leaning on the trees and the lamp-posts, or sitting on the edge of the pavement, that's how drunk he used to be, I saw him a thousand times in the street, many a time I went up to him, looked straight at him, nobody up that way saw him, he'd get home quickly from there, or only old Mrs Sándor and the other neighbours would see him, then help him in, and sometimes I was so ashamed of him I wished he'd die, die! and . . . I," *actually, this is the second story I came with ready, because I brought two,* said the Girl apologetically, *I'll start on that now, I'd still like to tell it,* and the Tear Man nodded all but imperceptibly with his eyes for her to go on and look into his eyes: ' . . . years ago now my mother gave me a folder containing Daddy's writings, and in it there were all sorts of yellowed newspaper cuttings from '67 and '68 up to about '75, she'd put them together, she'd written on top of the articles the year and the month, I recognized her illegible handwriting— oct. 1967 and iul. 1968, half in Romanian for some reason, that's how she wrote the months, in Romanian—it may be that Father's articles appeared before and afterwards as well, but nobody had collected those, and we didn't find any in his belongings . . . because my mother—though I never thought so, but this folder proved it—had loved him, loved my father and admired his writings, thought he was clever, she used to say *Sharp as a needle, your father,* I don't know why a needle precisely, on the other hand Father didn't love himself, well, since then I haven't opened this folder, I simply couldn't, not because I was afraid to, but I was afraid that I'd feel ashamed of what I read, I was waiting to go to University, I'd won Olympiad prizes, my essays had been published and I used to write poetry, I'd even published my first book review in *Utunk* (on *Óz, the great magician*), the University was going to accept me, Hungarian and Russian faculty, almost for sure, if I couldn't get in who could?, but I was afraid of my father's pitiful articles, his clumsy, ill-written theatre criticisms, the way he rambled on like an ignorant theatre buff, had the wrong idea, or I was afraid that I'd find even more alarming articles—*Igazság* on top of the pile with the strident front page of *Făclia* underneath gave me a fright, with that photograph that's in schoolbooks, and I immediately slammed it shut—I was afraid that Father had perhaps even written leading articles, laudatory speeches, eulogies and homages, you know what I'm thinking of, though such things are generally unsigned, they're supposedly written by the people, the masses, or he might have written the sort of patriotic verse to "We sing of you, Romania" that you find in schoolbooks, and that it might turn out that he'd written all sorts of things, not for publication, I don't know, reports or something, anyway, I didn't cry at his funeral nor have I since, but I'm trying to find out all about him, to get his books together which we sold when he died, because there were duplicates, for Mummy and him, and I look in second-hand bookshops because he used to put his name in books, and we kept his belongings, such as they were, the pebbles from Zajzon, and I want to see the trees which he must have seen when he was a boy, if the famous avenue of poplars is still there between Brassó and Zajzon, we're going there next summer, Mummy's promised, and I make friends with people that knew him, Julika, for example, that he used to drink with, not him, I don't even speak to him, but the folder with his articles, the thoughts that he wanted to express, the notebooks which he wrote in enthusiastically, I can't open it because I'm afraid that I'll be ashamed . . .' and the Girl looked up at the clean-shaven man who, with his warm, spinach-green eyes, was listening to the silence of the client who sat facing him, because in that circular tent, as high as a man, pitched on the bare earth, in which the only furnishings were two folding chairs and a camping table, there was nothing to buy, no objects, old bric-à-brac, as on the Flea Market, not even other people's stories, there she could only sit and expose shame

and anger, and if possible weep, which the Girl had been unable to do
for five years, *since then*, and to appeal to the calm face—her father's
was now blending with the Tear Man's soft, blue-shaven, smooth face,
but they weren't at all similar—and think of where the story of cruelty
had begun, committed at the kindergarten, the teenager's, the by-now-
almost adult's, because after all that was all that she'd come for, to look
for the story of her insurmountable, dry, tearless cruelty, the origin of
cruelty in the ever-deeper and more innocent levels of time right back
to childhood: when the kindergarten had been full of anger, she had
already known how to act against her father, to cause him pain, and the
teenage Girl had behaved as a grown woman, a wife, a dragon, a mature
and thick-skinned man-hater who had screamed and thrown him out
in drunken fashion, the drunken man, *don't come and look for me*, she'd
written in a message to him, and *I've had enough*, and *I don't want to set
eyes on you again*, and *you were drunk*, the teenager had flung at him, she
was still a virgin but was disgusted, *you disgust me when you're drunk, I
can't stand you*, and *you make me sick*—the teenage Girl really did vomit
for a month, six weeks, two months, until her mother, who only noticed
after a long time that her daughter was losing weight, 48 kilos when
she was weighed in the hospital, and she was given an infusion and no
more was ever said about it—because that had been from disgust,
throat-tightening disgust, and now, in the Tear Man's tent, the shame
began to pour out: because in that horrid (her mother's word: horrid)
cobwebby room, the so-called wash house, where her father had never
done any washing, the Girl had found his trousers completely foul with
faeces—she faltered, swallowed dry, looked into the Tear Man's eyes
and spoke out inwardly—and she'd gone in drunkenly and thrown
them into the dark room when they were clearing out the house, she'd
found them, there'd been no smell any more, they were completely
dried, and she hadn't told anybody, put them in a bag and thrown them
out so that her mother shouldn't find them, or her sister or grandmother, put them in the rubbish bin on the corner, taken it out through

the gate, and the Tear Man had been softly following the Girl's every movement, all the time she'd been biting her thumbnail, and now there was blood all around it, she daren't chew it now, but she used to, and he watched, his eyes helped to steady her so that she shouldn't tear at her big, veined hand, not hurt it, and he nodded one last time, now she could go calmly into that cobwebby, dark room and look around, and that it was all over, there were no trousers there at all now, the rubbish had been taken away long ago, it was the end, it had happened, *consummatum est*, and she could bring out the folder now and read the contents, because she was no longer afraid, she wasn't going to find anything of the sort in it, and in the photographs she would only see the man whom she called her father, look at him, what a handsome, attractive, long face, thick, wavy, fair hair, his forehead high and bulging, as if there were two horn-like bumps on it, like the statue of Moses, his eyebrows thick and long, his mouth full and wide, always with a shy smile, his nose fleshy and finely curved, *A handsome man*, thought the Girl, and saw again the other, the collapsed, drunken face with glazed eyes and wet lips and in her nose was the bitter acetone smell coming from his mouth, and the sharp tang of tobacco from his clothes, but in the black-and-white photographs his green eyes were sparkling warmly, wrinkles were starting at the sides of his mouth, then appearing across his forehead, a crease or two, deeper and deeper, then at the corners of his eyes, like a fan, when he laughed, but this man had not waited for the other wrinkles and died aged fifty-nine.

DEAR PISTA!

'I'm going to talk about your *Demeters*—your book, your *magnum opus*, which I've received from you, I accepted the copy but only because you'd signed it, I'm already reading it—that is, your novel, on which first of all congratulations, I thought it was about us, the three of us, that we were the three Demeters, as you call us in the book, so I wanted to describe my thoughts to you in this letter, say that I thought that everything was at last falling into place, you'd written the story of the three of us and we could at least be together in a book, your book, because after all we were siblings even if we'd lived apart since we were two, and now here was this novel, your novel! and on its pages the novel would at last restore what our mother had displaced and at last we three, three differently woe-begotten "Demeters", could be together, no, you're not the woe-begotten one, I mean myself, me and Buci, but above all myself, but after fifty pages I realized how stupid I was and how wrong—you hadn't written about us, the three siblings, but about our father and grandfather, and first and foremost and above all—rightly so, of course—about yourself, in the third person, about women in general, about Mummy and Granny and, I thought, about the three siblings, and I felt so awful, so ridiculous when I imagined that I, I of all people, could be the heroine of a novel, it was simply nonsense, even that dimwit Buci, our damaged, epileptic brother, is a more artistic, novel-worthy character than me as he stares with his innocent, uncomprehending eyes as his mother leaves him, the same mother who takes you with her on the other hand, because she took you away, that's your gift of life, she takes you away because you're supposed to cry a lot as she's packing and because you're not what they call handicapped, you're not the backward child as Buci was called in the country, and I'm still little, have to wear nappies, take a lot of looking after, and Mummy doesn't like looking after children, you don't describe that packing of hers, and Buci didn't understand and led his own life until 1952 and beyond—I'll come back to that 1952—he looks at what happens to him in the third person, poor chap, like you in your book, he's helpless, it's as if this life had nothing to do with poor Buci's being the eldest, much more colourful, notable, lovable and worth writing about than me, because he doesn't grasp anything, forgives everybody, he's not like me, he's the unlucky sort that obviously nobody's ever going to write a novel about, because people write novels about survivors, not those that sink without a trace like Buci and as I shall, he's a poor thing, as you say, whose life has been a failure—but what lovely daughters he's got— you, on the other hand, who are certain to survive me, have a long and fascinating life, a career, a whole lifetime of success and now novels, always on the way up to the top, full of twists and turns and literary excitement, because survivors have lives of unrepeatable richness like you, because you're the envied, lucky second son, who became the first because Buci's only a half-failed little wimp and you're the real heir apparent, because Mummy took you with her when she left—the reason she's supposed to have taken you with her in 1927 when she left for Kolozsvár and deserted her husband and her sons was that you cried so much when you saw her packing, and father told her, "Take that child with you, Bőske, can't you see the way he's crying?! What am I going to do with him?"—but I really thought that the book, your *Three Demeters*, was going to be about us, and as I finished both volumes of it I had to realize that you'd made me appear in it twice, precisely twice, all of two half-sentences, that's exactly what I amount to in your book, as if you'd casually trash me in the course of reading, you could sweep me out of your autobiography, your *vie romancée*, at a stroke, without anyone noticing, but now, dear brother, I am actually the trashed hero of your book, and now I mean to reply to this biography, this literary creation, because neither our late father nor the late Buci can object, nor Uncle Pista, Daddy's brother, whom Nature also endowed with the loss of his mind, his self-tormenting half, so that he shouldn't understand what had happened to him in 1952—yes, we keep coming back to that—and not the women either, whom you don't put in because in your opinion history is only made by men, even Mother can't make herself heard because she's got nothing left to say, because she's deaf to everything, finally closed up, and most of all not Granny Annus, who brought me up in the end, the one woman from whom we received warm affection, even she can't ask you now, Pista, how you imagine that 1952, because if that date hadn't happened, or the second volume of your book, I wouldn't be writing now—a bit on the late side, I know, because the second volume came out much later, but still feeling the icy breath of your book, because I've finished it now and I hope that I'll have the strength to send this letter—because from your book I've discovered your scorn for our father, what in the first volume of *Three Demeters* in 1973 and in 1980 in the second volume you call hatred for his class and the past, and which you talk about countless times even though in 1980 you can't stress class alienation any longer, Pista, that you know, in 1980 such a thing is simply no longer possible, it's risible to hate a class, in 1980 the entire vocabulary's ceased to exist, the way you say *antipathetic folk* about the proud people of Zajzon—Bogát, as you call it in the book (were you thinking of Marosbogát? there are no medicinal springs there, but never mind)—*antipathetic folk* is a very clumsy expression, forgive me, where did you pick it up? and generally speaking this constant reference to people as *blokes*, whatever else our father was, he was never a *bloke*, a grumpy man, difficult and snobbish lower-middle class, a doctor of sorts, ungainly, but a hardworking Székely and obviously quite a bad husband and father, don't write that stupid word again, please, so what you and I thought at the age of twenty-five, after the war, we simply can't think now at the age of fifty after 1971 and the Theses, when all hope has died, though now

I'm evermore deeply suspicious of our thoughts at age twenty-five—
perhaps we were wrong from the start and have been ever since, perhaps
we imbibed error with our mother's milk, literally, from the breast of
the founder of the Romanian Communist Party, because we've both
run after our mother as if we were terrified that otherwise she'd desert
us again, and I can understand that in the book you quickly gloss over
Mother so as to deal only with yourself, but you could have put an illegal communist in it, not a Jew, of course, who was excluded as early as
'46 from the Party for which she'd spent ten months being beaten up
in Szamosfalu prison—that can only have been personal revenge, or do
you know why it was?—and by the way, when I first looked her up after
the war, in 1949 I think it was, I thought that Mother still played a
serious role in the Party, but she clammed up and said nothing when I
mentioned the Party, just like when I pestered Father about her, he
knew nothing, and I never found out why they kicked her out, not a
word was said about her deserting her sons, so it was best to gloss over
a mother with such a past, I thought when I read it, and of course I
realize why you put nothing about her being excluded from the Party,
so I understand that you gloss over her because as far as I'm concerned
too she's dead, long dead, been dead since she deserted us—Buci, father
and me, that is—but all the same you can't seriously be thinking now, in
1980, dear brother, you can't believe that in 1952, when Grandmother
Annus and her family (Anna Gödri was her maiden name) were relocated and Father went up to see you in the Ministry in Bucharest and
you were already a big name in the Ministry of Finance or the
Economy, whichever, and you had a lot to do with the currency reform,
and Father went up to ask for your help because you were the only person of influence that he knew as he was no longer in contact with the
village doctor (who'd had everything taken from him), and you not only
didn't help them and never even went to see them where they were
relocated in Erzsébetváros on the Küküllő in Dumbrăveni, where the
Armenians used to live, 150 kilometres from their home in Zajzon—

which neither of them was to see again—not only did you not go to see them because you were afraid for your career, and not only did you do nothing for them, but you prostrated yourself to your ministers saying excuse me, I'm very sorry, I've got these relations who've had to be relocated because they had a couple of acres of woodland and grassland and a number of houses in Zajzon and medicinal springs which they've used for healing people, they ran a clinic, so please punish me, and you were afraid of being kicked out of the Party, that too you would understand, but, as you say, when you were confirmed in post in 1949, when you got your first important job, you'd already written everything off, made a full confession of your family and the past of your social class and its unforgivable sins, you publicly denied our father, didn't even go to his funeral in 1959—*at the time* everybody understood that, it was a difficult revolutionary time and you were a big man—but to get back to the deportation, because the relocations had started in Brassó—or rather Sztálinváros, as it was then called—and the region, Grandmother Annus was living on nothing with poor Uncle István, her own son and Buci, her grandson, the two mentally retarded ones, and fortunately Buci got some sort of work helping a joiner, obviously people felt sorry for the old woman with her two hapless relations, but I can understand that you thought that was all right in 1952 and that you needn't offer any assistance to your grandmother and your sick brother, didn't even meet with any of them, but did public penance for them, we don't go visiting people that have been relocated, that could harm our career, very well, I can understand, in your position I might have done the same if I'd had a career or something to worry about, but that you wrote this down in 1980! Nineteen hundred and eighty! but not because you were describing the pitiless times and the things that one was forced to do against one's family's interests, how debased and merciless one was, how completely mad, trod on anyone for the sake of an idea, nor did you put it in your novel because conscience was troubling you for never again having seen our supposedly favourite grandmother, and your diabetic brother Buci as well was sent off there, got no medical attention, but how even now, in 1980, can you try by this novel to prove your self-sacrifice, your loyalty, and to whom?! in 1980 you can't be thinking that it was right even if in 1952 you believed so profoundly, if that's how your book is altogether to be understood, it's an autobiography to that extent, but how else could it be, if it were about someone else that person too would be you, and I can't believe that you're so blind, such a low-down villain or so stupid, and it wouldn't be possible to write coolly and impartially in the third person, it had to be that "I" did this, it's me that time has made ridiculous, the time that has since gone by, because it's made a mockery of you, laughed in your face, because in 1980 our ideals and the Party haven't been anywhere for a long time, or to be precise they're everywhere, in you and in me, and in my innocent children too, who stand there making a *tableau vivant* on his birthday, and now of course we know precisely that there was no point in sacrificing our gentle-eyed brother and our grandmother for the "cause", but in 1980 only a dead man can write such a thing, so of course we know that this woman too, Grandmother Annus, is completely left out of your book or is just a grey shadow cast like a blot on your past, because I too am ridiculous with my mistakes and my blind faith, when in August 1968 I put on a suit and went to join Lili and her family in the park, the Kányafő, because I was expecting the Russians to come from Bács, I waited for them wearing a dark suit and tie, formally dressed, and in the end, all the same, I was right, I whom you de-Stalinize, because if you remember in the August of '68 *he* shouted in our ears that foreigners weren't going to swarm all over our country, long live independence, he condemned the invasion of Prague, for which the stupid West applauded him and considered him a great hero because they didn't realize that it was just a smokescreen, all he wanted was to be able to remain dictator, to do as he pleased here, and I was dressed up and waiting for the Russians but I knew nothing, and as it finally turned out that was the last chance of stopping him, for anybody from outside to impose order and push him out, but at the time everybody applauded his daring announcements, and I was the wild Stalinist when I appeared dressed up on the dusty Bács road on that Saturday, 24 August, and afterwards too everybody fell down and worshipped as after '68 he sat down to talks with the Hungarians and there was a Hungarian publisher, books and new magazines and TV programmes in Hungarian, and there was a Petőfi-house and Hungarian rectors at universities and for a little while a facade of freedom, but no relieving army appeared on the Bács road, neither from there nor from anywhere else, but then came July 1971 and the July Theses at Mangalia, and bang!, that was the end of the three-year facade of freedom, in came ideological purity and censorship, because after July 1971 one couldn't believe in anything any longer, and it was just then, July '71, that my younger daughter was born, the first in '68 and the second in '71, the opening and closing points of freedom, and so all the same—I have to admit—I actually envy you managing to kill off your father at least in this book, you settled accounts with *the bloke*, one's father is nothing but punishment, punishment, a burden and handicap, I see it in my daughters, and for that reason too you must be so fit and strong a man because in principle at least you've disposed of your father—you don't drink or smoke, you haven't changed!, you play tennis, drive a car, go hiking, have a wide circle of friends and acquaintances, and if you want to see the amazing difference look at me, everything that I've listed does not apply to me, and you'll certainly outlive me because then you'll write your memoirs differently, you'll say in a fresh burst of brilliance how everything happened according to you: *How must it have happened?* or some such title, and that'll certainly be in the third person because you won't be able to say "I", "I was", "I did", everything in that done-by-another third person, he's guilty, and I'm afraid you won't remember a thing about 1952 but the currency reform and your State decoration with which they bought you, and the great communist bank-robbery of the late '50s, then too you'll write an official history book instead of an account of your own life and the things that happened to you, and you'll say that you didn't understand, didn't know, didn't notice or didn't suspect because you were naive, "IT was naive and unsuspecting", like that, because you won't even be able to put your name in that book, but then you'll believe that you're now really writing about yourself and that'll be your new role, if there ever is another world, and you'll write in your future autobiography that you were neither victim nor hangman, you'll explain yourself instead of describing something that happened in which you took a bad decision, on 23 August my younger daughter waved to you when you were on the platform and she was very proud that there was her uncle, and you were there in the stadium when his birthday was celebrated, that you might describe, for example, when you all watched the tableau of children in the January frost, or how do you see yourself?, as a chronicler?, someone who writes down word for word in the third person what is dictated to him? you're a pen-pusher who doesn't write his own words but is dictated to by Party discipline, the decision of the Central Committee was dictated to you when they shut down the Hungarian University of Kolozsvár, and you'll do as you're told, you'll do the dirty work, they'll dictate that you were to persuade the teaching staff to condemn the counter-revolution in November 1956, does someone dictate everything to you?, your own books are dictated to you and so you can't say "I", how many books have you had published to date?, let's just look, here they are on the shelf: *Two encounters*, 1949; *The first step*, 1950; *The other front*, 1959; *The forgotten man*, 1962; *Mist and sunshine* (your first novel!), 1965; *Daily bread*, 1967 and in Romanian 1974; *Three Demeters I–II*, 1973 and 1980, which is what we're talking about here, this 1980; eight books, Pista! that's a lot, eight, it's said that stenographers taking dictation don't remember a thing about what they take down at breakneck speed, the greatest secrets of State can be entrusted to them, news of the liberating end of the world, even their own death sentences—it all becomes signs which they turn both ways, letters into signs and signs into letters *ad infinitum*, but they've got no idea what they're writing, do you see?, and I'm afraid that if you're ever able to divulge the great State secrets that have been entrusted to you, what has been, *How it must have happened*, you simply won't remember them, it'd be as if you didn't have a memory of your own, take, for example, a totally insignificant detail, the blurb on *Three Demeters* says, obviously with your approval—or perhaps actually written by you—that your first short story came out in 1949, and perhaps, Pista, it would be better if the saving ray of memory were focused on that date, and according to this it was the revolutionary upheavals that made you a writer, whereas the only book that I rescued from Father's was wrapped in the *Brassó News* for Sunday, 5 November 1939, and recently I undid this out of curiosity and began to read bits, and just fancy!, on page eight I find a short story entitled *The Artist in the Blood* by one IT, aged fifteen!, how proud we all were of you, lower down is a feuilleton by Renée Heves, on the opposite page a review of *The Scales of Nationalism*, I just want to remind you, Pista, this little story is about a Czech conductor, Konrád— you chose a Jewish name for him—who infects an entire small town with the love of music, a symphony orchestra has been formed and is rehearsing for a special performance under his direction, but the double-bass player is forever playing wrong notes, and on the day before the concert the conductor ticks him off for the umpteenth time, that's wrong, and he informs him that perhaps it is, but he's the mayor, the head of the municipal administration, so that's how he's going to play it even if the conductor does think it's wrong, at which the special performance next day is cancelled because Konrád ups and leaves town—it's a pity you don't remember that piece of writing in which you spoke of the artist's attitude, the impossibility of compromise, with the obstinate faith of a teenager, and in 1949, of course, it could no longer have been written because the 'mayor' would perhaps have been taken by everybody for Gheorghiu Dej, the Party chairman, but after all it's surprising that you should be ashamed of your teenage story, of course it wasn't well written, and perhaps you weren't a hangman as you later assert, but it's immaterial who delivers the final kick to the man that is down—as an example of a man that is down, take László Földes, editor of *Utunk* until he was pushed out in 1959 and couldn't publish a single line until 1970 and then died in '73 (his wife committed suicide shortly afterwards in Israel, did you know?), or the poet László Szabédi, who threw himself under a train at the news of the closure of the university in '57—it's immaterial who kicked these two unhappy, condemned men and how often, and which kick was the fatal one that ruptured liver or kidneys, or whether one merely stood in the square when the sentence of death was publicly carried out, because there was a square, wasn't there, that's how people were seated at these executive Party assemblies: the committee, to left and right their supporters and those with something to say, and facing them the accused on the scaffold, and there you sat as the most important agent of the Party, and furthermore, to your misfortune, at the time you were an activist in charge of cultural affairs at precisely the most difficult of times, after '56, and there you sat because you considered it your duty to sit there, and you even presided in the case of Földes, in which you're unfortunate, because those that look on in silence and those who execute judgement are one in belief, dear brother, and there you sat on 9 January 1959 and you too voted to exclude Földes from the Party, evidently on account of some "ideological impurity", his literary criticisms, András Sütő pointed out to the Party Földes' ideological errors to a total of twenty-nine, and Földes was dealt with by a simple show of hands, and yours too was raised, carried out the sentence, it didn't matter whose wish, because now we're saying, aren't we, that we can settle accounts only with our own, can't we, you know, one in belief, those that look on and those that act, and I'm not forgetting that I too was among the onlookers, I wasn't sitting on any side of the table, I wasn't physically present, let's say, but I found out everything—from the next day's paper, for example, where it was beautifully put, surely you too remember:

eight didn't vote for Földes' exclusion, eight did not, though I grant you that this too was merely show because there had to be votes against and abstentions, and then in the end it didn't matter, after all it's possible that all the characters are held on strings, and then it doesn't matter which arms or whose move at the word of command, the 'cons' or the 'pros', and it's possible that someone will remember your accusatory speech at the session, like a skilful show of manoeuvring, but it doesn't matter, you were there, you voted, and perhaps the fact is that you couldn't do anything else, because you were on the merry-go-round: you became a deputy minister, Party secretary, member of the Central Committee, regional delegate, second secretary, then you were dismissed for a while, then you were needed again, went back, and finally became county trade chief, commuting between Bucharest and Kolozsvár, and so you went up and up, and sometimes down a little too to keep you disciplined, allowed the use of a villa in Snagov, special shops at the end of the '50s, a car and driver, a rented flat, and then again a reduced salary and back to production in charge of the furniture factory (this was the "low point" for you), but in the end *alispán* in charge of commerce in Kolozs county, *alispán*[46]—the word has survived from the hated previous regime, and you became an *alispán* like our grandfather of the same name as you!, because in our family everybody's called Miklós, István or János, and Grandfather was district magistrate of Kőhalma (he also had the good luck to die in 1948, so he wasn't relocated), and I know that you won't do it for yourself, that you've only got one car and a rented flat in Dávid Ferenc utca, not your own property, obviously a matter of conviction because you despise property, right, and you're always ready to lend a hand: if I'm needed I'll come, and if not, I'll modestly stand aside and keep quiet, until now you're slowly going into retirement, there'll be a private, intimate celebration in the private room of University House, the table covered with

---

46 The senior elected authority in an old Hungarian county,

delicacies that you never see in the shops, but—console yourself—you're the last Hungarian in the municipal authority, and at least there's been one, and perhaps after you've been retired your phone will no longer ring, perhaps your friends won't call to see you, and you must think that you've died as far as other people are concerned, but that happened long ago, Pista, both of us died, so then we're shortly to be assessed as to what will be inherited from us, what's the bequest, if our descendants can still read Hungarian at all, your son goes to a Romanian school, perhaps you're right and I shall leave nothing behind, only that sign, the one that our parents—it's a strange thing to say, to the best of my recollection Father and Mother were never in the same place, let alone under the same banner—that sign, do you remember?, used to be in the lounge of the hostel in Zajzon, and I rescued it: *Rugăm a nu face politică*! (Please do not talk politics) because at that time, in the '30s, there were still heated debates in three languages in our dining-room, and later it became more and more painful for the staff and so the sign appeared, it was mainly needed after 1940 when Transylvania was returned to Hungary but Zajzon was left in Romania, but I'll leave all that, there's nothing to be said today, but we're getting off the point, Pista, you'll feel as if you've died when you're retired in the autumn of 1984 and I too now feel that I shall be dead by that time, but it's as if I've never been alive, because for us life was over when Mother took you with her and left Buci and me with Father, and nevertheless I was grown up in mind and rushed after her, after her ideals, but we "Demeters" are all dust and ashes in your book, like our aunt and uncle, whom I never saw because Mother didn't think it important for us to meet them, relatives and family didn't exist as far as she was concerned, and the Jewish relatives have vanished like aunt and uncle and their children, a boy of four and a girl of three, our little cousins, whose names only you were able to write down, you knew them, because everybody, all Mother's relatives lived in Kolozsvár in those days as did you, and so it might be more important for you at least to preserve their names than to write *How it must have happened* with IT Number One in the third person so that you could leave behind those two little children's names—Frici and Sarlotta—and their mother's, because only you know that, because nobody can remember them any more, but the rest they will: the *főispáns*[47] and *alispán*s, the great historical deeds and actions which can be read about in newspapers and reports, in minutes and in your books, your novels, because they'll remember our lives, if indeed we were living persons or just heroes in a book, and if, dear Pista, I too manage one day to write this letter addressed to you.'

---

47 In the time of the monarchy, the governor of a county.

MY BELOVED COUNTRY

Then he continued on a following page in a different-coloured ink: 'And thank you for helping Lili and me so often, you got her that wonderful job in the store, and you see how she's got on, developed a lot, turned out to be not just a good maths teacher but also a marvellous economist, been promoted again and again, and not long ago she even graduated from the Party college, the Ştefan Gheorghiu in Bucharest, even though she's a Hungarian and a woman, and now she's chief economist, she's in charge of the supply of shoes and clothing to all the shops in the city, and all housekeeping items from furniture and crockery to mouse-traps, she's very ambitious, always was, she can work hard, of course these days there's not much by way of merchandise, it's getting to the point where you can only get hold of man's underpants if you've got connections, so anyway, thank you, Pista, she wouldn't have this job if it hadn't been for you, you've really been a good relative, and you've done me personally a lot of good as well, never turned me away even when I've put you in a painful situation . . . (*crossed out after "even when"*) but I wouldn't like to distrain on you further, nothing of the sort's going to happen, believe you me, no painful situation's going to arise, we'll be careful, that is, I shall, because I've got to be careful, I shan't ask you for anything ever again, and I promise that I really won't'—but at this point he broke off the sentence because he felt it too mechanical and outworn by now, he had so often made this always broken promise out loud to his wife and daughters, but he couldn't easily have torn these letters out of the thick notebook, it was actually bound, he'd written them into a hard-backed notebook, not loose sheets, as if he'd had no intention of ever sending them to the addressee, perhaps hadn't really meant them

as letters but had some deeper purpose for them, because this fat notebook with its red leather binding wasn't an ordinary one that came from
the shops, nor even something bound by a bookbinder, but a real hard-
back book: it's a blind book, as printers term it, such things used to be
produced by printers if they had a biggish job on so as to assess accu-
rately by means of this draft book the dimensions of the book to be
printed, so that everything went precisely where it should and by the
time that they started to print the book everything could be calculated
to a millimetre, and he'd written his letter in this blind book, this mock-
up book, as it was officially known, which he'd brought from the
printer's, or rather picked up, when he'd still been working there, a long
time before the scandal, in fact he'd stolen it, but he saw no harm in
that, it was the most natural thing in the world, everybody took what
they could from their workplace, and so he'd started writing in this
thick book of a hundred snow-white pages in which a silk bookmark
had been inserted, another thing that was always planned: his own
book, this blind book, on the title page of which there had not yet been
inscribed the long name of the creator of the golden historical age, two
words, seven and nine letters respectively on two lines one above the
other plus that certain little tail below the 's', because the name could
only fit into a single line in the large-format *Omagiu* (Praise) albums,
and below the name the lengthy, descriptive title of the book would be
printed, likewise in gold lettering, because these books never had a title
consisting of one or two words, and the photograph of the smiling face
wasn't bound into the mock-up book on the first page, just the so-called
chalked paper, its dazzling whiteness protected by pelure paper with
spider-web tracery, a blank page and yet full, excluding all doubt as to
what this page was for, as if the grinning portrait was already there, and
this book now gazed blindly into the void in the hand of the letter-
writer: it lay there, empty still but already full of writing, at once liber-
atingly pure and cripplingly full as if the virgin paper were already a
palimpsest, and the blind book had now been waiting long years for

the first spidery lines of his Great Works, because Janó had chosen this very blind and empty book to write down his every injury and pain and bitterness *as a response*, on the pages which were blank and yet full of recollection, a reply to Pista and everybody else, and as he took the book in hand in the rainy spring of 1984, when it was for a long time impossible to work in the neglected, swamped garden, it was not the great novel that he wrote but he filled it with letters to Pista, earnest, long considered, full of reproach, and perhaps he remembered that he also had his elder brother to thank for the fact that he had escaped the weightier punishment that he might have had for a printing error: his ex-wife's advancement at work certainly terminated with this mistake, and bang went his children's university admission too, such a husband, even if only an ex-, and father was a serious blemish on a family, because he must have brought this blind book home at will, but *after that* had no longer been able to lay his hand on anything, had to leave his job at the printer's as a thief: because on one night shift he made a printing error—only one, but a bad one, he didn't misplace a word or omit one, not even a single letter, but he omitted the cedilla under one letter in the poem entitled *Ce-ți doresc eu ție, dulce Românie* (What do I wish for you, beloved Romania) and was thinking of the Hungarian translation, his own version, or: *What am I to wish for you, my beloved country?*, and was thinking *This is too short, there have to be twelve syllables, though like this it would rhyme with 'my Romania' in the next line, that is, the best rhyme with that would be 'my mania', as my friend Bubi the sculptor is always singing 'It's my ancient mania, to drive a tank through Romania'* and he carelessly omitted the vital cedilla under the *-t-* , just in this poem in an innocent bilingual volume of Eminescu, which had to be set by a Hungarian printer, and so in setting the type he replaced the letters *ț* by *t* throughout the most important cult poem in the book, one which Pioneers and actors piously declaimed at every festival, their lips radiant, the work of the melancholy nineteenth-century poet, the Petőfi of Romania, who lived a wretched life, finally becoming deranged, and children recited this poem with such fervour that at that moment one believed that they would unhesitatingly lay down their scarcely lived, brief lives like the poet in the poem, for *ţara mea de glorii, ţara mea de dor* (my glorious country, my yearned-for country), but through the omission of that infernal cedilla the poet was no longer singing of the land of desire, the glorious fatherland (*ţara*), but of his burden (*tara*), and Janó found out, but only when he ventured much later to look up *tara* in Laci's pre-war two-volume Romanian–Hungarian dictionary, 'Hey, Laci, what's this about a bale? Some technical term?'—and now the sacred poem spoke of 'my weighty land, my burdensome land, *which is a burden even to behold*, added Janó to himself, because that little nothing of a cedilla had become as interchanged as the unspeakable name of God on the quill of a Bible copyist when his attention wanders and it is no longer with total self-effacement that he toils at his humble task but he, Man, is present in it too, Man, who errs, becomes weary, whose mind wanders, who dozes, is hung over or actually drunk, in that confusion of 't' and 'ţ' is revealed the man himself, who has now fallen into Satan's clutches and committed a grievous sin by his own hand, and for his infamous crime the executioner will have the sinner's head like that of a thief, so that he may never more have the chance to write a single defective line, and so Janó committed a similar fatal error at night in the printer's: five thousand copies had actually been printed and had to be recalled from sale and reprinted, and he was to make good the damage done to public funds over ten months by deductions from his wages in a different job, and the outstanding sum was written off under pressure from Pista, County Director of Commerce, because the press was the last place in which Janó had anything to do with letters, where his hand touched a letter, and the job in the cooperative furniture factory followed, which likewise *dear Pista* also obtained, because as he had been director of the Libertatea furniture factory for a short time he still had connections there, and then Janó merely copied invoices into grey and pointless ledgers, and as he now closed the book, on which there was still no one's name—though there might have been two inscribed, the one man's in letters of gold, and the other's if he had had a name that could be written and his own book to go with it—as he closed the book containing the finished letter he saw before him the bronzed, short, powerful figure of *dear Pista* as he had seen him not long before in the street: he'd been in a good mood, friendly and cheerful as always, wearing pressed linen trousers, a white cotton shirt and white Chinese trainers, his freshly shaven face redolent of lavender which could be smelt at a distance, and he was off to somewhere on his short legs with little agile steps, his tennis rackets protruding from his sports bag, it was a Sunday morning, and he was just crossing Kossuth Lajos utca outside the Sora, where there had never been a zebra crossing, and he'd called out cheerily *Hello, Janó, must dash, got a match at ten o'clock at the Babeş garden, wish me luck, I'm playing this chap from Bucharest, big noise from HQ, everybody's in, er . . . know what I mean,* and waved pleasantly and ran off, his new false teeth gleaming between his broad, flat lips, and he reassured himself by swinging his bag of tennis rackets towards him, his weapon of war, and in such a way that it seemed that he'd really been pleased to see his brother, and the white figure slowly vanished down the wide road leading towards Főtér, and Pista had been to Janó like a bright patch of summer sunshine in the morning, a sight for sore eyes as he ran through the town, while Janó was on his reluctant way, dishevelled, grey and hung over, to the class celebration at his younger daughter's school because Lili had an assessment to see to and couldn't make it, but he'd promised, promised ten times over to be there, and as he shut the book with the letter to his brother—but without the as-yet-unstarted writings—he saw himself as ridiculous and pitiable as he sat there in his damp flat that was almost never cleaned, with neither water nor WC, and he'd looked for a long time through the dusty window and struggled to find the most appropriate words for the letter to Pista, and yet he thought that he was right, there was a truth which was his, and this truth began and ended in 64 Nagy Antal utca, in the twenty acres of garden, and that furthermore others had different truths and different lies and fortunately they would go into oblivion together with the copy of *Brassói Lapok* for 5 November 1939, tattered and preserved for no good reason whatever, because there was no point in remembering details, and Janó felt as if he were still that bereft child whom his mother had abandoned and who now too depended on the support of others, a *burden*, a weight, a millstone round somebody's neck, mainly his own, a *tara*, tara mea, tara mea, *my burden, my burden, my most grievous burden*, he muttered to himself, meanwhile Pista was running lithely about the tennis court in the Babeş garden and the healthiness and confidence of his strokes could be heard a long way off, the force with which the ball was returned from the middle of his racket, and one could tell that he was really going to win, he was going to win, that afternoon he was really going to thrash that big noise, that fearsome and very serious tennis opponent, that chap from Bucharest—he had the nerve to do it, everybody would admire him and have their fingers crossed for him.

NIGERIA

Mummy, just imagine, I dreamt that—but she didn't know how to begin the complicated, octopus- or serpent-like dream of that morning, she'd talk about it over coffee, she thought, and Mummy put the coffee into the red-spotted enamelled mug, added three spoons of sugar, held it under the tap and turned it on, but the tap began to splutter and then in the tones of a chesty old man, gave a dry cough and fell silent: *Water's off*, she announced, then her eyes sparkled and she said cheerfully, *Then Würtl's coming today*, because unexpected arrivals of Sándor Würtl and the cutting off of the water supply had been somehow become mysteriously, but all the more markedly, linked: the indefatigable suitor from Budapest actually only came to call on them at holiday times, about Christmas or Easter, when the water was indeed regularly cut off, and sometimes it was on other days too, or only hot water would come out of the tap, and at such times the nervous Würtl would appear unannounced—like somebody that was already a member of the family, thought the girls crossly—on the late Baltic Orient express, and as could be made out from the mysterious omens that night too he turned up dragging two big cases on little wheels, *Sándor, for the love of God, don't come here again with these cases on wheels, you'll be seen, they'll know at once you're a foreigner staying with us, and I'll find myself in the police station*, because Würtl knew very well that he couldn't send a telegram or phone, it was better just to ring the doorbell, that way he would seem less conspicuous, because foreign guests could only be received in private homes if notified in advance and approved, and the grandparents were always terrified because of Uncle Zoli, and had been forbidden to go out into the town in the red Zaporozhets (it was parked over the

220

road, at Aunty Buba's), and it had been Uncle Zoli, Grandmother's approved relative, that had brought this Würtl to visit them the first time, but this was now his umpteenth unheralded visit, and his presents were laid out in the big room: a snakeskin handbag and belt for Mummy, and for the girls identical pleated skirts (too small for them, not reaching to their knees), an umbrella and a silk scarf and polka-dotted, beribboned blouses, *Don't imagine I'm going to put this rubbish on!* Juci laughed out loud when her mother wanted her to try them, and Würtl spent all night smoking his long, brown St Moritz cigarettes in the kitchen—on the third night he rummaged in the rubbish bin for his slender stubs—and drinking the Romanian brandy which Mummy had decanted into a Hennessy bottle and which he couldn't praise highly enough, and all night he argued and tried to persuade Mummy while the younger girl was trying to sleep in the big room, and suddenly she became aware of Mummy's sharp, high-pitched voice as she burst out: *How can you say that my children are Romanians?* at which Würtl began to placate her, that wasn't what he meant, *but why was the young one reading a novel in Romanian now?* and Mummy retorted, *The young one's just won the county Olympiad in Hungarian lit-erature, she's had her poetry published in* The Young Worker *and* Our Way, *I'll show you if you're interested—No, don't bother, I'm not interested*, stam-mered Würtl, *And the older one*, Mummy went on, *is going to university to do Hungarian and English, so how can you say such a thing, Sándor?* and a lengthy silence followed as Sándor explained something quietly and fully: America, contract, two years, Nigeria, and again the Romanian children, at which Mummy spoke up, *Sándor, that's not the point, you can't imagine what the situation is here*, and indeed he couldn't, because in the small hours Mummy brought in the cold stuffed cabbage for him off the balcony, made with five kinds of meat, *Absolutely the same as ollaputrida*, thought the younger girl, for dinner he'd had fresh roast sucking-pig in its skin with pickles and mayonnaised potatoes, and *salate de beouf*, downed Grandmother's *beigli* with poppyseed, orange and raisins, drunk the Hennessy brandy, appreciated the coffee (made with mineral water) with creamy buffalo milk, and felt the thick, half-metre long candle by which they sat in the night was romantic, indeed, thinking that Mummy was sending him a secret, amorous message (a Romanian colleague of hers had got the candle from the Orthodox church, because in winter the girls used it to study by when the electricity was cut off), and when Würtl came to call the cats hardly showed themselves because he hated them, believing that they spread diseases, were dangerous and above all completely useless, *To Nigeria*, was all that Mummy said when he had gone back to Budapest a week later, and as was her custom as a serious mother she had prepared the ground and in a conversation rendered immediately tense, *You're big girls now, I can discuss things with you*, she added, one was fourteen and a half at the time, the other seventeen, *We're going to live in Nigeria for two years, and after that we're going to America together*—and she looked encouragingly at the older girl—*because Sándor's American contract begins in Nigeria, so that first we're moving to Lagos, that'll be very exciting, won't it?* she assured them in a wheedling, high-pitched tone like the one she used on the cats, but with that the conversation was effectively ended, Mummy was dead beat after a week of entertaining and did not herself know whether she wanted to inform the girls of her decision or to confer with them, but both girls immediately got up from the table and went to their room, Juci took down the school atlas, turned the pages for a moment, then declared the future: *Nigeria's in Africa, capital Abuja, population 119 million, good Lord, official language English, that's all right, has the world's biggest deposits of columbite, what the shit is that?* and no more was stated, but the two girls also were worn out by the daily history lessons of Dr Sándor Würtl, the physicist with piercing piggy eyes, and by his analyses of the national mind of the Romanians and their low-quality inherited genes, which they had listened to with wordless fury for three years by then, ever since he'd been courting Mummy, in whom love was strongly supported by parental urging and considerations of the girls' prospects, *He's a tidy man, reliable, serious-minded, nice-looking, has a good salary and doesn't want any more children*, Grandmother listed the virtues, and the uncle from Budapest also interceded in the Sándor affair, because Mummy's short-lived move to Budapest, or rather Kelenföld, in 1976, when she went to be with a curly-haired, blue-eyed judo champion, *What did you expect from a dim-witted sportsman?* her mother asked Lili when she came home starry-eyed with the girls from a summer holiday by the Balaton after a brief acquaintance, but over that Würtl week, during which Mummy's double bed had creaked regularly late at night, and the two girls had deduced from the panting and exclamations that Mummy was now very serious about Sándor and was trying hard, even putting the cats out of her bedroom at night for his sake, and on the second evening Juci realized that if the plug was pushed into the socket in the wall between the adjacent rooms, less was audible of the sound of the distant union, but a month later, in a ten-page letter, Dr Würth took leave of them and gave a detailed account of the 'fatal wound' which 'your family' had inflicted on him, and left for ever for the island of Lagos so that afterwards he should long remain present in their lives in the form of some salted peanuts, two pairs of corduroy trousers and a quantity of instant coffee, because every six or twelve months mother was notified of a foreign-currency transfer—the sum was not stated—which after a little investigation they spent together in the dollar shop on the side of the Hotel Napoca: instead of farmer jeans they disappointedly bought green corduroys, *That dumb Würtl can't even send a shitty pair of farmers*, Juci fumed, *he might at least have sent the stupid money, we could have changed it with the Arab students and bought proper farmers at the Flea Market*, and their mother could only with great difficulty persuade them to have the velvet trousers, and the trousers bought with dollars, which Grandmother turned up, represented no value of any sort until their downstairs neighbour Laci, an architecture student at Bucharest university, admired them and asked where these beautiful girls' Levis came from, *Did you get them at the Flea Market?* to which the younger, the one with the unmanageable hair—*You've got a comb*, as Laci teased her, because her fringe stood on end like a cock's comb—asked in embarrassment what came from where, and Mother gave up perfume and they got chocolate, coffee, a big pack of salted peanuts, a tin of cocoa and a previously unknown chocolate cream with the dollars of Dr Alex Joseph Würtl, never more to be seen, and they set off from the shop for Grandmother's with a foil-wrapped 1-kilo bag of salted peanuts and there ceremoniously opened it, together with the chocolate and cocoa, and Klári was regretful and with tears in her eyes spoke of 'that decent chap' Sándor as of one dead, *he so worshipped my coffee, how much he helped us, even now we're drinking his coffee*, she snivelled, *But all you're interested in is that Romanian man!* she flung at her daughter, *If only you'd stop thinking with your you-know-what just for once!* shouted Grandmother, who, in Mummy's opinion, had never thought with her you-know-what, *Poor Granny's frigid*, she said sympathetically to the girls, *that's why she quarrels with your poor grandfather so much*, and Juci could never imagine how anybody could be frigid around Grandfather, who allegedly still took women to the weekend house at the Kányafő at the age of sixty-five, but Mummy wasn't prepared to divulge further details and the subject didn't interest the younger girl, and once she said to Juci that Mummy had certainly eaten a lot of octopus when she was a girl and that was what caused her man-dependency, she'd read somewhere, because girls ought not to eat octopus unless they were getting married, *Where do you suppose Mother ate any octopus?* asked Juci, *Perhaps she's passed it to you*, her sister laughed, because Juci by then had a boyfriend who often slept over, *Anyway it's a symbol, in case you don't know, it's a Basque legend*, at which Juci burst out laughing, *Ah, Basque, of course, Basque! Mind you don't lose your virginity, little lunatic, nobody wants to find it! Everybody laughs at you in school, the way you're always on about virginity!* but in any case they spent a nice afternoon at

Grandmother's with the salted peanuts and the coffee, and Grandfather
didn't join in the noisy conversation: *These are complicated woman things*,
he said to 'my pal', the younger girl, as if she weren't a girl, and she took
herself off to the mansard to cry because it was all her fault, and the
monstrous sentence still echoed inside her with which they'd driven
poor, decent Würtl away, because she'd read about the unfamiliar country in the library, *People go to normal countries: they emigrate to Hungary
or escape to the West, but who goes to Nigeria, Ni-ge-ri-a?* she blubbered,
because after Würtl had left she looked up the article on Nigeria in the
Encyclopedia Britannica in the cold, dimly lit Academy Library—she
had to use a lens to read the tiny letters crammed into the two-volume
micro-edition, the library had been presented with the copy because it
couldn't afford the dollars for the full edition, and there was a special
drawer in the slip-case for the rectangular magnifying glass—and
through the lens she'd read the first line in shock and disbelief: *It is one
of the poorest countries in the world*, read it over twice to make sure she'd
understood that its GDP (the first time she'd heard of it, evidently the
means of assessing poverty, because according to that a unit of poverty
had been invented) was much lower than that of Romania, and she
would have looked up her own country in the second volume to compare the two figures but there was no data, only under 'Hungary',
though the pinhead-size letters were careful to point out that the
data there too were not from the most reliable source, as the country
in question had reported on itself, furthermore she found out what
columbite was good for, America was the biggest customer, used it in
space exploration—so Würtl had something to do with columbite, she
thought, he was studying it—and that Lagos was a snake-infested
island, and what the climate was like and the flora and fauna, and then
she opened the *Bolshaya Sovietskaya*[48] as well, all fifty-seven red-bound
volumes of which were within arm's reach, but in that the huge African

---

48 The Great Soviet Encyclopaedia.

country appeared much more harmless and attractive, and so that day she went home by a very roundabout route, the sentence beginning *one of the poorest countries in the world* pulsing in her throat and choking her, which as an objective and unquestionable opinion had settled their fate once and for all, the snow had left off, her thick hair had frizzled up completely by evening, *It's as if there were snakes growing on your head*, said Juci, and next day in the small hours in the unheated bedroom—on the wall on the street side a persistent patch of mildew disfigured the paper, they kept drying it out with an electric fire—once again she woke sluggishly after dreaming of snakes: in the morning, when she wanted to comb her hair, she looked in the mirror and on her head, like a moving hairdo, little snakes were coiled up, she was like a Greek statue come to life, and after a conference at the weekend the two serious girls confronted their mother on Sunday evening—she'd just switched on the TV to see an old American film and was about to do the ironing—and spoke in unison, *We're not going to Nigeria because it's full of snakes*, at which Mummy gave them a long, surprised look, *And crocodiles*, Juci added quietly and uncertainly, and looked at the floor so as to remain serious, but Mother gulped, which the girls took to mean that snakes sounded like a bad proposition, because Mother was petrified of frogs and any kind of reptile—when the younger girl had been in Year Five she'd brought back a little green frog from an excursion to give her shock, and she didn't speak to her for a whole week—she couldn't bring herself to touch a worm, screamed at lizards and would have passed out at the sight of a grass snake, and Juci had to pack up Würtl's present of a snakeskin handbag and belt—Mother dared not lay a finger on it—for her to take in to work, where fat Mrs Bruckenthal in Accounts gave her a good price for it, and now she was thinking of spending two years with Dr Alex Würtl, atomic physicist, surrounded by snakes in Nigeria, *The poorest country in the world*, said the younger girl seriously, with Würtl, who, furthermore, detested cats, instead of waiting for the other, unsophisticated V, as that evening and always in the past ten years, and it suddenly seemed such stupidity that she began to laugh in ringing tones, as since then she'd not been able to, at the water being cut off one morning in between two holidays, and at the way a few years later the determined teenage Girl quickly picked up *Utunk* to see if her latest poems were in, and her eye caught the front page, to which she usually paid no attention, as if it were not part of the paper, but the word AFRICA brought her up short: 'African visit' she read in March 1988, the President was visiting Nigeria and other African countries to bear, prophet-like, the news of world peace to the Negroes, *So he'd have been to see us there as well, wherever we go he comes after us*, she thought with a shiver, and among the names of the distinguished writers, beside Lajos Létay and Jorge Luis Borges, she read for the first time her own name, and as at half past seven she picked up the Friday paper at the kiosk outside her mother's office in Deák Ferenc utca and set off up Minorita utca, then crossed Farkas utca, because the class was no longer in the little classrooms of the Reform College but in the big building, and where she came out into Petőfi utca beside the grey Academy Library the school was on the left, but it was not the one where she would have liked to go, but teaching in Hungarian there had been stopped, and on the right was the former prison and the Hangman's House, and she paused for a moment on the corner as if unable to decide which way to go, and it was after eight o'clock, *There's nowhere to go*, she thought, she could have gone into school late, she didn't care about lateness and detentions, she was always getting into trouble, *There's nowhere to go*, she thought, and looked to the left: perhaps she'd go and sit in the dimly lit rooms of the library, there it was behind her, and be able to go on with what she'd left off the day before: her essay on 'The figure of Pan in mythology' which she was writing for her school-leaving examination, or, as the sun was just beginning to shine, go for a stroll in the cemetery, where not so long before there had still been executions, or the Hangman's House! because she'd heard it was being demolished and you could see inside, and because the world was boundlessly rich and interesting in Petőfi utca too, *Ah, there's nowhere to go*, she decided, and although she was late, went in for the shorthand lesson.

MEN'S SHIRTS

And after the incident with the yellow *ushankas*[49] she declared, *I'm not ironing any more men's shirts!*—though a certain pink, purple or pale apricot (according to the girls, 'Romanian colour') shirt she would be happy to iron every day, the shirt of the always elegant, quietly spoken man who left Mother to herself every year or eighteen months without saying a word, but his *horrible Romanian scrubber*, as Mother called her, did his ironing, because only Grandmother took exception to V, that is, Vasi (the girls' none-too-witty nickname for him)[50] or Vasile's origins, and felt that it was a betrayal of our family, but Lili meant the sentence *I've finished; I'm not ironing any more men's shirts* to mean the break-up of her marriage, whereas she never had to iron for Father, partly because they'd been a young and very poor couple (more precisely, Mother was the younger of the two) and there was neither iron nor board, nor poplin, linen or cotton shirts, and the mythical start of this marriage, going back to before the children's time, began with a piece of farce in Mother's cheerful account: at half past four Father would get up when his Soviet alarm clock rang and go to the printer's to proofread *Igazság*, at which Mother (Kitten) purred to him that she would get up with him: Father: *To make me a coffee?* Mother: *No, there isn't any coffee.* Father: *A cup of tea, then?* Mother: *No, there's no tea either.* Father: *A glass of warm milk, then?* Mother: *No, sorry, there's no milk either.* Father: *Then, to feel sorry for me?* at which point the listeners would laugh and

---

49 Russian word, a cap with flaps to cover the ears (*ushi*).

50 The wit comes from the blend of Vaszi, the standard corruption of his name, and *vas* 'iron', whence *vasal* 'to iron', so this is a colloquialism like *fagyi* from *fagylalt* (ice-cream), *süti* from *sütemény* (cake), etc.

clap their hands, and the story was called on as an example of love and poverty—in Mother's view the two were inseparable spiritual conditions—and the farther we went from divorce and the brief marriage of evil memory the softer the voice in which Mother purred forth the touching tale, because the young couple (she twenty-five, he forty-two) lived together happily in the Monostor flat, but for a short while—according to another evaluation, for a short while but happily—and Father wore fashionable shirts in artificial fibre, and a pullover and a singlet under them, and checked flannel, and in that marriage Mother didn't *need* anything at all because she was basking in the almost paternal love of the older man, undemanding, accepting, and she didn't cry out for 'it' at all, not after the incident of the yellow *ushanka*, and with that sentence she scratched out the faces of the entire male sex, even to the extent that *I'm not ironing any more men's shirts* summed up her entire experience, and it had to appear and quickly disappear from the stage of Mother's temptations as did Naszvadi, the smart judo champion of Budapest, Dr Sándor Würtl, the well-off atomic physicist of Budapest and USA via Nigeria, Gábor Nagy from the Gödöllő-Pécs–Szombathely axis, artistic intellectual of unknown occupation, antiques dealer and marriage cheat, a kind of *thieving swinish villain* according to Grandmother, because he turned up in his red Lada, ate a lot, cracked political jokes, brought 'dangerous' newspapers, and then vanished with the eighteenth-century portraits on paper of the 'ancestors', Great-grandfather's sword, a big photograph album with a brass clasp, sundry small items of silverware and the thirty-volume edition of *Jósika*, and in the meantime the greatest mountebank and humbug for years—Vasi Vajda, aka Vasile Vaida, the softly purring married man who played fast and loose with Mother, aka Tompuss—he was from Kolozsvár itself, *din Cluj, din Cluj*, as the country people emphasize, as if it were not a word but a concept that anyone should be a Kolozsvári, that is, actually born and living in Kolozsvár as distinct from Méra, Bács, Tordaszentlászló, Apahida, Szamosfalva, Kolozs, Gyalu or Fenes, nor even some deportee from the Olt or Moldavia, a real Romanian of ancient Kolozsvár stock (Grandmother: there's no such thing as a Romanian of ancient Kolozsvár stock)—so this Vasile Vaida, who for fifteen years, in his shirt of *Romanian blue*, hung about Mother's pretty, slender, white neck like a millstone, not letting her escape or even die, in short, Mother's experiments, her attempts at conquering her fear of men, were a series of border raids and incursions in which on the one hand she was hopeful and on the other had was forced into decisive situations: to go or not to go, to go to Budapest, Nigeria, USA or Gödöllő, and whether to marry again, because the two went together, marrying and ironing shirts, and marriage would involve the further care of existing children and possibly more yet unborn, together with the bringing up of fractious teenage daughters in the hard years of the '80s, but Vaszi Vaida, as if he were a secret agent, *un securist*, knew precisely when to reappear on the scene in his blue shirt—Juci maintained that Romanians in the country painted their houses blue so that flies wouldn't settle on them—and with his fawning, Mother-charming, feline voice and with renewed vigour set about further Mother-deception: he was getting a divorce once the mortgage was paid off as the children (his own and Mother's) would be grown up, he'd be able to get an independent flat as the children would be off to University (none ever went), or, 'Iulia' went on to herself, when you're old and decrepit, when certainly flies will no longer land on you, when you're like a skinny, mangy cat such as those outside on the rubbish heap, when even the dogs won't want to know you, even then you'll be scrabbling on my doorstep—but burdens like that, *Aşa o povară, Iulia, frunza mea albastră* (my blu-u-u-e le-e-e-af, a phrase from the love-song they both liked, a pan-pipe, that is, a *nai* played the opening bars, after which Mirabela Dauer sang in her full, resonant voice), Iulia, I don't mean to heap things like that on your weak female shoulders, purred V about the ever-uncertain shared future, whereas nothing of Mother's was strong except her shoulders and hands (and her temper), and the girls were slapped for the last time at the age of fourteen, after which Juci had asked in a menacing tone *Will you leave me alone?* and caught hold of her mother's hand, but Vaszi Vaida—otherwise the girls liked the big-nosed, slim football fan because he didn't play at being a father, didn't slap anyone, and altogether didn't expect anything, as the men around Mother usually didn't (with the exception of Würtl)—*He's a real gentleman* was Mummy's opinion, on hearing which Grandmother burst out *How can you call a Wallachian a gentleman?* Vaszi brought her flowers, kissed her hand, paid her compliments, was there and gone, didn't have to be taken seriously or feared, but how had Janó, the forty-two-year-old, divorced, uneducated father—he hadn't managed to finish university (or anything else), but entirely through the Party line became a lecturer in Philosophy (but according to the register, Scientific Socialism) at Kolozsvár Theatre Academy while it still functioned (his kindly, powerful elder brother had had a hand in the so-called unification of the Hungarian and Romanian universities, that it, the closure of the Hungarian one), which lectureship twenty years later had been elevated into Aesthetics and Philosophy, how had this worthless father, who, apart from wavy blond hair, a pleasant self-irony, wide erudition, a certain good taste, but all the more defective other forms of knowledge, had nothing worth speaking of to bring to the establishment of a marriage, with his occasional published articles, his scattered, disorganized family and his repressed childhood, how had he attracted Lili of the 58-centimetre waist (she'd made her father make her a stiflingly tight belt which she wore under her dress, and when she sat down it dug into her ribs), the eminent, self-assured student and mother of challenging beauty, who by then had a degree in Mathematics—she'd gone in for maths because the hefty Tibor Barabás had also enrolled for that, and the previous week, just before the entrance exam, she'd broken off with Laci Tóth, who was going to study Philosophy and become a teacher of Hungarian—whatever did that radiantly lovely girl want, because Janó was marrying the daughter of his friend, who came of a *good* family, and Father, who'd been attracted to this good family—indeed, to any family, any human warmth—married not only Mother but also Grandmother and Grandfather as well, and in the end Grandfather became his best friend (he'd been born in 1910, Father in 1925), and thus Father also acquired parents in place of his own (his mother lived in Kolozsvár, but they hardly ever met and never warmed to each other, while his grim father was in retirement in Zajzon) and Mother and Father, that is, Lili and Janó, had never spent any time together until June 1966, when the lecturer had to be replaced in Mother's final exam in Scientific Socialism and Father was available and took over in the big hall of the proud building in Farkas utca, and there she was in front of him, Lili, daughter of Laci Kühn, whom he'd known since she'd been seven, Laci's daughter, the Laci in whose garden he'd spent so many Saturdays and Sundays, and for a while had taken his first wife Nuci, the ballerina with a marvellous figure and big breasts, during their brief marriage: by Nuci he's had a lovely Romanian daughter Karmen, or Carmen, Romanian child of Hungarian parents, half-sister to the girls, who at Father's funeral in faulty Hungarian demanded her due, a share in his estate, *These flowers have a nice smell,* said she of the tuberoses which her younger little sister (what a thing! she'd suddenly acquired two little sisters for the afternoon) was holding —in Romanian there is no different word for 'scent', so a flower has a nice smell or a big smell, and Mother too used to say, when the sharp-scented boletes were being dried in the roof space, that they had a big smell—*I not yet sit in Kolozsvár,* said Karmen after the funeral (she'd come from Germany—East Germany, Mother made it clear) on holiday, her ballet contract kept her there but she'd been able to come to the funeral because it was the summer break, but *I not yet stop,* she added hastily, *as tomorrow I must to go back,* but even before that *I must to run quite to the doctor and my contract was now approved for the next season, I must only to receive the invoice, if there is such a thing here, or some document from the finances that my social is paid in, social security, I not know how I must to say it here*, all with an unmistakeable Kolozsvár accent tinged with Frankfurt-an-Oder—and with the said social-security certificate in her hand she vanished for ever from the green-grey eyes of her sisters, because as they sat up on top of the Kányafő in Laci's garden the two equally tall figures of Laci and Janó were all but indistinguishable at a distance, because despite their difference in age Janó aged quickly but Laci held the process in check, but Laci was Janó's better self: he didn't drink, cared for his family, kept the house and garden in order, pruned the trees, trimmed the bushes, painted the summer house in spring, was in constant motion from morning to night like a man possessed, like a busy, hard-working Székely, and after Janó's death he took care of his garden too for a while until it was sold, and Laci hadn't even been present when Lili was born, met her only when she was three, and later used to escape to the garden and his customers, to which Grandmother would say every evening W*ell, you've had a good sit-down* and glance coldly at the kitchen clock, but it seemed that his wife couldn't forgive him for being the cause of her giving up her 'painting school', and Janó was Laci's better self: he was a warm-hearted, affectionate, sensitive young man, could almost have been called cultured, and perhaps gave the girl, his future wife, precisely what she'd never had from the taciturn Székely father who ruled her life rigidly and had expectations which differed from hers, because Janó blamed himself for everything, the way alcoholics do, and Laci and Janó, Janó and Laci were equally astounded when she said yes to the seemingly casual question, intended at the most as flirtation or teasing: *Well, Kitten, will you be Janó's wife?*, because the two of them had been to a big barbecue one Sunday afternoon in the garden on Kányafői út and were strolling up through the Bács forest to the viewpoint, and on the way had picked a few bitter indigo weeping milk caps, and Mother carried off the finds in the apron of the pretty pink dirndli that she was wearing—both teenage girls were too big for that dirndli while Mummy at the same time fed us and sighed that there was nothing to eat, and the 58-centimetre waist and the belt became the female pattern to follow—and after the official announcement Grandmother baked the fungi that evening with sheep's cheese, bacon and parslied potatoes and they ate them in silence in the solemn middle room of the house in Dohány utca, opening out the big table ceremoniously so that as there were only the four of them they should sit farther apart, so how could Laci have said to his best friend look here, this is nonsense, Janó, you're an alcoholic (the word was never uttered, *poor Janó had one fault*, was what everybody said, and kept quiet, or *It was the drink that carried him off*, or *If only it hadn't been for that stinking pálinka*— though actually Father didn't like *pálinka*, only shop vodka), because Laci had had a quite different husband in mind for his precious daughter, and Janó, who had by then reviewed all Lili's suitors, was taken aback at his own proposal and had added, on the dusty Bács road, *Lili, little Kitten, wouldn't you rather marry Tibor Barabás or Laci Tóth?* and was about to list the reasons why he was a poor choice, but Lili wouldn't listen to a word of it but made a cross gesture and said *Now listen here!* and was seriously annoyed, *I'm not interested in your salary! Is that all you care about in life?*, and then there they were in the recently purchased flat on the first floor of the four-storey block in Monostor (Is that why you're getting up, to feel sorry for me? goes the marriage oath), three rooms bought with the proceeds of Lili's grandmother's jewellery—in fact, she was very generous to them, but neither she nor Lili's parents went to the ceremony (of course Janó's didn't attend) because this was a *modern wedding*, light-blue minidress, brown suit, no church, no wedding breakfast, no honeymoon, just the two witnesses—*We shan't have the children baptized*, Mother had stated during the fungi meal, and Janó, lecturer in Scientific Socialism, nodded, *No insolent priest is going to tell me that God's created my children when I've produced them, I've created them*, and it seemed that Janó had already to move away from that act of creation, but Grandmother was to slip away with the yet-unborn girls (*Don't want a son!* exclaimed Mother, *I'm leaving him in the hospital!*) and hold the two in the water of baptism

in St Peter's church round the corner—at the wedding there were only
the two witnesses and the totally mindless love between two unlikely
people, Mother was radiant, her body, to which the blue satin minidress
clung, her firm legs, her pointed breasts—the cups of the tight silk bra
were conical in shape, like funnels—her resolute face, her tall, lacquered,
blond coiffure, she was all passion, looking purposefully ahead, blue
eyes shining, broad cheekbones delicately rouged to make her face, her
pretty, longish face look even thinner, pointed nose immaculate, because
there Mother stood at the moment of the first big decision in her life:
now she was going to bear children, cook, keep house, and she took the
pen and dynamically, proudly, signed her new name because this was
something that indeed she wanted! and Father at her side in his soft
brown suit and narrow crocheted tie looked on warmly, romantically,
like a man that was only imagining it all, as if this wedding were not
wholly real but rather some scene in a puppet play, a pleasant green
mist rose before his eyes and, like a snowy winter landscape seen from
a speeding train, the fine detail wasn't visible, but it was August, and
Father reached slowly and carefully for the pen, not wishing to frighten
off the picture which was so indistinct in his dream, because he was
standing beside the last and only Woman, the twenty-five-year-old,
slender, self-aware and determined Woman, *This is the woman I have
always loved, in her mouth and in her heart I have been,*[51] seventeen years
later he read Ady's lines to the younger girl, who wanted to become an
actress (or was it her father who wanted that?) and they both knew of
whom Father was thinking, read to the Girl who was to be born in
Laci's house, in the mansard room where her mother had studied, 3
metres by 2.5, there the first and second children were born between
paper-thin walls, because it was only later that they moved up into the
new prefabricated flat for just a few months, until for Mikulás presents
Mother bought the fatal yellow *ushankas*—the warmth of love hadn't

---

51 Lines from Ady's *Hiába hideg a Hold* (It matters not that the Moon is cold) of
1909.

yet cooled, it was just a cold winter—and Father's Mikulás present was an inflatable Mickey Mouse *of mouse-skin*, he added, because mouse skin is *stroky*, soft, and as early as that same evening it had burst, the little girl, Father's favourite, began to cry and Father put on his hat and went out to look for another, *Janó, don't go, you won't get one*, Mother begged him as if she knew where he'd go in his desperation and that he'd only come back late in the evening when the children were asleep, *So I deserve it*, she shouted, *so you aren't ashamed of yourself, so you want me to kill myself*, and Mother got the girls up, dressed the two half-asleep children in the front room with impatient, rough movements, *We're going shopping*, she declared, and put the new yellow *ushanka*s on them, fake-fur caps as she called them, white and yellow fur and pompoms, and the sentence *We're going shopping* was the first that remained in the eighteen-month-old girl's book of souvenirs together with the rough, almost painful way in which her mother tied the flaps of the hat under her chin, and the leather cut into her and chafed and was all wrinkled up underneath, she was sore when it was taken off, *We're going shopping* although it was late evening, and she bundled them out of the flat, and all that could be seen of Father were the soles of his shoes as he lay full length on the yellow settee in the big room, *Daddy—on the settee—in his shoes*: the first of a long series of images that the girls carried away: 'man drunk in bed', but Mother shut the door and the children, torn from their beds, waited shivering for the Number 4 that took them straight to Grandmother's house, and it was on this trolleybus that the little one learnt her first words of Romanian: *Coborîţi? Coborîţi?* she asked twice in swift succession like adults did to people standing in front of them, are you getting off? *Coborîţi? Coborîţi?* she asked Mummy at the corner of Dohány utca because there they were, back at Grandmother's, and she opened the door without a word, asked no questions, and Mummy herded the girls up to the mansard, and none of them ever set foot in the Monostor flat again until Mummy got her new flat in the prefabricated block—*my own*, she stressed, and shared it with just her children and the cats—in the Györgyfalvi district on a twelve-year lease, and she announced that *I'm not ironing any more men's shirts*! because in Father and Grandfather, both the former, the father who as an abandoned child had likewise abandoned his own children and couldn't handle responsibility, and the latter, who had met his child at the age of three after coming back from Romania to his family who were stuck in Hungary, embodied the entire male sex, and it was no good their supporting one another, sharing their trials and tribulations, 'men' remained something incidental, unreliable and erratic, nobodies, blokes, here today gone tomorrow, a faceless generality, a technical necessity for procreation, a *must-have*, and in the fourth year at school the younger girl drew her family tree—her chest swelling with pride all the same—as Mrs Károly Soket *née* Mária Szabó, under that Mrs László Kühn née Klára Soket, all framed by thick lines, and to the side, as if only a sibling, László Kühn, then below that her mother and at the bottom herself and her sister, and she connected Father to Mother with a dotted line but didn't connect him to herself as if he were nothing to do with her, *This is our family*, she held it out proudly to the teacher because what a careful and detailed drawing it was, to be sure, but the teacher didn't like to enquire why the men were left hanging in mid-air, perhaps they'd all died? and Mummy said of her former suitors, those whose children went to the school in Brassó utca on the Number 3: he was almost your father! and the Girl had the strange feeling that the town was full of her older siblings, their relationship involving a sort of foreseeable, excessively logical and calculable failure of Father and Mother which only the protagonists had failed to see, because they had taken the crazy risk of getting married, having children, going back to their parents from whom they would hear for years *I told you not to go and marry that wastrel Janó*—then less forcefully but sympathetically, *Poor chap, a nice man, but a weak character*—and the Girl adduced the first memory in this very logical and, in terms of historical inevitabilities, calculable plot—that of the yellow faux-fur *ushankas*—every time that she wanted to punish her mother who, moreover had brought her up alone, because she couldn't forgive that yellow *ushanka*, and in revenge she told Janó in the summer of 1984— Juci was off to the seaside again with Levente and Mother, for the first time in her life, had gone to the lakes for a few days with Vaszi, because one day he'd appeared with his snow-white Dacia with a 1000 number, considered a veteran car and kept under a tarpaulin and which regularly had to be push-started in the morning in winter, and the girls laughed aloud as they watched from the window as Mummy, in her high heels, tried to push Vaszi's car and sprawled flat on the ice like a frog, anyway, Vaszi had appeared, purred something to Mummy in his beautiful, deep voice at which she'd melted, packed a bag and said apologetically that they were going to the lakes, and the black-haired Vaszi, smoothly shaven, well-groomed, perfumed, sat and smiled in the kitchen, *You'll be going over to your father's, I suppose?* said Mummy—in Hungarian, to show that it concerned only the two of them, perhaps some rare piece of good news—but the Girl went as far as the garden, not into the smelly house where there was no bathroom, but into the big, well-stocked garden, in the middle of which she stood and in answer to her father's timid question *And your mother . . . ?* she told him about the white Dacia and the lakes, *I think they've gone to Tarnica, Beliş or Fintinele,* she realized something, *they haven't taken a tent, so it's Fintinele for sure, because there's a hotel there, for a few days,* she added out of spite, but whom she was cross with she herself didn't know: with her mother, for taking a holiday with a man-friend who was not at all unpleasant and was kind to them all, but she never took them away anywhere, *How can I afford it? And when? Shall I steal the money? I work all summer, don't you realize?* she would burst out, because just once they'd been to Mamaia on a holiday voucher, or was this Girl angry with her father because once more . . . he was in a 'what do you look like' condition, and he'd promised never to do it again, or was it with that man who, of course, was never going to get a divorce, as everybody but Mother knew, *What d'you expect from him? He's a Romanian! It's in their blood*—they were all lies according to Grandmother, I tell you straight, I wouldn't like two Romanian brothers, added Juci, or perhaps she was cross with Juci for going to the seaside without her, *Begging your pardon, but we can't look after little ones, so sorry you haven't got your own boyfriend that would take you*, and the furious, impotent Girl felt that everybody had left her, she was of no account and wasn't getting a holiday! and there she stood in the middle of the garden and out of spite told him all about the white Dacia owner's last evening visit, what there'd been for dinner—stuffed eggs, fried liver, cutlets, aubergine salad, baked paprika—and they'd listened to their favourite records, that fat, backside-swaying Mirabela Dauer, one after another in the sitting room and danced to *Frunza mea albastrăăăă*, and then she came to the description of their secret wine, they'd drunk Perinița, the sweet Murfatlar wine, from Great-grandmother's goblets, and *perinița* that Romanian children's kissing game, played with handkerchiefs, which they too had played in the yard with the Romanian children, the boys had to catch and kiss the girls, but the previous evening not only had there been no *perinița* but neither had there been V, because he'd turned up unexpectedly that morning, and the offended Girl also told of how the previous time Mummy'd bought a savarin, that cake made of semolina pasta which you dip in syrup and cover with whipped cream, she always bought one from Katona's in Deák Ferenc utca when V was coming because he had a sweet tooth and Mummy was no good at making pastry, *According to her we don't even like it*, and even for V's sake she hadn't learnt, the most she could do was mix custard if some were brought from Budapest, but when they went to Bucharest on an assignment (by sleeper, added the Girl) they always brought back Turkish sweetmeats, but nothing had been said about V.'s having disappeared for six months, and Mummy had sworn she'd never speak to him again, *the dirty swine, she'd chuck him out so fast his feet wouldn't touch the ground*, because V always slunk back into the family nest in

Caragiale utca, where the Romanian woman perhaps made the same threat to chuck him out, and so father and daughter chatted, the one blinking in the sunlight, looking into the distance and putting together the pieces, trying to condense them into a single picture with the title 'Mother being happy' out of which he had fallen ten years previously, or before that had featured in it only faintly, as if the invisible photographer had focused on Mother and in the hole where Father's face had been, like in the sheets of coloured cardboard outside circus tents, somebody else's face appeared from time to time—Naszvadi, Würtl, Vaida—and then Mummy would burst out *I'm not ironing any more men's shirts*, and in that picture of her mother on a trip to the lakes which the angry teenager compiled in early July there had suddenly came the chance of vengeance, now betraying her to Father, revealing the secret which she at least had kept until then, or it was a kind of spoken incantation for Mother to be happy and not only for three days, Monday to Wednesday, because that was how long V's business trip was lasting, but she was looking into the distance as if seeking distant obscure details, as if there she'd be able to glimpse the solution, which still didn't seem logical or make any kind of sense, and Father, unsure of himself, unsteady on his feet and stinking, with whom this Girl was now very angry, who had slowly fallen completely out of the family picture, accidentally hit the stem of an almost fully grown tomato plant with his sharp hoe as he worked the soil—six weeks from then he wouldn't be hoeing it, it would be pulled over him—and finally this Girl was furious because this was all just delusion, Cicánka and Ciculescu making eyes at each other as in an animated film, rubbing together, little pink hearts fluttering above their head wherever they went, farther and farther away, towards the lakes at Tarnica and Bélis, but it was all at the most two or three days, well, a week, say, and another official trip to Bucharest, and after that Mummy's lips would thin and she'd assert in rage that she was never going to iron another man's shirt.

CATS

L and L were linked by a passion for cats like a kind of umbilical; a lifelong affinity, a secret, almost morbid alliance, an almost disease-like cell proliferation, which originated in 1938 from a single cell called Jozefin, a little dark grey cat found in the Rio cinema in Patak utca, when, at the start of the matinée showing of *Bluebeard's Eighth Wife*, as the principal male character was buying himself some pyjamas in a store, L asked for the hand of the future mother of L., who was sitting beside him, to which she without a thought, with lips pressed together, aware of her fine picturesque profile, nodded curtly as she looked straight ahead, but she was as disturbed by the sight of male pyjamas on the screen as by the proposal of marriage, and the pyjamas, Gary Cooper, Bluebeard, Laci and the two proposals, on screen and in the cinema, were completely mixed up in her head, and on the way out afterwards Klári heard frantic meowing behind the leather-padded door from the cinema foyer and bent down for the singing Jozefin, to be named after the Rio cinema and Josephine Baker, took her into her arms and away only so as not to have to look at Laci, and then this Jozefin travelled to Vásárhely to call formally on Lili's parents, then to Parajd to be introduced to his parents, to Szováta for an engagement holiday, from there to the sea at Constanca, then back home, and a year later was purring in the office of the salt mine at Ocnele Mare, under a reading lamp on the engineer's desk, with two legs on one side folded under her, *She's having kittens*, said Laci, and with her big belly the cat could scarcely jump up to warm herself under the green lamp, and shortly afterwards the first litter was born, which they succeeded only with great difficulty in giving away to local Romanian colleagues and peasants in the area, who regarded cats as useless creatures, but from the next Oncele Mare litter Laci kept a soot-black tom, because their old house—the new one wasn't yet ready—was full of mice, and this Lajos, more exactly Lajos I, came immediately below Jozefin, honoured as ancestral mother, on the family tree drawn up on a sheet of Klári's old drawing paper folded into four which Laci made for Lili's eighteenth birthday in February 1960, passing to his daughter an enthusiasm for cats and to his grandchildren one for family trees: with regard to the precise ancestry of the then Mercedes and Samu IV, Laci said *How do we know where we originate*, and handed over the creation with both direct line of descent and lateral branches, who had appeared meowing one fine day over the rooftops, through the roof void or through the hole made for the cats in the pantry door and, as future wives and husbands, at once acquired equal rights in the cats' lawful territory so as to spawn in swift succession their one-colour, tabby, patchy and spotted descendants—indeed, they made nonsense of the laws of genetics—or they had simply strolled in off the yard through the open kitchen door and announced with drawn-out meows that they were there and hungry: from then on they all belonged in the family and found their way into the genealogy kept in Laci's tiny sloping hand, and Klári couldn't bring herself to dispose of the kittens but Laci kept a sharp eye open, and any descendant of the forbear Jozefin—especially if it was pure steely grey (blue, as it's called, from which the breed takes its name), with short, dense fur, blue-tinged skin underneath, and eyes with a green glint like the great ancestor—was to remain in the house, and Laci and Lili then honoured the blues like superior beings, Egyptian godheads, blue-blooded aristocrats, to whom special delicacies were given—chicken liver or heart, gizzard to chew, or Laci's very favourite, the parson's nose—they were not turned off beds, they were allowed to curl up and doze of an afternoon on the warm top of the big Philips radio console, and there was even a kitten named Csombi, *Look at the way she dozes with her chin between her paws*, said Laci at the time, and he spent a long time admiring his favourite, he added the years to the names on the family tree when he remembered, and the big lacquered root-wood box served as a reminder as the photographs that it contained were dated on the back: *Lili and Samu, aged four* (Samu, that is), *Klári with Balti and Szüri, Mother with Petymegy and a cat that turned up today* (and underneath in a child's hand, *Kormika*), *Mother in court dress with Árpi on her lap* (he died tragically shortly afterwards, trampled by a mounted policeman), *Lili's birthday, the guests holding Szüri and her five kittens* (we gave them away, to Auntie Gizi, Mother, Janó, and the night watchman at the Dés brickworks, and a cross when one had died), *Laci and Lili with Ananchita* (the picture was taken by Klári with Laci's precious Voigtlander, but Ananchita moved, and the picture looks as if she's got two heads), and finally the last picture of Christmas '59: a small Christmas tree in the snow with black decorations, when Lili and Laci made a joint present to the pussies, Samu and Merci, this naughty girl who presents us with additions twice every year, said Laci proudly: in December 1959 Laci and Lili made a real cats' Christmas tree, decorated with spleen and liver, tying the delicacies onto the tree with thread—*You've mucked up the whole hall*, grumbled Klári, *so now clear it up*—and as a surprise they placed it outside in the border, but by the time that Samu and Merci appeared in the evening the spleen had frozen solid, and the cats weren't interested in celebrating the birth of Christ the next day either but went out on Christmas Eve when Laci, Klári and Lili lit the sparklers and didn't appear for two days, and it was only on the third day, when everybody had gone to visit Auntie Gizi, that they sniffed around the Christmas tree inside and started to hit the balls and whipped cream kisses from underneath, then they tore down the tinsel, and when the big tree, which was as high as the ceiling, fell sideways with a crash as the little tree with the spleen stank untouched in the hall, *They wouldn't even sniff at your tree*, said Klári with satisfaction and stripped it, 'this nonsense that you've done, what a waste of spleen!', and she burnt the tree, but Izabella and Ludmilla and the slowly growing grandchildren, who liked to tease the cats, considered spleen a treat, and Laci built up a special relationship with the restaurant owners, kitchen staff, washers-up and waiters so as to be able to feed the cats and later the dog left by Janó, he took them soap and stockings (which Lili obtained, but in her position she couldn't use tipping in restaurants as a means of persuasion), half a bottle of *pálinka*, a basket of Beszterce plums or morellos from the garden in Kányafő út, which made Klári cross, *You bring those plums that keep you regular home, I suppose your Romanian pals don't want those!*—she'd remark, and the neighbours too were always saying, why keep cats at a time like this? but even then Lili and Laci continued to support each other: Lili acquired the contacts and the presents that served as regular items for barter, and Laci, by that time retired, would get on his dilapidated woman's bicycle every two or three days and set off for the ring road and the Főtér, and then to the suburbs, park his precious bicycle at the back doors of restaurants and cheap eating-places and wait humbly—his younger granddaughter often saw him at the restaurant opposite the Viktória cinema but never spoke to him, she was ashamed at her grandfather begging at back doors—and Laci just waited until the hefty women in charge of the kitchens called him in, or simply passed the bag of unknown contents out in silence and took in what was offered in exchange, and Laci waited, motionless, lighting one cigarette from the stub of another, like somebody conscious of their wicked and these days completely inappropriate, even crippling passion for cats but who can't help giving in to their enthusiasm, and he thought himself that he deserved the humiliation of waiting in the street, then saying 'thank you' for the bag with its valuable contents, and if they had understood he would have said quietly *May God reward you, give you a thousand times as much for it*, then take spleen, lights, bits of chicken, once even frogs' legs, because he accepted anything raw, even suet, from which Grandmother made grey washing soap, or to everybody's great delight he got marrowbones, which restaurants usually threw away because the Romanians didn't appreciate them, and the cats' favourite in those days was *tacîm*, chickens' heads and feet, 'scratchings' as people say, such as you could buy in kilo or kilo-and-a-half bags, though there was serious competition for them between the children and the cats, and the two grandchildren loved to suck chickens' feet that had been cooked in soup, only Klári didn't care to make soup from 'scratchings' just as she didn't cook chickens which weighed hardly 20 decagrams, frozen and inexplicably bluish-purple in colour—the little bruised birds were vulgarly termed 'Petreuşi brothers' after two cheerful, popular folk-singers from Maramureş, well-known figures in *curáj* music, both suntanned and bursting with health, who were on the TV every Sunday at about lunchtime, *You have them with your cats*, Klári would say crossly and fling the 'Petreuşi brothers' onto the cat shelf in the fridge, and later Lili once tried the cats with some smoked pig's trotter, which was called *Adidas* because they were sold in pairs: she singed them, cooked them with greens and put them out on the balcony to cool, and by next morning they'd become a nice wobbly brawn which the girls ate with mustard, but the cats wouldn't go near it, and by evening Izabella of the broad head and bushy tail, the yellow-speckled tortoiseshell and the graceful Ludmilla were wailing sorrowfully and sniffing reproachfully at their empty bowls because *our furry friends*, the posterity of Jozefin and Juci, remained insolently indifferent to the time and the changed ways, their obstinate nature didn't permit them to evince any understanding of the contents of the fridge, to be converted to potato, chew bread or lap up spinach even if smothered in sour cream for them, and by next day the two girl cats from the block of flats had secretly been chewing the asparagus, but Lili burst into helpless tears because her children ate up everything but the cats couldn't be prevailed upon to have greater insight and she daren't send the younger girl to the shop again for a final desperate attempt— *Kandúrbandi*, she would call her nickname in a sing-song voice and hang on to the end of the word, and the child knew that she was supposed to go hunting for cat food—and even in her teens the Girl was passionately fond of going into shops, which to her amounted to a treasure hunt, she knew how to queue up and get hold of things and to come home with surprises: eggs or cold cuts or a packet of pink twists of assorted coffee, or at least some fresh bread, but Lili was by then reluctant to impose such a burden on her teenage daughter and went to the shop herself, and in the end the younger girl ran after her, Lili stopped in the front part of the long, dark shop, at the meat counter where there was nobody, she waited a little then tapped on the counter, at which a man appeared and looked questioningly at her as if to say what can a customer want here, where there's nothing on sale, at which Lili pointed sternly at the only item on sale on the counter, frozen sea fish, on which no price was marked because as far as the teenage Girl beside her could remember no one had ever yet bought any, and she drily told the assistant *One kilo*, and he raised the huge axe and brought it down on the mass and fish flew in all directions like when the fresh catch is pulled from the sea and the shining merchandise is shed from the net into the boat, and Ludmi and Bella hurled themselves upon the pieces of herring, now none too fresh and smelling very fishy after much thawing and re-freezing (the result of regular power cuts) and for which a separate chopping board and knife for cats' fish had to be used, because Lili's own cats, Ludmi and Bella, and Laci's, Jucika and Zsiga, just crunched up the chicken heads and feet, the bluish-purple pieces of 'Petreuşi brothers', and finally the fish, which cost 8 lei, with its penetrating smell and dark red juice, because by then they, Ludmi, Bella, Jucika and Zsiga, had become the copy-book dream citizens, the best customers, who took and ate precisely what the shop offered, as if the whole meat trade of the city were kept going just for them, because as the blue-eyed pair maintained, the father and daughter incapable of restraining their shared wicked passion for cats, the world had always revolved around these soft, selfish, proud carnivores, of whom, in the end, no time had got the better.

A LONG DAY

Now she didn't say *I'm out of steam*, as she usually did in fun when she came home from work, or late in the evening when she stopped typing, now she just sank without a word onto the red plastic folding kitchen stool, her eyes glazed, and in fact she was worn out, dark purple grooves stretched beneath her swollen eyes, even in her youthful photographs there were rings around her eyes as if she were always tired, and she tried to cover them with powder, but now more than one long day had gone by since she'd applied powder, her skin colourless and creased into tiny wrinkles, the wooden slides in her hair *all squiffy*, as she used to say, and on her right hand, which rested on a half-copied juridical notice left lying on the table, there was a broken nail on the middle finger (on which she wore Granny's ruby ring), but she always carried a nail file in her handbag—the younger girl had typed the court summons at her mother's instructions, even though a university student she still enjoyed typing, and going to the country with her mother to assess the division of the property of divorcing parties, when Mummy inventoried the goods on behalf of the court, it wasn't hard for her, everybody had the same sort of furniture, pots, pans and ornaments, and Mummy valued them, and in the end the court's decision on the chattels of the parties that had been incapable of dividing them was based on the list that Mummy typed up at night, because her third, evening, night and weekend job as property assessor, which she'd been able to obtain through important connections, was indispensable not because of the modest state salary but for the trips to the country which, despite the long bus journeys at the weekend, were more valuable than legal cases in town, because Mummy never came back from the country empty-handed: eggs, honey, sausage, fat bacon, chickens, cheese, sour cream, jam, fresh bread, *pálinka* and vegetables came her way, she accepted everything, even bags of apples or potatoes, even a can of petrol which was brought back to town by car (there were no vegetables any longer, Janó's house and garden had been sold five years previously because minors couldn't inherit and possess real estate), because in the country it was understood that it was usual to make a gift—or absolutely imperative, compulsory, the assessor had to be kept sweet, as if the court would otherwise be unable to reach a just decision about them—and the Girl had often been able to notice that the woman in the divorcing couple carefully wrapped the groceries in newspaper and put them all in a damaged shopping bag which she wasn't going to see again, while her husband looked on saying nothing, like a stranger, as if the result were nothing to do with him, only the procedure, when every animal or plant existed as such, was a little pig or tomato, alive and to be cared for, which the man described to himself as work, but not inanimate produce or merchandise, and the silent man, with his grey, dejected face and his rubber boots, reminded the Girl of her own father, and then the woman would hand the package to the other woman without a word, hopefully, or give it straight to the teenage Girl as she loitered nervously there, knowing that she should accept it, accept everything, otherwise Mummy would make a lower valuation of the heavy carved furniture or the mass-produced Persian rugs, writing off not 10 but 30 per cent of the original price because the woman was keeping the living-room furniture, but the kitchen furniture, which was going to the man, she had long wanted to replace (she whispered in Mummy's ear), and Mummy would note down in her book 'nearly new, 10 per cent', and the man had nothing to suggest or wish for when she went out into the pantry for the sausage, but from divorcing parties in town the most that came was coffee, toiletries or hideous gifts from the shops which Mummy was then able to exchange for cash in the central store, but that day they had bet on where Mummy had spent the night (a book was the stake: next day they were going to call on their university lecturer, who was leaving the country and was disposing of his library, and they had been given 150 lei each by Mummy to buy books, and so the terms of the bet were that the winner could pick a book at the loser's expense): the older girl said that Mummy had told her that it was going to be a long day, she was going somewhere a long way out of town and wouldn't be able to get home, and the younger disbelieved that, because it had never happened that Mummy had had to sleep on the job, as she put it, on a professional valuation because she never went out of the county, could get home from everywhere by bus or train, and so the Girl was hoping that Mummy was somewhere completely different, that she would come home happy, tired, travel-worn but happy, like after her short official trips to Bucharest or when she went to Arad, Iași, Korond or Szeben to *contract*, to order goods *with Him* (to the four-storey, empty, echoing warehouse, where the invisible goods which had not got onto the shelves had perhaps never arrived), with Him, whom Grandmother referred to as *the Wallachian man*, and the younger girl christened *Ficăţel* (Little Liver), because Mummy always cooed to him as she did to her cats, making everything that she set before him a diminutive, and when, at the expense of no little effort and trouble, she laid on a veritable feast for V's special visits, on her name-day or birthday, she gave everything pet names: *muşchiuleţ, cafeluţă, cartofiori, supică, prăjiturică, castraveciori* and, of course, *ficăţel* (sirloin, coffee, potatoes, soup, pasta, gherkin, liver), but V would address her quietly in his deep, soft voice: *Júlia*, and she came back happy and tired from their official trips by sleeping-car, bringing at least a tin of caviar, sardines or Vietnamese crab, but first and foremost she unwittingly gave the girls their own momentary, sparkling happiness, and on such occasions V stayed another night with them after the journey: and Mummy's big double bed, which had been nearly impossible to get into the flat and took up the entire room, remained silent all night as if nobody were sleeping in it, the sleepers were merely floating above it—the younger girl had once managed to catch a glimpse of them, she'd skipped school that morning, but Mummy never shut the door, and they were lying motionless on top of each other, *afterwards or before?*, she'd wondered, because she couldn't decide, their eyes were closed and nothing indicated that they'd ever moved or were ever able to separate, as if they'd always been lying like that, like the calcified lovers in Pompei whom the destroying fire had surprised together and they had weakly submitted to it, thus immortalizing their hour of happiness, and they were not embracing in wordless, ecstatic love but holding each other, and now too the younger girl hoped that Mummy had been there again, in V's arms, somewhere in the country or in a hotel in some other town where, on the basis of their grey ID cards (the one was divorced, the other married) they had to take two rooms, or perhaps they'd escaped to their secret love nest, the lake two hours away, where—as Mummy said, at least—they'd sworn eternal faithfulness to each other (which the very same day had to be broken) in the church at Béles, they'd rowed in a boat borrowed from the hostel through the high, arched windows into the church, the wooden frame of which had stood untouched for a quarter of a century, because when the 20-kilometre lake was created Jósikafalva was evacuated to higher ground—Lili was unaware that her former brother-in-law Pista had been the instigator and director of the creation of the system of dykes and lakes at Béles, Tarnica and Fîntînele, and very proud of it—but of the village there remained in the valley, in the eternal peace of the waters, only the church and the bones of Pál Vasvári,[52] because he'd had no relatives in the village to move him with the other dead up to the new settlement, and a sultry silence filled the church, the words that they whispered, meant only for each other, were not re-echoed, and afterwards they slept away the afternoon among the pines in a narrow, fern-ringed inlet and set off for home late in the evening because then too they could have only one

---

52 1826–49, writer and prominent figure in the 1848 revolution.

251

long day like that day, and the younger girl hoped, although she'd laughed openly at her mother's cooing weakness when she had been shamelessly happy, shone and effervesced, filling with hope anyone near her, that perhaps she would be like that this day too: after her two dull Russian seminars that morning she'd gone up to Mummy's office in Főtér, but had not found her there: *E la casare*, that is, *She's sorting out some rubbish*, the secretary gave the official response, but what further rubbish could there be to sort out in this warehouse?, thought the Girl, and remembered all the broken toys she'd been given as a child from the *kászálások* (write-offs), which at the time she and Juci had called *kaszálások* (reapings), and she didn't dare enquire whether her mother had been in at all that morning, she regarded the answer as a good sign and on the way out stole a look at the *kondika*, the dread signing-in book, where beside Mummy's name was her hasty signature, timed at seven o'clock, but the Girl knew for a fact that her colleague uncle Nuszi must have written that, as they could forge one another's signatures undetectably, then she looked into the two coffee bars opposite, where Mummy often met Him but only found the coffee-drinking idiot Lulu there, and then in the late evening and night she didn't want to call Grandmother, she'd only have been needlessly anxious and would at best vilify that chap *who only uses your mother, and spends her money*, but when, early in the evening next day, Mummy sank onto the seat, drenched in perspiration, her bag over her shoulder, wearing the same dress as the day before and with her stockings laddered, staring in front of her and not speaking, because she didn't complain of how tired she was, nor was she smiling a mysterious, betraying smile, but just sitting, and meanwhile the cat sidled into the kitchen and rubbed against her legs and she didn't even give it a stroke, and the younger girl knew that it wasn't anything to do with V, Mummy would be laughing or crying if it were, *Where've you been?*, she asked coldly and severely, and her mother shivered, looked anxiously at the reproachfully empty cats' dish, then began to look around the floor and on the stove, which was full of empty saucepans, for something to eat for the cats and the girls, because it seemed that it had only just dawned on her that she owed her children an explanation of her first unannounced absence all night, another time she would have shouted self-assuredly *I'm not accountable to you for anything! Not for anything, and that's flat!* and the Girl asked a second time *Where've you been?*, as if sensing the weariness and desperation that would let her advance easily and unopposed until she'd squeezed the answer out of her mother, *Tell us where you've been!* Juci shouted at her and was about to threaten, as she'd learnt from her mother, what punishment would ensue if she didn't speak out, *Mummy!*, yelled the younger girl straight away, as if shouting at her own teenage daughter who'd stopped out all night, as if she ought now, in adult fashion, to be thinking not of punishment—that could come later—but of an immediate answer to the problem while it could still be resolved, because the Girl who had become officially an adult three months before and who still obstinately guarded her virginity, changed, that late October afternoon, into a parent, and in front of her sat a child, in a state of collapse, defenceless, but perhaps not yet beyond redemption, *If you don't tell us at once where you've been, I'm going to ring the* . . . but Mummy didn't let her finish the sentence and the Girl wouldn't have been able to say whom she might have meant to ring—her late grandfather, of whom Mummy was afraid? The Hungarian teacher to whom she would run for help? the police, whom they would never ever under any circumstances ring up?, because the Girl only knew the emphases, the role, as she stood over a lightly bowed mother and shouted at her, but she didn't yet know the solution, *Girls, my little girls,* Mummy said suddenly, quietly, as if she herself didn't know whom she was talking to, as if she'd decided to confess the unbearable truth to her parents after all, she gave a gulp and looked her severe-looking younger daughter in the eye—and that afternoon there appeared a vertical crease on her forehead between the bushy eyebrows that she inherited from her father, *I can't stand it any longer, now they come up into the office every day, until now I've only had to go in during working hours, but now . . . I don't know what they want*—she said in one breath, in a dull voice, *I'm going to telephone*—replied the Girl decisively and almost unfeelingly, and pretended that the announcement that she was going to telephone was nothing to do with what she'd heard, and she confidently left the kitchen as if she knew that in October 1989 there was only one solution: to spend all afternoon telephoning, all evening, both that day and the next, to friends, teachers, Grandmother, neighbours, acquaintances and people that she'd heard of, the Hungarian teachers, beginning with the Évas and the Júlias, the important and the dangerous, to talk into that grey plastic handset and say that it was only needless expense, we don't need it, and then the girls persuaded her all the same to put in the request and in exchange for seven pairs of white men's underpants—which for a long time then had only been obtainable by barter, not bought, but the seven cotton underpants were even then a suspiciously ridiculously low price for the telephone, and then next day they came out again and carefully checked the equipment, and she had to say into this grey telephone that Mummy's been *there*, not *Mummy keeps being called in*, and after a pause, seriously: *she was detained last night*, or to tell someone that doesn't understand clearly *in Traian út,,* and to tell Grandmother even more precisely still: *Which is Traian út? I don't know these new names*, grumbled Granny, who hadn't known the new names for forty years—At the Security, the Girl answered, as if she were only saying in the market or in a beer garden, but Grandmother didn't hear: *In Horthy út? Or what did you say? Because that goes down to the station as well, so do you mean Árpád út or Szent István út: What did you say they call it, Trianon? Have they made a street of that now! Goodness that's not . . .* and then she and Grandmother talked about streets and roads and squares and houses that had been demolished, but Grandmother still had no idea where on earth Mummy had spent the night, and it seemed that Grandmother, with her bent back and bleary eyes, was no longer able to travel that long

street from the street named after the emperor Traian as far as those
named Horthy or Árpád or Szent István, it seemed that that conversation too, like the others, had only been started in order to make it clear
that Szent István út ran from the railway to the Szamos (then that's
what is now Karl Marx, thought the Girl), and that Árpád út was
Külső-Király utca in the old days, and had only been so named in 1940,
and ran from the Szamos to Kajántói út, and they also had a long talk
about the city which existed only in Grandmother's still-permed head,
and the two university students took it in turn for hours on end to telephone, so that everybody should know, *they* too, and in the end they
were passing information on two channels: to the person that they were
speaking to, who had a five-figure telephone number, and the silent,
nameless stranger, incapable of replying, who now, not for the first time,
was also a person addressed, and the clearly enunciated message was
for them both, because at the time one could be silent or speak in a
whisper only in exceptional circumstances—in love, in the fern-fringed
inlet in the Béles lake—because from now on Mummy could only thus
be protected, but still she protested feebly from the kitchen, wailed
*You'll be the death of me, you mustn't say a word, don't even tell your
Grandmother, least of all on the phone*, but that tapped telephone was
now the only refuge, as good as having an announcement made on
Radio Free Europe or Kossuth Radio, joked Juci, *Thank you, boys!*, they
called into the phone to sign off, or *Mulțumim, băieți!*, *you got it all
down, didn't you?—You think they're all boys?*, asked Juci pensively, thanks
to our in-built eavesdropping equipment, you can see that we treat it
properly and use it, only give you valuable information: that in a room
with a barred window on the ground floor of Traian 27, the former
Hungarian-language metal-industry school, a piece of paper was put
in front of Mummy, the door was locked for the entire night, and she
had to consider what foreign connections we have, she and her grown-
up children, whether we're still in touch with 'the poets'—with the poet
who was expelled to the West, with the other one who moved to

Budapest, and the third, the writer whose son is now serving as a soldier in Temesvár—who was preparing to put their papers in and with whose help, and finally she had to sign the *statement* and a further blank sheet too, *Did you sign it?*, asked Juci, meanwhile the younger girl was telling the story of Mummy's night for the twentieth time, colouring it and embellishing it with details, now it was not only Mummy's stockings that had laddered, as happened regularly in any case, she was always using ladder repairers, the two girls teased her about it all the time, because she wore stockings all summer, but *there* her blouse too had been torn, and under the influence of the story and the details and the ever increasing flow of narrative she began to calm down, *Tomorrow we'll tell the whole of the Hungarian department and all the students in our year, and at least it will become clear which of them . . . I suspect Noémi*, because she's been suspected for a long time, and Mummy's notebook had been taken out of her handbag and examined to see who else they had to speak to, the humorous Puiu Gîngă, who was brilliant at translating Romanian and Hungarian words literally, and Mr Hosu, the lecturer who taught Romanian grammar in the university, Mummy knew him as well, and to Jil, the former German teacher, and of Mummy's colleagues to Márta, the fat Mrs Bruckenthal, and no doubt to Uncle Nuszi and the pretty Aunty Magdi, *Don't ring Magdi, she was selected yesterday as a delegate to the XIVth congress, she's going to Bucharest*, said Mummy wearily, *Then I will so ring her! And do you know V's number?*, asked Juci, he and his family live somewhere on Traian as well, *I'll tell him tomorrow*, Mummy replied and added impatiently *Now that's enough, we'll get everybody into trouble*, but nobody could be got into trouble any more because whether anybody had been in 27 Traian, or whether they'd had a house search, or whether shadows had trailed them in the street, the trouble had already been with them and in them for a long time: *There's nothing to be afraid of*, said the two girls to their mother in the deep, calming, reassuring tone in which Aunty Mózes spoke to them when she came to give them an injection when they were little because they were ill and Mummy soothed their fevered brows, *We aren't alone, you'll see how many know by this time*, said the younger girl, and would have liked to soothe Mummy's fevered brow, *And*—Juci went on seriously, imitating her sister's warm, quiet voice, her slow, murmuring speech, *if you pick up the telephone you don't have to dial anybody, just tell it what's on your mind, how lonely you are and it'll be heard, they'll come running to cheer you up, you'll see, we can't ever be alone again, Mummy*, and at that the other girl too began to laugh aloud, *a frog's chorus*, Father used to call it in the old days, like when once at dinner, ten years previously in Dohány utca, they'd been eating corn porridge and spluttered the yellow, milky liquid at each other, and in the end Mummy put an embroidered cushion between them and went back into the sitting room to give a lesson, but by the time she came back out, *Good heavens, what's been going on here!!*, they'd spat all over both sides of the decorated cushion, and this time too she didn't dare laugh but tried to control the smile that played at the corners of her narrow mouth, *Ludmi*, she bent kindly to the cat, *you're hungry as well, aren't you? Now you two stop this at once*, she tried to speak seriously to them, but laughter was still bubbling from Juci and one could scarcely make out the broken words, *Whahahay did you puhuhut that cuhuhushion betwehehehen us?*, because when they laughed uproariously she still threatened her daughters, now twenty and eighteen, that she'd put a cushion between them, and the blood-red uvula could be seen in Juci's wide-open mouth, tossed in the gale of laughter that tore, free and unrestrained, from her throat, like the heavy, bloodstained but victorious banner of a fighter for freedom standing proud atop the peak.

OLLOPUTRIDA

Two scientific works on nutrition appeared at almost the same time: the first in the usual way, on the front pages of all the papers in the form of a table; it contained the presidential directive on scientific nutrition, the latest theories, expertly laid down theoretical quantities of carbohydrates, proteins and starches mandatory for the health of the population irrespective of region and natural environment, and at the same time all these carbohydrates, proteins and starches were, by a system of allocation worked out by another scientific method and based on population records, available—if indeed they were—in regional distribution centres, within the framework of a traditional allocation system, long opposed but in the end known as pre-booking or reservation (an *abonement*, like the trolley buses that seldom ran), worked out by István Tompa, the girls' great-uncle and Kolozs county director of commerce, in the summer of 1981 and introduced on a voluntary basis, in the first place as a personal recommendation and then as a scheme under the title of rationalization, primarily so as by rationing to put an end to the distressing emptying of the shops and arguments which had gone on for more than a decade and which chiefly gave the city a poor appearance (before that, workers had 'had a share' in all shops at the same time, both in the morning and at four in the afternoon as they left the factories), but shortages of cooking oil and sugar were followed by shortages of butter, flour, meat, cooked meats, eggs, bread and all produce—and of all textiles, especially underwear, men and women's, and of nylon stockings, for which the ideal system of rationing was never achieved, this, on the other hand, could have been to Mummy's credit as chief economist of the county branch of the *ICS Textile-*

Încălțăminte, the State supplier of clothing and footwear, true, rationing was achieved for gas and electricity and a ridiculously low quota brought in, but not for water because homes did not have separate water meters, so the water was simply turned off, and at this time a car was allowed 50 litres of petrol per month, with queuing through the night, and the system of food rationing in fact began to operate first in Kolozsvár, though initially only as an experiment and with a degree of revolutionary illegality, and so the population was able, on the basis of personal registration, to receive those carbohydrates, proteins and starches the quantities of which fell far short of those stated scientifically and officially: half a litre of oil monthly, half a block of butter, a kilo each of sugar, flour and cornflour, seven eggs, together with a chicken and a kilo of pork—what actually developed, however, was that the Jews' rations were cut on 1 May 1944 and from then on they were each allowed 30 decagrams of sugar a month, 10 decagrams of beef or horse meat a week—the decree did not allow them pork—they could not obtain eggs or milk, on 3 May the ghetto was designated, and in June the papers announced what colour the Jewish ration card was, when there were no Jews left in the city—but the rationing system introduced in Kolozsvár in 1981, in collaboration with the Statistical Office, worked so well that it was brought in nationwide, and by this means to some extent the huge queues for sugar and oil were ended, but those for meat, bread and, as was customary, anything else that *was being distributed*, *se dă*, being given, as the expression was, but rather most of all not being given but exported, while the self-sufficient counties were made to surrender an ever-higher annual quota, the remainder being distributed to the population, and the scientific table that appeared once again in the papers was communicated in silence: nutrition had become a science, numbers, grams and calories, paper and novelty like the other fantastic or rather science-fictional work, *Anna Bornemisza's Cookbook of 1680*, which was considered harmless, according to the introduction definitely in the realm of scientific research and enquiry, something of a book of fables rather than a collection of recipes reminiscent of a thing of use, which slipped past the censorship in 1982 in a way that a simple, contemporary cookbook tailored to everyday reality would not have done because the sharp-eyed censor, a member of *Comitetul de Cultură și Educație Socialistă* (the Commission for Culture and Socialist Education), would have discovered an ironic allusion to the present day in every recipe, although Anna Bornemisza's cookbook had been translated for the princess by János Keszei from a German original, Max Rumpolt's *Ein new Kochbuch*, which Keszei, as secretary to Mihály Apafi I, 'began in Fogaras and finished in Radnót among his other tasks', and this harmless cookbook proclaimed a lucid and admirable *doctrine*, a biblical ordinance, which, in Keszei's childish drawing, an angel resembling a handsome teenage boy held in his hands: *Let every moving and living creature be to your sustenance*, words with which the Lord blessed Noah and his sons, and they had complied with it but the inventors of rationing did not, though they were close relatives, who, like everybody else, had their own system: if friends came to call, even though they came often, it was their custom to boast before dinner, *We've killed a hog*, and then, on seeing the listeners' look of astonishment, to add *A hedgehog, hahaha!*, but after the publication of Anna Bornemisza's cookbook of 1680 the hedgehog joke seemed paltry and stunted beside the opportunities in the book for 'every living and moving creature', not all of which they recognized, and the pig, furthermore, remained a sacred animal, seeing that Mummy was never able to use a single pork coupon because she hadn't the time to stand for hours queuing, but the steward —whose profession the learned book apportioned between master of ceremonies, captain of the court, head cook, sommelier, steward, cup bearer and head carver in separate chapters—or rather the younger girl enlisted as steward only liked short, predictable queues in which the purpose was shared by all and the outcome certain, or displays of ingenuity, cunning feats, for example buying, in addition to the ration of seven eggs monthly, unrationed pale-yolked cracked ones which were kept almost out of sight in a glass case under the shelf behind the vendor, as if the fate of cracked eggs had not yet been decided on, whether or not they could be sold, whether they counted as stock or just happened to be on the shelf as wastage along with the fat, grubby ledgers on the basis of which the monthly grocery quota was issued, or perhaps cracked eggs too likewise counted as merchandise, but because there was no settled, *rationalized* arrangement for cracked eggs, they retained the incalculable supply and demand element of the market, the spirit of the vendor's whim and the purchaser's acuity, because cracked *hen fruit*, as they are called in Master Keszei's translation, were not covered by the rules of the system, and the clever steward girl—who in all respects met the prescriptions of the book—'comely, cheerful, industrious, immune to boredom, pretty, clean and of good morals'—had only one fault, that she had been born a girl—at times Grandmother would watch from the fourth-floor window with her opera glasses the delivery vans parked at the back entrance to the shop and assess the goods arriving by the size and weight of the plastic boxes so as to decide whether it was worth going shopping that day, because fresh bread and cold meats had arrived, otherwise she would just go down to walk the dog and look to see if anything was happening in another local shop, who had what in their shopping bag and where they were coming from, in case by chance something interesting had been put on the counter, say, some Bulgarian apricot jam, and elderly, head-scarved peasant women or a little man in a straw hat would often ask her to buy them 30 decagrams of bread, even if it was stale, even yesterday's, because the shops weren't allowed to sell bread to people from the country, according to the rationalizers they, collective farm employees, had wheat—land, of course, they might not have—and in this way they bought up all that bread for the young pigs, which they had almost nothing to feed with, and while Father had two pigs he often went round the local shops and bought a loaf in each, because they would only let him have one, but Mummy worked all day in the office, then at the court, and in the evenings she gave lessons at home, and after that did some typing, she didn't go shopping but she handled the bigger jobs: she obtained things, exchanged, discussed, established links, but chiefly invented things—puddings, soufflés, all sorts of hot-pots and casseroles, minced things and patés with nice, promising names, a series of unrepeatable foods because she never cooked the same thing twice, but like a culinary showman she would concoct a one-off from available ingredients, but she could never repeat her death-defying performances in the kitchen arena: cabbage and breadcrumbs became cabbage soufflé, a tin of Globus tinned meat or fish (which, as the results of significant 'acquisitions'—perhaps washing machines or colour TVs—were piled high in the pantry) with sour cream and mustard produced *crudd*, because that was the name of all food of an unknown nature, *doovery, gunge, shredded oojah*, as Juci said, a *mishmash* in which everything was God and amen, in which anything edible might be found and which was downed at once, sometimes standing, without bread, *puppypoop* (a word of Juci's coinage) if tiny rissoles were baked of it and she found them, or *sloppy puppypoop* if it came to the table in a sauce, but in summer, if it often rained, we had chanterelles, boletes and big, white giant puffballs (Father once picked one weighing 3 kilos, it was as big as the biggest medicine ball in gym lessons, and he carried it home in his arms like a newborn child), blue milk or bitter mushrooms, which they also picked in the Hója, and for the perfumed, spongy bolete Mummy had no end of recipes, and in spring they picked a great amount of lesser celandine in the forest, and once they ate fresh veal for a whole week because, as their mother said, that was what people in the country had paid her with for valuing their belongings, and at the last birthday party to which he came the poet put a piece of fried veal between two fried boletes, said delightedly *A Hamburger*, and swallowed it, but the girls weren't to be caught out by fried semolina, whatever sour cream and roasted garlic Mummy piled onto it, but both of them announced *I hate it! And the awful smell!*, and Laci, the neighbour downstairs, who was studying architecture in

Bucharest and who often dropped in about lunchtime, always trotted out his favourite expression: *We're eating tubers and roots,* and pulled a pious face at it like a hermit in the forest, the hedgehog joke too they got from Laci—his parents picked fungi, Krisztina's collected snails in the cemetery, while the Pápai family kept coypu, made sausage from them and smoked it, but Grandmother couldn't invent anything, *newfangled cooking,* as Master Keszei called it in the princess' book, remained beyond her ken, *She hadn't been able to get used to it, couldn't make anything of it,* Mummy regretted, because her mother didn't just fling things together, she only followed recipes, It's *goose risotto,* said she of a dish of tough old chicken and rice, but the grandchildren didn't enquire which was the goose part because they'd never eaten real goose —their father had some, but he wouldn't let them be slaughtered—and Grandmother spoke dismissively of her daughter's cooking, including pizza, *Well, I don't know what this is, we didn't cook things like this in our house,* and she didn't taste piquant, sour-creamed udder soup (Mummy got that too from a client in the country) though it was tasty, *it's meat with no bones,* nor Romanian tripe soup, towel soup, as Juci called it, *Leave it for the Wallachians!,* said Grandmother, and indignantly told us how her neighbour, old Mrs Török, had cooked bologna in the apple soup! but for special occasions even in Mummy's kitchen everything was done according to regular recipes: after lengthy accumulation the five kinds of meat were ready and waiting in the little freezer for authentic stuffed cabbage, in which 'many kinds blend together' as in Master Keszei's best dishes: *On the bottom of the pot comes a layer of smoked fat bacon, pork rib, because it is meaty and thick, and a nice big smoked knuckle, but not the trotters, that is not good, because there is no meat on it, though in time of great dearth we put that in too, all this goes into the pot of chopped cabbage, for the filling minced meat, and into that too a nice smoked knuckle—Well, does that take five? Were you counting?* Mummy explained, *And hand of pork, doesn't it call for that?,* asked the youngest, and Mummy cooked the whole thing in two enormous pots (one of salted cabbage, in the other the filling) for two days, *It's really a sort of olloputrida*, Juci was well read in the scientific specialist literature, an olloputrida, which had to be made of ninety-two ingredients on the occasion of a visit by a prince or king or elector when the host princess gave a great feast—during the visitations which fell to the lot of Kolozsvár too every year or two the shops were shut all day so that the queues should not spoil the appearance of the city, surrounded as it was with sprawling estates of dwellings and heavy industry alike, and the employees, together with those that worked in the city, the schoolchildren and university students stood shoulder to shoulder from the airport at Szamosfalva to the Főtér and waved, in the front row the reliable cadres of the enterprises preventing the couple who waved from the open car from being inundated with letters, which was unsuccessful in the year of the two scientific works, the table published in the papers and the old cookbook—that olloputrida which, as Juci informed them during lunch, because reading at table was permitted, had consisted of ninety-two ingredients including, in addition to the usual four- and two-footed creatures—wether, calf, kid, chickens old and young, game small and large and birds—seal, spiny hedgehog, beaver, sea rabbit, elk, buffalo, Indian pig, lark, starling, eagle, pelican, heron, crane, peacock, turtle dove and *habarnica*, that is, spider crab—every moving and living creature, in accordance with the doctrine—a *karakutya* too, by which a kind of carp is meant, because in translating Master Keszei met with much difficulty over Hungarian names for the denizens of the waters, and furthermore a marmot, all separately baked or boiled, marinated in black sauces and chopped herbs, and finally placed in a great cauldron between cabbage leaves, and the cook had to take great care that everything should blend together, like Mummy had to with the five kinds of meat, and so she did, because olloputrida was not entirely harmless and risk-free and perhaps it was the 'clear and worthy doctrine' of the simple truth that from Moses to the present day *everything that moves is edible* that contained the hidden intention of the learned publisher, Dr Elemér Lakó, and so all three of them looked forward most to the monthly barbecue, in other words, in Keszei language, the *chicken feast*, when on Mummy's payday the three of them would buy a whole chicken, cooked on the premises, in the Gospodina, the 'house-wife', a standing-only buffet—the name of a nationwide chain—where otherwise it was possible to get only fish-paste balls and tart *salate de boeuf* a few days old, and most of all beer on tap, and they would take it home and even eat it out of the paper it was wrapped in, the monthly ration, Mummy had established this fruitful, or rather meat-productive, link with the Gospodina in '85 and tended it carefully once a month, because then she no longer had Father's garden with the chickens, and men's and women's underwear, mainly knitted nylon underpants, formed the regular barter trade, and medium-sized Chinese towels which the Orthodox required for burials instead of the embroidered shawls used in the villages—at wakes, sweetbread and *pálinka* were set out on them—but a huge, red, flower-patterned, artificial-fibre carpet finally opened the fridges in the restaurant, and there was no payday when the three of them did not sit in the fourth-floor kitchen eating a chicken: the two girl started with the tastiest part, the wings, the roast chicken skin, because most often they were given chicken pieces, and so that was what they liked, and Mummy's favourite was the back, Juci got the neck (to her regret it wasn't cooked with the head on, but when it was cooked in soup she could enjoy the thrill of sucking out the brain), her sister got the parson's nose, then they continued with the legs but left the breast to last, and with no words save mmm's of appre-ciation ate the pure, boneless, white meat, both from the scientific point of view and in Grandmother's opinion the most valuable part, they divided the tender flesh of the breast into three, the youngest put mustard on it so that the dry, boneless and skinless meat should slip down more easily, and Juci also sucked out the marrow from the bones and then graciously gave them to the cats for further chewing, and the three would sit for a long time at the kitchen table after the invisible remnants of the chicken feast, because to be together and eat a chicken was a rare special occasion, and finally, like a blessing after lunch, Juci read out the epilogue as if grace were being said: *And this is called* ollop-utrida *or* alaputréta *because many kinds are brought together, and it is fit to set before kings, emperors, princes and lords.*

SNOODLING

That was what everybody in the house called it—the mansard, and the word even began to spread in the streets: 'You can go round, the light's still on in Laci's family's mansard,' said Dudus, or old Mrs Boci, the next-door neighbour, 'It's so quiet nowadays up in your mansard, is Lili away?' because they were the only people in the street with a mansard, Laci had boarded out the roof void, put in electricity and installed gas for the ancient cast-iron stove which had been brought down from Apponyi utca, but although he understood all about installations and had every licence and professional qualification, as one that bought his freedom by this means, he did not have it registered, and the little room was not officially part of the house, didn't count for consumption of gas, nor had planning permission been obtained for it, and so officially it didn't exist, but remained an illegal refuge, a secret hideaway, and so the Girl had heard the word 'mansard' and that was what it meant to her, in the past Lili and Janó had kept their secret finds up there and later on Lili had 'taken refuge' there with the children after suddenly one evening moving out of the Monostor flat, bought with Great-grandmother's earrings, and eventually the younger girl took herself up there every summer, in her teenage years referring more and more often to studying and getting away from Mummy's nocturnal typing because of which—said she—she couldn't sleep, and Laci too kept his secret papers there in boxes, his licences, plans, out-of-date land-registry seals which represented an office and country that had ceased to be, and his military insignia, and there Grandmother hid her love letters from Bandi Klájn, the black-haired, stylish lawyer's clerk in Vásárhely that she wasn't able to marry, and her paintbox and easel which was likewise disapproved of after she was married: around the little room, scarcely 3 metres by 3, stifling in summer and draughty in winter, stretched a big roof space, the empire of the cats, where at night they sparred and called to each other as they pleased, and it was full of cupboards and boxes, because Laci, who had originally been a mining engineer, thought that every house had its secret place, like a secretaire or a wallet: there had to be ever such a tiny room above or beneath the house, a pantry or a passage, in which one could live should need arise: *There's always another room*, Janó wrote in the diary which he started to keep in the winter of 1983, but instead of ending the sentence he drew in ballpoint in the middle of the page a wild monstera with pinnate leaves, *Monstera deliciosa*, and as he drew he was perhaps pondering how to end the sentence, but the ground-floor rooms below the mansard were at the time as he described them: the windows fitted badly and the rooms were always full of the dust that came through the gaps, and although Klári did the housework every week nothing was done in the house for thirty years, it wasn't painted or rewired, the hardboard flooring that Laci put down wasn't sealed, the taps in the kitchen weren't plastered in, and in winter everything froze, nothing was fixed at all: Klári believed that they had known that in six months' time, or the following year at least, the house was to be demolished and 'we can be put into a block' like the Hóstát people, so there was no point in mending the gate or the snake-headed well in the garden, Laci just replaced the tiles one biggish storm after another, the front of the house was crumbling in several places under the window, the outside render kept falling off, and as lorries replaced horse-drawn carts in the streets the house shook in the early morning as they set off for the construction work in the Mărăşti district, shook and trembled, because in the summer of 1984 all the houses with gardens around the nearby church of St Peter were demolished: thick wooden shutters were the only significant improvement at the end of the '70s, when Klári's eyes were becoming so bad that she could only sew at the desk in the window, and she was afraid that she would be seen by the electric light and Laci now went out to work at other people's homes, refurbishing the house, installing gas or water, varnishing, painting, plastering or just going round on his rusty lady's bicycle picking things up, but the younger girl, if she was there on holiday or asked to go down to her grandparents', got up late, tottered down from the mansard, stayed in her nightdress until lunchtime and went about the house barefoot or lay down with a cat at her side—they too liked to sleep in the daytime —on a bed downstairs which Grandmother hadn't yet got around to making, and Grandmother would call at about midday, *Are you still snoodling there?! We're having lunch right away*—because the evermore dilapidated house in Dohány utca was the best of all places for a snoodle: when one had nothing to do, no aims or plans, in just her nightdress or pyjamas that Grandmother had made, or a frilly-edged silk négligée of Great-grandmother's that she'd found in the attic, or just in her briefs and vest, to drink a milky coffee and nibble a bit of dry, leathery toast left over from breakfast, spread with softened margarine—or rather cut some off or chop it up because it was too hard to spread—not to wash, brush her hair or clean her teeth, and meanwhile read the paper or a book, and so she would still be in her nightdress mentally too, neither planned not wanted anything, not a cloud in the sky cast a shadow on the snoodling—*lipisteskedés* was her word for it, which came from her great-grandmother, as did the heavy, sunflower-decorated dressing gown which trailed on the floor behind her as a teenager, as if both the special item of clothing and the feline snoodling and stretching in it were passed down as a lifestyle in the female line from the Orzas, the Szabós and the Sokets, and snoodling and dressing gown also meant being at home in the house, only men could find no place in there, were always pottering about elsewhere: Laci was restlessly in and out all day, always had something urgent to do and a definite purpose, and Janó would be at work in his garden until evening, *There's someone at the door, you're snoodling there, go and see who it is*, Grandmother would say, and even if she was snoodling she could answer the door to the milkman who came on Fridays with expensive cottage cheese, cheese, sour cream and milk from Mera, the Gypsies who wired pots back together, the retired postman, the bottle man and all sorts of pedlars, because this street connecting Külső-Magyar utca and Honvéd utca was that known formerly as Alsó Kereszt and was only named Dohány utca (or *strada Tutunului*) after the tobacco factory established by a decision taken in Vienna in 1850—that had been the first effect of a Vienna Award in their family history, the moving of the tobacco factory to Kolozsvár—but by this time the evermore rickety house in Alsó Kereszt was itself both cross and consolation, and snoodling was the essence of the house as it waited, brought to a halt in time, for someone to take a decision on its fate, whether to shore it up in its unstable condition or to demolish it once and for all and in its place build a row of ten-storey blocks of flats, not upwards from below, as was usual, but by first running up a long, ten-storey-high facade as on Mărăşti tér, so that the blue sky couldn't be seen behind it, sticking flowers on the nonexistent parapets, and in front of the houses hastily planting trees, cut and rootless, which in three days had withered to nothing, for the high-ranking visitor on a tour of inspection to raise his right hand in his open car, turn the palm towards himself, wave and drive past towards Szamosfalva airport, noting *en passant* the bewildering speed of construction, and then for the entire wall to be demolished in a few months' time and building to begin again, with the cranes leaving behind their massive metal rails to sink slowly into the earth, and as no objection could be raised to its demolition the house in Dohány utca, bit by bit and unobserved by the occupants, was demolishing itself: thus it took revenge as if its careless owners were the only ones responsible for its collapse, as from the outside the house looked as if its occupants had long ago abandoned it to its fate, and only the annuals, planted from seed and watered several times daily—marigold, zinnia, pink, purslane, night-scented stock, calendula, cockscomb, antirrhinum and, of course, the night-scented tobacco-flower—intimated that anyone still lived there, *Where there are no flowers at the window, nobody lives there,* because Klári believed it as the Gospel truth that they too were to be bulldozed in autumn like Pata utca and the odd-numbered side of Honvéd, that is, Budai Nagy Antal utca, *Janó's house has got away with it,* she repeated, raising her thin eyebrows, *There must be somebody on the even-numbered side preventing it being demolished* (by that time they didn't care, Janó's house and garden had been sold in 1984), but there was nobody that they could look to in Dohány utca, only elderly people lived there that had been resettled after 1949, and paupers and old people eked out an existence in the long, cobbled, gloomy back of the courtyard, resettled country people and penniless students: because lined up behind the houses in the street stood dwellings which in the front were bigger and had bathrooms and kitchens while those behind had poorer dwellings around courtyards, as if they had grown out of the others without any kind of preliminary planning: they clung tightly together in the secure warmth of one another's poverty, each new wall extending another, on top of one another and underneath, every which way, with lavatories installed in communal cellars (neither gas nor water was brought into the dwellings at the very back), and at the end stood pens and sties which, as the confined space in the yard was built on and used up, imperceptibly became habitable dwellings, as if, in its helpless condition, the court-yard, bloated into holding ten dwellings, were re-enacting the process of being populated, but the rumour was circulating in the city that houses much more important than those in Dohány utca were to be demolished: the Hangman's House, for example, or the whole of Fő tér, but the perennials, the ceiling-high diffenbachia, the huge monstera, which were presented to a sculptor's studio, and the constantly spreading begonias, ferns, tradescantia, parlour palms and all the plants which Klári hadn't had the heart to inhibit in their growth and expansion and then had replanted, as if all that wild proliferation wouldn't obey and insisted that it had a future, it had somewhere to grow, spread and develop, and it wasn't a question of faith or the unshakeable quality of human endurance but merely a weakness for chlorophyll, and although every week Klári made up her mind to sell the two chandeliers or the chest of drawers, the double bed or the ornamental cast-iron stove from the mansard and the travelling chests, because there would be no room for anything in the apartment block, and she did in fact sell the majolica stove with the lilies to Zoli Karácsonyi, the dentist who was emigrating to Hungary, and one by one all sort of little things from the display cabinet, which had nothing to do with the removal, although she kept repeating that the chests and cupboards in the attic must be looked through, *Where am I to go with all this stuff, into a flat?* she asked in despair, *There's nowhere,* she muttered to herself more and more, especially after Laci died, and heavy tears ran from her cloudy, vacant eyes, but there was still the weekend house on Kányafő, at the top of the hillside that was becoming more and more developed, Cabin Number 101, built of plywood, one room and a veranda, surrounded by a garden full of big Beszterce plum trees, with a terrace with red pillars and white wooden rails which Laci brightened up every year with expensive oil paint as he did the tubs that held geraniums and indeed the whole house, he renewed the roofing felt, trimmed the stumps of the trees and the garden beds, oiled the two water-butts and the posts that held the rings, and the whole place would shine in the early March sunshine like an operetta set, and the freshly varnished name of the house glistened too—*Megkínlódtalak,* Hardgrind House, because over the years Laci had pushed everything in house and garden up there on his bicycle, he hadn't dug a foundation for the house, its walls were of thin, flexible panels as if it were intended for a single summer like a shelter built of leafy branches, the green leaves which provided hardly a month of shade before they wither, but when he bought the piece of land Laci believed that the hillside would never become so built up that it would not be possible to look down on the sprawling town, water and electricity would never be extended so that blocks of flats could be built, said he triumphantly, because as he stood in front of the terrace and looked over the recently trimmed holly bushes through his binoculars he could make out, surrounded by those modern dinosaurs, the skeletons of blocks of flats under construction, the single-storey houses of Dohány utca, obstinately lurking between the buildings of prefabricated panels, Dohány utca, the odd and even numbers of which for some mysterious reason remained alive, and the only explanation for that was a miracle, that is, in its impotence it rotted slowly on in the toils of the laws of gravity and the depredations of time, though it would have taken a long time still or the deliberate intervention of the hand of man to bring about the ultimate destruction without trace of Number 26: and so the house in Dohány utca outlived the Hangman's House, which was allegedly set on fire one night as an act of reprisal—that too could have been seen from the Kányafő, had they been there that day—and the Gypsy inhabitants of several local streets left the district and encamped at once between the smoking walls of the dread house, only to be removed in the course of a single morning by the dread vans.

THANK YOU

The last letter from Ocniţa came on 26 August: by then Laci had sent Klári on ahead with the furniture and something else, of which in the middle of summer neither she nor he could have had any inkling, and Laci promised that when he'd sold the house he'd follow her, but she travelled up to Kolozsvár with some misgivings and only after his lengthy pleading—by the time the letter reached there on 31 August Kolozsvár was in Hungary—because to Klári neither the war nor the Vienna Award had been good enough reason for the sudden removal and the separation for an indefinite period, and the ten-page letter of 26 August contained no explanation—'Not everything is as you think in your beautifully waved little head'—wrote her husband, only an account of how much the house might fetch, the young lady, that is, the Domnişoara, would give 170,000 lei for it, the chief engineer's relative 180,000, and the most that the rest offered was 150,000—he wouldn't let it go for that—so he'd rather sell to the young lady, only she hadn't got the cash, and by the time that she'd raised it . . . the other half of the house likewise belonged to a young Romanian lady, Domnyisóra, as Klári pronounced it, because Laci liked designing semi-detached houses 'and clever little passages into the cellar'—Klári recalled the painful and unexpected expression—'so that he could sneak through to the young ladies at night'—a similar narrow passage existed under the Linzmayer house in Apponyi utca, Kolozsvár, even in 1935, but the secret passage connected not the adjacent houses, but Numbers 36 and 37, which were opposite each other: Laci also qualified as a fitter of both gas and electricity so as to conceal his work, took up all the flagstones in the street and thus constructed a passage under the roadway, 1.40 metres in height and 13 in length, lit by electricity, and the road was closed while the work was in progress, but Klári didn't know of the narrow passage under Apponyi utca until 1May 1944, only when late in the evening after the usual bridge party Lili, one of the Salamon girls, wife of the tenant opposite, said in an undertone as Klári was shutting the door after Gizi and Pőtyi, *my sister Arany is escaping to Romania, Brassó, tonight, and I'm staying here in the cellar, if you like, I'll show you, but it's better if you don't know about it,* and Lili, who was short, scarcely had to bend down, *I'm not taking my cat across, it would run back, you know how cats stick to their homes rather than to people, only please, go over once a day and feed it.—What about your husband?* asked Klári, taken aback, *He knows nothing, and doesn't even want to believe what's happening, he even told Arany to sit tight, you know how naive Karl is, but I won't tell you where the entrance from your end is, I don't want to get you into trouble, Laci knows,* but at the time Laci hadn't been home for years, *And what about food? What are you going to eat in there?* but Lili brushed the question aside, it was all arranged, but Klári would have liked to ask Laci what made him think of having a low, narrow passage made between two houses, which in Apponyi út, Kolozsvár, turned out to be a spell, an incantation, but the one in Ocniţa? in south Romania, what was it for? wondered Klári, because at the time she only knew about the one in Ocniţa, but why was it necessary in the Romanian salt country, down south near Ocnele Mare, on the main road from Sinaia to Tîrgovişte, to make a secret subterranean passage between two modern villas in that cul-de-sac if not for the purpose of 'it', because that was the only ready explanation in Klári's view: so that Laci could go over to see the girls, and now too she searched the letter for the sign that would betray why Laci hadn't answered her letter for five days when she'd sent him two in a week, but by the time that Laci wrote his letter, now to a foreign address and costing three times as much, it didn't enter Klári's really lovely curly head, didn't occur to her, that letters with Romanian stamps were being delayed in the main post office in Kolozsvár until the portrait of the recently abdicated Károly

II of Romania had been over-printed with 'Kolozsvár has returned' before being sent on their way in leisurely fashion, as there was no longer anywhere to go in a hurry, but light eventually shone on the delay from Laci's ten-page letter: the weekend of which it gave an account, he wrote, *I spent in prison*, as if he had been having a good time, an adventure lasting a few days, and an excursion not without risk: he'd been arrested at his workplace early on the Friday afternoon, the report began at the top of page three, because up to that point it had only been about important matters, the sale of the house, and a charge-sheet of thirty-eight points was laid against him, he couldn't remember all thirty-eight, he wrote, because it was only read aloud to him, it wasn't put into his hand, but at all events a few accusations *concerned you, my dear heart*: 'Just because I kill chickens Hungarian fashion?', snorted Klári on reading the accusation made against her, that the wife slaughters chickens Hungarian fashion—*When once that stupid Romanian maid used an axe to cut the head off my lovely guinea fowl, which I'd brought straight from home and raised in the kitchen, and she didn't get the blood out, and all the flesh was as blue as if it had frozen to death, that precious meat had to be given to the cat, it would have turned my stomach over, that purple meat, so of course, after that I killed them properly, just a single cut, and what lovely white meat there was! And I can't speak Romanian! And I introduced kosher rites to the village! If the Jews slaughter animals that way as well, what can I do about it! And the things those stinking Romanian peasants plot between them! Because I taught that Wallachian scumbag how to kill a chicken and make consommé, because peasants like her throw away the liquid after cooking the chicken!*—she burst out, and according to the letter Laci had spent two nights in prison, but the reason must have been, he guessed, not really the chicken or the proud Hungarian wife but that his colleagues and well-wishers in the construction work had put a German map in front of him for him to translate, to provoke him, but he hadn't realized that immediately and had readily translated it and commented on it, so that was the mistake, he wrote, that he'd told them that the German map could hardly be very accurate, what did the Germans know about us?, they ought to get a Hungarian map instead, they were more reliable ... 'We know this region a bit better, after all, it's ours', and then added hesitantly 'or was', but just then it became 'ours' again, because the Vienna Award came into effect at three in the afternoon on 30 August 1940 and Laci was locked up in jail by five o'clock, and in that last letter he gave a detailed account of the prison in Romînica and *my almost-miraculous liberation, because I got out of there absolutely like a Houdini,* that is to say, he got a very decent lawyer who didn't put him up before a military tribunal, because the total of thirty-eight accusations and eight witness-statements aroused his suspicion that such a thing could only be the result of personal animosity, as the Hungarian 'Domnu inginer' had offended the young lady's fiancé, a Romanian officer, *and he'd got designs on our house,* thought Klári, and in her next letter, in which she was much more gentle towards her husband, she enquired kindly about the cats, had the kittens been born yet and how many were there, she told him to sell the rest of the chickens when he came home, and—Klári left it to the end of the letter—she was afraid by herself and *he hadn't come in two months,* and she was being sick every morning, perhaps she was ... but it couldn't be the best moment, however much they wanted it, and in the end she crossed all this out and wrote the letter out again, but never had a reply for more than four years, only a card from the young lady: *Loţi e bine,* she wrote in her florid script, Laci was well, the card took weeks to arrive, and the young lady wrote only the one line, thinking that Klári wouldn't understand any more, or that a more detailed account would be none of her business, but Klári stared in desperation at the almost colourless letter-card—how did the young lady know about her husband, perhaps her officer had some information, or perhaps he was still at the salt mine? and why didn't he come home? because now it was certain that she was pregnant, it wasn't the best time, but she'd looked forward to it very much and she couldn't keep her food down, but even when she read the prison letter she had her suspicions, when Laci described in detail his common criminal cellmates and the Bucharest whores, and she felt relieved when he described their loathsome diseases, but after the young lady's letter-card she trembled and waited anxiously for more news which King Mihai's 15-bani portrait would bring to Apponyi utca, but no more *Loți e bine* came and Klári waited petrified until in 1942 she decided to have a little marble tablet engraved 'Bring Laci home' and to take it to be put up in the church in Egyetem utca and dedicated, it was done by the mason in the cemetery, two lines of gilded lettering, and she was going to have it hung on the wall in the University church for Laci to be brought home to her and Lili, who, aged eighteen months at the time, stood there in the side aisle of the cold church, which was full of votary tablets, *You'd like to order one saying* Thank you *as well, wouldn't you?*, the mason suggested, *He'll be home, you'll see, and I'll reduce the price for two, my dear Mrs Kühn, or shall we put* Danke schön? *You're Saxons, aren't you? Where were you born, Klári*, to which the answer was a scarcely audible 'Segesvár', *Or rather* Mulțumesc? *Your husband's in Romania, you mean? Anyway, all languages are the same price for* Thank you. *We can even put* Spasibo! *They say the Russians are coming. That's all we need! There's a man here that knows Russian, and I'll engrave it with my own fair hand, I've done Hebrew before now, you know! So will you take the* Thank you *now, see, it's ready? It's a pleasure to see the way it shines, I painted it yesterday,* and he held it out to the little girl, and Klári paid for *Thank you* as well, Bring our Laci home *is sixteen letters, should we put a name underneath? What's your name, little one?*—addressing Lili—*Well, not if you say not, all letters cost the same, accents don't count, it'll be ready in a week,* said the mason, at which Klári raised her plucked eyebrows because surely he'd been complaining earlier of having no work, all you could expect these days were shared graves and wooden crosses, but the mason just smiled, that wasn't the point, a mass of street names were being replaced, lots of streets were being renamed and there were lots of new ones too:

Hunyadi tér was becoming Adolf Hitler tér, and there was Horthy Miklós sugárút, the one that led down to the station, and a heap of Hungarian memorial plaques, at least a couple were set up every day, *There's as much work here, if you please, as there's shit on a battlefield, forgive my French in front of the little girl*, and Klári shrugged her shoulders and took the *Thank you* plaque, which the mason wrapped up in the previous week's number of *Ellenzék*, and he showed Lili the two-week-old puppies while Klári stood there impatiently and read the headlines: *Japanese–American sea battle off Santa Cruz; Apafi funeral at Farkas utca Reform church; 118 cabs and 103 taxis serve Kolozsvár; illusionist and conjurer Carloni at New York Grill; Buy 'Better Luck' lottery-ticket!; New primary school in Méhes utca; Budapest premiere of Jenő Huszka's new operetta 'Lieutenant Mária'; New number of* Termés *published, cinema programmes*, but she couldn't get used to the new names of the cinemas, how could cinemas be named Árpád, King Mátyás, Corvin, Rákóczi and Transylvania? previously they'd gone to the Rio and the Apollo and the Royal, and mostly to Janovics' cinema, the Select in Egyetem utca and, of course, to that little fleapit in Pap utca, on the back page the restored Magyar Bolt (Hungarian Shop) was advertising, it had now taken over the Sora establishments, and in big letters, framed: 'Goods of Christian Origin', and even the swinish Jenő Dajbukát was shamelessly advertising his ironmongery business, was the stinking Armenian not ashamed of himself!—and Klári angrily folded up her last week's newspaper and as she was about to close it there was the good news at last in huge letters in the headline: *On 15 November Kolozsvár celebrates 150th anniversary of Hungarian-language theatre in National Theatre on Hitler tér*—and she read the impressive programme, perhaps she ought to go, she thought, I'll ask the Linzmayers if they're coming to the National, we haven't actually been since we came back, and she read on in the programme, what Janovics was proposing if he now got back what he'd built, it would be *Bánk bán* or *János vitéz*, or the *Hamlet* that had been broken off in 1919, because she thought that Jenő Janovics had come back from the summer tour with his company, but the name didn't appear anywhere in the brilliant programme and his wife, Lili Poór, was only to appear as a 'guest performer', someone that wasn't a member of the Kolozsvár company, *Well, hello, world!*, the Romanians had ousted him from his theatre in 1919 and now the Hungarians didn't want him, *and Janovics had sat in his flat on Petőfi utca, writing a book about the Hunyadi tér theatre and nobody's ever going to publish it, the poor man's trying it with Singer and Wolfner in Budapest but nowadays they're very cautious, or perhaps he'll try at some Aryanized publisher, Athenaeum or Franklin, because here there's no chance, but even they won't want it in Budapest, they can delay it for ever and a day, or rather the State has frowned on his collection, that book'll never be published here, my boy,* and while she was cleaning the mud from her shoes at the cemetery gate she recalled that the previous day, as she was coming up Honvéd utca she'd seen a poster saying that the Jewish Theatre had been founded in the Ironmen's Club and was performing Ferenc Molnár, *So there, Janovics, a block away from your wonderful theatre, you can start over there, in that dark hole*, thought Klári, but Janovics had been in Budapest for a long time by then and she discovered that only in 1945, when he and his wife came back and took over the theatre on the Sétatér again, never again the one on Hunyadi tér that he'd had built, and now Klári was about to leave the cemetery on Petőfi utca, and as she was going that way she went into the church on Egyetem utca with the *Thank you* plaque: she stood in front of the statue of St Barbara who 'Lay in peace there beneath the altars of the faith', and who had been 'in the twenty-fifth year of married life', she read from the black marble tablet, on the cold stone which Barbara's husband had raised to her, and Klári looked at the plaster statue of St Barbara, as big as a ten-year-old child, and the two of them stood there face to face like an original and a miniature copy: thin, bloodless lips, long, pale face, sea-blue, wide-set eyes, straight eyebrows, narrow, light hands with manicured, almond-shaped fingernails—those must be size six hands, thought

Klári—and all that was missing from St Barbara, wrapped in a red shawl and holding in her hand a bunch of wilting lilies, was the short, thick, plaited hair, and Klári stood on tiptoe and looked around, then, with a sudden movement, placed the *Thank you* tablet in the statue's hands, and in the gloom with the little plaque in its hands the statue looked as if the fragile saint was off for a walk in the town carrying a neat little handbag, and when Klári felt the cold, dead plaster hand she shuddered, but her own hands were just as cold as Barbara's, in which the heavy marble tablet now lay as if she had put a pagan spell on her, *Laci, come home! Laci, come home! Laci, come home!* muttered Klári, and then suddenly turned on her heel and with her cold, dry hand seized Lili, who burst into tears, and there the shining tablet which she had just obtained from the mason was left, and Klári had begun to hustle Lili towards the exit when from the semi-darkness of the last pews there appeared a woman in black, her face tearful, who smiled wanly at them: *You mustn't cry, you must be happy and say thank you, because Daddy's come home, hasn't he?*—and she turned to Klári, who the following week went for the 'Bring Laci home' plaque that she'd ordered, but that she took straight round to Apponyi utca, didn't even unwrap it from the newspaper but put it in her painting box, which she hadn't touched since the wedding, the dried-up tubes in it were light, the varnish had started to come off the expensive brushes which she'd obtained from Vienna, but the marble tablet restored the box to its former weight, when it had been full of heavy oil-paint tubes two fingers thick, and as she held the box in one hand she felt a painful desire at least to give expression to that dark self-portrait which she had abandoned in August 1939, a week before the wedding, but a troubling sense of guilt stopped her bringing down the folder with the half-finished canvas, it was as if she would be cheating Laci, sinning against him, taking advantage of his absence, preventing his return or sending him straight to his doom, *If he comes back I won't paint again*, she decided, as if staking her most valuable possession, although as early as 1938 Laci had decided in a single sentence *I'm not having you painting, we don't need it, I earn enough,* the new well-off husband from Parajd, according to his marriage certificate Kühn, in Hungarian times Kun on his railway pass, and on his later issued 'passport', with which he travelled home to Kolozsvár Kohn, and Jewish, and finally on his pension-book Engineer Vasile Kuhn, and Klári took the black, lacquered *boksz*, on which she'd painted a delicate Japanese landscape, up to the mansard, but as she held it in her hands the box was again as excitingly heavy as in her unmarried days, and all that was missing from the complete equipment was the lacquered, iron-cornered basket-work chest in which she kept the box and the rolled canvases—that was to return with Laci, undamaged, the suitcase too, Laci too, who was standing there one morning in late autumn at the open door, thin as a rake, bald and brown as a Gypsy, a good year after the *Thank you* had been put in position, confronted by a three-year-old girl who stared at him with her big eyes of the same unmistakeable blue that shone back from his swarthy face, and before she could run away in fright he asked her if she'd like a little kitten, to which the little girl gave a silent and serious nod, and he opened the woven basket-work case with its iron corners which seemed to have been invented specifically for the transportation of cats, and took from it a young three-coloured cat, *I've brought this for you,* said he, *her name's Jozefina Señadora Ananchita, because her grandmother was Jozefina, her mother was Señadora, and Ananchita means 'First-born', like you, I think, because I'm your father,* and Lili took hold of the cat by two front legs and the helpless animal's back paws scrabbled at the floor, and with her heavy burden the child ran up to the mansard, calling from the foot of the stairs *I've been given a pussy by a gentleman, it's name is . . . I've forgotten,* and Klári shut the heavy painting boksz again and in a scarcely audible voice said *Thank you,* the little girl pushed open the door, the half-finished self-portrait fell off the easel as she went past, Klári bent down to the cat which the little girl was triumphantly displaying, and asked her sternly *Did you say thank you?*

TRANSLATION

Klári could only find one old newspaper from 1938 and from that discovered the address of the editorial office, because she wanted to place
a small advertisement: *Piaţa Unirii 1*, she spelt out, but letters had to
be sent to Calea Moţilor—which can Piaţa Unirii be?, she wondered,
the other was, of course, Mócok útja, the road to Monostor, but that
wasn't what she required, but the editorial address: *Cluj, Piaţa Unirii 1*
was given in small print below the headline in *Ellenzék*, and as she
leafed further down the pile collected by Laci she realized only then
that in the *Brassói Lapok* of 1939 there was also Braşov, strada Zizin, of
course, Egyetem tér must be Unirii where the library was as well, that
was where the editorial office must be if it hadn't moved, and she went
on reading the clipping that had been carefully attached to the banner
headline: 'Chief engineer dismissed for ignorance of national language
reinstated', followed by a brief account of the incident involving Oszkár
Tellman, Laci's contemporary at university, who had turned up at their
place once for a birthday celebration and who had been suing the Torda
glassworks for eighteen months, his lawyer had finally won suitable
compensation for him, but Laci had brandished the newspaper as he
explained to Klári, you see, you have to know Romanian, otherwise I
wouldn't have been able to get the job of junior engineer at the Ocniţa
salt mines, I could have gone and lodged a complaint, he always said,
because afterwards he'd really been the only Hungarian in the place,
he'd wanted to prove by getting the appointment in the Romanian-
speaking area that he couldn't only hold a job under the wing of his
strict father in the salt mines at Parajd, where he'd be for ever just 'the
managing director's son', but in the big Ocnele Mare mines in
Romanian country, *there was something else the matter with that Oszkár,*

in any case, said Klári quietly, but Laci dismissed the idea: 'You're imagining things', but when in 1941 Klári put in the advertisement: 'For
sale, Wirth upright cross-strung piano, Linzmayer House, Apponyi út
36, Mrs Kühn', she was advised in the office to give a box number for
fear of being burgled, and these names did not go down so well with
Hungarian purchasers, she would do better to put 'by Christian woman',
at which Klári considered the suggestion and asked how much per word
the advertisement would cost and said regretfully that she would rather
save those three words and the three *fillérs* that they would cost, but
next day, 18 May 1941, she bought *Ellenzék* to see if her advertisement
was in, but on page three, where general news of the city was printed,
she was surprised to find that the case of the Jewish engineer Oszkár
Tellman had been re-examined, he had connived with the Jewish
lawyers and the Jewish- and Romanian-controlled court, his claim for
compensation was dismissed, he was given a hefty fine and suspended
from his position, she turned quickly to the penultimate page and there
read on one side the extensive, framed advertisement of the new
Hungarian Shop chain and looked for her own among the other
columns of small advertisements on the right-hand side: 'For sale, coat,
fit slim person', 'Any business transacted in Bucharest', 'Lost in
Fellegvár út, bread- and flour-coupons in names of Goldstein and
Friedman', 'Wish to send money to relatives in Brasso, will pay in
Kolozsvár in *pengő*s to appropriate person to be handed over in *leis*',
'Permanent waving, Mrs Tompa, Mussolini út 12', 'Disappeared a
month ago, mentally ill son of Ágoston Vajda, aged 20—Worried
mother', 'Because of bereavement, wanted, loving parents to adopt
healthy six-month-old boy. Enquiries to Kolozsvár, Kővári L. u. 28',
and the paper shook in the expectant Klári's hand, she hadn't heard
from Laci in several months, 'Room in elegant flat of non-Aryan family,
suit lady, young lady or female student, address on request', 'Horthy
and Bocskay hats available, Fortuna hat shop', 'Hungarian Jewish Laws
available at Dr Mandel's translation bureau, Unió utca 24', at which

Klári realized that it was to the Mandel bureau that she'd been sent to have documents drawn up, but she persistently delayed in applying for citizenship, 'former Romanian subjects of Hungarian extraction' could 'opt for' nationality if they possessed the relevant documents, *They'll turf you out of the hospital if your papers aren't in order, you'll see*, said Irén Salamon the paediatrician, and Klári had been waiting and waiting, *When it starts to move I'll go that day, Dr Fazekas too says that if it starts to move it'll survive*, she decided, and by that time her parents had sent her certificate of baptism and she'd obtained the printed form, *You must produce your birth and marriage certificates*, said the official in city hall drily, and in Romanian translation also—*I recommend the Mandel translation bureau, Unió utca 24—baptism certificate, your parents' birth certificates and certificates of baptism, certificate of address and income not more than three months old and a treasury stamp*, and her parents also sent the certificate of income from Vásárhely, they had testified before a notary that they had been supporting their married daughter, *What about your husband?* asked another official next time, to which Klári said that he was working in Romania and, something about which she would have done better to remain silent, she hadn't heard from him for months, *This won't be easy*, and the uniformed man shook his head, *And your certificate of baptism, what's the date on it?*, as he turned over the new document, *When did you convert to Christianity?*, to which Klári crossly replied that the original had been lost while moving house and so a copy had had to be obtained from Segesvár, *Tell me*, the man turned the pages with leisurely indifference, *where does this name 'Soket' come from?*, to which Klári replied anxiously *We don't know, my father doesn't know—I see that your sister was actually put down as 'Schocket'—Yes*, said Klári helpfully, *the Saxons registered his name in Segesvár, but Father and my grandfather, Dr Károly Soket senior, medical officer in Petrozsény, wrote it like this, I can get his medical diploma sent along*, at which the official slowly raised his head, *Petrozsény's in Romania now, isn't it?*, and Klári suddenly recalled her father and mother's correspondence of 1905, before they were married, when Father had been sent to Segesvár as financial inspector, letters in elaborate, sloping handwriting which she'd been reluctant to read for a long time, then she'd suddenly come across them in a suitcase: Father wrote that in Segesvár there was no one to see but 'disgusting Saxon characters' in the cobbled streets, which were so rough that you wore out your shoes in a month, and nothing to hear but 'Saxon cackling', of which he could make nothing at all, but despite his mother's objections he'd sent Klári to a Saxon primary school because in his opinion it was stricter and better, *Well, all right*, the ashen-faced man made a tired, dismissive gesture, *I came here from Szolnok, I've been working in the tax inspectorate, I can't make head or tail of all this, I'll have to ask for your birth certificate*, at which Klári passed it over from the pile in front of her, the Romanian original and the translation from the Mandel bureau, typed and tied up with ribbons in Hungarian colours, *Excuse me*, and he looked up from the document, *but this translation has not been made from the original, you weren't born in 1919 but 1909, I'd be obliged for the original*, to which Klári said that the Hungarian-language original had been lost in 1919 when likewise they became naturalized, or, she hesitated and corrected herself: the documents were replaced, *You can only opt for citizenship on the basis of original documents*, declared the man, and closed the many-paged application that lay in front of him: *The taking of Hungarian citizenship isn't compulsory, the law doesn't insist on it*, said he in an official tone *as a point of information*, and carefully tied up the folder, which Klári had, with her own hand, decorated with Japanese water lilies, and in the same building in 1945, when once more documents had to be obtained, another official asked *Doamnă dragă, dar pîn-la urmă, cum vă cheamă?* (*Dear lady, I simply can't get people's names right here, what did you say yours was in the end?*), but on this occasion Klári completely failed to understand what she was being asked and Laci quickly interpreted for her *He's asking what your name is after all that*, because her certificate of baptism (now no longer required) gave Klára Gizella, the birth certificate had

Clarissa, *Originalul, vă rog* (The original, please—according to Laci, he sounded like a peasant from the Olt), to which Klári said that the original had been lost, but Laci interpreted her patiently, syllabically delivered sentences: all that she had was the 1941 Hungarian translation of the Romanian translation of 1919 of the Hungarian original of 1909, and in the meantime she began to write down the years on the back of an envelope which she took from her bag and to draw, so that O stood for original and T for translation, with little arrows between them, and at the same time she tapped with her sharp pencil that the one before had always been lost, and what she had was therefore a Hungarian translation which had been made from a Hungarian original which didn't exist, because in-between there had been a Romanian translation which didn't exist either, therefore the translation had to be original, did he see, *Aşa o prostie n-am mai auzit, doamnă, vă bateţi joc de organe?* (I've never heard such rubbish, madam, are you making fun of the authorities?) but this time Laci didn't interpret but answered direct, oh, not in the least, he had misunderstood, *Madam*, the gendarme went on, pushing the documents back to Klári, and her swollen belly jutted towards him, as she couldn't pull the chair up to the table, *if you don't produce clear documents you'll give birth to a stateless child. We're giving Hungarian citizenship to Romanian subjects of Hungarian ancestry. If you're Saxons I can't do anything for you.* But under the table Klári opened her handbag, took out the letter-card from the envelope in which her father-in-law had sent a photograph showing them standing at the entrance of salt mine Number Seven with the management and workers, with the handwritten words 'Parajd has come back, 1940', and tried to stuff money into the envelope, but the official stood up, like a man that has said his last word, *Don't do that. I advise you to go and see the Jew, Mandel, have the documents sorted out urgently, bring the originals here and we'll exchange them for you without another word,* and on the way out Klári still had the photograph in her hand, 'If only Laci had come back,' she thought tearfully, but four years later they sat side by side in the office smiling, because by then Laci had found work in the dairy at Dés, and from then on everything was going to go swimmingly: *Dear Father! Thank you for trying to help us again, and for offering me the vacant post of secretary at Parajd, but at Dés dairy* . . . and so he just had to take his documents in to the dairy or butter factory, some people called it one thing, others the other, in any case all the cats in Apponyi utca—they were living there until the Linzmayers' or Vályis' houses were sold—were getting fat as the result of Laci's daily deliveries, *Lili's got the original*, Klári was suddenly pleased, and she proffered the three-year-old's paper, *Poftiți* (Here you are), that was all she knew: Klári was happy that at least one of them would have documents, the child would be in order, *So, goodbye*, whispered Laci quietly, *we shan't be seeing that again*, and the perspiring man pointed crossly towards the wall, where two little metal plaques hung one below the other: *Timp de convorbire: 3 minute*, and *Vorbiți romînește* (Speaking time: three minutes, and speak in Romanian), but the man leafed lazily through the translations, tied together with ribbons in the national colours of red, yellow and blue, the Kühns' ever-fatter dossier, *Nu știu ce să fac cu voi* (I don't know what to do with you), and he shook his head, *faceți-vă hîrtii ca lumea* (have proper documents made), *mergeți la juriștii de pe strada* (go to the public notary in . . . street), and he began to search in his drawer for the address, *Da, acolo lîngă magazinul Herbak* (Yes, next door to János Herbák's shoe shop), *acuma nu știu cum se numește* (now I don't know his name) and Laci interpreted, *Is it Mandel?* asked Klári, *Da, aia e* (Yes, that's right), and at last Klári's application was accepted, *But Laci, what do other people do?* she asked when they were in the street, *Surely everybody's lost their original documents*, and as they left the cool shade of the city hall Laci reached into his shirt pocket and brought out a handwritten piece of paper which was folded into four, and which Klári had never seen: the original birth certificate of László Elemér Kuhn, issued at 'Deésakna' on 21 June 1910, he grinned broadly, his white teeth gleaming in his suntanned face: *I never surrender the original, know what*

I mean?, one never gives up the original, you have to say that it's been lost, the Romanians or the Hungarians or the Hottentots have stolen it, it was burnt when our house was bombed, Klári my dear, get it right, we don't give original documents to anybody, don't even show them, not even to the police, we'll go and see Mandel and make a statement that the original doesn't exist, and that'll be that, and even if the King of Romania comes back and asks for it in person we still don't produce it, right?—But in that case, asked Klári, her eyes wide, *what use is this document if we never show it to anybody?* Laci lit a cigarette and took his time answering: *It's so that there'll always be an original, get it?—But what's it for?*, Klári insisted, *what's the use of an original if we can make a notarized statement to this villain Mandel to the effect that its lost? Just think of the money that Mandel must have made, his bureau was set up in 1918,* and so they went down Magyar utca with Laci going into a long explanation that whenever a new regime happens to come in and ask for original documents and they're necessary, even then we don't produce them, but Klári was insistent that if a document is never to be shown it has no value *on God's earth.* Laci stopped dead in the middle of Főtér, held his three fingers together and explained, as if to a child, that once things were shown to people, believe you me, they got lost, and there was no knowing what would happen, and Klári shrugged her shoulders, she couldn't care less what happened, she'd never been asked for the documents before and even so they were lost, it was taking a lot of to-ing and fro-ing and money to have new translations made, and even then they were going to brazen it out, say that the original no longer existed, the Gypsies had the right idea, they never had anything put on paper, only thought and moved on, or crossed the frontier, didn't even know what country they were in, but as they reached the corner of Főtér they both acquiesced in the irresolvable contradiction of the two sorts of truth and turned into Unió utca, making for Mandel's bureau, from which by that time a long queue snaked out all the way down to the former Kötő utca, recently renamed Ion Rațiu.

K and K looked into each other's eyes for the first time above the cradle, but despite the fifteen-year difference in their ages, whenever Kocka and Klári might have met, their paths must have crossed several times as they both came from small towns in the east of the Dual Monarchy: Kocka was born on 19 April 1895 in Nagyenyed (Strassburg am Mirsch/Aiud) and Klári some hundred kilometres farther east as the crow flies in Segesvár (Schässburg/Sighişoara) on 20 March 1910, Kocka attended Nagyenyed college, and from 1915 we find her in Kolozsvár studying medicine, though she didn't defend her doctoral dissertation—also in Kolozsvár—until 1928 at the age of thirty-three, Klári, however, 'went up' to Kolozsvár to look around in 1928 (her parents had by then moved to Marosvásárhely, to live with her mother's parents—Segesvár was only where her father worked as a financial adviser), and on that occasion had her hair cut short, for which Károly Soket, her strict, already retired father, gave her a mighty slap, the only one she received in her life, as it seemed that at the sight of her fashionable Eton crop he was unexpectedly confronted with the fact that his daughter was an adult and took her own decisions, and this he could not forgive, but her mother burst into tears, and Klári announced that on leaving commercial school she meant to go to 'painting school', while Kocka after receiving her diploma went to Zajzon for five years as a spa doctor, and finally left there in 1927, a pivotal point in her life, while Klári went to Budapest and Vienna (with a passport, a *Passeport à l'étranger*, issued by His Majesty Ferdinand I of Romania, in which

53 In normal usage, *Kaiserlich und Königlich* is a colloquial allusion to the Imperial and Royal, institutions of the Austro-Hungarian Dual Monarchy (1867–1918).

the colour of her skin was recorded—not her religion—and a stern red seal stamped in it on the frontier informed her in Hungarian that she might not undertake any work or employment), and eventually she found a place in the studio of Aurel Ciupe, former teacher of Kolozsvár, and decided that 'I'm going to be *a painter*', at first she tried to live without help from her parents and designed carpets for a factory, Kocka married in 1921, Klári in 1938, *well*, both of them definitely married *well*, not very early but rather after due consideration, but although K and K lived in the same town, just a few streets apart, for forty years there was little reason for the 'communist Jewish woman' (as Klári thought of Kocka) and the 'petty-bourgeois gentry girl' (Kocka's term for Klári) to meet, and their careers were unlikely to impinge on each other until they met over a cradle: for the impossible and the parallel to be at arm's length from each other all it takes is a plump newborn child with wondering eyes in a cradle of woven rushes in the middle of the room: the cradle was in Klári's house in Dohány utca, in the middle of the big room, as if on a visit, or as if the casual call of the new arrival had thrown the unprepared family into a state of surprise, and they didn't know where in the house to put her and had only had time to bring the light, airy summer cradle which had been bought for the firstborn down from the loft and dust it, and the big, lazy child in it, that had not moved much in her mother's belly, looked just as surprised as those around her: Kocka looked at Klári, Klári at Kocka, and both at the child with the enquiring gaze, and at the foolish idea that the two of them, who for ten years—not ten, indeed, but twenty-five!—had regarded each other with such sincere disdain, should now have a grandchild in common, and they looked at her wide-eyed, like a supernatural miracle, to think that their *common* blood ran in that tiny, 4.5-kilo body, and the child too seemed to stare uncomprehendingly at them as if to say what were the three of them doing in one room, where the fragrant Klári, with her fine features and thin lips, and the short and swarthy Kocka with her wide mouth and her grey hair in an untidy chignon, were bending inquisitively over her, she to whom her parents hadn't yet given a name, as if her father hadn't yet accepted that it was not a son that had been born (that is, it couldn't be Andrej, after Andrej Bolkonsky), and her mother had said in advance that she meant to leave any boy in the hospital—*I don't want a son*! she had declared, but as it had been a girl she'd brought her home, because a daughter was what she very much did want, and now both parents were waiting perplexedly for a sudden inspired solution to realize their hopes, the name, while K and K were bending over the cradle, focusing on the white-clad infant, the third present, who would save them from each other because Kocka and Klári hated their own selves reflected in the other, as if they were both looking at themselves in that merciless mirror that did not intentionally distort but showed them nevertheless as unrecognizably pitiful and paltry, in which they were only half visible because that mirror showed the half of them that was actually lacking: because *K has been successful, but at what a price*—thought K, and *K has not been successful, but at what a price*—thought the other K, because in fact both of them had married *well*, Kocka the well-to-do protestant Székely doctor from a reputable family, who promised a secure, infinitely long and, as it turned out, dull future, but in any case a shared career in medicine, the rest-home, cure-village and medicinal springs in Zajzon, and sons, all of which Kocka—still Erzsébet to everybody in those days—felt was little or nothing, felt that in the taciturn, passionately industrious Székely family, which consisted mostly of men, she was even then the 'Jewish woman', even if she gave birth to the expected boy children, three in number and christened (compulsorily in their family) Miklós, István and János, whom she bore in that order, so as after brief consideration to abandon them: but she didn't return to her parents' house in Kolozsvár, where she, as a 'bluestocking', with university studies behind her, a protestant husband and Christian children, could never count as an ordinary member of the family, least of all as a Jewish woman, but she moved on to where, according to the best information, *ahead* was possible, where she could discover and create her own new family and religion of which she could become a member with full rights, and Klári too had married well, not early, if anything rather late at the age of twenty-eight, after going to art schools, also marrying a Székely with a good salary, though with a strange name for a Székely, a young engineer, in response to her parents' gentle and persistent encouragement when he courted her—Laci was a very good prospect, a steady sort, with a decent salary and a tidy family—because apart from her talent, her loyalty, a few pieces of porcelain and some table- and bed linen, Klári's dowry was merely an elegant wardrobe, because in the Romanian period her father had been unemployed—previously he'd been a civil servant, but with the extinction of the State he couldn't serve the new regime for lack of knowledge of the language—but Klári's mother brought the modest-sized, rented flats in Vásárhely into the marriage—they were ever less in number and were slowly swallowed up by time, the inability to keep house and most of all by Great-grandfather's passion for cards (to which a bullet put an end one dawn, after he'd staked his two daughters and lost), and Klári was a so-called modern woman: she rode a bicycle, played tennis, swam, went hiking, was a passionate reader and listened to records brought back from Budapest, had her thick, curly hair cut short, and went dancing at the Sétatér Club and the Ursus beer hall—sometimes with Bandi Klájn, which her parents either didn't know or preferred to ignore, merely sent the money—which they found somehow—for the art school (from which, in the end, there was no qualification) and the escapades in Budapest and Vienna, and mentioned less and less frequently the strong, stocky boy whom she met bathing at Szováta, who persisted in writing short, succinct letters and sending modest bunches of flowers, so that in 1938 Klári too should feel that marriage to László Kühn made sense, as did Kocka's to the doctor, though in the latter case there was more passion and discouragement at home, but in any case 'marrying well' meant marrying without love, and Klári's love had actually been Bandi Klájn, who sent long, passionate letters from Vásárhely but never ventured to ask for her hand because marriage to him couldn't be *good* in any respect, Kocka, on the other hand, had no lover (nor had Erzsébet), and if she had she might perhaps have left Zajzon to go to him rather than the Party, so instead Kocka married the Party only for the said Party to desert her on the spot shortly after their nuptials—dangerous and life-threatening for a long time, but demanding eternal loyalty—had been officially and openly announced (after August 1944), because Kocka was excluded from the list of founding members in 1946, and she married badly a second time too, because during the war she married the Romanian artist Viktor Constantinescu, who spoke excellent Hungarian and who sent her the application for divorce to Szamosfalva prison, because he felt that like her relatives, a Jewish woman that had been caught in an illegal organization wasn't going to survive the war, so it was best to divorce her, and Klári's Bandi Klájn also married and went off to Palestine, and as Klári looked at Kocka's grey, solid figure she felt then too that she'd married *well* (Laci was at the time smoking a cigarette in the courtyard and mending a wheel on the pram), even if at the very beginning of their married life he had made it clear that *I don't want you painting, we don't need it*, not so much forcefully prohibiting something as designating a whole new course for their fifty-one years of marriage, then just beginning, not as if painting were something forbidden or harmful, just completely superfluous and unprofitable, but Klári didn't know how to be a wife and mother *and* paint all at once, and while she was thinking about this war broke out, Laci was trapped in Romania, and during the difficult months of her eagerly awaited but then unbearable, lonely pregnancy Klári felt it risible to be yearning for her palette and painting box in a Hungary which afforded her little if any pleasure, and even in her own eyes was ashamed of this inexplicable and irrational, and moreover inappropriate desire, and by the time they'd moved to Dohány utca and Laci had built the perfect place for painting on top of the house, the peaceful mansard with its big windows, which could have become her own real little studio, of which she'd always dreamt, Klári could see in it nothing better than a lumber room and a place to dry clothes which remained there above the house and Klári's head as if intended, with its emptiness and unused motionlessness—in winter the plants off the veranda were put there to dry out—to serve as a permanent reminder of her plan, her erstwhile, now-abandoned, desires, and her dark ('quite clever', in Laci's words) pictures—a female nude, a Gypsy violinist, a portrait of her sister and a self-portrait that was slowly darkening completely—hung on the wall in the gloomy, windowless middle room that was used as a dining room: she had portrayed herself in black, veiled in mourning for her sister who had died young, and by then the material of that veil had become thicker and thicker as if coming to independent life in the picture, while the face behind it was less and less discernible, so that in the end it shrouded the painted face like a prophecy or a threat, as if Klári had used it literally to veil her past, her former desires: *I'm going to be a painter, a theatre set-and-costume designer, or an industrial artist, and plan huge modern carpets and furniture*, she wrote of her dreams to the handsome, curly-haired Bandi Klájn, at whose side she imagined all this, only—instead of painting and designing and Bandi Klájn—to keep herself and her tiny, fatherless daughter in wartime by making men's underwear out of monogrammed bed linen and selling it at the Ószer, and later she sewed for the whole of Dohány utca, altering and mending things for friends and especially the family, and then, at the age of sixty, there she stood face to face with Kocka, by that time she'd worked under a real industrial artist making mass-produced things, hundreds of dresses of the same sizes and patterns, because the one had truly given up, and at what a price, while the other had not given up, and at what a price, the one had actually messed up, but at what a price, and the other had not, but at what a price, and as they stood face to face in wordless loathing they no longer bent over the low cradle that rocked between them but looked with scorn and anger at the half of themselves that was lacking but present in the other, and this cradle was the only link between the two women, who otherwise would have had no reason to meet and speak to each other, because neither the fact that both had moved to the same town, nor that they spoke the same language, was sufficient reason for anything—that they were 'Transylvanian Hungarians' seemed too broad a term, devoid of handholds and, surprisingly, limits, an outmoded, shapeless thing, an empty, unfilled frame, at least as incoherent and various as Kocka's Jewish relatives with their differing aims and lifestyles (her brother Pál became a Zionist and moved to Israel, Jenő was a communist, and their parents had remained Orthodox Jews like the four brothers who, together with their children, were herded into the ghetto at the brickworks), because in the Dual Monarchy, the country which had given equal rights to the one K's ancestors and a living and a civil-service salary to the other K's, the two women found themselves in an unexpected and inconceivable, alien and ill-defined concept which others called Transylvanian Hungarian, but it was, and even in 1971 still remained, Kocka and Klári's sole common possession, when Kocka was seventy-six, Klári sixty-two, that women *therefore* had chosen, chosen something, and not chosen—Klári had not chosen painting, Kocka had not chosen her family, and correspondingly: Kocka had quickly and easily borne three sons, while Klári, after years of waiting and suffering, in the depths of despair and after twenty-four hours in labour, had borne one daughter, after whom there could be no more, and then that Kocka's deserted son and Klári's hard-won daughter should then chance upon each other *in a less than good marriage*, in which at first there was love—Klári could not forgive that marriage, she didn't go to the wedding, and though she loved Janó like a son she could not accept him as her daughter's fiancé because Lili *was not marrying well*, while Kocka didn't give a damn—and now the second fruit of this brief, mindless love was rocking there to right and left between K and K in the cradle that had been brought down from the mansard, wondering in silence at two such different faces bending over her, two women, by then two old women, who had had no reason to meet before 4 July 1971, Kocka had refused to look at the firstborn child but the second had had to come for her to relent and make the kilometre journey from Brassai utca to Dohány utca, and the little girl was shortly to call these two people, who were inconceivably remote from each other, her grandmothers, that is, Kocka and Granny.

THE TOWN IN SUSPENSE

When the lions were boarded up at the Romanian Theatre—perhaps they'd been like that for weeks, surrounded by wooden slats, people took no notice, perhaps the theatre was going to be refurbished, though there hadn't been an announcement and nobody knew anything about it, and perhaps the renovation would have started with the two little turrets, the two Roman charioteers, born winners, wearing laurel wreaths—there was somebody that certainly did know something about it: under cover of darkness the lions had been removed to Bucharest to the palace that was under construction, the biggest in the country, and only their now-vacant places were covered by the wood-work, because those that had their suspicions were afraid that the town would be taken to pieces in the same way as the stones of Rome: there were also those that one night saw the enormous cross on the church in Főtér, covered with gold-leaf said to weigh 7 kilos, replaced by a heli-copter with a new one which, when expert eyes examined it in full day-light, caused some surprise because, good heavens!, it was less shiny than the original, it was only a poor imitation, and there were those that thought that the gold leaf had been stripped off long before and we hadn't noticed, but people became used to the new one because there was nothing to compare it to, they hadn't known the old one, but if the cross hadn't yet been stolen it would in any case have been next: the removal of the lions and the cross on the church, which one fine day were simply seized and taken away, not even at night, secretly, but in broad daylight for all to see, *In bright sunshine, the great heavy cross was carried down the public street on their shoulders, do you see, just as on that occasion, only now it is not He that carried it but* . . . and he that said that crossed himself quickly, and the lions were taken and the statue of Mátyás, people were reassured, there were to be excavations around it and it had to be moved to facilitate discovery of Daco-Romanian antiquities, and it was removed because it emerged that under Főtér, precisely under the statue of Mátyás, there was another city to be discovered, a buried city, the real Claudiopolis, with forum, circus, theatre, baths, Roman palaces and olive oil and grain remaining in amphorae, or the whole thing was removed without any reason being sought, destroyed, or if it couldn't be moved from where it was, just blown up—the statue had been the cause of great anxiety during the Second World War, and Grandmother told us that one day as she was coming out of Egyetem utca she saw it being photographed from every angle, and it said in the papers that a bomb-proof shelter had been excavated at the end of Donát út, in case it had to be dismantled, because there would be bombing, and eventually there was, but the statue wasn't moved and it escaped damage—but in 1984 everything was trembling, began to move and collapse as if there was a war on then too, it seemed that the ground on which the city stood was about slowly to fall in, threatened by earthquake, volcanic eruption or floods, or some yet unknown natural disaster which would wipe the city off the face of the earth: the churches, the palaces, the whole Főtér, the New York hotel, the castle wall and the bit of remaining bastion, it would sweep the Hangman's House out of Petőfi utca all the way down Farkas utca, the Házsongárd and the Jewish cemetery and the Biasini house in Avram Iancu utca, where a plaque still reminded us that 'Sándor Petőfi and his wife stayed here 21–24 October 1847'—the house where Petőfi stayed was then in Avram Iancu utca, but the street where the Romanian revolutionary and innkeeper Avram Iancu lived (and who, compared to Petőfi, lived to a ripe old age), was named Petőfi utca, but the two streets were ironically continuations of each other, Petőfi found a place in Avram Iancu and Iancu in Petőfi Sándor, as if in this city in the end nobody could find the way home because they couldn't agree what to call what in the

'20s when the naming took place—and Petőfi's house was demolished or moved, or just driven out of town: *Out of here, away from this town* as he wrote about Kolozsvár, and the house found a more modest place, somewhere beyond Főtér, perhaps actually in Donát utca, and the name has been changed now that the building of the tobacco factory no longer exists, and nobody can remember why Alsó Kereszt utca is named Dohány utca or why that too might not be Petőfi utca, and in 1984 the earth rumbled beneath the gardens in the Hóstát and on Kerekdomb, under the single-storey houses, the earthworks, the Gypsy row and the villa quarters too, under the confined cobbled yards of the city centre, Sétatér and the Officers' Club, because by that time the Malom-ditch had been covered over, the Szamos too in places, the Cigánypatak and the Nádas had vanished for ever, the boating lake was still there, there was a plan to cover the market, it was said, the cattle-market square and the whole of theÓszer, things would be removed, demolished, moved or covered over and made invisible like the entire city of which the poet, who stayed in the Biasini house for three days, wrote one poem entitled *Out of here, away from this town* in which he took his leave of the city *Away then, quickly away hence!* but anyone that looked at the city from above, from the Fellegvár, the Kányafő or the Torda road, or who looked through binoculars from the Bükk, could see that the lions, the cross and the statue were in place, and that the ten-storey blocks of flats were rising only on the outskirts, in Monostor, the Hajnal area and Mărăşti tér—the blocks appeared at the start of the '70s, then factories increased in number on what had become the industrial estate in socialist competition with the counties, and they required more housing estates to which the future workers and their families were relocated from other parts of the country, beyond the mountains, Moldva and the Olt region, which everyday speech suspiciously referred to as blatant Romanianization: people were given housing and jobs here, so they were here for good—and from above it could be seen that those outskirts were becoming squeezed inwards by their matchbox-like blocks towards the houses in the Hóstát, as most of the kitchen gardens in the Hóstát or Hochstadt had been destroyed by 1984, and the area around St Peter's church had been cleared by then—there was a rumour that the church too was to be moved, then in the end only the fence was moved, and the church, now stripped of its fence and defenceless, was hemmed in in the middle of the new quarter, like a fragile body in the aggressive mass of concrete—and the bulldozers were by then close to the centre in Kossuth Lajos utca, where Number 25 was demolished, the former Neumann family's three-storey house, and those next to it, because the earth was moving, but it was not the all-obliterating natural disaster that ensued but the work of men's hands: because two kinds of wrath can destroy a city, that of Nature and that of Man, and in the suddenly adult teenage Girl too there was a constantly growing anger with the city and, by degrees, simply anything, and in 1984 the great passion for demolition reached its peak: attention was turned to Bel and Külmagyar utca (Magyar utca, in Granny's parlance), the present Lenin út, rumour reached the teenage Girl that the school where she had been able to go for an altogether happy year in Year Ten was to close, and the house in Dohány utca and the rest of the street were to come down, said Grandmother confidently, because they, they had always lived out there on what had once been the edge of the city, the Kühns had lived out there in the lower town, they had been able to live for just a short while as tenants near wealthy Hárompüspök tér, in Apponyi utca, while property was being nationalized, then came Dohány utca from 1949, then Mummy and Father's first (and last) shared flat in Virág utca in Monostor, which was built in the early '70s, the new version of which, consisting of blocks of flats, was named after the poet and folklorist Grigore Alecsandrescu, and finally a three-room flat in a block in the street named after the mathematician Nicolae Pascaly, in a micro-region in the Györgyfalva district, likewise built on the Hóstát people's gardens, the allotments—because the city had at one time consisted of *tizedek*s and *fertály*s, then of *kerület*s, then *negyedek*s and finally *micro-region*s, *Zona 7*, the taxi dispatcher called it, pronouncing it peasant-fashion *sépté*, to distinguish it from Zona 6 (*shásé*), but a car couldn't be sent, they were short of them, and petrol was almost unavailable, they preferred not to answer the phone, left it off the hook, only responded to the special number which Mummy had discovered from somewhere together with the password, and indeed a taxi came when called, and Mummy gave directions: *La casa lui Matei Corvin* (to King Mátyás' house), but the driver grumbled bad-humouredly back *Şi eu de unde să ştiu unde mai stă şi ăsta* (And how am I supposed to know where everybody lives), but they too lived on others' ground, in a block, because that was what Mummy had been given a loan for, in a block which was still being built near Grandmother's, it was spreading, threatening the city centre too, while the heart of the city waited motionless, like a person that has remained alive too long, or who has been given up and is unexpectedly alive—or rather just a weak old woman—panting like someone whose fate is in the balance, and would himself rather forget his uncertain date of birth which takes him into the distant past, who has lived too long and seen all manner of things, the centre lay motionless, waiting, because no decision had yet been taken about it, whether it was to be finally destroyed or left alive and rendered unrecognizable by building, like the surface to be scraped off, as in plastic surgery, and a new, youthful, pastless face stitched on, *Out of here, away from this town*, wrote the poet on his autumn journey because at the side of his long-sought beloved, Júlia, he was afraid that he would deceive her, fall in love with this town, which would delay him in his hurried journey, distract his attention from his task and the purpose of his journey, and now the town, in 1984, alarmed and on tenterhooks, like a person anticipating a very, very great misfortune, a deadly, sudden shower of lava which would bury him leaving not a trace, likewise didn't notice that the surface of its beautiful body was already cracked, the tiny, at first trifling wound had become full of pus, its tissues infected, the disease beginning to deform its face beyond recognition, because the town looked upwards, to the high places, its own summits, to the lions and the cross and the aquiline nose of the stern but just king, his palaces, his proud town centre and didn't even notice that one Tuesday morning a start was made on clearing up *The shame of the city, Ruşinea oraşului*, said those that were assembled indignantly in their own languages, clearing up Csipke, Árva, Varjú, Munkás, Nyúl, Szántó, Cimbalom, Agyag and Hangász utca, the nameless quarter of tiny alleways that was set upon from four directions so that there should be no escape, it was attacked by bulldozers from the direction of Timotei Cipariu (formerly Széna) tér, *What have these been doing here all this time, in the heart of the city?* protested the serried ranks of the onlookers at the public execution as if their eyes had suddenly been opened to some ancient wrong, and they were at last able to name the true cause of their offence, the admirers stood in rows behind the Teachers' house opposite the Tailors' bastion to watch the quick and painless carrying out of sentence, *At last there'll be order here*, said someone in satisfaction, *and they're clearing the shanty town*, the Gypsies cursed and wailed in three languages, *They deserve it if they wouldn't get out, they were warned*, and the machines crumpled the houses with their light iron-sheeting roofs and mud-brick walls as if they were pushing paper pellets along, because the so-called useful Gypsies from Agyagdomb had in the past made their home outside the city walls and didn't come into the city of their own volition but Ulászló II (1490–1516) ordered them in, *five bands of Gypsies*, and entrusted to them the public cleanliness of the town, so that they became known as the stink-kings, lords of refuse, lavatories and carrion, and at one time the town hangman was of their number, a respected person with a monthly salary—he can't have lived in the Hangman's House in Petőfi utca, he wasn't rich enough to have a two-storey house—but it wasn't the Gypsies that moved deeper into the town, they never moved in five hundred years, but the town that expanded, outgrew the superfluous and cheaply removed stone town wall, but in 1984 the public toilets in the town were closed, the State enterprise was charged with refuse removal, which was never seen to, in every housing estate there were enormous stinking heaps, but on this particular Tuesday morning, with the increasing support of the onlookers the new hangman, the *justitiae executor*, and his wordless servitors swept them away in a single morning and at eight o'clock the Girl, as she tried to get into the former Reformed Church college, the Ady-Șincai (the Ady was to be removed from its name, and the Hungarian class abolished), could scarcely push through the crowd, and she too stood and watched the slow and thorough work of the machines, a fat woman with her hair in plaits and coins woven into it carried with her only a big, steaming pot of half-cooked soup from which protruded yellow chicken's feet, a man wearing a hat and corduroy trousers brought a quilt on his back, chickens flew up in one yard as a machine removed the fence, at the next pass the pigsties went too, dogs howled and children wailed as they clung to their mothers' skirts, everybody fled, the old Gypsy woman picked her way over the debris with the steaming pot and left the now-flattened street, went beyond onto what was now unoccupied, bare earth, found a few bricks among the ruins of her house, gathered some bits of wood and started a fire to cook the food, and in the excited crowd, as it cheered on the hangman, the Girl in Year Ten was quite fascinated by the unprecedented sight of devastation, but by then it was after eight o'clock, she was late for the Ady-Șincai literature and history school, where neither sympathy nor compassion were taught as they had been in the kindergarten in Majális utca or earlier in the élite Hungarian grammar school, and that afternoon, by the time the Girl came out of the main door in Petőfi utca and looked to the left the last of the lorries was leaving with the debris of the Gypsy row, the satisfied crowd had dispersed, and she never thought again of what she'd seen that Tuesday morning, *It's still not Dohány utca, those are only Gypsies*, she consoled herself, she had then never heard of Ulászló and the almost five hundred years—where she'd been to school they were only taught about the Roman period and the union of 1 December 1918,[54] Gypsies weren't in the book—and she didn't even tell Grandmother about the terrible scene that had been enacted *because we're Hungarians, after all, they can't treat us like that*, but next day the paper carried the news of the successful clearance of the area around Cipariu tér, the city fathers' effective action, and gave an account of the plans for the valuable central region, which in the end remained inexplicably undeveloped— neither factories nor blocks of flats took the place of the Gypsy row, and it seemed that a sort of disability had settled over the site, and on the morning of 22 December 1989, when they were marching blissfully through the finally confident town, a man in the crowd said loudly that . . . *if that's blown up the whole town'll be flooded*, and during the demon- stration the Girl, now in her first year at the university, knew that what could be blown up was only the dam at Tarnica: the lakes where they went camping in summer, and she'd known ever since they'd been going there that the city could be inundated at any time, because the dam, built in 1968, was guarded by soldiers, but who could be going to blow it up, who was the enemy that morning, she didn't ask herself: *they*, obvi- ously, who had previously meant to blow up the city, *and it's better*, thought the Girl, *it's better if it vanishes for ever*, she thought crossly, because she was angry like the poet, *Out of here*, said she to herself, as rage was bursting her apart, *it's better if it is destroyed*, but why she wanted it to vanish precisely then, when . . . *when we're marching here a new world's beginning*, but they'd had to wait so long for that new world that it would disappear at once, she thought in the morning of 22 December 1989, and as she was warmed by the shouting, the crowd and her hope that perhaps if it did disappear under water then it would begin a new life as an underwater city, a fairy-tale city, a city of hope,

---

54 The Union of Transylvania with Romania was declared unilaterally on 1 December 1918 by the assembly of the delegates of ethnic Romanians held in Alba Iulia. Romania's national day, Great Union day (also called *Unification Day*) commemorates this event, which anticipated the Treaty of Trianon (1920).

the legendary Russian Kitezh of which Tatyana, the blue-eyed Russian teacher, had told her, Kitezh, which had miraculously moved to the depths of the lake to escape the marauding Tatar-Mongol hordes because it was completely undefended, had never thrown up any sort of fortification around itself, had not even supposed that it would be attacked and was forced to flee, and since then it had flourished as a fabulously happy city at the bottom of the lake, and the church tower of this submerged city might be seen like that at Jósikafalva in Béles Lake, where you can go boating and actually row into the church, perhaps the defenceless city would escape its enemies by going underwater and the huge golden cross with the seven kilos of gold would be seen, because in some inexplicable fashion the cross would be there as would the gold, because no building higher than St Michael's church could be built in the city and Kolozsvár, alias Claudiopolis, among the many cities the only one named after Claudius, alias Cluj-Napoca, alias Klausenburg, would escape under water and then perhaps have some luck as a submerged city and be able to begin its life afresh.

THE KING'S FOOL

'Kukumay, Kukumay, there'll be no more Tenth of May!' the children sang to Kukumay on Hárompüspök tér, in the wealthy quarter: Lili, the two Attilas and Csaba, however, had no idea what 'Tenth of May' meant, they just knew that you had to shout that to Kukumay and then run indoors because then you had to be frightened of him, not like you were of the little old woman in the wedding dress that was worn to greyness, who seemed to have been left behind by a travelling circus, all you had to say to her was 'He'll be along, you'll see!' because her stalwart fiancé was supposed to have perished in the war and ever since she'd been waiting for her man, and when she was grown up Lili knew that you had to give the coffee-beggar 50 bani, or at least 25, so that he could have his coffee of the day—was it the eighth? or the fifteenth?— in the erotically charged 'sand coffee shop', where Turkish coffee was still brewed on hot sand, or in the Orient or the Zöld patisserie or the Kárpáci in Főtér, otherwise the coffee-beggar would be cross and wouldn't leave you alone and would go on grinding out in his monotonous voice, 'Buy me a coffee' until you were tired of him, while to the man in the leather coat who hung about between the blocks at the end of Rákóczi út and fired bursts from an imaginary machine-gun at incautious passers-by, to the great alarm of children, you had to shout *Vin nemții!*, dragging out the '-*i*' like in films, the Germans were coming, and he would at once start a wild machine-gunning, but the drunken General (his uniform blouse covered to the waist with every medal awarded this century, even including some given to Pioneers and huntsmen and '*Mama eroina*', the 'hero mothers' who had had ten children) would not pause as he smoked and drank, but if anyone went his way or looked at him then out would come the tales of his heroic deeds and he would seize the arm of the unsuspecting passer-by and say excitedly—*Then I let him have it, at which . . . and the other one got away, but then round the corner came a Horthyist and I waited for him in a doorway and knifed him, like this . . .* and all the rest: Bubulina, the Russian 'bag lady', to whom you had to say '*Zdravstvuyte tavarishch*'— Greetings, comrade—and at once she'd start rattling on in plaintive Russian, and Ragged Laci, and Imola, who sold newspapers, hawking them round Főtér and shouting out as she went: *Lőre, Lőre, Előre*! and *Gazság, Gazság, Igazság!*[55] and if she found a male customer she would immediately start to bargain with 'the Count', to weep and wail, she'd do simply anything for 25 lei, and what a poor thing she was, that was why they nicknamed her Cunty, and you had to say something to all of them, shout at them or make them jump, as Grandmother said, so that they should come out of their day-dreaming and start to talk, because the monarchist Kukumay was always waiting for the Tenth of May, in Romanian *zece maj*, the festival of the royal house, the day on which Károly I was crowned King of Romania in 1866, when such great happiness or misfortune came upon Kukumay that in the end he lost his mind, and the machine-gunner was always waiting for the Germans so as to settle accounts with them heroically once and for all, and all the rest who were trapped in the delicate web of time had some unfinished business with history, and their anger against the world was permanently stuck at that point, and they would spit it all around on the streets of Kolozsvár, angrily or mournfully, at the bidding of the townsfolk and children when they wanted a little amusement and who at times showed them little sympathy and at times were downright cruel, because for them—Kukumay, the bride, the machine-gunner, Bubulina, Ragged Laci, the General and the rest—time did not go by, it was always at the start, only their bodies aged and their illnesses and the

---

55 Plays on words—*Rotgut, Rotgut, Forward!* and *Villainy, Villainy, Truth! Előre* and *Igazság* are the names of newspapers.

filth on them increased, but their time ticked always on the spot: forever 1939 or 1944 or 1933 or 1959, whatever year from the distant past, as any year, day or moment can maim a frail human being, and sometimes political agitators too were trapped, declaiming speeches in stentorian tones as on the TV, but they rather inspired fear in the passers-by, who gave the dangerous orators a wide margin in case he too were swept away into trouble, and then under the influence of swift police action they would vanish for a little while from the comparatively free haven of the city and spend some time in the yellow house in Majális út, but only Iosif Covaci—nobody in the city knew his real name—who had been born into a family of six children in Nagyesküllő (Aşchileu Mare), Kolozs county, had no unfinished business either with people or with man-made history, nor yet with fickle nature: all day he went round the city on his short legs, in his coat which brushed the ground, like some-one who had business in the world, affairs to attend to, he went into shops, the Főtér, the market, the station or the cemetery, or just rode the buses, he was everywhere, because the city was his and he was the city: he would greet everybody in his deep, harsh voice and they usually returned his greeting, *Serus!* he would exclaim, sounding rather like Donald Duck, to women he would say '*I kiss your hand*', to the elderly '*Good day*', and after the glum and wordless who didn't favour him with an answer he would call *De ce eşti supărat?* (Why are you angry?), and if anybody smiled at him or was disposed to talk he would interrupt his circumambulation for a few sentences, he accepted croissants, pretzels, acid-drops or apples, even small change—paper money he didn't rec-ognize, *Mai bine dă-mi un leu* (Rather, give me a lei), he would say firmly, if anybody were to offer a brown 5-lei note, as if he had his doubts about paper money, though after the 5-lei note was replaced in 1978 by a big, light aluminium coin decorated with a factory chimney he quickly became accustomed to it, he sometimes presented girls and children with white carnations which he had been given by florists, because he was regularly given things in shops, Mummy's staff in the big warehouse gave him a shop-soiled pullover from the children's department, socks and a scarf, and in exchange he tried to make himself useful in the Central, for example, he helped a big lorry which, judging by the number, had come from Iaşi, to park in the parking space at the back, and the unsuspecting driver, a stranger in the city, entrusted himself to the snub-nosed little man with the brisk gesticulations who beckoned him on and on and on, until suddenly crash! and the driver leapt angrily from the cab, shouted *Fuck it!* and raced to the back, where the little man stood, hands on hips, pointing indignantly and saying *Na, acuma uite ce-ai făcut!*—Well, look what you've done!—and the doorman on the rear of the building had to rescue him from a thrashing, and he would go to weddings, burials and christenings to sing, and on such occasions his rasping, monotonous speaking voice would become a deep, warm baritone, and he could sing folk songs, ceremonious greetings and Greek Catholic hymns, he was there at Uncle Nuszi's retiral party, for which Nuszi had prepared for months, getting together the five kinds of meat for the kosher *sólet*, which he brought in in two 20-litre cooking pots, and the little man turned up after the top management had left, stood at the door, greeted people and offered wine and beer as they arrived but refused it himself decisively and offendedly: *Nu sînt nebun*, said he in his usual voice, *I'm not fool enough to get drunk like all you, and lie under the table, I'm not that daft!* and indeed nobody ever saw him drink, and Nuszi's colleagues, almost all of whom were women, cheered and applauded him like a clever child because he was the city and hope, the naive holy man who never talked politics, never mocked or imitated anybody, didn't know the meaning of hatred, nor cared about paper money, the metric system, attendance lists or alcohol, was never in the Falcons of the Fatherland or the Pioneers, never went to communal work or parades, and his sister, with whom he lived, drew a disability allowance of 650 lei on account of him, *He'll be buried like a king*, prophesied Uncle Nuszi when Lulu made a hurried departure after singing for half an hour and eating a little dish of *csólent* and a big slice of gateau, *but the king will be shot like a dog*, he added with a laugh, bending towards Mummy's ear, because the harmless child, 140 cm in height, had an unconscious power over the city and finally conquered the king too: in the local elections of autumn 1988, when the rumour went round that everybody, but everybody, had to vote (the girls may have heard it in school, certainly nothing was said about it in Mummy's workplace), *Granny, will you absolutely have to go and vote?* asked the younger girl, to which Grandmother replied crossly *I can't get as far as the front door, let alone go to the Someş to vote!* and her granddaughter promised *I'll go with you, you can take my arm, we'll get a taxi if you like*, Grandmother shrugged her slender shoulders, *A taxi! Well really, that'll be the day!* But the Girl went on persuading her *But it's very important, you must see, everything's going to be different*, but Grandmother just waved it away with her grey hand, Oh really, what's going to make any difference, the elections were all rigged, but she knew that voting was compulsory and by evening the hundred per cent turnout would be reported and once again Mocuţa (or whoever they had to vote for) would be county First Secretary, *The whole thing's an absolute circus*, but all the same she dressed smartly at her grand-daughter's request, curled her hair, polished her nails and limped out because she was afraid that if she didn't participate the house would be demolished as punishment, *But you'll mark the paper, I can't see to do it*, said she, leaning on the Girl who was by then a head taller than herself, *Are you coming like that?* she asked on seeing her in a shabby sweater and jeans, *Granny, we're not going to the theatre*, said the Girl, and in the voting station which was set up in the former tobacco-factory building, a grey room, empty apart from the booth, she explained to the authorities that here was her grandmother and her identity card, but if you don't mind, she can't see very well so they would like two voting papers, and Grandmother took a seat while the Girl went on with the two voting papers, sat down in the solitary school desk and carefully laid out in front of her the two flimsy, faintly printed, grey sheets, but this time she didn't put what she had before, when she'd first been able to vote at the age of fourteen, didn't scribble, no crossing-out, didn't draw a death's head or an executioner's axe, no twirly writing or stupid message, but like a serious adult who was taking her fate in her hands and knew that now she alone was responsible for it, printed in the blank line on each of the papers the only correct and possible response: LULU, then she folded them over and put them in the box, which was covered in brown paper, because in 1988 there was only one real man living in the city, one man on whose hands there had never been any blood, because it was he, Lulu, that won the local elections, not Iosif Covaci, born 9 December 1951, according to the papers at the time aged thirty-six, a citizen of Kolozsvár, but the pleasant, dark-haired, sensitive Lulu, who was far removed from time and had only a single name like saints and kings and fools, Lulu, the great lover of children, who next day was congratulated and winked at by several people in the street as they stuffed croissants and pretzels, acid drops and toffees into his capacious pockets, and he in return distributed carnations to the girls and little children, and by noon his pockets were full, weighing down his big, dark coat so that both skirts were dragging on the ground, giving the impression of an angel with a damaged wing that was forced to remain on earth, and Lulu hurried past the decorated city hall in Kossuth Lajos utca happily and good-humouredly (for which he had cause every day), because he, Lulu, had been the winner, even if next day *Gazság, Gazság, Igazság* and *Făclia* were, true to their custom, totally silent about his sweeping victory.

FRONT

She'd been standing out in the street since early morning, outside the open window, *It's like it was in July 1974*, she recalled, when there was the flood, they still lived there and the water was thigh-deep all up the street, *It was an amazing flood*, thought the Girl, with a shiver, she'd been three, and the muddy river had surged along Dohány utca—but which river? the Szamos? or the Malomárok?—she'd sat, terrified, on Grandfather's shoulders in the doorway as the rain poured down, *It's a tempest*, he'd said, and it seemed that they were silent witnesses of unlikely biblical events, because the mighty flood would sweep them away too, the house and all the city, and at the time the window on the street side, the 'front' as Grandmother called it, was open as well, as it was now too, and the Girl's empty stomach was quivering with excitement as it had then, because the three windows were only opened in the morning to let some fresh air in, otherwise they were kept shut even in summer, *People will be able to see in, they'll see me sewing, or they'll listen under the window to find out what we talk about, they'll know we've got visitors from Budapest, that we're speaking Hungarian, or drinking coffee*, Grandmother went on sternly, and as time went by she listed more and more things to be afraid of, and so the front window was only opened on special occasions, when there was a *tempest*, as if it were not a human hand that opened it from inside but time, the unstoppable time of the street, as if the front really were here like at Torda during the war or just now in Dohány utca, because inside the house time didn't even exist, it seemed to have stopped for a morning snoodle and be going by outside in the one-way street, and from the outside it seemed that the house, with its three windows and crumbling wall, was itself the front which had to be held, firing positions manned inside and constant defence, *You'll see, one day the even-numbered side'll be in one country and the odd-numbered in the other, and we'll need passports to go over to Aunty Buba's for coffee,* Grandfather used to say, as if Aunty Buba's grey house opposite and her coffee too were equally eternal and immortal with the collapsing Number 26, only the street would change—its name had been changed time and again, as had the direction of traffic along it, sometimes it had been one-way, sometimes not, and the whole of Dohány, including their house too, was under constant threat of demolition—but this morning there was nothing unusual to be seen outside, people were coming and going as on other days, stopping under the open window for a moment, listening to the TV which the people in the house had turned up for the benefit of passers-by, *Have they caught the swine?* Grandmother would call from the kitchen when the shouting on the TV grew louder, people were calling back and forth in confusion, emphasizing a point, or maintaining a long, tense pause before what could be expected to be a dramatic report, because although Grandmother couldn't understand the words she knew precisely what was happening, and the passers-by asked the same: *L-au prins?*—Has he been caught?—of the long-haired Girl as she stood outside the house wearing a nice, warm sheepskin jacket turned inside out, a personal find on the Ószer which she wore proudly and for which her mother had knitted sleeves in thick wool and Grandmother had made a lining, *Nu, nu l-au prins,* she replied calmly to all that asked, *They haven't caught him yet but they're not far behind him,* she also informed the people who went past the house, whether they asked her or not, replying to everybody self-confidently like someone that knew more that she was telling, and she also addressed those who scurried past the house as if indifferent to the latest news, and Kossuth Radio from Budapest was playing loudly in the kitchen too and Mummy was on the telephone non-stop in the middle room, though the Girl ran into the kitchen now and then to warm up, drink a quick coffee which

Grandmother made unperturbedly—this day was not at all like ordinary days for that reason alone, as at other times she kept strictly to one coffee a day—then she went back to her sentry-post to wait, *They're on their track*, she tossed excitedly to an enquirer like someone that knew a great deal more than they did, but the time hadn't yet come to divulge it, and there she stood, hands deep in pockets, skipping from foot to foot like a reporter working in two shifts, at one moment belonging to the pursuing group and keeping the viewers fully informed on whether they'd surrounded the monster, *odiosul*, the novel usage had suddenly become current (did it mean 'hated'? she wondered, she'd never heard this terribly literary word in school), because as she ran impatiently between the street and the house she seemed to have in the pocket of her jacket a tiny weapon, invisible to the passers-by, which she meant to fire if he was caught, when the time came, I can kill, she thought brightly, almost with relief like somebody that had just done well in a difficult examination, I've grown up, because in fact she hadn't long turned eighteen, of course everybody can kill, adults and children, it's not a question of age, and just at that moment Mummy called out from indoors, Yes, Mummy too can kill, of course, she couldn't bring herself to drown little kittens, 'I'd absolutely die if I had to kill them!' she wailed in a piping voice and certainly left the dirty job to Grandmother, who had an aluminium washtub for the purpose in the mansard, and since I was a child they lied to me that the cats had taken their little ones away because they were afraid of what we might do to them, but Granny used to drown the poor things on Mummy's instructions, and then Mummy, of course, wouldn't show herself for the rest of the day and in the evening would look accusingly at her mother without saying a word, as if she were a child-killer, and they thought I was stupid and accepted the story, but I'd always known that the kittens were drowned, Grandmother was good at killing, she knew how to kill a chicken, everybody did, even Grandfather, haha, poor Granddad always used to say: 'You'll be the death of me with this incessant nagging', and my sister killed her three-month, no, four-month-old foetus when she was pregnant, and Mummy killed Daddy when she left him, and it was Mummy who had Rachel the pig killed, and Father killed himself, and then too they tried to keep it secret, but I'd been the last to see him that afternoon, but today I mean to kill! today I mean to kill! today I mean to kill, I shan't go to bed until I have!—she skipped about, hands in pockets, her heart in her mouth, and then Lili called out again more loudly, she had to make herself heard above the TV in the big room and the radio in the kitchen, *Come inside, girl, you'll freeze, I've just heard on the phone they're still only near Várad*, to which Grandmother jumped up from the kitchen seat as if she'd been stabbed, *Jesus, they're near Várad already, and I'm not dressed*, then the pantry door creaked and Grandmother set off unsteadily up the stairs to the mansard, and the TV was saying that the court had now been set up and he would be prosecuted in accordance with law, the charges read out to him, *What for?*—the Girl was astounded, *That's idiotic*, and suddenly her ears began to ring, so furious was she, because she felt that it was her rightful business, her personal rightful business, and didn't call for legal arguments and charges, everybody knew precisely what his crimes were, so the sentence had to be carried out without delay and personally, and she wasn't disposed to share the news of the impending court action with the passers-by, she thought it was a mistake that would be corrected at once, why mess about with legal action, and she clenched her fists, he must be shot down or beaten to death, people must demand that the hangman carry out the sentence at once! and I want to be the hangman! because as Grandmother said, *I could throttle him with my bare hands*, and she imagined Granny, at that moment tottering up the stairs to the mansard on her bad legs, setting to with her slender, veined and blotched, but still beautiful and soft hands and throttling him, but just at that moment round the corner skipped the Cselinszki boy—they lived in the wood-store at the back, where the single damp room had neither gas nor water, and Mother taught the boy maths free of charge—and Mihály was wearing a dirty, light-blue nylon jacket which bulged oddly in front as if he were pregnant, torn tracksuit trousers and gym shoes, he was picking something out of his mouth and as he came nearer the Girl realized that he was eating a banana complete with skin and spitting out the latter, he grinned and called from a distance that bananas and oranges were being distributed to children in Főtér, *I should go if I were you, I've been three times*, and he undid his zip fastener to show her what he'd got: the gleaming oranges shone so brightly in gloomy Dohány utca on that misty morning, they were like a big, shiny, blood-red pond being shown on black-and-white TV, *Go on*, said the skinny little Cselinszki boy, because he was going straight back, *I'm not a child, they won't give me anything*, replied the Girl proudly and firmly, *We're just off to the airport with the relief supplies*, she added significantly and went indoors, because anybody with serious matters to attend to hadn't got time to chat in the street with such a youngster, but all the same she went back to tell the boy how to eat a banana, *Look, you have to peel it, see? Like this, at the end*, and in the house her mother was still sitting by the telephone and organizing things, *Seventy lorries*, she called out self-confidently and looked up at the Girl as if the whole consignment were to be hers any minute and she'd be able to deal with it, *What do you need?* she asked the telephone and made notes in an old diary, she was calling orphanages, old people's homes, nurseries, parish priests, obstetricians, *I don't know when we'll deliver, who'll receive it? Name of the person in charge?* and Grandmother, breathing heavily, came down from the mansard clutching a big dusty bag, put it down carefully on the kitchen seat, cleared the table of the little pots and pans in which she had stored the remains of lunch from the previous couple of days, *Well, I don't know if it'll still fit me, it'll certainly be no good to your mother, the poor thing's put on weight, but perhaps my mother's will fit her*, and she began to unfold the tissue paper, *I can't find the skirts*, she complained, *They're right here, and I also meant to unpick the sleeves and the lace off the front to wash it, but now there isn't time, and the headdress is here for one of them,* and she spread out the two gowns, smelling strongly of mothballs, on the table, and the Venetian lace sleeves were yellow under the armpits, where the black velvet met the lace there were two big perspiration stains, *Mother perspired a lot last time she wore it,* she said, *It was a very hot day and we were standing in the sun in front of the statue, by the horse's tail, as you put it, and waiting, it was the fourth of September, it's a good thing it's December now,* she smiled, *this time we'll freeze instead, yes, the black, my mother's, wasn't laundered before it was put away and it should have been, it always happened so suddenly that she had to put it on, and the last time before that when she wore it was in the theatre in September 1919, and even then she'd had to bring it out without warning for Hamlet, and the poor thing perspired so much because there was such a crowd and the performance went on until night-time, and we thought the Romanians would surround the theatre, and the cast would be taken straight over the frontier, and it had been said earlier on, in spring, because this was in autumn, in September, that poor Janovics, the director of the theatre, was in the lunatic asylum, that's where he hid, because he didn't want to hand his theatre over to the Romanians, and he was there for about six weeks in the building with the green roof, it was in the same place as now, in Majális utca, and he took refuge there with a group of Hungarian officials, so my poor mother told me, and that's why he was able to play Hamlet so well afterwards, because he'd been in the mad-house, and they say that's where he wrote his study of Hamlet, a whole book, which of course these stinkers never ever published, because in those days there was a very famous doctor in the asylum, Károly Lechner his name was, and he helped, and then in 1919 he left the country or was expelled*—and both of them stared at the purple-grey perspiration stains below the two arm-holes, like the calyces of flowers which had opened seventy years, two months and twenty-three days before under Great-grandmother's armpits, and seventy years had not been enough for them to be washed out, perhaps out of respect for the stains which alone preserved the perfume of the body of Mária Soket from 30

September 1919, when she had watched the last stage performance by Jenő Janovics and his company in the theatre in Hunyadi tér, at which the actors decided not to take the Romanian oath of loyalty and not to leave the theatre until they had played *Hamlet* for the last time, in which the censor would no longer allow the liberator, the worthy Fortinbras, to arrive, because even so the performance was drowned in an expectable demonstration and hours of standing ovation, the militia surrounded the theatre but Great-grandmother hadn't been able to hear a word from the stage after the line 'report me and my cause aright To the unsatisfied', nor had the sleeves been undone when in August, twenty-one years later she had perspired into them once more when the Hungarian military had processed, *People always sweated into these dresses*, thought the Girl, *when they went out in them, That is, to the front*, she recalled, as if this dress had been a military uniform worn by women at the front, exclusively for wear in the street, which had always been ready and waiting, and so it had not been possible to clean the stain, which had slowly faded as time went by, in case by taking off the sleeves for washing it was made impossible even for a single day to put it on, as was perhaps then necessary, whereas festive clothes were made for single occasions, such as a wedding dress, and Great-grandmother's had been originally for the dedication of the Mátyás statue in 1902, and yet owners of such dresses often wore them to be married, and Great-grandmother had worn it in 1919 in the theatre, and a third time in 1940, each time uttering the same tremulous 'yes', in hope of happiness and believing that it was for the last time, and Grandmother had only once shown her granddaughter the dresses preserved in the mansard, so that if ever the Girl needed them she should know where to find them, and Grandmother had carefully unfolded them, wouldn't let her try them on, but the Girl, who all through her teens was a passionate explorer of the only partially revealed domain at the top of the house regularly took these dresses out in secret and looked at them— their origins and purposes were unknown to her, and she felt that she was handling costumes for masked balls or ancient scientific instruments of unknown function and intention, she looked at the clumsily worked rosette on the head-dress, the torn lace apron, the two pearl-trimmed velvet tops with lace sleeves, she tried them both on and they fitted, and like somebody that knew that these clothes were no longer wanted she put them back, but now Grandmother was beginning to mend the black-pearl decoration, *Great-granny was photographed in this dress in a rocking chair, with a cat on her lap, and since then the poor thing didn't want to go to the theatre, she said she'd seen the best performance in her lifetime, there couldn't be a better one, to which Grandfather always added that that performance might have been dispensed with in the Hunyadi tér theatre, in 1941 it was renamed Adolf Hitler tér, I don't know what it's called now*, and this 'now' had lasted forty-five years, which in Grandmother's mind must have been at the most an intervening period of a few transitory months, *in my view this theatre's more beautiful than the Víg in Budapest, more friendly, I only went there for the first time in 1941, but I hear that you and Juci go to the Romanian Theatre—we saw The Taming of the Shrew*, interrupted the Girl, and *Hamlet* at the Sétatér theatre, but that she didn't divulge, it would have sounded like a profanity with the dress spread out there—*Your father used to go as well, now, if the purple's no good to your mother you wear it, men's clothes weren't made, at least not in our family, Janovics wore a braided velvet suit, Mother had a photograph of him, when the Hunyadi tér theatre was opened in 1906, after that he's supposed to have given it to the wardrobe because he'd put on too much weight, well, after 1918 how would he get into it? Not even in the theatre, but we never had things made for your grandfather, the poor man missed out on everything, in 1940 as well he was trapped in Ocnele Mare, and Daddy put on his frock-coat or his uniform, I can't remember, your poor grandfather, if he hadn't smoked all those stinking Nationals at least he would have been alive today*, but at that moment out came Mummy with the news that they were now at Hunyad, and moving with a police escort, *Bánffyhunyad?* exclaimed Grandmother, *What kind of police escort?* she asked, *We call them gendarmes,* she corrected her daughter and added: *Lili, look here, try the purple on, I'll wear the black, the purple used to be mine but now I'm too old to wear purple,* at which Lili laughed, *Sure you don't want to wear court dress to wait for the lorries?,* but then the TV suddenly announced that there was to be a very important newsflash within minutes, and the announcer, the same balding, bespectacled man who'd read the news for years, kept looking around confusedly, and behind him noise, footsteps and shouts could be heard, then, again confusedly, he read from a sheet of paper that shortly a very important statement was to be made, Grandmother came in and was glued to the TV, *What's all that noise?* she asked, watched the screen for a moment longer, then asked uncertainly were *the Hungarians* coming now or not? and should she get dressed? but nobody answered her and she limped back into the kitchen and her granddaughter went after her and picked up the long, torn black lace veil that Granny had dropped as she came in, caught her up in the middle room and took her arm— Grandmother was by then a head shorter than her—*Granny, lorries are coming and bringing sugar and flour and oil and medical supplies, the frontiers have been opened and there's freedom, do you understand?* to which Grandmother replied irritably *I know that,* but the Girl went gently on, *Granny, a new world's coming, do you understand?* to which Grandmother replied more gently *There's been a new world every time before,* and, she added, *you might get some decent oil out of these relief supplies, because what they give you on your ration card is full of water and it spits, look at my hands,* and she held out her brown-spotted hands, and the Girl replied *We won't be able to bring anything away, Mother's said in advance, it's not for us,* to which Grandmother made an angry gesture, *Who's it for, then?—And,* the Girl continued, *our friend's going to be killed, we're going to kill him, understand? Perhaps they've caught the swine by this time, that's what they're going to announce on the TV,* at which Grandmother calmed down, *I'll believe it when I hear it officially on Kossuth Radio as well,* but Mother ran out, *Good Lord, they're here, they've turned into the street, I'll put my shoes on,* and she grabbed her tables and notebook and ran out, and the Girl called after her that she wanted to go and help, but Grandmother was leaning out of the window on the front and outside the house Lili was gesticulating frantically to the lorries to stop, here was the chief organizer, she'd got the tables, she knew what was to go where, then she got into the first one, a surprisingly small three-and-a-half tonner, at which Grandmother too began to wave and tears came to her eyes, *At least we could have brought the flag down from the mansard,* she muttered, but the Girl had never found a flag at all, apart from the red one, *if I couldn't wear my dress just once more, and Lili's gone off just as she is in that tatty nylon jacket of her father's,* and the TV announcer was repeating emphatically and syllabically that shortly extraordinary news was to be announced, a little patience was requested of the honoured viewers, but Grandmother stood there while all the lorries rolled past, waving and tearful, then happily shut the front window and turned off the TV, on which she was never going to believe anything, but the Girl waved down the biggest and most powerful of the lorries that surged along like a river of grey, which turned right with her out of Dohány utca and headed for Szamosfalva and the airport, and from her elevated seat she looked down on the city below, her face flushed, her hands back in her pockets, and with a tingling sensation she leant back in the warmth of the cab like a fully trained and experienced marksman about to deliver the first great accomplishment of her life, because on the threshold of adulthood she had been entrusted by way of initiation with a very weighty, flattering task, and she felt a calm, the calm of the wielding of hatred and justice, because she knew that she was thoroughly prepared, she would certainly make no mistake, her hand would not tremble, and as Antal, the biology teacher, had taught her, the first bullet was going to pierce precisely the middle of that narrow forehead.

A TURN TO THE RIGHT

Let's see how we get on, then, the Girl urged herself as she ran on the anniversary, the fifth, she was only now coming down the hill and she'd meant to run round the lakes five times because it was the fifth anniversary—five years, five circuits—but not actually five times, she decided suddenly, ten! or more likely fifteen, *yes, fifteen times, I can do it,* how far round was the biggest lake? Something like 700 metres? 800? but now she was running for the first time, she'd made a point of not smoking that morning because she'd decided: she was going to run, even on that hot day, because it was August again, but she hated running, always had, she used to skip PE lessons taken by teachers who were inclined to slap you, who shouted and smelt strongly of cigarettes, and when she was supposed to run round the statue of St George in Farkas utca she would turn in by the library and cut out half the circuit, but today she was going to do it, on the anniversary, because she was going to do something difficult and out of the ordinary, she'd made up her mind weeks before that there by the lakes she was going to run, that was where her father had taught them to skate, and while he was slithering about on the ice he'd broken his arm, by the lake, where she'd once found a tiny fish that had somehow been flung onto the bank and was still alive, the dog found it, and afterwards the fish was christened Aladár and lived for a long time in a goldfish bowl, outlived her father, in fact, because her father used to go there with his long-legged spaniel and let it run, and there . . . the Girl was out of breath, though she hadn't even run a hundred metres, starting was so hard, it felt as if she were carrying a rucksack full of stones, her chest was hurting, she could hardly breathe . . . this was where he'd once cried, the only time she'd ever seen her father in tears, and had promised not to drink any more, but I didn't cry either then or later, she thought with satisfaction, *but now it's 'then' once more, let's see how we get on this time,* and she was very careful about where she put her feet so as not to trip, the old Chinese trainers were extremely soft and she could feel the pebbles under the soles of her feet, and she was careful about her ankle which she'd once sprained, because now, as she dared for the first time in five years to go back in thought to the house, she was there again, in the August of 1984: *but now let's try the way you go into the house, through the kitchen, into the room, catch sight of him and come out, don't turn left towards the way out but right, to where he's lying, go on in,* she encouraged herself, and perspiration was now dripping from the thick, strong, blond eyebrows that she'd inherited from her father, but she was only a third of the way round the first circuit, *go in, go back, look at him, take a good look and turn to the right! Turn right!* not like five years ago when she'd turned left, because that was her sole memory of that day, she'd turned left, out, away, away, away from the house, and run all the way home, but now *in you go again, get the key out, because the door's locked,* the paint on the battered, green door was blistered by the sun but the brass of the handle was shiny, *you listen, you hear the dog inside,* they'd bought Andrej, the pedigree spaniel, five years before, and at the age of four months he'd had longer legs than a greyhound, and he chased the chickens like a hunting dog when they flew out of the pen, *you take out the key, you open the door,* only the top lock was locked, the Yale lock, there'd never been a key to the bottom one, so he was in because the dog was in as well, you knew that he was in, *the dog rushes out,* we'll never see it again, *suddenly never again,* that day everything was suddenly never again, the Girl is panting, fifteen circuits? she won't even manage five, two at the most, and she struggles with herself not to give in, not to stop, *you go through the kitchen,* there wasn't a hall, on the left was a table, on it a worn oilcloth with cigarette burns, the stove was sticky with dirt again, there was yesterday's soup on it, the first soup the Girl had made—she was thirteen at the time—the day before in the morning she'd picked the vegetables for it—carrots, parsley, celery, lovage, a whole sprig of lovage off the big bush, green beans, kohlrabi, no, certainly not kohlrabi, because even now she hated that, green peas, no, there weren't any, they were no longer any good, it was August, spring onions, salt, what else was needed, pepper, there wasn't any, a couple of potatoes, cabbage preferably not, it would have been a waste to take a whole head, oh yes, and a nice big tomato, almost the year's first big, rough, ridged tomato, she'd had to ask for some paprika from the garden next door (why had he never planted paprika?), and from the marvellous, perfumed vegetables she'd made what turned out to be tasteless soup, and they'd eaten it out at the back, and the cook, like a good housewife, criticized what she'd cooked, but he for whom it had been cooked praised it, enthused over it, was grateful, ate it in slow spoonfuls as if he were recovering from a long illness and could only now eat freshly cooked food for the first time, ate it, swallowed, chewed, struggled with it, cleared his dish to the last drop, mopped it up with bread, 'One must confront Death, Confront it, János, charge, János,' she encouraged her father, he should have some more if he loved her, and half a saucepan of putrescent left-over soup was still there next afternoon, smelling strongly on the stove, *the door of the room is half open, you go slowly in,* it was half dark, the solitary window was so dusty that daylight scarcely filtered through, *on the left is a bed, that's where he's lying, on the right is a table, no telephone, what would have happened if there'd been a telephone? why is there no telephone?* it had never occurred to him to ask for one, on the right was a table and a bookcase, one shelf of yellow-backed French thrillers, another of hardbacked volumes on Marxism–Leninism, *then you look to the left, there he lies, you stop beside the bed, you look at him, did you? did you really look at him? was he alive? Was there any other possibility? and have you've realized that you're now on the second circuit, it's still dreadfully difficult,* to turn left, head for the door and through the kitchen for the way out, to take the bunch of keys and toss it onto the table because the Yale lock could be locked without the key, you only had to pull the door to, so you needed only to toss the bunch onto the worn oilcloth on the table by the entrance so that anyone leaving the house now quite certainly wouldn't be able to come back in, *but now I want to go back! now for the first time, it's been five years, back into the house, and to take a look at what happened,* this is what is known as a premeditated intention because she slammed the door shut—no, she didn't slam it at all, but quietly and delicately pulled it to, because the dead are fragile and must be treated delicately—therefore she closed the warped door behind her, so weak that it could be opened by just a shoulder, not, of course, by a thirteen-year-old girl whose first door this was, when *she alone took a decision* and silently closed such a door behind her, and there was no going back because the key had been left on the table, *you left it there!,* and the man behind the door was motionless and at peace, fully dressed despite the baking heat of summer, even wearing shoes and a checked flannel shirt, not snoring, though he used to when he lay on his back, especially when he was drunk, as the vodka bottle on the table and the smell of acetone coming from his stomach and permeating the room revealed that he was, but his mouth was shut, and dark, dried blood clung to his handsome, full lips, and a little had trickled onto the threadbare blanket and the dirty embroidered pillow under his head, and on the documents was stated: cerebral haemorrhage, *I've lost count of the circuits,* she suddenly realized, but today, today she'd set herself a really big achievement, going back there, into that house which had been sold a long time ago, she looked down and noticed that her Chinese trainers too had turned grey, as had her white towelling socks, as she determinedly pounded the circuit around the lakes in the Györgyfalvi quarter, *there would have been no turn to the right, even if there'd been a telephone,* because the decision began with the bunch of keys left on the table, the tangible evidence that conspicuously revealed that *somebody had been there,* though we shall learn no more about that moment, not the facts: when this scene was enacted—opening the door, key, Andrej the dog rushed out, the Girl walked in—was he already dead or not, and in any case that turn to the right had already taken place exactly a month before, when the first skirmish with death was successfully won, and János promised—as so many times—that he was going to stop drinking, that he wouldn't deceive the children, wouldn't desert them—promised, in his weak, faltering voice, that he would confront death: because at that time, a month before August, the door was left open, and Andrej vanished, only reappearing next day, and the door was left wide open, but the Girl rushed into the next street to her Grandmother's, *did I rush? Then this isn't the first time I've run*, and by evening there had been stomach-pumping and infusions, but late in the evening, when he opened his eyes, he asked almost inaudibly '*Did you see to the watering?*' at which her mother, who was standing there beside her, immediately said that it didn't matter now, but she said in embarrassment that she had done it, and from the hospital ran into the garden and watered everything, gave the cucumbers special attention, let the hose run for at least ten minutes on every bed, and she picked the first tomato, it was becoming huge, and at the end of August they made more than a hundred litres of tomato soup, she really detested pulping them, but it had to be done, she had to turn the handle on the ancient tomato press, they were nice just raw, but as tomato soup simply divine, it lasted until February, *there'll be tomatoes but without you,* because she that even in July had managed to turn to the right, in August, when the final column was reached in the schedule of death, turned to the left and flung the key onto the table, shut the door behind her, and with that turn set off on one of the possible routes in the labyrinth, without any conception of the layout of that labyrinth nor yet of its existence, to wander for years among orders of left turn! right turn! and she hadn't been able to escape because there was nothing but left turn! or right turn! because she couldn't escape from the twists and turns between the hedges of Jerusalem-thorn, impossibly high to climb, and again and again it was five o'clock in the afternoon of 4 August

1984, and she asked which way now? which way should I turn? Left, left, she urged herself, but János, János was no longer able to reach his own death, *but I couldn't have done it, couldn't have dragged him out, couldn't have dragged his helpless body all that way,* but the thirteen-year-old Girl, now almost as tall as she would ever be, still knew nothing, that there were left and right, a father who had been alive and by the next day was certainly dead, *but it's possible that then, then he was still alive,* and since then this turn to the left had become the universal unit of measurement, an involuntary movement at five in the afternoon, not even a decision, just an action, *I'll have to do the watering tomorrow as well,* she said to her mother quietly and tenderly, and on the third day, when they were in their father's house, and after the funeral, until the garden was sold she did the watering in the evenings because she couldn't get up at dawn, the cucumbers had to be picked and the tomatoes, the raspberries were beginning to ripen, there was constantly something that had to be picked, everything was growing and ripening and getting out of control, only the flower garden had turned black, because that same day she'd completely wrecked it when her mother made her go with her to the store where she worked to get her a black blouse and skirt: *No, trousers won't do, you'll wear a skirt,* a horrid, pleated skirt, *But Mother! It's a Pioneer skirt,* she objected, *But it's black!* and she bought her a short-sleeved black blouse with an embroidered collar, *It's exactly what the peasants in Szucság wear, I'm not putting that on,* to which her mother replied *Your father's funeral isn't a fashion show,* and—*In that case I'll wear my black trousers!—I'm not putting that old rubbish on,* and in the middle of the shop she burst into tears, she was going to look like an Aunt Sally, and her mother said quietly *You should be ashamed, behaving like this at your father's funeral,* and she went on: *I don't want to buy black nylons, Mother, it's August, nobody's wearing stockings, only gormless peasants and ignorant churchgoing women in nylon headscarves and Jehovah's Witnesses—I'm taking the decisions, and you'll have to have a black ribbon.—I'm not tying my hair up, just leave it alone, it's all you can think of, you and the school, nothing but how I'm supposed to do my hair—You look terrible, I'll comb it out and plait it,* but after that she left it alone, and in the end she didn't have to tie her hair up, but in the store she said with a sigh to one of her staff, *Now I can wear black for a year, it's all very well for these youngsters, they don't have to, I'll take clothes home, you can go, you'll be home by six, see what I mean? I've still got to order the wreath, what shall we put on it?—No need for a wreath, Mother, we'll get a great big bunch of flowers from the garden, there's lots of zinnias and gladioli—*On the one hand, I hate gladioli, she retorted, why does everybody in our family hate gladioli? she wondered as she panted, and now she noticed that a dirty white stray dog was running beside her, not after her but with her, and if everybody hated gladioli why did we plant them? *On the other hand, this is a funeral, not a birthday party, so we're taking a wreath,* and the Girl rushed out of the ready-to-wear shop in Szentegyház utca, which was full of uniforms, where only country people shopped, *rushing about again? See how much I've run about for you? Now it's getting twilight and I'm still running, but I didn't believe in it for a moment, I was just being big-headed, telling myself I could do it*—she ran all down Deák Ferenc utca, then past the Romanian Theatre, then along Budai Nagy Antal utca, straight into the garden, didn't look at the house as she didn't have a key any longer, borrowed secateurs from next door and cut down all the flowers, all the dahlias, the zinnias, the gladioli, even the chrysanthemums, though they weren't open yet, the few dwarf carnations, the orange-yellow Japanese lilies and the solitary scented white one, and the few roses that they'd tried for the first time—and evidently the last—that year, and the two cherished tuberoses, put them all into tidy piles, went back into the vegetable garden and cut down the little flowering sunflowers that had been planted as decoration beside the beds, *Because they'll come to nothing, they're so sickly,* she said, then back into the flower garden and uprooted all the plants, the peonies, which had shed their petals, the daffodils, the hyacinth bulbs, piled them all up and watered the bare roots and the flowers so that next day at the funeral she wouldn't forget to tell Mrs Sándor (she didn't want to call in then) that they were all hers, the roots and bulbs, certainly she'd be able to make use of the roses and the dahlias (they were hard to uproot, she had to dig round them), and she worked until late in the evening, she still had to water the vegetables and pick them, and she took at least 10 kilos of vegetables home, and her mother said nothing about her being late in, and next morning she'd have to ask next door for the wheelbarrow to take the flowers to the cemetery, but her mother wouldn't let her, *I've ordered three wreaths*, she said, *one for you, one for your sister and one for myself, that will have to do—'your loving daugter'* it said on the black ribbon protruding from under the other wreath, she couldn't read the start of the sentence, *The Hungarian florist wasn't there, so the other one wrote the ribbons, that's why there's a mistake,* Mother complained to Grandmother after the funeral, and on seeing 'your loving daugter' the Girl burst into tears, *It doesn't matter now,* she thought as she ran, the long-eared, black-nosed dog still keeping pace with her, but though she'd said nothing her tears were tears of rage, because the ribbon on her wreath was the one that protruded from the rest, and it was only when Mrs Sándor came up to offer her condolences and kissed the Girl (she hadn't been able to kiss the body, the coffin was closed, though Mrs Sándor would have liked to look at him) there on the spot she put in her hand four crumpled purple 100-lei notes, the sort the Girl had never had, because Mrs Sándor had been out to the market first thing and taken all the cut flowers, and she whispered into her ear *It was clever of you to cut them, and you'll need the money, so I've cashed up all that loose change, but next time don't pull them up by the root—What next time, Mrs Sándor? It's a pity I forgot to ask*—and there she stood with the four 100-lei notes beside the coffin, no pockets in that stupid blouse or skirt, but never mind, she clutched them and made up her mind not to give them to anybody, she'd buy a fur coat with the money, yes, *And I've had a nice wreath made from the zinnias, the gentleman's favourites, and your chrysanthemums, and took the cost out of the takings, and I had a card written as well, there, you can see it, from 'your loving daughter' and your names, so there you are, enjoy the money, I'll hang on to it for you until the funeral's over,* and the Girl really did buy a goatskin coat with it and she still wore it, not then in August, but in winter, and sometimes used it as a bedspread at home, because it was cold in the block, and in school she kept it on in lessons because there too they were freezing, but now the perspiration was running off her, the white sweater was clinging to her and it was fortunate that there was a bit of a breeze, but she went on and on with the hard, liberating circuits, and the dog still ran with her, it was panting, its pink tongue hanging out, and the Girl suddenly looked up and realized that there were other runners too, she wasn't alone, she didn't know how many laps she'd done but she kept going, decided to run for as long as she could, until evening if need be, and to start again next day until she'd finally truly escaped from that high, thorny labyrinth by an appropriate turn to the left.

CHRISTMAS 1989

But she was wrong, because in the end the lorries didn't go to the air-port but in that direction—Kolozsvár airport! she wondered, when she got into the lorry, an imaginary concept, it must be an imaginary place because nobody's seen inside it, nobody that she knew had ever even landed at Kolozsvár airport, but many of them had come from abroad, and aircraft didn't take off from there, only the . . . his, because long ago, very long ago, when Mummy was little and her grandmother had still been alive, people went by air to Vásárhely for All Souls' Day, because in those days there'd been direct flights between the two, so she said, although later Mummy could also have gone to Bucharest by air but preferred to go by sleeper and with him, or rather Him, V, and so the Girl was now imagining—and not imagining, she knew for cer-tain, although nobody had told her—that they were going to the airport to pack things, because she thought that, as of then, perhaps from next day, this airport would become a reality and people would get on and off there, Paris, London, Berlin, Vienna, Moscow, America! they'd no longer need to change planes but would travel directly because as of then Kolozsvár could suddenly become part of the world, a city with an airport, a travel destination, could feature in travel books, because the world was big and Kolozsvár was part of it, arrivals, departures, vis-itors! she exulted and felt a thrill of excitement in the overheated cab, now the relatives from Budapest would be able to come and go, though by that time they were all dead . . . but she was wrong, because in fact they had been going towards Szamosfalva but in the thick fog they'd turned off the Szamosfalva road towards the huge warehouses, never even half full and always covered in cobwebs, and the previous morning

Mummy had brusquely commandeered the warehouses by telephone, firmly requesting the loan of them from their startled owners, warehouses belonging to the central textile, footwear and foodstuff-trading organizations which had for years yawned hungrily into the snow-covered yards on which the lorries—smaller, larger and quite alarmingly huge—drove one after another with the cooperation of the military authorities—because Mummy had called on the assistance of the military who were 'on our side', as she put it, and her two daughters—they had come of their own accord, pleaded to be allowed to come, because they wouldn't for the world be left out of the revolution—and under Mummy's guidance the incalculable volume of goods here, enough to fill seventy lorries, began to be organized: the soldiers brought in the big items, unpacked, classified and repacked them so as to dispatch them as aid in accordance with Mummy's previously prepared tables, the girls sorted and piled the smaller packs, boxes and sacks, and the younger girl, like a scribe, was responsible for the letters, greetings cards, messages to be passed on, and drawings made by children and gathered the collection of books and magazines, mostly from IPM, Ludas Matyi, Élet és Tudomány and Nők Lapja, *it's a pity I can't take Élet és Tudomány for Granddad*, thought the Girl, and there were a few copies of *Erdély Története, Mozgó Világ és Film, Színház és Muzsika* too, of which they had a lot, their grandfather had carefully bound them up, and perhaps a copy of an unknown paper called *Színház*,[56] Mummy would certainly be glad of it, but outside, Mummy, like the statue of Mihai Viteazul in Széchényi tér, was standing like a military commander on a platform which the soldiers had brought out for her so that she could have a better view of the warehouse yard, and instead of a drawn sword she was

---

56 *Ludas Matyi* is a comic paper, *Élet és Tudomány* (Life and Science), *Nők Lapja,* (Women's Journal), *Erdély Története* (History of Transylvania), *Mozgó Világ* (Moving World), *Film, Színház és Muzsika* (Film, Theatre and Music). The reference to the 'unknown *Színház*' is an ironic touch: the author is currently the editor of a periodical called *Színház* (Theatre).

brandishing a big, old notebook, and when they were setting out early in the morning she'd put on shiny, light-blue eye makeup (obtained from Budapest) as if she were going on a date, powdered her thin nose, put her hair in papers overnight and now the blond ringlets were dangling on her shoulders, she'd put on her long, blue, hand-painted skirt and her high-heeled boots, she was beautiful and brave and her eyes were shining because now she was beginning her final great business battle, at last real merchandise was coming under her strict supervision —she'd got a megaphone, a tin funnel, from an officer, then one by one she was letting the vehicles in, discussing their contents with the drivers, then sending them to one or other of the warehouses, where they began to unload, and every half-hour she announced that it was prohibited to take anything from the area of the warehouses, the donations were intended for those in need, and she listed them in Romanian, then suddenly had an idea and spoke in Hungarian as well, the soldiers ran up to her every minute with queries about what to pack for where, and in the warehouses piles of boxes, bags and sacks grew steadily— sugar, flour, oil, cleaning materials, clothing, medical supplies, preserves, sweets, coffee, chocolate and powdered milk, toys, blankets, alcoholic drinks, coloured soft drinks, domestic utensils, footwear—and slowly there developed in the warehouses huge shops, enormous supermarkets, such as there were in the West, the sort that Würtl had spoken of— he'd been to America—but had not been believed, and then suddenly a spotty-faced young soldier stood in the doorway of the biggest warehouse and stared for a long moment, open-mouthed, with wondering eyes at the tins of food on the pallets and in a deep voice struck up the hymn *Ţie-ţi voi da pămîntul Canaan* (I will give you the land of Canaan) and, hands clasped together, bowed low several times before the idol, and nobody laughed at him, they all got on with their work, the girls too went on unpacking bags and sorting them, making piles behind them, and it looked as if some people had run round to the corner shop, bought up what they could and even left the till receipt in the Christmas parcel, and as they worked they read out to one another the cards, letters and poems, and in the end only the first lines: 'Dear Compatriots', 'Székelys! Hungarians!', 'Dear Unknown!', 'We've risen again!', 'You're our much suffering brothers', 'The sea has risen, the sea of the peoples', 'Dear Romanian Friends', 'Death to the Communists', 'Dear Jolika and Pötyike, dear children, I hope . . .', wrote the letter-writers, all addressing somebody, and now and then the girls ran outside for a cigarette with the soldiers, youngsters from Oltenia and Moldova that were stationed in Szamosfalva, who were in their shirt-sleeves because by midday the sun had come out and it was like spring, and the boys made strong, sweet Turkish coffee in a big pan and offered them some, and at noon everybody, including Mummy, was given an aluminium bowl of grey official stew, and as she spooned up the hot potato soup up there on her platform, like a general who dared not leave the battle before it was won, a swarthy youth ran panting across the yard towards her and shouted from a distance, like a child that had discovered something *Tovarăşa comandant* (Comrade commander), *conserva aste este de pisică* (this tinned meat is cat), *noi românii nu mîncăm aşa ceva* (we Romanians don't eat things like that), and Mummy reached down from the platform with her hand, reddened by the cold, took the longish tin and scanned it with an expert eye, *Asta lasă aici*, she began slowly, addressing the soldier in the singular as a friend, that is, leave this with me, put the rest with the other tinned things but keep it separate, *Trebuie analizată* (It'll have to be checked), she pronounced officiously, and put the tin into the pocket of her thick coat, *Eu răspund* (I'll deal with it), *Yes ma'am*, replied the boy, saluted smartly and ran back with the instruction that the strange consignment had to be treated separately, and Mummy repeated in Romanian and Hungarian that there would be a check at the gate on leaving and that nobody might take anything away without permission, but late that night, when an officer from Iaşi offered to give the girls and *Doamna directoare* a lift home, there was no longer anybody on duty at the gate, everybody was absolutely worn out after the day's packing, and before leaving Mummy designated sentries for the night and arranged for them to be relieved, had the warehouses locked, examined the night-watchman's key cabinet, even joked with him that it was all done, what was there for him to watch, eh? the dog would come in useful now, by that time the well-groomed wolfhound had made friends with everybody, *Hoțul*! (Thief!), called the watchman (all Romanian dogs had that name) when Mummy raised an admonishing finger to the dog telling it to be on the lookout in the night, *Hoțul, nu sare, bă*! (Thief, don't jump up, now) and the toothless watchman smiled, he'd been on guard for fifteen Christmas nights, *De cinș'pe ani sînt de serviciu de Crăciun, dar niciodată n-am avut nimic de păzit*, he'd been on duty on fifteen Christmas nights and previously he hadn't had anything to guard, *Good Lord*, sighed Mummy, *look at the time*, she muttered, as if she'd still be able to make something of Christmas Eve, and opened her eyes wide, the blue eye-makeup was smudged, the powder was completely rubbed off her nose, *how could I have forgotten*! and she gave the girls a conscience-stricken look, but in the end they were home before midnight, *We could at least have brought a fresh loaf*, she said regretfully, as there'd been a lot of bread in the consignments, *You're the one who said we couldn't bring anything*, said Juci with a grin, *We ought to have something hot*, said Mummy, standing in the middle of the kitchen and pulling off her boots, *my feet are killing me, I'll make some chips—Ah, there's no need, there's some stale bread left, it's the day before yesterday's, no, even older than that, we'll moisten it and toast it, that'll do, it'll be toast*, she said, opening the metal bread-bin, *And there's all that meat for the stuffed cabbage in the freezer, but I forgot to take it out this morning*, Mummy apologized in a high voice, *I managed to get all the meat this year, it's been five years since I was able to make stuffed cabbage like this, two knuckles of ham I got, some loin of pork, some nice lean belly, I didn't get any sauerkraut, of course, I always get that on the day from the Hóstát people, but who'd have thought it would turn out like this, and the tree as well, we've never had such a nice tree, I got it off a couple that were divorcing in Almásszentkirály, it would have been too big in the flat,* she sank onto the kitchen stool and Ludmilla immediately jumped onto her lap and began to rub against her, *We won't phone Granny, it's late, and in any case we're having lunch with her tomorrow,* and Juci suddenly asked her sister—was it an interrogation or just an enquiry, wondered the Girl—*Didn't you bring anything away?* and her sister looked at her in embarrassment not knowing how to reply, *Yes, yes, of course I did, so there,* she felt braver by the end of the sentence, *What about you?—Me?*—Juci returned the question uncertainly, *of course I brought . . . something—It's Christmas, after all,* laughed the younger girl, *of course I did,* because she thought that when all was said and done everybody had brought something, and it had been no use Mummy saying so a thousand times, and if anybody couldn't resist taking, that is, stealing, a single cigarette or a bit of baking powder or a newspaper or some soap, that, in the final analysis, according to Mummy's rules, constituted theft, *And we owe that Albanian confectioner half the price of a kilo of Christmas sweets,* said the younger girl with a laugh, a fortnight before she'd been to Mr Fizula's in his flat on the third floor of the block in Pata utca and they'd ordered Christmas sweets for the first time in their lives, it was the first time that Mummy'd had the money, she'd said that this time she wanted a real Christmas, everything the way it should be: the tree, the stuffed cabbage and the sweets, and the Albanian's three-room flat (he spoke Romanian rather oddly) was a proper sweet shop, there was no furniture in it, the whole place was just a big kitchen, fine white powder everywhere, and Mr Fizula showed them the three sorts of Christmas sweets for them to choose from—two white and one pink—and sliced off a bit from each, but the Girl took it nervously and then enquired about the price and in embarrassment asked for the cheapest, which even so was terribly expensive, and had to pay half in advance—*We didn't bring anything away,* she repeated, *But this we did,* replied Mummy, softly and sweetly, and reached into her coat pocket and slowly drew out the tin of meat, *cats' meat*, said she slowly and looked at the floor, looking for her pussies, *Juci, bring the tin-opener*, but Juci took the tin and with a single movement pulled off the top by the ring, by which time Bella too had appeared in the doorway, *You're the only ones to have presents, Ludmilla, Bella, come here to Mummy*, she purred to the cats, *Yours are in the office*, she looked up at the girls, *We'll give you yours tomorrow as well, then*, Juci consoled her mother, and in the meanwhile she got out the three-day-old bread, sliced it, turned on the tap and sprinkled it like clothes to be ironed, and Mummy fed the cats with the tinned meat, *This year we've really got the lot, tree, cabbage, presents, sweets*, she said in satisfaction, and there was nothing missing, and she finally took her coat off and laid the table, *There's some dripping if you want any to put on it*, she said, and Juci began to heat up the iron baking-sheet, *No thanks, we're on a diet*, she said, because she was slimming, and slowly the familiar Sunday morning smell began to spread in the flat, *Let's have a glass of pálinka*, said Mummy, and began to eat the toast, which Juci had done very thoroughly, it crunched so loudly that they could scarcely hear one another, and for a long time there was silence in the kitchen, then the younger Girl asked quietly, *Now what shall we do?*— and Mummy raised her eyebrows as if she didn't understand when 'now' was, tonight? or tomorrow, when they were going to Grandmother's? and she said something but the Girl couldn't hear because of the resounding crunching in her ears, only the end of the sentence, their names, their real, complete, adult names, because that was how Mummy used to address them and said something else before, something like *you do* or *you go* or *you want*, or *you are*, but in any case she never addressed them formally but always talked to them like adults, *Let's take the bug out of the telephone, one of the soldiers in the office showed me how*, Juci proposed, *it's not much of a job, he told me how to dismantle it—Leave it till tomorrow*, Mummy waved the idea aside, by this time it really didn't matter, but Juci went on *And why didn't we ever think of it?* to which Mummy replied defensively *Well, we didn't know!—What, that we were being eavesdropped?* the girls roared with laughter, and indeed the whole thing was a little black plastic gizmo 8 centimetres long from which pieces of aluminium protruded, and they looked at in disbelief— that was all it was, *Oh, surely not, if that was all there was to it we'd have taken it off ages ago,* and they hung it on a red ribbon from a branch of the bronze chandelier, below the little bronze angel, as if it were a Christmas tree decoration, and there it dangled and the cats stared at it fascinated, watching intently for the chance to pounce on it, but Juci went and stood under the little black box and said *Álo* to it as Mummy did, because that was how she always answered the telephone, she could never be persuaded to stop doing it: in her view the telephone was a Romanian thing and had to be addressed in Romanian, and she couldn't hear any difference between *Hallo* and *Álo, And now what shall we do?* asked the younger girl again uncertainly, but it seemed that she wasn't interested in Mummy's response, rather in her own, that in future she ought to reply, because it was midnight, and the adult person born at Christmas 1989 was still alarmed and defenceless, clung to her weary Mummy and her elder sister and her grandmother, who by then was almost blind, and the soft, sedentary cats, to the gloomy flat in a Kolozsvár block, was still afraid to go into her room—her own room, because at last she had her own room, she'd got the sitting room, as she was a big girl—and was afraid to go to bed because next day she might not wake up as she had been before, and next day she had to reply to what they were to do, but Juci swallowed the last of her toast, and mentioned casually that she'd heard from the soldiers that passports could be obtained, that people were queuing all night at the police sta- tion, perhaps they might go next day, to which the Girl retorted *Are we travelling somewhere?* and quickly added *it's Monday tomorrow,* and she looked encouragingly at Mummy, who pulled a face—she might have to go into work, she didn't know what was going to become of her State employer, and she shook her head, she couldn't go standing in queues for passports just then, *And where could we go, anyway?* the Girl asked suddenly, and looked enquiringly at Mummy, but Juci replied impassively *You can go by yourself, you're an adult, you don't have to have your hand held, you just go, get your passport and you're away,* but the Girl swallowed the mouthful that she'd hardly chewed, the hard crust stuck in her throat, the roof of her mouth hurt, the toast had scraped it, and tears came to her eyes, as much from the pain as from the three exhausting days, when there'd been the shooting, next day the demonstration, then the relief workers had come, and truly it had been the best Christmas in the last eighteen years, when in reality everything had been right, as Mummy had said: the tree, the cabbage, the sweets, the presents, but there hadn't been anything, next day she could go for her passport if she wanted, *you can go, you can do,* repeated Mummy, or as the girls said again and again *we're going to go, going to do,* only there was as yet no telling where to and what, but in any case Mummy was going to bed because *my feet are killing me, but you do as you please, girls.*